MW01148211

# DARK NOTES

PAM GODWIN

Copyright © 2016 by Pam Godwin
All rights reserved.
Editor: Lesa Godwin, Godwin Proofing
Interior Designer: Pam Godwin
Cover Artist: Pam Godwin

This is a work of fiction. Names, characters, places, and
incidents are the product of the author's imagination or are
used fictitiously, and any resemblance to actual persons,
living or dead, events, or locales is entirely coincidental.
No part of this book may be reproduced in any form, except
for the inclusion of brief quotations in a review or article,
without written permission from the author.

Visit my website at pamgodwin.com

# IVORY

Poverty.

It used to be easier.

Maybe because I don't remember it much as a child. Because I was happy.

Now all that's left is grief and yelling and unpaid bills.

At seventeen, I don't know a lot about the world, but I find that being unwanted and unhappy is harder to endure than having nothing to eat.

The knot in my stomach tightens. Maybe if I puke before I leave the house, it will loosen my nerves and clear my head. Except I can't afford to lose the calories.

A deep breath confirms the buttons on my nicest shirt are holding together, my considerable cleavage still conservatively hidden. The knee-length skirt fits better this morning than it did in the thrift store, and the ballet flats... Forget it. There's nothing I can do about the cracked soles and rips in the toes. They're the only shoes I own.

I step out of the bathroom and tiptoe through the kitchen, combing shaky fingers through my hair. The wet strands fall against my back and soak my shirt. Shit, is my bra showing through the damp fabric? I should've worn my hair up or dried it, but I'm out of time, which further hardens my stomach.

Jesus, I shouldn't be this anxious. It's only the first day of school. I've done this numerous times.

But it's my senior year.

The year that will determine the rest of my life.

One mistake, a less-than-perfect GPA, a violation of dress code, the tiniest infraction will steer the spotlight away from my talent and shine it on *the poor girl from Treme*. Every step I take in the judgmental, marble halls of Le Moyne Academy is an endeavor to prove I'm more than just that girl.

Le Moyne is one of the most recognized, elite, and expensive performing arts high schools in the nation. It's intimidating. Fucking terrifying. Doesn't matter if I'm the best pianist in New Orleans. Since my freshman year, the academy has been looking for a reason to expel me, to fill my competitive spot with a student who brings talent *and* financial endowments.

The stench of stale smoke roots me in the reality of my life. I flick the kitchen wall switch, illuminating piles of crushed beer cans and empty pizza boxes. Crusty dishes fill the sink, cigarette butts litter the floor, and what the hell is that? I lean over the counter and squint at the burnt residue in the bowl of a spoon.

*Motherfucker.* My brother used our best utensils to cook coke? I toss it in the trash with a surge of anger.

Shane claims he can't pay the bills, but the jobless bastard always has money to party. Not only that, the kitchen was spotless when I fell asleep, notwithstanding the mold blooming on the walls and the laminate flaking away from the countertops. This is our *home*, goddammit. The only thing we ïave left. He and Mom have no idea what I've endured to ïeep us current on the mortgage payments. For their sake, I ïope they never find out.

Soft fur brushes my ankle, drawing my attention to the floor. Huge golden eyes stare up out of an orange tabby face, and my shoulders loosen instantly.

Schubert tilts his scruffy chin and rubs his whiskers against my leg, his tail twitching in the air. He always knows when I need affection. Sometimes I think he's the only love left in this house.

"I have to go, sweet boy," I whisper, stretching down to scratch his ears. "Be a good kitty, okay?"

I remove the last slice of banana bread from its hiding spot in the back of the pantry, relieved Shane hadn't found it. I wrap it in a paper towel and attempt to make a quiet-as-possible escape to the front door.

Our crumbling house is one room wide and five rooms long. No hallways. With the rooms set up one in front of the other and all the doors lined up, I could stand on the back stoop, shoot a shotgun at the front door, and not hit any walls.

But I could hit Shane. Deliberately. Because he's a fucking burden and a waste of life. He's also nine-years older, a hundred-and-fifty-pounds bigger, and the only sibling I have.

The hundred-year-old wood planks groan beneath my feet, and I suck in a breath, waiting for Shane's drunken roar.

Silence. *Thank you, Jesus.*

Holding the wrapped bread against my chest, I pass through Mom's room first. I walked through thirty minutes ago, half-asleep and shuffling for the bathroom in the dark. But with the kitchen light shining through the doorway, the lump in her bed looks unmistakably human.

I stumble with surprise, trying to remember the last time I saw her. Two...three weeks ago?

A flutter stirs behind my breastbone. Maybe she came home to wish me luck on my first day?

Three quiet strides carry me to the bed. The rectangular rooms are cramped and narrow, but the ceilings soar twelve feet or taller. Daddy used to say the pitched roof and long front-to-back layout was a ventilation design to ensure all his love could flow through.

But Daddy's gone, and all that's left circulating through the house is the musty, sputtering coughs from the window units.

I bend over the mattress, straining to see Mom's cropped hair in the shadows. Instead, I'm met with the bitter stink of beer and weed. *Of course.* Well, at least she's alone. I have no interest in meeting the man-of-the-month she's been shacking up with.

Should I wake her? Instinct tells me not to, but dammit, I ache to feel her arms around me.

"Mom?" I whisper.

The lump shifts, and a deep groan rumbles from the blankets. A man's groan, one I know with horrifying intimacy.

A chill grips my spine as I scramble backward. Why is my brother's best friend in Mom's bed?

Lorenzo's thick arm swings up, and his hand catches the back of my neck, pulling me toward him.

I drop the bread in my attempt to push away, but he's stronger, meaner, and never responds to *No*.

"No," I say anyway, fear amplifying my voice, my pulse roaring past my ears. "Stop it!"

NOTES

He wrestles me to the bed, shoving me face-down beneath his sweaty body. Hot beer breath smothers me. Then his weight, his hands...oh God, his erection. He jabs my ass with it, rucking up my skirt, his heavy panting scraping my ears.

"Get off me!" I thrash wildly, my fingers clawing at the blankets, taking me nowhere. "I don't want this. Please, don't—"

His palm slaps over my mouth, shutting me up as his strength confines my movements.

My body grows cold, numb, collapsing like a dead thing, separating from my headspace. I let myself slip away, my concentration on the safety in what I know, what I love, as I wrap my entire being with dark atmosphere, light strokes of piano keys, atonal rhythm. Scriabin's Sonata No.9. I see my fingers walking through the piano piece, hear the haunting melody, and feel each quivering note pulling me further into the black mass. Away from the bedroom. Away from my body. Away from Lorenzo.

A hand snakes under my chest, squeezing my breast, pulling on my shirt, but I'm lost in the dissonant notes, recreating them with care, distracting my thoughts. He can't hurt me. Not here with my music. Never again.

He shifts, shoving his hand between my butt cheeks, inside my panties, probing roughly at the hole in back that he always makes bleed.

The sonata shatters in my mind, and I try to reassemble the chords. But his fingers are relentless, forcing me to endure his touch, his palm muffling my scream. I gasp for air and frantically kick my legs near the bedside table. My foot collides with the lamp and sends it crashing to the floor.

5

Lorenzo freezes, his hand tightening on my mouth.

Loud banging vibrates the wall by my head, a fist pounding in Shane's room. My blood runs cold.

"Ivory!" Shane's voice booms through the wall. "Fucking woke me up, you worthless fucking cunt!"

Lorenzo leaps off me and backs into the beam of light from the kitchen doorway. Tribal tattoos blacken his chest, and baggy sweatpants hang from his narrow hips. An unassuming person might consider his beefed-up physique and strong Latino features attractive. But appearances are just the skin of the soul, and his soul is rotten.

I roll off the bed, shove down my skirt, and grab the wrapped bread from the floor. To reach the front door, I have to pass through Shane's room then the parlor. Maybe he hasn't crawled out of bed yet.

With a trembling pulse, I dart into the pitch-black cavern of Shane's room and— *Oomph!* I slam into his bare chest.

Expecting his reaction, I swerve out of the path of his first swing, only to expose my cheek to the hard slap of his other hand. The impact sends me back into Mom's room, and he stays with me, his eyes drooping in a haze of alcohol and drugs.

To think, he used to look like Daddy. But that was before... Every day, Shane's blond hairline recedes farther, his cheeks sink deeper into his pasty face, and his belly hangs lower over those ridiculous workout shorts.

He hasn't worked out since he went AWOL from the Marines four years ago. The year our lives went to shit.

"Why. The. *Fuck*..." Shane says, shoving his face in mine, "are you waking up the goddamn house at five in the fucking norning?"

Technically, it's almost six o'clock, and I have a quick stop o make before the forty-five-minute commute.

"I have school, dickhead." I straighten my spine, standing taller, despite the awful fear souring my stomach. "What you should be asking is why Lorenzo is sleeping in Mom's bed, why he puts his hands on me, and why I was screaming for him to stop."

I follow Shane's focus to his friend. Faded ink scrawls up the sides of Lorenzo's face, indiscernible beneath the dark shadow of his sideburns. But the fresh tattoo on his throat burns as bold and black as his eyes. *Destroy,* it says. The way he's glaring at me, it's a promise.

"She came onto me again." Lorenzo's gaze stays on mine, his expression an open canvas of malice. "You know how she is."

"Bullshit!" I turn back to Shane, my voice pleading. "He won't leave me alone. Every time you turn your back, he's pulling off my clothes and—"

Shane grabs my neck and throws me face-first into the door jamb. I try to dodge it, jerking against the force of his rage, but my mouth connects with the sharp corner.

Pain bursts through my lip. When I taste blood, I jut my chin out to keep the mess off my clothes.

He releases me, his eyes dull and heavy-lidded, but his hate stabs through me sharper than ever. "If you flash your tits at my friends again, I'll cut them the fuck off. You hear me?"

My hand flies to my chest, and my heart sinks as my palm slips through the gaping *V* of my shirt. At least two buttons gone. Shit! The academy will write me up, or worse, kick me out. I desperately scan the bed and floor, searching for little plastic dots in the sea of scattered clothes. I'll never find them, and if I don't leave now, there will be more blood and missing buttons.

I turn and run through Shane's room, his furious shouts propelling me faster. In the parlor, I grab my satchel from the couch where I sleep, and I'm out the door in the next breath, exhaling my relief into gray sky. The sun won't be up for another hour, and all is quiet on the vacant street.

As I take a step off the front lawn, I try to shed the past ten minutes from my mind by compartmentalizing it into baggage. The old-style kind, bound in brown leather with those little tan buckles. Then I picture the baggage sitting on the porch. It stays here, because I can only carry so much.

A short jog takes me toward the 91 line. If I hurry, I still have time to check on Stogie before the next bus.

Veering around the potholes that dimple the stately tree-lined streets, I pass rows of cottages and shotgun houses, each vibrantly painted in every color and adorned with the trademarks of the deep south. Wrought iron railings, gas lamps, guillotine windows, and gables etched with ornate scrollwork, it's all there if one can look past the sagging porches, graffiti, and rotting garbage. Empty, overgrown lots pockmark the streetscape, as if we need reminders of the last hurricane. But the resonance of Treme thrives in the fertile soil, in the cultural history, and in the weathered smiles of the people who call the back of town their home.

People like Stogie.

I reach the heavily-barred door of his music store and find the handle unlocked. Despite the dearth of customers, he opens the store the moment he wakes. This is his livelihood, after all.

The bell overhead jingles as I enter, and my attention compulsively darts to the old Steinway in the corner. I've spent every summer since I can remember pounding the keys on that piano until my back ached and my fingers lost feeling. Eventually, those visits turned into employment. I handle his customers, bookkeeping, inventory, whatever he needs. But only in the summers when I don't have the means to earn my *other* income.

"Ivory?" Stogie's raspy baritone warbles through the small store.

I set the banana bread on the glass counter and holler toward the back. "Just dropping off breakfast."

The shuffling sound of his loafers signals his approach, and his hunched frame emerges from his living quarters in the back room. Ninety-years-old and the man can still move fast, crossing the store like his frail body isn't wracked with arthritis.

The cloudy glaze in his dark eyes denotes his poor eyesight, but as he nears, his gaze instantly finds the missing buttons on my shirt and the swollen cut on my lip. The wrinkles beneath the rim of his baseball cap deepen. He's seen Shane's handiwork before, and I'm so grateful he doesn't ask or offer pity. I might be the only white girl in this neighborhood, and I'm definitely the only kid with a private school education, but the differences end there. My baggage is as common in Treme as tossed beads on Bourbon Street.

As he takes me in from head to toe, he scratches his whiskers, the little white hairs stark against his coal-black complexion. Visible tremors skate across his arms, and he squares his shoulders, no doubt an attempt to disguise his pain. I've been watching his health decline for months, and I'm helpless to stop it. I don't know how to support him or ease his suffering, and it's slowly killing me inside.

I've seen his finances. He can't afford medication or doctor's visits or even basic things, like food. He certainly can't afford an employee, which made my last summer on his payroll bittersweet. When I graduate from Le Moyne in the spring, I'll leave Treme, and Stogie will no longer feel obligated to take care of me.

But who will take care of him?

He tugs a hankie from his shirt pocket, his hand trembling as he lifts it to my lip.

"You look mighty smart this morning." His shrewd eyes bore into mine. "And nervous."

I close my eyes while he blots the blood away. He already knows my strongest ally at the academy resigned from her position as the head music instructor. My relationship with Mrs. McCracken was three years in the making. She was the only person at Le Moyne who had my back. Losing her endorsement for a scholarship is like starting over.

"I only have one year." I open my eyes, locking onto Stogie's. "*One year* to impress a new instructor."

"And all you need is a moment. Just make sure you're there for it."

I'll catch the 91 line a few blocks away. The bus ride lasts twenty-five minutes. Then a ten-minute walk to the campus. I check my watch. I'll be there, missing buttons, lip busted, but my fingers still work. I'll make every moment count.

I run my tongue over the cut and cringe at the fatness around the broken skin. "Is it noticeable?"

"Yes." He slides me a narrowed glance. "But not nearly as noticeable as your smile."

Unbidden, my lips curl up, which I'm sure was his intention. "You're such a charmer."

"Only when she's worth it." He opens the clutter drawer at his hip and digs a quivering hand through the guitar picks, reeds, nails... What is he looking for?

*Oh!* I snatch the safety pin beside his probing finger and search for another. "Do you have any more?"

"Just the one."

After a few strategic adjustments, I manage to pin the front of my shirt together and give him a grateful smile.

With a soft pat on my head, he makes a shooing motion. "Go on. Get up outta here."

What he's really saying is, go to school so I can get out of that house. Out of Treme. Out of this life.

"I plan on it." I slide the bread across the counter.

"Oh no, now. You take it."

"They'll feed me at school."

I know he hears the lie but accepts it anyway.

As I turn to leave, he grabs my wrist with more strength than I thought he was capable.

"They're lucky to have you." His dark eyes flash. "Damn lucky sons-a-bitches. Don't you let them forget it."

He's right. Just because my family can't offer wealthy donations or powerful connections doesn't make me a charity case. My four-year tuition was paid in full when I was ten-years-old, and I passed the required auditions when I was fourteen, just like my peers. As long as I continue to outshine the others in coursework, recitals, essays, and behavior, the academy might not be so hard-pressed to drop me.

With a kiss on Stogie's wrinkled cheek, I head toward the bus stop, unable to stop the dread from returning to my stomach. What if my new music instructor hates me, refuses to mentor me or support me in the matriculation process for college? Daddy would be devastated. God, that's my greatest ache. Is Daddy watching me? Has he seen the things I've done to make ends meet? The things I'll have to do again, as soon as tonight? Does he miss me as much as I miss him?

Sometimes the terrible hole he left behind hurts so badly I can't bear it. Sometimes I want to give into the pain and join him, wherever he is.

Which is why I'm moving my biggest challenge to the top of my task list.

Today, I'm going to smile.

# EMERIC

As the early morning faculty meeting adjourns, my shiny new colleagues file out of the library in a monochrome of starched suits and clicking heels. I remain seated at the table, waiting for the herd to disperse while watching Beverly Rivard out of the corner of my eye.

She hasn't shifted her authoritative stance from the head of the table, hasn't given me so much as a glance since she introduced me at the beginning of the meeting. But she will, as soon as the room clears. No doubt she has one more agenda item to discuss. Privately.

"Mr. Marceaux." Her eyes cut to mine as she glides across the marble floors, surprisingly quiet in her pretentious pumps, and closes the doors behind the last staff member. "A quick word before you go."

It'll be more than a word, but I won't use semantics to unbalance the position she thinks she holds over me. There are more inventive ways to put her on her knees.

Folding my hands in my lap, I recline in the leather chair, an elbow on the table and an ankle on my knee. I give her the full force of my gaze, because she's the kind of woman who wants something from everyone, something powerful she can manipulate according to her own will and vision. For now, all she's getting from me is my attention.

Beverly strolls around the long table, her modest skirt-suit tailored to fit her slender frame. Twenty years my senior, she carries her age with remarkable elegance. High, pronounced cheekbones. Narrow, aristocratic features. Barely a wrinkle in her pale complexion.

Hard to tell if her hair is gray or blonde where it gathers at her nape. I bet she never wears it down. Attracting attention from men isn't her especial vanity. No, her ferocious pride lies in her sense of superiority in giving orders, and watching subordinates scramble to kiss her ass.

Our first and only face-to-face meeting over the summer exposed some of her nature. The rest I deduced. She didn't become the dean of Le Moyne through the goodness of her heart or by shrinking from competition.

I know firsthand what it takes to oversee a prep school like this one.

I also know how easy it is to lose that position.

As she saunters toward me, her sharp eyes pass over the nooks between the mahogany bookcases, the empty librarian desk, and the vacant couches at the far end. *Yes, Beverly. We're alone.*

She lowers into the chair beside me, legs crossing at the knees, and regards me with a calculated smile. "All settled in your new house?"

"Let's not pretend you care."

"Fine." She drags trimmed fingernails over her skirt. "Barb McCracken's attorney contacted me. As it turns out, she decided not to leave quietly."

Not my problem. I shrug a shoulder. "You said you'd

1andle it."

Perhaps Beverly isn't as competent as I assumed.

She hums, holding on to her smile, but it's tighter now. "I 1andled it."

"You threw more money at it?"

Her smile slips. "More than was warranted, the greedy bit—" Her lips thin as she leans back in the chair and stares across the room. "Anyway. It's finished."

I relax my mouth in half-smile, a deliberate signal of amusement. "Second guessing our arrangement already?"

She flicks her gaze back to me. "You're a risk, Mr. Marceaux." Her eyes taper into frosty slivers as she swivels her chair to face me. "How many job offers have you had since your fiasco in Shreveport? Hmm?"

Her taunting awakens a torrent of anger and betrayal that kicks up my pulse. My throat burns to lash out, but all I give her is an arched eyebrow.

"Right. Well." She sniffs with insolence. Or uncertainty. Probably both. "Le Moyne has an inimitable reputation, one I'm responsible for upholding. McCracken's departure and my willingness to hire you as her replacement have stirred unwanted suspicion."

While Shreveport destroyed my professional reputation, the reason for my resignation was never made public. Nevertheless, people talk. I suspect most of Le Moyne's faculty and student families will hear the whispers. I'd rather air the truth than subject myself to judgments based on twisted rumors. But Beverly's terms for the job offer require my silence.

"Remember our agreement." Her elbows press against her

sides, her eyes overly bright, almost glassy. "Keep your mouth shut and let me herd the sheep and their frivolous chatter."

She says this as if I should be impressed by her unethical business practices. But what she's inadvertently done is shown her hand. Her fear is palpable. She wrongfully fired a tenure-track teacher and paid the woman to shut up, all to bring me here for her personal gain. If she truly had control of the situation, she wouldn't have felt the need to initiate this conversation. She's cold-blooded enough to destroy people's lives, but that doesn't mean she's prepared to play this game. *My* game.

I rub a thumb over my bottom lip, delighting in the way her eyes reluctantly follow the movement.

The skin above her buttoned collar flushes. "It's paramount that we keep the attention on your achievements as an educator." She lifts her chin. "I expect you to set a professional example in the classroom—"

"Do *not* tell me how to do my job." I was a well-respected instructor before I climbed the administrative ranks. Fuck her and her self-righteous audacity.

"Like most teachers, you seem to have a problem with *learning*. So try to pay attention." She angles forward, her tone low and clipped. "I will not have your perversions darkening the corners of my school. If your misconduct at Shreveport is repeated here, the deal is off."

The reminder of what I lost sparks a fire in my chest. "That's the second time you've mentioned Shreveport. Why? Are you curious?" I level a challenging look at her. "Go ahead, Beverly. Ask your burning questions."

She breaks eye contact, her neck stiffening. "One does not

ᴀire a whore to hear about his exploits."

"Oh, I'm a whore now? Are you changing the terms of our deal?"

"No, Mr. Marceaux. You know why I hired you." Her voice ʀaises an octave. "With the explicit stipulation that there ᴡould be no indiscretions." She lowers her tone. "I don't want to hear another word about it."

I've allowed her the upper hand since the moment she contacted me. It's time to see how she navigates through a little humiliation.

Angling forward, I grip the armrests of her chair and cage her in. "You're lying, Beverly. I think you want to hear all the dirty details of my *indiscretions.* Shall I describe the positions that were used, the sounds she made, the size of my cock—?"

"Stop!" She sucks in a breath, a hand trembling against her chest before clenching her fist and plastering on the dignified expression she shows the world. "You're disgusting."

I chuckle and rest back in the chair.

She jumps to her feet, glaring down at me. "Stay away from my faculty, specifically the women in my employ."

"I checked out the offerings in this morning's meeting. You should really update the scenery."

There were a few tight-bodied teachers, plenty of interested glances my way, but I'm not here for that. I have dozens of women ready to bend over at my call, and my mistake at Shreveport... My jaw stiffens. It's one I won't make again.

"You, on the other hand..." I let my gaze travel over her rigid posture. "You look like you could use a good hard fuck."

"You're out of line." Her warning tone loses its effect with the wobble of her heels as she backs away.

She turns and flees toward the head of the table. The farther she moves away from me, the stronger her gait becomes. A few more steps and she glances over her shoulder as if expecting to catch my eyes on her flat ass. I shudder. The arrogant bitch actually thinks I'm interested.

I stand, slide a hand in the pocket of my slacks, and stroll toward her. "Is Mr. Rivard not meeting your demands in the bedroom?"

She reaches the end of the table and gathers her papers, refusing to meet my eyes. "Continue this behavior, and I'll make sure you never see the inside of a classroom again."

Her illusion of control makes it damn hard to keep my proverbial teeth sheathed.

I step into her space, crowding her. "Threaten me again, and you'll regret the outcome."

"Move back."

Leaning in, I let my breath brush her ear. "Everyone has secrets."

"I don't—"

"Is Mr. Rivard warming another bed?"

It's just a guess, but the slight tremor in her hand tells me I'm onto something.

Her nostrils flare. "Outrageous."

"What about your perfect son? What has he done to put you in this precarious position?"

"He's done nothing wrong!"

I wouldn't be here if that were true. "You're trembling, Beverly."

"This conversation is over." She steps around me, eyes on the door, and trips.

Her balance teeters, papers tumble from her hands, and she falls to her knees at my feet. *Perfect.*

She casts me a startled look, and as she realizes I made no move to catch her, her upturned face deepens into a self-effacing shade of red.

Snapping her eyes to the floor, she collects her things with angry movements. "Hiring you was a mistake."

I step onto the page she's reaching for and glare down at the top of her head. "Then fire me."

"I..." She stares at the snakeskin-embossed leather on my Doc Martens, her voice hushed, dejected. "Just use your connections."

To get her undeserving son into Leopold, the highest ranked music college in the country. That was the deal.

She gave me a teaching job when no one else would, and I'll hold up my end of the bargain. But I will *not* bend or cower like her subordinates. She has no idea who she's dealing with. But she'll learn.

I toe the paper toward her fingers and hold it down with my shoe. "I think we're clear on the terms"—I lift my foot, allowing her to snatch it—"as well as our positions in this arrangement."

She stiffens, her head hanging lower.

Humiliation complete.

I turn and amble out of the library.

# IVORY

*"I heard she stuffs her bra."*

*"What a slut."*

*"Didn't she wear those shoes last year?"*

The murmurs ripple through the crowded hall, spoken behind manicured hands yet intended to reach my ears. After three years, how have these girls not come up with new material?

As I pass their whispering cluster of brand names, limited edition iPhones, and black American Express cards, I reinforce my smile with the reminder that, despite our differences, I deserve to be here.

*"I wonder whose bed she crawled out of this morning."*

*"Seriously, I can smell her from here."*

The comments don't bother me. They're just words. Unimaginative, immature, hollow words.

Who am I kidding? Some of those jabs are true enough, and hearing them voiced so hatefully sucks the wind from my lungs. But I've learned that tearful reactions only encourage them.

*"Prescott said he had to take three showers after slumming with her."*

I stop in the center of the corridor. The flow of traffic parts around me as I pull in a deep breath and walk back toward their huddle.

When they see me coming, several of the girls scatter. Ann and Heather remain, watching me approach with the same morbid curiosity tourists give my homeless neighbors. Unblinking eyes, backs straight, their dancer's legs motionless beneath knee-length skirts.

"Hey." I lounge against the lockers beside them, smiling as they exchange glances. "I'll tell you something, but you have to keep it to yourselves."

Their eyes narrow, but there's interest there. They love gossip.

"The truth is..." I gesture at my boobs. "I hate these things. It's hard to find shirts that fit"—*let alone afford them*—"and when I do, look at this." I poke at the safety pin. "Popped buttons." I give their flat chests a once-over, and while I feel a pinch of envy for their coltish figures, I hide it beneath a sarcastic tone. "Must be nice to not have to worry about that."

The taller girl, Ann, gives an indignant huff. All lean and graceful and full of confidence, she's the highest-ranked dancer at Le Moyne. She's also intimidatingly beautiful, with her appraising eyes and full lips set in a dark brown complexion sharpened with cool, midnight undertones.

If Le Moyne had formal dances, she would be the prom queen. And for some reason, she has always hated me. She never even gave it a chance to be any other way.

Then there's her sidekick. I'm certain Heather made the shoe comment, but she's coyer than Ann, much too squeamish to be cruel to my face.

I lift a foot, twisting it so they can see the holes in the

lastic. "I wore these last year. And the year before that. And the year before that. In fact, these are the only shoes you've ever seen me wear."

Heather fingers her long, brown braid and stares at my beat-up flats with a furrowed brow. "What size do you wear? I could give you—"

"I don't want your hand-me-downs."

I do want them, but there's no way I'm admitting that. It's hard enough to stand up for myself in these halls. I'm sure as hell not going to do it in borrowed shoes.

Since day one, I've confronted their barbs with directness and honesty. That's what Daddy would've done. Yet here we are, a brand new year, and they're already mocking me with enough venom to burn through my skin.

So I decide to try a different tactic, a harmless lie to shut them up. "These were my grandmother's shoes, the only things she owned when she immigrated to the States. She handed them down to my mother, who passed them to me as a symbol of strength and resilience."

I don't have a grandmother, but Heather's guilty expression tells me I may have finally burst her precious golden bubble.

Triumph spirals its way up my spine. "Next time you open your patronizing mouth, consider the fact that you don't know shit."

Heather sucks in a breath, as if *I* offended *her.*

"Moving on." I stoop toward them. "Here's the thing about Prescott Rivard..." I glance around the crowded hall, like I give a shit who can hear me. "He has a sex problem. All guys do. They want it, and if you don't give it, they *take* it, you know?"

Ann and Heather stare at me blankly. Clueless. How do they not know this?

I adjust the strap of the satchel on my shoulder, my skin itching with the truths I'm leaving out. "Someone has to step up and make the guys happy. I'm just doing my part to keep sexual violence out of our school. You should thank me."

I made that sound a lot more charitable than it actually is. I do what I do to survive. Fuck everyone else.

Ann glares down her scrunched nose at me. "You are such a slut."

A label I've worn since my freshman year here. I've never discouraged their presumptions about me. Sexual misconduct requires proof. As long as it doesn't happen on school grounds and I don't show up pregnant, I won't get kicked out. Of course, the rumors tarnish my already loathsome reputation, but they also distract from the real reason I spend time with the guys at Le Moyne. *That* truth would get me expelled in a heartbeat.

"A slut?" I lower my voice in a conspiratorial whisper. "I haven't had sex in a while. I mean, it's been like forty-eight hours." I turn away, wait for their gasps, and spin back, grinning at Ann. "But your dad promised he'd make up for his lapse tonight."

"Oh my God." Ann doubles over, gripping her midsection and cupping her gaping mouth. "Gross!"

Her father? I wouldn't know, but sex in general *is* gross. Horrible. Unbearable.

And expected.

I leave them in shocked silence and slip through the first

half of the day without losing my smile. Mornings at Le Moyne are a breeze, comprised of all the easy A/B block classes, such as English and History, Science and Math, and World Languages. As midday approaches, we disperse for an hour to eat lunch and work out before switching gears and heading to our specialized classes.

Daily exercise and food are required as part of the *balanced musical diet,* but eating is an inconvenience, seeing how I don't have food or money.

As I stand at my locker in Campus Center, the empty ache in my stomach awakens with a groan. Layered on top of the hunger is a tight bundle of dread. Or excitement.

No, definitely dread.

I stare down at the printout of my afternoon schedule.

*Music Theory*
*Piano Seminar*
*Performance Master Class*
*Private Lessons*

The last half of my day is in Crescent Hall. Room 1A. All taught by Marceaux.

During English Lit, I overheard some of the girls blabbing about the hotness that is *Mister* Marceaux, but I haven't worked up the nerve to wander over to Crescent Hall.

My insides coil tighter as I mutter aloud, "Why does he have to be a *he?*"

The locker door beside me swings shut, and Ellie angles around my arm, glancing at my schedule. "He's really pretty, Ivory."

I whirl toward her. "You saw him?"

"A glimpse." She wiggles her little mousy nose. "Why does the *he* part matter?"

Because I'm more comfortable around women. Because they don't overpower me with muscle and size. Because men are takers. They take my courage, my strength, my confidence. Because they're only interested in one thing, and it's not my ability to play the last bars of Transcendental Étude No.2.

But I can't share all this with Ellie, my sweet, sheltered, reared-in-a-strict-Chinese-home friend. I think I can call her a friend. We've never really established that, but she's always nice to me.

I stuff the schedule in my satchel. "I guess I was hoping for someone like Mrs. McCracken."

Maybe Mr. Marceaux is different. Maybe he's gentle and safe like Daddy and Stogie.

About a head shorter than me, Ellie smooths a hand over the cowlicks of her inky-black hairline and does this bouncy thing on her toes. I think she's trying to stretch her height, but mostly it just looks like she needs to pee. She's so tiny and adorable I want to tug on her ponytail. So I do.

She bats my hand away, smiling with me, and drops back to her heels. "Don't worry about Marceaux. It'll be fine. You'll see."

Easy for her to say. She's already locked in a cellist spot at Boston Conservatory next year. Her future doesn't hinge upon whether or not Marceaux likes her.

"I'm headed to the gym." She lugs a backpack half her size over her shoulder. "You coming?"

Instead of an organized PE class, Le Moyne provides a full
fitness center, personal trainers, and a myriad of conditioning
classes like yoga and kickboxing.

I'd rather cut off my 5-4-3 fingers than jump around in a
mirrored room with disapproving girls. "Nah. I'm going to
run the track outside."

We say our goodbyes, but my curiosity about Marceaux
has me calling after her.

"Ellie? *How* pretty exactly?"

She turns around, walking backwards. "*Shockingly* pretty. It
was just a glimpse, but I'm telling you, I felt it right here." She
pats her stomach and widens her angular eyes. "Maybe a little
lower."

My chest tightens. The prettiest ones have the ugliest
insides.

But I'm pretty, aren't I? I'm told I am, less so by people I
trust and more often by people I don't.

Maybe my insides are ugly, too.

As Ellie bounces away and flashes her pretty smile at me
over her shoulder, I stand corrected in my generalizations.
There's nothing ugly about Ellie.

In the locker room, I change into shorts and a tank top
then head outside to the track that encircles the twenty-acre
campus.

The humidity deters most of the three-hundred students
from venturing out of the A/C this time of year, but a few laze
on the park benches, laughing and eating their lunches. A
couple dancers practice their synchronized warm-ups beneath
the imposing steeples of the Campus Center building.

As I stretch my legs under the shade of a large oak tree, I

stare out over the lush green grounds and rubberized walking trails. The same trails I walked with Daddy when my head barely reached his hip. I can still feel his big hand swallowing mine as he led me along. His smile was so full of sunshine when he pointed out the old cathedral-like stonework of Crescent Hall and speculated on the grandeur of the classrooms within.

Le Moyne was his dream, one his parents couldn't afford. He never seemed sad about that. Because he wasn't a taker, not even when he dreamed. Instead, he gave his dream to me.

Bending at the waist, I reach for my toes and let the stretch heat my hamstrings as the memories warm my blood. I look like Mom with my dark hair and dark eyes, but I have Daddy's smile. I wish he could see me now, standing here on the campus, living his dream, and wearing his smile.

I grin wider, because his dream, his smile...they're mine, too.

"Holy mother of God, I missed that ass."

I snap straight, smile gone and my body too stiff to turn toward the voice that makes my shoulders hike around my ears. "What do you want, Prescott?"

"You. Naked. Wrapped around my dick."

My stomach caves in, and a bead of sweat trickles down my temple. I straighten my spine. "I have a better idea. How about you tuck your dick between your legs, dance like Buffalo Bill, and go fuck yourself."

"You're so nasty," Prescott says with a smile in his voice as he prowls into my line of sight.

He stops an appropriate distance away, but not far enough. I step back.

His long hair stops at his jawline, the blond strands bleached by the Caribbean sun or wherever he spends his summers. If his tie and button-up are stifling him in this heat, he doesn't show it as he takes his time unnerving me with his wandering gaze.

I don't understand why the girls at Le Moyne fight over him. His nose is too long, his front tooth is crooked, and his tongue squirms like a worm whenever he shoves it in my mouth.

"Jesus, Ivory." His focus zeroes in on my chest, burning my skin beneath the top. "Your tits grew another cup size over the summer."

I fight my shoulders into a relaxed position. "If you're asking for my help this year, try again."

His eyes remain locked on my chest, his long fingers tightening around his sack lunch. "I want you."

"You want me *to do your homework.*"

"That, too."

The huskiness in his voice makes me shiver. I wrap my arms around my chest, hating how noticeable my boobs are, hating the way he flagrantly stares at them, hating that I depend on him.

His gaze finally lifts, landing on my mouth. "What happened to your lip? Catch it on a cock ring?"

I shrug. "It was a really big...ring."

His expression darkens with jealousy, and I hate that, too.

"You should get one." I tilt my head at the forced sound of his laughter. "Why not? It increases the pleasure." I don't know anything about piercings, but I can't pass up the dig. "If you had one, you might actually make a girl come."

His strained laugh cuts off with a cough. "Wait, what?" His eyes harden. "I make you come."

Sex with him is a lot like removing a tampon. A quick tug that leads to a repulsive mess, one I discard from my mind until it has to be done again. I don't bother telling him this. He can see it all in my glare.

"That's bullshit." He charges forward, crossing the boundary of what onlookers would consider friendly conversation.

When he reaches for my arm, I glance up at the Campus Center building and find the empty window of the dean's office. "Your mom's watching."

"You're a lying bitch." He doesn't look up, but his hand drops.

"If you want my help, I'm going to need an advance."

He barks out a disgusted laugh. "Hells no."

"Suit yourself." I take off at a sprint, keeping to the grass along the track where it doesn't burn my bare feet.

It only takes a couple seconds for Prescott's long legs to catch up. "Hang on, Ivory." Sweat forms on his face as he jogs beside me in his collared shirt. "Will you just stop for a minute?"

I slow my strides, anchor my fists on my hips, and wait for him to catch his breath.

"Look, I don't have any cash on me right now." He pulls at the pockets of his slacks. "But I'll pay you tonight."

*Tonight.* My stomach buckles, but I smile through it and pluck the sack lunch out of his hand. "This will do until then."

Lunch is the only advance I needed anyway. He has an

nlimited balance in the cafeteria, so it's not like he'll go
 ungry.

He looks at my bare feet, at the paper bag in my hand, and
 auses on my busted lip. For a guy who struggles with
 lgebra, he's not stupid. More like disinterested. Disinterested
 n my problems. Disinterested in the curriculum.

None of us are here to study quadratic equations or cell
biology. We came for the arts program, to dance, to sing, to
play our instruments, and to get accepted at the music
conservatory of our choosing. Prescott would rather devote
his time to fucking and playing classical guitar, not writing a
history report *en Français*. Lucky for him, he doesn't have to
bother with academic coursework. Not when he can pay me
to do it for him.

He isn't the only entitled prick at Le Moyne, but I limit my
services to those with the biggest wallets and the most to lose.
We all know the risks. If one of us goes down, we all go down.
Unfortunately, my little circle of cheaters is largely made up
of Prescott and his friends.

And sometimes they take more than they pay for.

I peer into the lunch sack, salivating at the sight of roast
beef on crusty bread, grapes, and chocolate cookies. "Tonight
where?"

"The usual."

Which involves picking me up ten blocks from school,
parking his car in a vacant lot, and doing a lot more than
homework. But I'm the one who established the rules. No
swapping homework assignments on school property or
public places. It's too risky, especially with the way the dean
watches her son.

"See you in class." He strides away, his attention locked on the dean's window and the shadowed silhouette within.

He swears she doesn't suspect anything, but she's been gunning against me since she stepped in as *Mother Superior* my sophomore year. Maybe it's my slutty reputation or lack of wealth. Or maybe it's my choice of college.

Leopold Conservatory of New York is the most selective university in the country and only accepts one Le Moyne musician each year. That is, if they accept any of us at all. Dozens of my peers have applied, including Prescott, but Mrs. McCracken said I'm the best. I'm the one she was going to recommend. Which makes me Prescott's biggest competitor. At least, I *was*. Without her referral, I may very well be back to square one.

Curled up beneath a tree, I devour Prescott's lunch and convince myself not to worry about him. Marceaux will like me. He'll see that I deserve the spot. And tonight... Tonight, I won't get in Prescott's car. We can go over his assignments on the sidewalk, and if he has a problem with that, I'll leave. Let him fail his coursework and drop out of the running for Leopold. I'll find another slacker to make up for the loss in income.

As I run the three-mile track that winds around the tree-covered property, I strengthen my mind and body with the solidity of that plan.

When the five-minute warning bell rings through the buildings, I'm showered, dressed, and weaving through the crowds in Crescent Hall, my stomach lurching into a roil.

*All you need is a moment.*

Stogie's confidence in me lightens my steps, but it's the

memory of Daddy's energy that lifts my lips. If he were in my
shoes, walking the halls he dreamed about, he would've been
humming with unrestrained enthusiasm and gratefulness. I
can feel it, his infectious dynamism, pumping my blood and
hurrying my strides as I enter Room 1A, the same music
room I was in last year.

An impressive display of brass, string, and percussion
instruments line the far wall. Six or so of my fellow musicians
gather around the desks at the center of the huge *L*-shaped
space. If I walked around the corner, I would see the
Bösendorfer grand piano in the alcove. But my attention
snags on the man in the front of the room.

Perched on the edge of the desk, arms crossed over his
chest, he watches the congregation of students with a
brooding, irritated expression. Thank God he hasn't noticed
me yet, because I can't seem to unglue my feet from the floor
or look away.

He's unexpectedly young, not student young but perhaps
my brother's age. His profile is ruggedly sculpted, his jaw
cleanly shaved, yet so dark I suspect the sharpest razor
doesn't scrape away the shadow.

The longer I stare, the more I realize it's not his face that
looks youthful. It's his style, so unlike other teachers with
their conservative suits and modest demeanors.

It's the way his black hair is arranged, short on the sides,
long and messy on top, like a shove of his fingers left it falling
across his brow in perfect chaos. His long legs appear to be
encased in dark jeans, but closer scrutiny confirms he's
wearing slacks that are cut like jeans. The sleeves of his plaid
button-up roll up to the elbows, and his tie has a different

plaid design, which doesn't match but somehow totally works. His brown fitted waistcoat is the kind a man wears beneath a suit jacket. Except there is no jacket.

His overall look is casual cosmopolitan, professional with personality, challenging the dress code without violating it.

"Take a seat." His booming voice reverberates through the room, jarring my insides, but it's not directed at me.

I exhale a moment of relief before he swivels toward me. His blue eyes move first, followed by his whole body. His hands grip the edge of the desk as his face comes into full view. Sweet merciful fuck, words like *shockingly pretty* dilute the effect of his image. Yeah, the first glimpse is a shock, but it's not just his attractiveness. It's his presence, his projection of self-assurance and command that makes me feel disoriented, breathless, and really fucking weird deep in my core.

He stares at me for an eternal second, expressionless, and his dark eyebrows pull into a *V*.

"Are you...?" He glances at the hall behind me and returns to my face. "You weren't at the staff meeting this morning."

"Staff meeting?" Realization punches me in the gut.

He thinks I'm a teacher, and now he's looking at me like guys do, his gaze dragging over my body and arousing a twisted sickness in my belly. It reminds me how different I look than other girls my age and how much I hate those differences.

I pull my satchel over my chest, hiding my most noticeable parts. "I'm not..." I clear my throat and force my feet toward the nearest desk. "I'm a student. Piano."

"Of course." He stands, hands slipping into his pockets, voice gruff. "Sit down."

# DARK
## NOTES

His stark, icy eyes follow me, and goddammit, I don't want o be intimidated by them. I attempt to fortify my swift steps with the confidence I felt walking in, but my legs are wobbly.

As I lower the satchel beside a vacant desk, his impatience thunders louder, sharper. "Hurry up!"

I drop into the chair, hands trembling and my heartbeat a heavy hammer in my head. If I were stronger, more confident, I wouldn't care that his gaze is drilling into mine and tripping my pulse.

If I were stronger, I'd be able to look away.

# EMERIC

Blindsided. That's the best explanation for the stern volume of my voice and tightness in my usually-composed expression. I wasn't prepared for this. Not for a tall, voluptuous, sexy-beyond-all-reason woman to walk into my classroom. My first thought? Beverly Rivard found the hottest music teacher in the country to place in my employ. To test me.

*But she's not a teacher.*

I relax my fingers on the edge of the desk. Christ, that would've been a terrible inconvenience.

Except this is worse.

Distrust steels the girl's gaze as she studies me from the front row. Sitting stiffly in the chair, she tugs the hem of her skirt over her knees and keeps her legs closed. Not the reaction I'm used to from women—or high school girls, for that matter.

I pride myself on being a strict, respectable educator. I know how female students look at me, and I'm immune to the bubbly-hearted infatuation in their innocent eyes. But there isn't a hint of naïve adoration in the deep mahogany eyes staring at me now. In my six years of teaching, I've never encountered a student who regards me as if she's summed me up in a glance and disapproves of my intentions.

Maybe this girl heard about the mistakes I made with Joanne, the *debauchery* that led to her taking my job. Well, fuck that job. Only my parents know the depth of what I lost in Shreveport and the nature of my intentions.

Whatever this girl thinks she knows, I'm not beyond using intimidation or a show of power to demand her focus in the classroom.

I hold her incisive gaze as I speak to the class. "Find a seat and put your phones away."

Several more students trickle in, and a quick count of eleven girls and nine boys confirms everyone is present.

As the bell rings, the latecomers choose their seats. I recognize Beverly's son from the pictures displayed in her office. Prescott Rivard is cockier in person, wearing a smirk instead of a photogenic smile. He settles next to the brown-eyed beauty and leans over her desk to twist a finger through her hair.

She jerks away. "Stop it."

The hipster boy on her other side angles toward her, his skinny body squeezed into tight pants, a checkered shirt, and a plaid bow tie. He stares at her mouth through black-framed glasses and whispers something too low for me to hear.

Her lips thin into a line, and the dark expression on her face seems to come from a place much deeper than simple irritation.

I need to know what he's saying to her. It's a weird sort of curiosity, pulsing in my chest, as I level a look at the whispering boy. "What's your name?"

He reclines, flippantly slouching with his legs stretched out beneath the desk. "Sebastian Roth."

I walk toward him and give the toe of his shoe a warning kick that propels him to sit straight. "What did you say to her, Mr. Roth?"

He leers at the girl, rubbing his mouth to hide his grin. "I was just commenting on how big her...uh..." He looks at her chest and lifts his gaze to her mouth. "Her lip. How big her lip is."

Prescott bursts into laughter, followed by several boys sitting around him.

That's when I notice the segregation in seating. Girls on one side. Boys on the other. With the exception of the girl who looks like a woman. Whether she chose her seat out of urgency or to deliberately sit where hard-dicked boys could flock around her, I intend to find out.

With the tips of my fingers in my pockets, thumbs out, I shift to stand before her. "Your name?"

Her bottom lip is, indeed, cut and swollen. She sucks it between her teeth as her shoulders make a slow decent to self-assurance. Then she raises her chin and meets my eyes. "Ivory Westbrook."

*Ivory.* That conjures an image of paleness with hard, worn edges like piano keys or teeth. Doesn't fit her at all. She's a dark portrait of soft curves and chestnut hair with deep golden skin that seems to absorb shadows in the room I hadn't noticed until now.

Fuck, I'm definitely going out and getting laid tonight.

"Miss Westbrook, find a seat with fewer distractions." I point toward the girls.

Ivory's enormous doe eyes stare up at me, as if caught in the glare of stage lights. She blinks, glances at the girls, and looks down at her desk when they cast her uninviting sneers. That answers my question about her seating choice.

"I'm not here to indulge in your sensibilities." I slam a hand on her desk, making her jump. "Move."

With a ragged inhale, she grabs her satchel and walks toward the snickering girls, her gait leaden yet determined.

Every male in the room watches her stride along the front row of desks, and I don't have to follow suit to know what they see. Stripper-pole legs, tits almighty, and a high, round ass that flexes with each step.

The primitive, hungry part of me wants to join in their appreciation while the protective part wants to cover her with an over-sized coat. Instead, the disciplinarian takes over and lands an admonishing smack on the back of the closest juvenile head.

Sebastian flinches and casts me a startled look. "What was that for?"

I pluck his phone from his hand and toss it in the vicinity of my desk. It overshoots, slides off the other side, and hits the floor.

The rest of the room erupts in a flurry, shoving phones into pockets and bags. Everyone except Ivory. Hands folded together on the desk and no phone in sight, she watches me with a guarded expression.

Sebastian plays with a clump of his over-oiled hair. "If you broke my phone..."

I arch my eyebrow, my tone hard. "Go on."

He shrugs. "My dad will buy me a new one."

Of course, and it would be hypocritical of me to condemn this kid for being an entitled prick. I was no different at his

...ge, with wealthy parents and an inflated sense of self-
...mportance. Hell, I'm still a prick, only now I'm held
...ccountable for my actions.

I move to the front of the room, hands clasped behind my
back. "Welcome to twelfth-grade Music Theory. I'm Mr.
Marceaux, and I'll be your music director for your last year
here at Le Moyne Academy. After this class, you'll head to
your master classes in specific disciplines. Piano students will
remain with me. Before we begin, what do you want to know
about me?"

The Asian girl who Ivory chose to sit by raises her hand.

I gesture toward her. "Introduce yourself, please."

She stands beside her desk. "Ellie Lai. Cello." She bounces
on her toes. "What's your background?"

I give her a nod and wait until she settles in her seat. "I
hold a Master of Music from Leopold Conservatory of New
York. I'm a member of the Louisiana Symphony Orchestra.
And my most recent employment was Head of School at
Shreveport Preparatory, where I also directed the music
program."

Prescott makes a show of stretching and smiling. Then he
nonchalantly tosses an arm in the air and speaks without my
prompt. "What are you, like...twenty-seven? Twenty-eight?"
His voice drawls with antagonism. "How did you get a
master's, do the teaching thing and become dean, all in such a
short amount time? What's up with that, Mr. M?"

*I worked my fucking ass off, you lazy little cocksucker.*

And to think, in one hasty slide of a zipper, I lost it all,
including something I never set out to have, which ended up
being the only thing that mattered.

The very thought of Joanne sitting behind my desk in Shreveport makes my rib cage vibrate with rage. But imagining her continuing her life without me evokes a toxic fume of poison so invasive I can smell the betrayal with every choking breath.

I slowly roll my neck, clearing my thoughts and reining myself in. "I received my undergrad early and taught high school in Manhattan while I worked on my master's. Any other questions?"

Ivory raises her hand.

"Yes?"

She remains seated, doesn't fidget, and her dark gaze hones directly into mine. "You play piano? I mean, of course you do, since you'll be my tutor. But you play piano in the Symphony Orchestra?"

Christ, her voice... It's not lazy and high-pitched like girls her age. It's complex and entrancing, like raindrops at midnight.

"Yes, I play piano in the Orchestra."

Her smile is a slow-building nocturne, a tranquil expansion from her mouth to her eyes. "Solo?"

"Sometimes."

"Wow."

Not only am I shocked by her line of questioning, but the reverent way she's looking at me makes my goddamn skin hum. I don't like it. I'm proud of my achievements, but not when that lofty feeling distracts me from my hard-earned bitterness.

I dismiss the remaining raised hands with a sharp tone. "Open your Music Theory books to chapter three. We're ʒoing to jump right into..." My attention snags on Ivory as the entire room follows my directive except her. "Do you need a hearing aid, Miss Westbrook?"

"No." She drops her hands in her lap and meets my gaze head-on. "My other teachers gave me the week to buy my books."

"Do I look like your other teachers?"

"No, Mr. Marceaux." A female voice pipes up in the back. "You definitely do not."

A chorus of giggles follows, and irritation curls my fingers.

I swipe my text book from my bag and drop it on her desk. "Chapter three." I lean in, putting my face in hers. "Try to keep up."

She blinks rapidly. "Yes, sir."

Her whispered response strums at a pulsating, destructive, very adult hunger deep inside me. My skin heats, and my palms slick with sweat.

Jesus, I'm going to need a screaming-hard fuck tonight. Leather, rope, and chafing strokes. No safe words. No clingy aftercare. Chloe or Deb will do. Maybe both.

*Focus, Emeric.*

"Take out your tablets and open a browser to my website." With my back to the class, I continue talking while scrawling the url on the whiteboard. "You'll find all my lectures here. I expect you to follow along."

When I face the room, Ivory hasn't moved to follow my directions.

I feel a vein throbbing in my forehead and anchor my fists on my hips. "Let me guess. No tablet?"

"She can sit here," Prescott says, patting his lap, "and share mine."

She clenches her jaw and flips him off.

I waver between wanting to punch Prescott's face and whip Ivory's perfect ass. Neither is a lawful option, and the latter boils my blood just for thinking it.

My focus dips to her lips for a breath too long before I address the class. "Read the chapter and answer the questions at the end of the lecture."

I curl a finger at Ivory in a follow-me gesture. "I'll see you in the hall."

# IVORY

I follow Mr. Marceaux out of the classroom, my mouth dry and hands damp. As the door clicks shut behind him, my insides writhe under the barrage of a thousand fists.

He's not a huge man, but he seems gigantic in the empty hall, a towering pissed-off mountain of repercussion.

If my future depends on his first impression of me, I've fucked my life to hell.

He rubs a hand down his face, over his mouth, and glares at me for an eternity. "You come to my class unprepared and—"

"I cleared the text book issue with the front office. They always give me the first week to—"

"Do *not* interrupt me," he says harshly and leans in, bracing a hand on the wall beside my head.

A rush of blood heats my cheeks beneath the intimidating blue of his gaze. His mouth is so close I can smell the lingering scent of cinnamon gum on his breath, and my stomach turns with unease.

"Are you deliberately trying to waste my time?" His jaw hardens. "No sniveling excuses or lies. You have five words to explain why you don't have your supplies."

Five words? Is this guy serious? He can eat a dick, because

I'm only giving him four.

"I live in Treme."

"Treme," he echoes, deadpanned.

I hate how stiff and uncomfortable I feel in the confines of his glare. I want him to look away, because I hate his eyes, hate the vivid facets of sapphire and the way the icy specks sharpen under the fluorescent lights. Nothing could ever be gentle or safe in that gaze.

His throat moves in the deep pocket of shadow above his tie. "Why?"

"Why what?"

"Why do you live in Treme?"

He doesn't just ask the question. He snaps it like a whip. Like a punishment I didn't earn.

I'm only inches away from him, my back against the wall, and I feel defensive, cornered, my hackles bristling with vindication. "Oh, right. I forgot you have a big fancy degree, so I'll dumb it down for you."

"Watch your fucking tone."

It's barely a whisper, caught and held in the small space between us, but I feel it vibrate through me like a thunderous roar.

He said no sniveling excuses or lies? Fine.

I wipe the attitude from my voice and give him raw, unpolished honesty. "I live in Treme because my family can't afford a mansion in the Garden District, Mr. Marceaux. I can't afford a cell phone or *any* kind of phone. I can't afford running shoes or food for my cat. And those...those electronic bracelets all my classmates wear when they work out? I don't know what they do, but I can't afford one of those, either.

And right now, I don't have the money for school supplies. But I will. I'll have it by the end of the week."

Straightening, he steps back and lowers his head. Is that a fucking smile he's hiding? I swear to God I glimpsed one. Is he actually enjoying the pathetic appraisal of my life? What a horrible fucking person! *This* is the teacher I'm supposed to look up to? The one who will make me or break me? My lungs heave and slam together.

When he lifts his head, his mouth is a flat line, and the frigid depths of his eyes seem to manipulate his entire expression, twisting it into a collage of other faces that haunt me when I sleep. "Am I supposed to feel sorry for you?"

"Never," I seethe through grinding teeth. "I never want that."

"No? Then what? Seems you expect me to make exceptions for you?"

"No. Just—" I've never met a more callous, self-righteous dick. "Just write me up or whatever you're going to do."

I know something isn't right the moment he looks down the hall and checks to make sure we're alone. I know this entire confrontation is inappropriate when he bends toward me and places his hands on the wall, trapping me in. And I know there isn't a goddamn thing I can do about it as he whispers through the pounding in my ears.

"Don't worry about your punishment." His attention falls to my lips, returns to my eyes. "I'll take care of that later."

Just like that, my strength, my bravery, all the things I wish I had right now abandon me in the heavy arms of fear. I've been in this position countless times. This is a first with a teacher, but he's no different than the other takers. I could report him, but who are they going to believe? The girl with a slutty reputation or the former dean of Shreveport? And while I can't overpower him, I know I'll survive it. I might even master my emotions while it's happening, like a Chopin nocturne in D-flat major.

I'm startled when his hand lifts, not to grab my breast but to pinch my chin so he can see my lip. "You need to go to the nurse and have her put something on this cut."

It's not until he releases me and slides his hands into his pockets that I realize I'm shaking. He steps back, elbows wide, shoulders loose. A heavy chill diffuses through my body.

He watches me with those arctic blue eyes, and I'm not sure if I'm supposed to head toward the nurse's office or wait to be dismissed. For some reason, it matters. Like he's testing me. So I wait.

He's a mercurial, heartless asshole, but he also surprised me. He didn't force his mouth against mine, didn't dig his fingers between my legs. He...stepped back?

Maybe I still have a chance to prove I'm not just a poor girl or a five-minute grope in a hallway.

A recurrent of sharp clicking sounds fills the silence between us. I follow the noise with my gaze, trailing over his tie and waistcoat, visually tracing along the dark dusting of hair on his exposed forearm, and pause on the mechanical watch on his wrist.

Moving wheels with tooth-like points whirl inside the enormous face, ticking, measuring the rhythm of time, like a metronome. Will each ticking moment I spend with him be an irreversible succession into the future? Or will he hold me here, stuck in the present, in this life?

"Miss Westbrook."

I snap my attention to his face, the angled lines of his jaw, the darker shades of his cheeks where stubble will grow in, and the curve of lips that haven't been injured by circumstance. He seems untouchable. Maybe his fists are as brutal as his beauty. Just looking at him feels like I'm inhaling a lungful of fire.

Because he's dangerous, and he seems to know this, too, as he thrusts an impatient finger in the direction of the nurse's office, his voice fueled with urgency. "Go."

I turn and hurry down the hall with the weight of his gaze pressing against my back.

# EMERIC

As Ivory darts down the hall, she doesn't look back, doesn't dare meet my eyes. But the frantic rush of her steps tells me enough. I affect her. Not my professional bearing, but my masculine presence. I terrify her.

A wide grin stretches my mouth.

Separated by the length of the corridor, I still feel the *what-ifs* firing between us. I know she imagined us together when I corralled her against the wall. I'm certain she felt the power exchange, maybe even detested it, as it stuttered her inhales and dilated her pupils. And still, she waited for my permission to leave.

Knowing that, watching her run away, the sight of her curvaceous body swaying innocently, all of it ignites a predatory need inside me. The need to chase.

But I won't. Not here. Not ever. I release a breath and wait for my hard-on to receive the message.

The moment she vanishes around the corner, I slouch against the wall.

She's exactly the kind of woman I'm drawn to. A woman who flees when hunted and comes alive when she's caught. A woman who bends beneath punishments and seeks acceptance in her humiliation. A woman who bites at a heavy

PAM GODWIN

hand, only to melt around the unforgiving grip when it cuts her air.

I demanded her honesty—*no sniveling excuses or lies*—and expected her to recoil, disobey, or tell me to fuck off. But she didn't, *couldn't.* It was the moment I realized it's her nature to give me what I want. When she exposed the embarrassing details of her poverty, offering up her vulnerabilities for me to mock at, heaven help me, it was beautiful and tragic and seductive—a trinity of temptation.

A greedy throb tightens the front of my pants, but the reaction means fuckall. It's simple, really. I want sex. Filthy, kinky sex. Nothing more. As raw and enraged as I am about my last mistake, I'm unwilling to move on, unable to let go of Joanne. But I'm also vicious in my resentment and vindictive enough to fuck as many women as possible with the brutal dominance Joanne craves and can no longer have. Maybe she'll choke on her poisonous jealousy.

Which makes Ivory a tantalizing tease. I can give her exactly what she needs. I can train her, objectify her, and defile her, and she'd let me, because surrender is the very fabric of her sexuality.

But I could also lose myself in her, because she's the kind of woman I make mistakes for.

Except she's not a woman.

As a senior, she's at least seventeen, the legal age of consent. But she's still a child, ten years my junior, and sexual conduct between teacher and student is punishable by imprisonment, regardless of age.

The notion is sobering, deflating my dick and making it a hell of a lot easier to keep my hands to myself.

52

Back in the classroom, the students bombard me with questions about the chromatic scale and the circle of fifths. Slowly, my fixation with Ivory slips into the recesses of my mind.

Until the door opens, and her dark eyes instantly find mine.

I continue the lecture as she slides behind her desk, her bottom lip glazed in a sheen of ointment. I don't give her more than a half-second glance. I'm the adult here, the one in control of our interactions. Ignoring my fascination with her, pretending I don't want to devour her with my gaze, sets appropriate boundaries. I'm here to teach her, and that doesn't include instructions on how to properly suck my cock.

To be honest, despite my disgraceful end as Head of School in Shreveport, I'm excited to be back in the classroom. Nothing fills me with a sense of belonging like standing before a rapt audience and commanding attention with the sound of my voice. This isn't a job. It's a creditable use of my need to influence and dominate, a place where I can discipline weaknesses, mold trustful minds, and inspire students with my passion for music.

My veins thrum with energy as I listen to the class discuss the application of an invariant hexachord. I straddle a chair at the front of the room, nodding in encouragement and interjecting only when they stray off topic. They look to me for knowledge, shiver beneath my directives, and I get off on it.

This is why I didn't fight to keep my job in Shreveport. I need this...this freedom to leave all the administrative bullshit behind and focus on my love of teaching.

The class discussion grows in volume, voices clashing, as a debate arises about the use of tone rows. I'm seconds from putting an end to it when Ivory jumps in.

"You guys, ordinary relations of tones *are* stereotypical." She furrows her brow. "But you can still obtain an emotional thrill from the music." She quickly backs up her points with valid examples in Schoenberg's Concerto for Violin.

Not once does she reference the textbook. Not even as she cites ornamental compositions by opus number. The classroom listens quietly, and by the time the bell rings, she's brilliantly persuaded the debate.

I find myself...impressed. She knows the material, almost as well as I do. If she plays piano with the same aptitude, I'll have to punish her just for making me so goddamn enamored.

Her eyes catch mine as the classroom thins out. Five students remain, but I'm too focused on one to make note of the others. There's something recognizable in her gaze. Distrust? Accusation? *Abuse.* Whatever she's exposing is both offensive and haunting.

I harden my eyes, a silent reprimand. She looks away, her emollient-lathered lips rubbing together, as she surveys her peers.

Three boys and two girls make up the senior pianists at Le Moyne, including the hipster fuck, Sebastian Roth. He moved seats between classes, sitting closer to Ivory while leaving a row between them. I'll let it go as long as he doesn't look at her, not one fucking glance.

Since the student files didn't land on my desk until lunchtime, I haven't had a chance to read them. But I knew the final classes in my schedule would be an intimate group. The perquisites of forking out an expensive tuition are many, all illustrated in Le Moyne's glossy brochure with an entire page dedicated to its 1:5 teacher-student ratio.

"So this is what Le Moyne's top pianists look like?" I pitch my voice with doubt, making it clear they'll have to prove themselves. "You think you have what it takes to become piano virtuosos, composers, professors...something other than privileged, snot-nosed brats?"

Except Ivory. Her tattered clothes and shoes, her inability to buy textbooks, nothing about her reeks of privilege. How does a girl from a poor neighborhood land a spot here? It's bizarre. And distracting.

Forcing her out of my mind, I stroll along the rows, hands folded behind my back, and study each of the five students without registering individual features. I don't give a shit what they look like. I'm searching for straight spines, parted lips, and alert gazes.

Five pairs of eyes lock on me, their bodies angled to follow my movements, breaths hitching, waiting, as I pass each desk. I have their attention.

"We'll be spending three hours a day together, every day, for the rest of the year. Music Theory, Piano Seminar, Performance Master Class, and for some of you, private lessons... This is what Mommy and Daddy shelled out the big bucks for." My leisurely walk ends at the front of the room, and I turn to face them. "Don't waste my time, and I won't waste your parents' money. Don't take me seriously, and I will seriously fuck up your prospective futures. Are we clear?"

I can almost smell the mix of trepidation and startled

respect in the silence that follows.

"I'm not going to lecture or put you on a piano bench today." I glance at the student files on my desk. "I'm going to use the next few hours in one-on-one conferences with each of you. Don't think of it as an interview. Just a brief meeting to help me become acquainted with your backgrounds and academic goals."

Unbidden, my thoughts dart to Ivory and all the ways I *can't* become acquainted with her. I push a hand through my hair, avoiding the prick of her gaze. I'm itching to talk to her again, to learn how a girl from Treme affords one of the most expensive tuitions in the country.

Maybe I don't want to know.

But I do know I need a moment to gather some damn self-control. "Mr. Roth, I'll start with you."

I'll save the temptation for last.

# IVORY

I twirl a pencil between my fingers and try not to chew a hole in my lip. Sitting on the floor in the back corner of the *L*-shaped room, I watch Mr. Marceaux through the maze of chair legs while he conducts private meetings at his desk.

A huge space separates us, the length of two normal classrooms filled with desks and instruments. But when he glances my way, which he does unnervingly often, I can see him. I can also shift ever-so-slightly and obstruct the eye contact.

Sometimes I don't move, my gaze paralyzed under the force of his. Why? It's the strangest thing, this preoccupation I have with him. I want to learn more about him—what he eats, the music he listens to, and where he goes when he's not here. I want to study his calculated movements, watch the path of his fingers along his jaw, stare at the hard angles of his face, and memorize the way his slacks outline the shape of him. He's enchanting, distracting, and positively terrifying.

Why can't I just focus on something else? This has nothing to do with my ambitions for college and his role in it. Good lord, I haven't even thought of that. I just want... What? For him to look at me? I hate his eyes, yet I watch them, wait for them to shift my way. That's so fucked up.

He told us we could use the free block of time to study, but I can't concentrate. I can't think about anything except the enigma in the front of the room.

Two of the students, Sebastian and Lester, left after their meetings. Sarah chose to hang out after hers, and Chris is up there now, perched stiffly on the edge of his chair, nodding at whatever Mr. Marceaux is saying.

That leaves me, and the wait for my turn is flaying my insides.

"Psst. Ivory."

I turn toward Sarah, who mirrors my cross-legged position—our loose skirts stretched over knees for modesty—at the other end of the back wall.

"C'mere," she whispers.

I shake my head, unwillingly to give up my view.

With a sigh, she sets her textbook down and crawls toward me.

This should be interesting. I think she's talked to me twice in the last three years. I gave up trying to be friends with her when she said the hamburger I was eating was made of greed, lies, and murder. I don't have the luxury to choose food that saves farm animals and boycotts political agendas.

Her brown, stick-straight hair is so long it drags along the floor as she edges toward me on hands and knees. She has an old-school hippie look about her, with ropes of multi-colored beads dangling from her neck, a long flowing dress that she hitches up her thighs, and a mischievous twinkle in her eyes. I'm pretty sure she's not wearing a bra, but she has the kind of svelte build that doesn't require one.

She tumbles into a sprawl beside me, all arms and legs and

smiles. What is she up to?

In a volume too low to be heard beyond our huddle, she asks, "What do you think of him?"

Kill me now. I'm not going there with her. "He's stern."

She glances at Mr. Marceaux, and lines form in her forehead. "Not *him*. I mean, yeah, he's stern and sexy and... hello? Didn't you hear about his *other* uses for his belt?"

His belt? I shake my head. "What do you mean?"

"It's just hearsay. I want to talk about Chris Stevens."

I don't have an opinion on Chris, other than he tried to sleep with me sophomore year, and I've been avoiding him since. "What about him?"

"Have you fucked him?"

My cheeks burn. "What!"

Mr. Marceaux cuts his splintery eyes at me.

Shit. I lower my voice, clipping the words. "I haven't done anything with him."

"Sorry, sorry. It's just...." She separates a lock of her hair and proceeds to plait it into a skinny braid. "I know you've been with Prescott and Sebastian and...others. They don't shut up about it, and well, never mind. It was rude to assume." She drops the braid and flashes me a pair of dimples. "Are we gravy?"

"Yeah, we're good." I guess?

"Cool, because I need some advice." She lowers her chin, whispering, *"On sex.* And since you're...um..."

*A slut? A tramp? A dirty whore?* I fight my shoulders into a relaxed position. "I'm what?"

"Experienced."

I grit my teeth.

She doesn't seem to notice. "Chris and I are kind of a thing. Like, we've made out and stuff, and I've been...I don't know, saving my *V*-card for something special, you know?"

No, I don't know. I can't imagine anyone or anything being special enough to go through that for.

She puts her face so close to mine all I see is freckles. "What's it like?"

I tilt back, growing increasingly uncomfortable by the second. "What? Sex?"

"Yeah." She licks her lips. "That."

Just the thought of sex makes my stomach swarm with a thousand bees. Enduring it is worse than licking an oozing cold sore covered in dead skin and pus. But I don't know if it's like that for everyone—people act like girls are supposed to like it—so I shrug.

She cocks her head. "Does it hurt? The first time?"

"Yeah." My voice cracks, and I clear it. "It hurts." It never stops hurting.

"How old were you?"

I don't want to talk about this, but at the same time, my chest aches with an overwhelming need to share. No one has ever asked me about my sexual experiences. Definitely not my mom, and I've never had a close friend. Isn't this what I've always wanted? Girl talk without judgment?

I search her face for signs of cruelty and find only bright-eyed curiosity. It produces a warm sensation deep in my core. She's interested, maybe even envious. Because I have something she doesn't. *Experience.*

Stretching my legs out, I rest my head against the wall. "I was thirteen."

"Wow." Her face glows with wonderment. "Who? How? Tell me everything."

The words come easily, pouring from a memory that's tattooed on every cell of my body. "My brother had just come home after serving time in the Marine Corps, and he brought one of the guys from his squad with him. His best friend."

I was so taken with Lorenzo then, so giddy over his good looks, battle-honed muscles, and rugged charm. And he looked at me like I was the most beautiful girl he'd ever seen.

He still looks at me, and I dread it down to the marrow of my bones.

Sarah covers her mouth, her smile escaping around her fingers. "You gave your virginity to your brother's best friend?"

Prickles race up my spine. "He was staying with us until he could get his own place. I woke one night, couldn't fall back asleep, so I stepped outside to sit on the back deck."

Daddy had only been gone a month, and the loss was still so very painful, a constant constriction in my chest. He used to say, *Nothing is inconceivable, and everything is possible. The proof is in the magic of music.* So there I was, humming his favorite Herbie Hancock song, wishing for the inconceivable, and willing him to come back.

Sarah crowds in, her expression radiating far more enthusiasm than the reality of that night deserves. "What happened?"

"My brother's friend came outside and pinned me on the stairs. He was so big. Big *everywhere.* And strong. He knew what he wanted, and I couldn't stop him from taking it."

Couldn't stop the concrete steps from scraping my chest

and legs as he took me from behind. The hand on my mouth muffling my screams. The ripping sound of my nightie. The smell of his breath rotting the air. And the hurt between my legs...the tearing, the blood, the soreness for days after when he took me again and again.

"Dude." Sarah slouches against the wall. "That sounds so hot."

It does?

"You're so lucky." She plays with the ends of her hair. "You have boobs and experience and guys like that falling all over you. I want that. I guess I've been scared, but I'm definitely ready to...you know...with Chris."

There must be something wrong with me, because boobs and sex and everything she just said makes me want to puke my guts out. "Sarah, don't—"

"Between you and me, the girls around here are only mean to you because they're jealous. I mean, look at you. Guys want that." She waves a hand to indicate my body. "No wonder you've slept with half the school."

Bile hits the back of my throat, and I swallow repeatedly to keep it down.

"Oh, look. He's done." Sarah jumps to her feet, grabs her books, and rushes through the room, making a beeline for Chris.

Part of me wants to tackle her to the floor and beg her to stay away from him. But the other part, the selfish part, craves her acceptance. If she has sex with Chris, she'll be just like me. Maybe she'll talk to me more, confide in me. Maybe I can share other things, scarier things, about men and their needs.

"Miss Westbrook." Mr. Marceaux stands from his chair,

fists on his hips and a chill in his eyes. "Don't keep me waiting."

# EMERIC

I attempt to read through her student file, but the words run together. I'm too distracted, my every thought funneling toward the girl on the other side of my desk. I sent the other students home, and now it's just Ivory and me and this inconvenient attraction.

Her slender fingers fold together in her lap, her back straight and dark hair falling around the graceful lines of her neck. A smile anchors her lips, an expression that seems to come naturally to her, but this one is smaller than its predecessors. Shakier. The kind of smile little girls wear when they're scared.

I drop the file on the desk and lean forward, breaching her invisible bubble of tension. "What are you worried about?"

I know the answer, but I want to hear what it sounds like on her lips.

"Nothing." She brushes a finger against her nose. A tiny, telling gesture. She's lying.

I slam a fist down on the desk, hard enough to make her gasp.

"That was the last time you will ever lie to me." I'll whip the godforsaken truth out of her if I have to. "Tell me you understand."

A vein bulges and flutters in her throat. "Yes, I understand."

"Good." My gaze dips to the *V* of her shirt, the deep line of cleavage, and the safety pin precariously holding it all together. Just as quick, I avert my eyes, training them on her face. "Now answer the question."

She rubs her palms on her thighs and holds my gaze. "You, Mr. Marceaux. *You* worry me."

Ahh, much better. I want her to spoon-feed her honesty to me, breath by trembling breath. "Explain what you mean."

She nods to herself, as if summoning her courage. "You're smart and strict like other teachers, but you have the approach and temperament of a barbaric di—" She clamps her lips together.

"Language is permissible in my classroom, Miss Westbrook." I narrow my eyes. "As long as it's used in a constructive manner."

She narrows her eyes right back. "I was going to say dickhead, but I'm not sure that's constructive."

At least she's thinking about a dick.

"Give me an example of my alleged behavior, and I'll decide how constructive it is."

Her mouth falls open, as if flabbergasted by my response. "How about when we were out in the hall? When I told you my financial situation, and you...you *smiled?*"

Fuck, she saw that?

I can't tell her I smiled because her vulnerability made me high on lust and hard as a fucking rock. But I can give her sincerity.

"You're right. I was wrong, and I apologize." I pick up the

file and flip through the printouts. "Let's talk about your circumstances."

I scan the bio page and confirm her Treme address. Skipping over the summary of her exceptional GPA and SAT scores, I latch onto the facts I care most about.

Date of birth?

She'll be eighteen in the spring.

Parents?

*William Westbrook. Deceased.*

*Lisa Westbrook. Unemployed.*

That explains her shortage of funds, but not how she pays for private school. Wait...

I jump back to her father's name. "William Westbrook?"

Her eyes drift closed. I look back at the page, trying to connect the details. Westbrook, dead, from Treme, daughter plays piano...

Jesus, I can't believe I didn't place her name earlier. "You're Willy Westbrook's daughter?"

Her eyes flash open, bright and hopeful like her smile. "You've heard of him?"

"I grew up in New Orleans, sweetheart. Everyone around here's heard of Willy's Piano Bar."

Her gaze turns inward, her smile softening. "I hear it's a cool place. Tourists love it."

She says this as though she's never been, which contradicts the image I have of her sitting behind Willy's famous piano after-hours and dreaming of filling his talented shoes.

I rest my elbows on the desk, angling closer. "Don't you live down the street from there? You've never been?"

She raised her eyebrows. "It's an eighteen-and-over bar. I

can't get in."

My brain chugs through a cloud of confusion. "You don't go there when it's closed to help run the business? It's still in your family, right?"

Except her file says her mother's unemployed?

Her stare falls to her lap. "Daddy sold the bar when I was ten."

I hate when I can't see her eyes. "Look at me when you're talking."

She snaps her head up, her voice quiet, flat. "The new owner kept the name and let Daddy continue to play piano there until..."

Until a fight broke out in the bar, shots were fired, and Willy caught one in the chest while trying to subdue the brawlers.

My familiarity with the story must be written on my face, because she says, "You know what happened then."

"It was all over the news."

She nods, swallows.

Willy's death garnered a shitload of attention. Not only was he a white jazz pianist in a black neighborhood, he was also adored and respected by the community. His bar brings a great deal of tourist dollars into Treme, and from what I hear, its popularity has kept the surrounding businesses afloat for years.

I specifically remember watching the televised reports of his murder while visiting New Orleans—that particular visit back home had been a pivotal point in my life. It was...four years ago? I'd just received my master's from Leopold and was waffling on whether to keep my teaching job in New York

City or look for work closer to my hometown.

That same week, I accepted a job offer at Shreveport Preparatory. And met Joanne.

I was twenty-three then, which means Ivory was thirteen when her father was murdered.

She sits across from me, watchful and quiet. As the silence stretches, a subtle transformation works its way into her posture, curling her body into itself and making her appear smaller. She picks at a thread on her sleeve, bringing my attention to the stitching in her shirt and all the places the seams are unraveling. Her clothes are cheaply made, old, or worn from use. Probably all of the above.

There's not a smudge of makeup on her tan face. No rings, bracelets, or jewelry of any kind. Not a whiff of perfume, either. She certainly doesn't need enhancements to make her pretty. Her bare beauty outshines every woman I've ever laid eyes on. But that's not why she goes without.

I won't pretend to understand what it's like to live in poverty, let alone to lose a parent the way she did. My father's a successful physician, and my mother retired as Provost and Dean of Leopold. When I returned to Louisiana after college, they moved back with me to remain close to their only child. Their love and support for me is as dependable as their fortune, and to say they're wealthy is an understatement. The Marceaux family holds the patent on the wooden bracings used in pianos. I'm set for life, as are my children, and their children, and so on, as long as pianos are in production.

Old money is rife among Le Moyne families. Except Ivory's. So why did Willy Westbrook sell his booming business only to continue working there as an entertainer, earning the kind of menial salary that left his daughter destitute?

I leaf through her file, searching for the payment schedule of her tuition. A small notation on the last page indicates all four years were paid in full seven years ago.

*Daddy sold the bar when I was ten.*

I meet her eyes. "He sold his business to send you here?"

She shifts in the chair, back hunching, but she doesn't look away. "He received an offer that was just enough to cover the four-year program, so he..." She closes her eyes, opens them. "Yeah. He sold everything to secure my position here."

And three years later, he died, leaving her so goddamn broke she can't afford textbooks.

I don't bother hiding the contempt in my voice. "That was extremely stupid."

Twin flames ignite her eyes as she jerks forward, her hands clutching the lip of the desk. "Daddy looked at me and saw something worth believing in, long before I believed in myself. There's nothing stupid about that."

She glares at me like she's expecting me to jump on the bandwagon and believe in her, too. But really she just looks like a defensive, angry little girl. It's unbecoming.

"You're not thirteen anymore. Grow up and stop calling him *Daddy*."

"Don't tell me what I can and can't call him!" Her face reddens in a lovely shade of vehemence. "He's *my* father, *my* life, and it has nothing to do with you!"

Christ, this girl has baggage, and given the cut on her lip, it goes beyond Daddy issues. Physical abuse is easy to detect. Sexual trauma, however, is a huge leap. But I'm suspicious by nature and far too curious about her. Despite those bold sparks in her eyes, her posture has a tendency to curl inward in self-defense, evidence that someone in her past or present hurts her.

I want to dig around inside her, carve out the useful facets of her misery, and obliterate the rest. "He *was* your father, and you have your own life. Move on."

A twitch bounces in her cheek. "I hate you."

And I hate how badly I want to punish her mouth by shoving my cock in it. "You've succeeded in showing your immaturity, Miss Westbrook. If you want to remain a student under my tutelage, you will stop bellyaching like a schoolgirl and start behaving like an adult."

She sniffs, shoulders squaring. "You don't have a very high opinion of me." She stares across the room, her gaze roaming the wall of instruments. "I've really screwed this up."

"Look at me."

She does, instantly.

The cloying perfume of her obedience licks along my skin. I want to bathe in it, taste it, and test it. "Why are you here? Because your father decided when you were ten that you would become a pianist?"

Her brows pull together. "No, this is my dream, too, and 'I'm obliged to be industrious.'"

She can quote Bach. Good for her.

"What is your dream, exactly?" I open the file to the college acceptance section. "According to this, you have no goals, no ambitions. What are you going to do after high school?"

"What?" Outrage screeches through her voice. She

launches across the desk and rips the page from my hand, her gaze flying over the empty columns. "Why is this blank? There must be some mistake. I've...I've... God! I've been adamant about—"

"Sit down!"

"Mr. Marceaux, this isn't right. You have to listen..." Her voice weakens, trailing to frightened silence under the force of my gaze.

She lowers into the chair, face flushing and quivering hands rustling the paper.

I steeple my fingers against my chin. "Now tell me, in a calm voice, what you expected to see on that page."

"I'm going to Leopold."

*Not a chance in hell.*

Except the unwavering strength in her glare argues she has the determination to make it happen, and the lift of her chin challenges me to claim otherwise.

I accept that challenge. "You realize only three percent of the applicants are accepted each year? Dozens of your peers have applied, even though Leopold hasn't accepted a Le Moyne student in three years. Maybe, just *maybe,* one of you will make it in next year."

There's no *maybe* about it. My mother still holds a seat on Leopold's Board of Trustees and has the means to push one of my referrals through. I'm confident she'll do it. For me.

However. While slipping *one* student application past the stringent acceptance process won't raise suspicion, *two* would most definitely sound alarms and put my mother's integrity in question. I would never ask that of her.

I lean back in the chair, flipping through the printouts to

make sure I didn't overlook notes on Ivory's college goals. "You should've applied for the matriculation process by now. There's nothing here indicating you have an interest in pursuing such an impossible venture."

"Everything is possible, Mr. Marceaux." She tosses the blank page on my desk. "And I did apply. *Three years ago.* In fact, Mrs. McCracken intended to refer me as the leading applicant."

That explains why Beverly forced Barb McCracken into retirement and brought me here as her replacement. When I accepted the deal, I knew there would be students more worthy of my referral than Beverly's son. But I didn't expect to feel this much guilt tangling in my gut.

Ivory Westbrook poses a moral dilemma, and I haven't even heard her play. Maybe her talent is mediocre, and I can shove this conflict of interest aside.

She stares at my tie, a fugue of thoughts flickering in her eyes. Long seconds pass. Somewhere down the hall, a clarinet plays in perfect key.

Finally, she meets my gaze. "My presence isn't exactly wanted around here. I don't wear the right clothes, drive the right car." She laughs. "I don't even have a car. And I certainly don't bring endowments or glamorous connections. The only thing I have to offer is my talent. It should be enough. It should be the only thing that matters. Yet this school has been against me since day one."

Nothing she said surprises me. She's a little lost lamb among a pack of cutthroat wolves. So why doesn't she aim a little lower? Try for an easier college and remove herself from the cross-hairs? Why Leopold?

PAM GODWIN

I hold my expression impassive, deferring my questions until she's finished.

She touches the blank page and scoots it toward me. "Someone deleted my proposition for Leopold, along with all the prep work I've done to support my eligibility. Mrs. McCracken told me she put it all in my file. I don't want to point fingers, but someone in this school doesn't like me, and that someone has a son who is competing for my spot."

Beverly Rivard wiped her file, a conclusion I'd already come to. "Why Leopold?"

"It's the best conservatory in the country."

"So?"

"So?" Her eyes light up. "The rigorous education students receive there is unparalleled. They have an elite faculty, top-notch facilities, and the best track record in propelling students into musical careers." Ticking off names on her fingers, she lists notable alumni, such as world-renowned composers, conductors, and pianists, then adds, "And you, Mr. Marceaux. I mean, you're in the Louisiana Symphony Orchestra."

I'm about to call her out for being a brown-noser, but then she surprises me.

"I don't just want to perform." She clasps her hands together, her gaze losing focus. "I want to occupy a principal chair in a major symphony and sit beside the best of the best, in a sold-out venue, shivering under the stage lights. I want to be there, part of it all, when the music begins."

This isn't a pitch she prepared in advance. The passion in her voice is a thousand decibels of intensity, her entire body vibrating with the prospect of her words.

74

She lowers her hands and meets my eyes. "Also, as you already know, every single student accepted into Leopold receives a full-tuition scholarship. Doesn't matter who you are or what your background is..."

We share a look, and in that space of understanding, I mentally finish her sentence. Leopold has enough prestige and wealth that it doesn't concern itself with student bank accounts. The school evaluates its applicants on talent alone.

"Very well." I rub the back of my neck and hope to hell she's a terrible pianist. "I'll update your file, and we'll go from there."

Under normal circumstances, being best in her class would get her into Leopold. But Beverly hired me to ensure that wouldn't happen. Leopold will accept Prescott Rivard because I'll make it happen. Everyone else from Le Moyne will be overlooked. That sucks for Ivory, but life's a bitch.

"Thank you." She smiles, her posture loosening.

"We have one more matter to discuss."

I tuck the file away, rise from the chair, and walk around the desk to sit on the ledge beside her, facing her.

With her legs pinched together, she stacks her feet—one bare foot atop the other—against the leg of my desk. I scan the floor and spot her beat-up shoes beneath her chair. I suspect the torn plastic edges irritate her skin after wearing them all day.

When she looks up, I place a finger beneath her chin, holding the position of her head. "What happened to your lip?"

As expected, she tries to lower her chin. An evasive response. Every instinct in my body tells me someone hurt her.

I apply a small yet unmistakable pressure against her soft skin. "Stand up."

Her breaths quicken as she lifts from the chair, guided by my touch beneath her jaw.

When she reaches her full height, I drop my hand. "I asked you a question, and before you answer, remember what I said about lies."

She presses her lips together.

I try another tactic. "As your teacher, I'm a mandated reporter. Do you know what that means?"

Her eyes, like liquid ebony, blink. She's distressingly beautiful, and I'm so fucked.

I unfold from my perch on the desk. Standing over her, I'm a head taller and a lot bigger. "It means I'm required to report suspected child maltreatment to protective services."

"No!" Her fingers fly to the cut on her lip. "You don't need to do that. My brother...he and I got into it this morning, like siblings do. It's totally normal."

Normal? I don't think so. "How old is he?"

She leans a hip against the edge of the desk, a casual pose, but she's not fooling me. "He's twenty-six."

Twenty-six is ten years past knowing better. If the fucker hit her, I won't report him. I'll find him and break his fucking face. "Did he hit you?"

"He...uh, well, we were arguing and uh..." She picks her words carefully, forehead pinched in concentration, no doubt trying to avoid a lie. "I ended up eating the frame of a door."

"Did. He. Hit you?"

She releases a breath. "He backhanded me. This"—she

points at her lip—"was the door frame."

A raging fire erupts inside me, rushing to the surface and searing across my skin. "How often?"

She hugs her midsection, eyes on the floor, further enraging me.

"Answer me!"

"Don't do this. I can't...I have enough problems to deal with right now."

"Lift your shirt." What am I doing? Fuck, this is a bad idea, but I have to know. "Show me your ribs."

She peers around me, her eyes locked on the hall.

"If someone walks by, they can't see around my body." I bend my knees, putting my face in hers. "I'm required to hotline you, Miss Westbrook. Prove to me you're not covered in bruises, and I won't make a report."

I'll beat the shit out of her brother instead.

Her fingers grip the hem of her shirt, her expression tight, eyes squeezed shut. She's so still I'm not sure she's breathing.

"This is just an examination, for your own good. Nothing inappropriate." It's illegal as fuck, but I can't stop myself. "I'm waiting."

She directs her gaze on the buttons of my waistcoat, up to the knot of my tie, lingering there, before she drags her focus upward in a painfully slow trip over my mouth. When she connects with my eyes, a sharp hum rattles in the back of her throat.

Then she raises her shirt.

# IVORY

*He's a teacher. He won't hurt me.*

Slowly, shakily, I gather the hem of the shirt above my navel.

*He's just doing his job.*

Goosebumps shiver across my skin from the unwavering press of his glare, the rush of my heartbeat, and the chilly air as I inch the cotton higher, baring my ribs.

*He promised nothing inappropriate.*

So why does this feel so wrong?

It *is* wrong.

I shove the shirt down and turn to collect my belongings. His hand catches my upper arm, fingers digging in as he swings me back into position. "Show me or I'll report the injury."

His voice ricochets through my skull, sharp and uncompromising. If he reports me, I could lose my home, my education, and my cat. And Shane... God, my brother would strike back with a wrath of pain.

My stomach quivers as I lift the shirt. He releases my arm as I hold the fabric beneath the weight of my breasts and meet his eyes.

All I see is blue ice, an endless arctic landscape, like I'm staring into an unknown world.

His nostrils flare, and the muscles in his face harden with emotions I don't understand. I'm not hiding anything. Nothing under my shirt anyway. Other than the cut on my lip, Shane hasn't left a scratch on me since the night I walked in on him fucking some poor girl on the couch—on *my* bed. Failing to knock on my own front door earned me a nasty bruise on my stomach. But Mr. Marceaux won't find that. The discoloration faded last week.

He lowers into a squat, his glacial gaze traveling over my torso, the low waistband of my skirt, then dropping to the knee-length hem. "Now raise your skirt."

I snap my attention toward the doorway and the empty hall beyond. His bent position puts him eye-level with my pelvis, his body no longer shielding me from hallway traffic. The final bell rang an hour ago, but lots of kids stay after for private lessons. Even now, the legato of a clarinet sings down the hall.

Anyone can walk by and assume the worst. Here I am, the resident slut, flashing my body for the teacher.

The cold floor beneath my bare feet makes me feel even more naked. I wish I hadn't slipped my shoes off during our meeting. "There's no privacy. Someone might see me."

"That's for me to worry about." His arms drape over his bent knees, his strong hands flexing in the *V* of his thighs. "I won't give the order again."

I shove the blouse down and cover my stomach. Now the skirt? Holy smokes, what should I do? Physically, he's in an unusual position for a man, lower than me, his face below my waist. More vulnerable, right? Yet he's still trying to take in a way. I could knee him in the nose and run. But I'm not sure I need to. Or want to.

Shit. I curl my fingers around the front of the skirt, bunching and lifting until my legs are exposed to mid-thigh.

"Higher."

I raise the hem another inch. Surely he can see my legs shaking? How high does he want me to go?

"Higher."

His voice whispers roughly into the foot of space separating his face and my thighs. His hands are right there, too, dangling between us, close enough to grab me between the legs if that's his plan. A slight tremble twitches through his fingers, and my muscles tighten.

*But he's a teacher. He's not allowed to touch me.*

As his student, I'm supposed to trust him and do what he tells me.

I wad the loose material of the skirt against the crotch of my panties and cup my hand there, giving him a full view of my legs without revealing too much. "What are you looking for?"

"Widen your stance."

I slide my feet out, wobbling with the effort.

"Just like that," he breathes. "Good girl."

His praise wraps around me like a warm hug. I can't remember the last time someone embraced me without hurting me, but if Mr. Marceaux spends the next nine months calling me a good girl, I might never need a hug again.

He dips his head, angling closer. "I'm looking for marks on your inner thighs."

Lorenzo has left marks there, along with numerous other

guys. The mean ones always do, grinding and bucking and lasting too long. But Mr. Marceaux doesn't know about those other guys.

"My brother would never—"

"I'm not suggesting *he* would."

My throat closes up. Has he already heard about my reputation? Is he checking for evidence of my behavior?

"You have a fairly dark complexion." He looks up, studying my expression, too steadily, too deeply. "Easier to hide bruises."

I choke on a nervous laugh. "My mom tells me I'm too pale. Hell, she complains *she's* too pale, and she's half-Black."

"Lower your skirt." He stands, hands anchored on his hips. "Tell me about your mother."

I straighten the fabric around my legs. "Everyone says she looks like Halle Berry but—"

"I don't care what she looks like. What does she *do*?"

Drugs. Men. When she doesn't have both of those, she sits in her room and cries.

If I share that with him, he'll probably smile at my misfortune. "She's between jobs."

"What was her position on your father selling his business for you?"

She hates me for it, so much so her lip curls whenever she looks at me.

"They argued about it." I adjust the pin and buttons on my shirt. "She's not happy about losing that fight, so don't expect her to show up for parent-teacher conferences."

"Human beings are miserable disasters. They make mistakes. Do the wrong things." He rubs the back of his head.

"If she doesn't come around, that's on her."

Wow, that was...unexpected. Surprisingly thoughtful and really quite profound. Though now I wonder what kind of mistakes *he* makes. Hopefully none that will affect my goals.

He lowers his hand and makes a swirling motion. "Turn around and show me your back."

My pulse spikes. More examinations? Only this time, I won't be able to see his hands.

I open my mouth to argue, but the hard look in his eyes changes my mind.

With a deep inhale, I give him my back, hook shaky fingers under the shirt, and drag it from hips to armpits.

The creak of his leather shoes, the whisper of his breaths, the heat of his body, everything about him feels like a violation of privacy. I wish I could see his expression, because he's likely abandoned his search of bruises to stare at the tattoo on my back. The faded scrollwork wraps from one side of my waist, up my spine, and curls around the opposite shoulder.

I brace myself for one of his sharp-voiced reprimands. *I'm too young. Tats are too trashy.* But I don't care what his opinion is about this. The tattoo is personal and treasured and mine.

Without warning, his hands land on my back, not on my skin but on the folds of my shirt. He yanks the material from my grasp and shoves it to my waist.

Startled, I spin around. "What's wrong?"

He's farther away than I expected, several feet between us, with his hands clasped behind his back and his attention on the doorway.

I follow his gaze just as Ms. Augustin walks in.

She pauses on the threshold, clutching the strap of her purse against her shoulder. "Oh, I didn't realize you were with a student." She flicks furtive glances between Mr. Marceaux and me, back and forth, up and down, and stops on me. "Hi, Ivory. Did you have a good summer?"

I curl my toes against the marble, longing for my damn shoes. "Sure."

"Awesome." She returns her attention to my teacher, her hand lifting to trail up her neck, sweeping up and combing through a tendril of blonde hair. "Mr. Marceaux, will you be...uh...heading out soon?"

She stares at him the way my mom looks at her boyfriends, with over-bright eyes filled with adoration and stupidity.

Of all the music teachers, Ms. Augustin is the youngest and prettiest. She's also annoyingly nosy, but Ellie raves about her, so I guess she's a good strings teacher.

Mr. Marceaux cocks his head. "Miss Westbrook has private lessons until seven every night."

*I do?*

A sudden lightness lifts my chest. Mrs. McCracken kept late hours to tutor me, but I hadn't worked up the courage to ask him for extra time.

He stands so tall and confident beside me, feet planted wide, every inch of his posture sculpted with authority as he studies Ms. Augustin. "I won't be heading home soon. Tonight or any other night."

"Oh." Her face falls, and her whole body seems to deflate. "Okay. Well..."

The only thing she moves is a long slender leg as she drags the toe of her high-heel backward and rocks it on the floor behind her, lingering. Waiting for him to say something else?

Finally, she straightens. "I'm headed home." She points down the hallway, laughing softly, smiling, and acting really fucking weird. "So, I guess, have a good evening?"

The question in her voice bugs the piss out of me. He already told her he's staying for my private lesson. She should go.

But then I would be alone with him again. How is it possible that I feel both possessive and terrified of him?

He ends her embarrassing shuffle with a firm, "Good night, Ms. Augustin."

As she vanishes into the hallway, I replay their conversation with subtext. "She just asked you out, didn't she?"

He turns toward me with an irritated frown on his face. "That's none of your business."

Probably so, but I feel wonderfully dizzy about the whole exchange. I mean, he told her *no*. Not tonight or any night. Because he would be with me, helping me.

Maybe I didn't screw things up as badly as I thought. "We're doing piano lessons tonight?"

Cords twang in his neck. "No."

"But you just said—"

"Here's tonight's lesson." He erases the distance between us and leans into my space. "Don't question me. Don't lie to me. And never look away from me." He straightens. "Sit down."

Those are ridiculous demands, but I find myself falling into the chair and locking my eyes on his.

He scratches a finger down his whiskered throat and yanks

on the collar behind his tie. Giving up on his attempt to loosen it, he crouches before me. "When did you get the ink?"

There's no way I can answer his questions about it without lying, but I can give him this. "I was thirteen."

Something flickers in his eyes. Comprehension? He knows how old I was when I lost Daddy— My dad. My *father*. God, even in my thoughts, I'm trying to please Mr. Marceaux. But maybe he's right about my immaturity. If my dad were alive today, would I still be calling him *Daddy*?

Instead of asking questions about the tattoo, Mr. Marceaux reaches under my chair and drags my shoes toward his feet. His bend puts his face inches from my lap, but he keeps his eyes on mine as his arms move around my calves.

With his knees on either side of my legs, I don't feel trapped, but my stomach squirms all the same. I don't understand why he's holding my beaten up ballet flat, why he's examining the inside, or what he has planned for me next.

With my shoe in one hand, he reaches for my foot. The moment his fingers graze the back of my ankle, I jump in the seat.

He pins me with a flinty glare, his scowl at odds with the tender stroke of his hand. Unhurried, he caresses along my ankle, traces the bony knobs on the sides, and cups the heel of my foot, lifting it.

I'm tongue-tied, confused by the gentleness, lost in the sensation. The entire world narrows to the warmth of his palm, the careful way he slides my toes into the shoe, and the absolute concentration he gives the task.

He lowers my foot to the floor, and I exhale a chestful of

air. Then he shifts toward my other leg.

Why is he doing this? What does he get out of it? Will he expect me to show him my boobs? Give him a blow job? Sex?

I jerk my foot out of his reach. "I can do this."

He fists his hands on his legs and imprisons me with those frigid cobalt eyes. "What's tonight's lesson?"

"Don't question you?"

Maybe this is a small thing to him, but it's not to me. Men don't touch me unless they want something, and his touch is freaking me out. It's too nice. Too intimate. Way too intimate for a student and teacher.

He holds his palm out, waiting. I want to ask him what he wants from me, but that would be failing the lesson.

I move my foot toward his hand, and he gives it the same attention as before. Fragile strokes. Fingers like velvet wrapping around my breakable bones. Taking? Giving? I don't know what this is. Every brush of his fingertips shoots tingles up my legs, making my heart flutter and my whole body hyper-aware. It scares me. *He* scares me.

When he slides the other shoe on, I tuck my feet beneath the chair, knees pinched together, dreading what he'll demand next.

He rises, his expression dark beneath black brows and his breathing noisier than it should be. I know that needful look, that hungry sound. My blood runs cold.

Now is the time to run, but my feet aren't moving. Why? I need his permission, I think.

I *want* his permission.

Turning toward the desk, he presses his hands against the surface. "Go home, Miss Westbrook."

Relief shimmies down my spine, but it gets cut off by my next thought.

I can take any one of the exits out of Crescent Hall, race through the parking lot or the park, zigzag along the streets to the bus stop. Doesn't matter which way I go. Prescott will catch up. He'll find me. He always does.

Then home. Where Lorenzo might be waiting. Where Shane might be fucking on my bed.

Which is scarier? Prescott? Lorenzo? Shane?

*Mr. Marceaux.*

I grab my satchel and hightail it toward the hall.

# IVORY

The muggy air clings to my skin as I make the ten-minute walk from Le Moyne to the 91 line. Oh man, it feels good to get a breather from that classroom. I don't know if it's Mr. Marceaux or the frightening sensations he inflames in me, but I couldn't run from there fast enough.

He's aggressive and powerfully built like other men. More so. But he had numerous opportunities to take and didn't.

Because he's a teacher? Or because he's not like other men?

I'm not ready to trust those thoughts or the way they make me feel.

The crescent moon hangs high in the sky, painting a dim glow over the antebellum mansions that fringe Coliseum Street. The brick sidewalk is paved in a herringbone pattern and bordered on one side by wrought iron fences, gas lamps, and blooming vegetation that infuses the air with the fragrance of summer.

The foundations of the towering homes butt right up against those fences, and illuminated windows give me a peek of interiors twinkling with chandeliers, grand staircases, and rich woodwork. Luxury cars line the narrow street and pristine gardens adorn the side-yards. Everywhere I look boasts generational wealth, the kind that came from sugar, cotton, and shipping.

Does Mr. Marceaux live in one of these mansions? Maybe his family is old money? Le Moyne attracts a lot of residents in the Garden District, including Beverly Rivard.

I don't know which house is Prescott Rivard's, but he knows which paths I take home. There are only so many options between school and the bus routes. My legs itch to walk faster, to put him off for another day. But the longer I delay touching base with him, the harder it will be to cover this month's bills.

Halfway to the bus stop, the familiar rumble of a motorcycle interrupts the quiet street. It approaches from behind, growing louder, faster.

The tiny hairs on my nape stand on end. I peer over my shoulder and glimpse a black helmet, black jacket, and obnoxious orange fairings. My heartbeat slams into overdrive, and I pick up my pace. If the rider lifted his chin, I would see *Destroy* inked across his throat.

Every step hammers vibrations through my thin soles. I should've known Lorenzo would come looking for me. He often does when he grows tired of waiting. It's been two weeks since the last time he took from me, and I bled from my butt for hours after.

My stomach cramps as my mind spins through my options. The next cross-street is a thirty-second sprint down the road. Maybe I can lose him.

I quicken my gait, scanning for a cut-through between the mansions. I won't find one. Fences encircle the generous plots, equipped with security cameras and alarms. Wrought iron and brick brackets the street on both sides. I have nowhere to go as he motors up beside me.

"Get on the bike." Even muffled by the helmet, his shout is hard and unkind.

"I'm taking the bus." I walk faster, hunching my shoulders with my satchel banging against my leg.

He revs the engine, rolling the bike alongside me. My legs shake, and the toe of my shoe catches on a chipped brick. Momentum whirls me forward. I maintain my balance but...goddammit, I lose the shoe.

I spin back, my pulse thrashing in my throat, and shove my foot inside the cracked vinyl.

A pair of headlights emerge on the road behind Lorenzo's crotch rocket. I stare blindly into the beams of light, waiting, hoping. For what?

*Black hair, blue eyes, commanding presence...*

As if.

Lorenzo stops beside me, just out of arm's reach, his helmet tipping in my direction. "Not gonna tell you again. Get your ass on the bike."

The approaching car slows, veering around Lorenzo. Wide front grill, metallic silver paint, fat tires, the Cadillac CTS Sedan makes the perfect toy for rich juvenile idiots to cruise around in.

Idiots like Prescott.

He pulls to a stop in front of Lorenzo, bends across the front seat, and swings open the passenger door.

Lorenzo's helmet swivels toward the car. "Who the fuck is that?"

*That* is a diversion. Thank God. I won't be able to evade

Lorenzo forever, and I certainly don't relish climbing into Prescott's car. But right now, I'll take Prescott over Lorenzo. Prescott never forces himself from behind and in my ass.

I lurch forward, running a wide circuit around the bike, and slide into the front seat of the Cadillac. "Go."

The motorcycle's engine sputters as it jerks forward. I slam the door shut on the noise.

Prescott leans over the console, twisting his neck to glare at Lorenzo. "Who is that guy?"

"Just some creep. Let's go."

He hits the gas, and the burst of propulsion presses my body into the leather seat. My anxiety and fear tumbles behind us in a fume of exhaust. I relax, a small degree anyway. Now I'm stuck with Prescott.

His long body sprawls in the leather seat, his finger punching through various glowing gadgets in the dashboard. I can't begin to guess how much this car costs. His parents certainly have to make bank for them to be able to buy it for him. Is it a badass car? Absolutely. Am I jealous he has it?

I prefer not to be jealous of anyone, especially Prescott. I peek over at him, taking in the sharp angle of his jaw, the tuck of blond hair behind his ear, and the long, straight profile of his nose. He's skinnier than Mr. Marceaux. Less developed muscle. Smaller hands. Smaller dick. Not that I've seen Marceaux's dick, but I bet it's bigger.

That's not a good thing.

My heart skips. Why the hell am I thinking about that? Why am I even comparing them?

Prescott shifts gears then reaches over to hook a finger beneath the hem of my skirt. "I'm going to make you come tonight."

I smack his hand away. Jesus, I never should've baited him with that comment about piercings. Stupid, stupid, stupid! "Where's your homework?"

He downshifts around a curve and thrusts a thumb over his shoulder. The seat belt indicator screams as I kneel backward through the gap in the front seats.

I gather his binders from the floorboard, and a single headlight fills my view through the back window. "He's following us."

Prescott throws the car into high speed. Mansions blur by. Stop signs and intersections come and go. Guess he's not worried about breaking the law. Thankfully, Lorenzo doesn't share his recklessness. The motorcycle maintains the speed limit and stops at every stop sign. Maybe Lorenzo has drugs on him or outstanding warrants. Whatever the reason, he falls behind and eventually out of sight.

Releasing a heavy breath, I collect the rest of Prescott's folders. "You lost him."

Prescott yanks my skirt up to my hip and pinches my pussy through the crotch of my panties. "Baby, I'm gonna fuck you so hard tonight."

I spin back toward the front, falling into the seat, and try to control my breathing.

My hand shakes as I buckle the seat belt. "No, you're not."

There's a heavy dose of conviction in my response. And maybe a tiny smidgen of doubt. I've escaped Prescott's advances before, but I can count those times on one hand.

He laughs. "We'll see."

When he turns onto Jackson Avenue and heads away from

the river, I don't have to ask where he's going. During the six-minute drive to our usual spot, I use one of the overhead lights to skim through his assignments and notes. He's pretty organized for a guy who's not interested in homework, his tasks outlined in neat penmanship and notated with due dates. Everything he's detailed is doable, easy enough to work in with my own assignments.

He pulls into an empty lot, hemmed in by a jungle of weeds and boarded-up homes that didn't survive the last hurricane.

Shutting off the engine, he turns to me. "I have a proposition."

A tremor shivers through my insides. Anything he has to offer comes with a painful price.

He bends toward me, his face inches away and cast in darkness. "I know you're *doing homework* for a lot of my friends and who knows how many others."

I haven't had a chance to talk to the other guys about schedules and assignments. Another dreaded task on my to-do list.

His hand snakes over my thigh, making its way to the gap between my knees. I jerk away, and my legs collide with the door.

With a grunt, he faces forward, posture stiff, his fingers curled around the steering wheel. Fingers I don't want anywhere near me.

He tips his head against the headrest. "I don't want to share you."

"Too bad."

"Fuck, Ivory! You're so—" He rubs his hairless cheek and

softens his tone. "I got an increase in my allowance. I'll pay you more, enough to cover what you're making from everyone else, if you stop seeing them. Give me a price."

He can't afford it. I mentally sum up the monthly utilities, mortgage, groceries, and tack on a little extra for school supplies. Shit, that's a lot of money. Pulling in a deep breath, I give him the number.

"Done."

What? His fucking allowance covers the sum of all my bills?

I wrap my arms around my midsection. "All I have to do is stop helping other people?"

*"That.* And stop fighting me on *this."* His fingers wrap around my knee, pulling my leg toward him.

"I—I..." My breathing quickens as I try to pry his grip away. "I can't." My chest heaves, my fight against his hand useless. "Let go."

"I'm going to get this anyway. Stop making it so damn difficult." He releases me and holds his hands up. "What's it gonna be?"

I sway against the door and cover my face with my hand. Fuck, what choice do I have?

I can walk away from Prescott, forget his money, and try to make up the loss with all the other guys who want the same things he wants.

Or I can tell them all to fuck off and let the mortgage default. I'm not eighteen yet. I can go to social services and explain my situation. Maybe they'll step in and put me in foster care. But there's a good chance a new home would be too far away to commute to Le Moyne. Can I put my future in the hands of some grown-up who decides where I go to school? And what about Schubert? A temporary family may not let me bring him. My heart pinches just thinking about that. He's not just a cat. Schubert is the last gift my dad gave me before he died. He's the only living form of love I have left to wrap my arms around.

Or I can accept Prescott's offer, endure just *one* high-school dick, and keep my house, my school, and my cat.

The pressure of tears burns the backs of my eyes as I force my lips around my answer. "Okay."

"Okay?" He sits up, his entire body shifting to face me. "Okay...uh..." He twists around, scrutinizing the emptiness of the overgrown lot, and pauses when his gaze lands on the back seat. "Get out."

With trembling hands, I put the binders on the floorboard, open the door, and step into a tangle of vines.

He's out of the car and around to my side in a flash. A huge grin contorts his face as he opens the door to the back seat. "In there. On your back."

*No, no, no.* My lungs labor for air, and every muscle in my body locks up.

"Ivoryyyyy," he growls. "That's not how this works. I'm not paying until I get my dick wet."

Oh God, he already has a condom in his hand.

Tall grass itches my ankles. The chirrup of nighttime insects creeps from the shadows of broken concrete. Somewhere in the distance, a dog barks. Another joins in. But it's the godawful sound of a zipper that screeches past my ears.

He holds his dick in his hand, the bulbous thing swollen to

fullness and pointed right at me as he rolls on the condom. Nausea simmers, and saliva rushes into my mouth.

When he meets my eyes, his determined expression looks ghostly and sinister in the moonlight. "We doing this the easy way or the hard way? One of those earns you more money."

A sheen of tears blurs my vision. I made this deal, knowing what came next. *Suck it up and eat it, Ivory.*

I turn toward the waiting door, press the heels of my hands against my eyes, and slide into the back seat.

My brain is already reaching for the dark notes of Scriabin's Sonata No.9. The melody plays in my head as the weight of his body presses my back against the bench seat. I envision the complicated key strokes as he wrenches my panties to the side and shoves inside me, grunting, thrusting. So dry, so fucking painful, the fire between my legs coaxes more tears from my eyes. I focus inward, blocking him out. I'm nearly lost in the discordant music of my mind when a ring tone chirps from Prescott's pocket.

"Fuck." He fumbles around his legs and pulls his phone from the folds of his trousers. "Goddammit!"

"Get off me."

"No. And I have to answer this, so keep your mouth shut."

I shove at his chest, but he doesn't budge. His hips thrust harder as hatred leaks in huge drops from my eyes.

"It's my mom." He sets the phone on the seat above my head, the cheery ring tone bleeding into my ears. "If she hears you, the most I'll get is a loss in allowance. But you..." His finger hovers over the screen as his hips drive against mine. "You'll get kicked out of school."

Before I can tell him he's a fucking moron, he taps the

screen and puts it on speaker phone.

"What's up, Mom?" He lifts his pelvis and slams back against me, the hunger on his face illuminated by the glow of the screen.

"Where are you?" The dean's severe voice barks through the phone.

"Avery's house."

*Who is Avery?* I squirm beneath him, aching for this to be over with.

"You sound out of breath," she says.

He cups my breast and squeezes. "Lifting weights. She has a sweet workout room."

"Oh? Well, tell her mother I said *hi*. We need to do tea soon."

"Yep."

"Keep your hands to yourself, son. I don't want any problems with her parents."

I bite down on my lip to keep from crying out. His movements quicken, growing erratic. Thank God, he's getting close, but how can he do this while holding a conversation with his mother? He's so disgusting my skin recoils everywhere his heat penetrates my clothes.

"I saw you talking to that Westbrook girl at lunch," the dean says.

My pulse skyrockets, but Prescott's in a whole other dimension. His mouth hangs open in a silent shout as his body flails and jerks through his release. The moment he's finished, I shove him off me.

"Prescott?" The dean exhales through the phone. "Are you listening?"

"Yeah. Ivory's nice." He stares at me and mouths, *A nice fuck*. Without looking away, he says aloud, "I don't know why you have a problem with her."

"She's trying to steal your Leopold spot, Prescott. Not only that, she has a reputation with the boys at school. Stay away from her."

He drags a finger over his eyebrow. "Yeah, okay. Gotta go."

"Prescott—"

He hangs up and tosses the phone in the front seat. "Did you come?"

I angle away from him, covertly wiping away the tears as I growl, "Of course, I didn't come, you idiot."

He seriously thinks I enjoyed that? I've never had an orgasm, at least not that I know of. But if I'm capable of having one, it wouldn't be with him.

I fix my panties and yank my skirt down. "Who's Avery?"

He pulls off the condom and adjusts his slacks. "My girlfriend."

"Girlfriend?" A thick lump forms in my throat. "Why are you cheating on her?"

"She's a prude. But you're not, are you?" He reaches for the *V* in my shirt.

I knock his hand away and grab my satchel from the front seat.

"Bet you've fucked more guys than there are keys on a piano."

Eighty-eight guys? Heat tingles my face as I open the door and jump out. Truth is, I'm not sure of the number. Maybe half that? Maybe more.

He climbs out the other side and meets my eyes over the

roof of the car. "Fifty-two white guys at Le Moyne and thirty-six black guys in Treme. Am I right?"

*Fifty-two white keys, thirty-six black keys.*

He thinks he's clever with his sick analogy, but he has no idea how hurtful his comments are. Yes, I've had a lot of sex with a lot of different guys. Not all of my experiences have been like this one. Sometimes I'm too weak and don't have the physical strength or size to stop it. Other times, I feel tricked, bribed, trapped...sweet-talked. When I was younger, I let guys touch me in my stupid desperation for affection, but I eventually learned there isn't anything affectionate about a swollen penis. Still, there are moments when I wonder, *Will this time be different? Maybe this one will hold me close and love me. Maybe it will feel good*, and I fall back into the trap.

But after Prescott's hateful remarks, I don't even want his fucking money. I stride away, hooking the strap of the satchel over my shoulder. The projects of Central City stretch out around me, but I know the way, having walked this road every time Prescott fucked me in that lot. Five blocks from here, I can catch a bus home.

The Cadillac's engine starts, and a moment later, it rolls up beside me.

He extends an arm out the window, his hand filled with a wad of bills.

I stare at it, needing it, hating myself. "How often do I have to do this?"

"As often as I want." A strand of blond hair falls over his eyes. "My first assignment is due on Monday, so we'll meet again this week. Next time, I'll make you come."

A surge of anger scorches through my veins. I hate him.

But I need him.

I swallow my pride and snatch the money from his hand.

He flashes me a sated smile and drives off, leaving me standing on the side of the road like the whore that I am.

# EMERIC

With the address from Ivory's file mapped on my phone, I turn my old GTO onto her street. This doesn't feel stalkery, but it doesn't seem completely sane, either. What can I say? I've never needed an excuse to beat someone's ass. I just didn't imagine the ass I'd be beating tonight would belong to her brother. Yet here I am.

I don't have a plan, only that Ivory can't know I'm here. I should've reported her swollen lip. I damn sure shouldn't have searched her body for bruises. But this? Showing up at her house? Definitely crossing into *what-the-fuck-am-I-doing* territory.

Dusk grays out the horizon, and there aren't any street lamps. Maybe I can coax her brother outside without her seeing me and punch his lights out before he has a chance to memorize my face. Of course, if she glimpses my car, she'll know. The 1970 Pontiac GTO is too recognizable. If she didn't see it in the school parking lot tonight, she will before the year's over.

I should've taken a cab, but I wasn't exactly thinking when I left the classroom and drove straight here.

Following the GPS, I sneak along a row of sagging houses. No, not sneaking. The American muscle under the hood is a

455 V8, and its thundering dirty rumble has residents leaning forward on their porches. Pedestrians stop walking and gawk. It occurs to me that I won't be able to leave the car on her street. It would be jacked within minutes.

Just a couple blocks north of the French Quarter, Treme is the place tourists are warned not to go, not in daylight and definitely not at night. I haven't visited this area since I was a rebellious teen. I forgot about all the graffiti, boarded-up windows, and huddles of men on the street corners looking around like they're hiding something. How does she live here and not get mugged every day?

*She has nothing of value to steal.*

Except her innocence. Though I'm certain that was stolen long ago. The niggling question is, how much damage was done? I understand her reactions to me, the looks of both fear and desire to please. They're her natural reflexes to a dominant man. But layers of obscurity lie beneath her expressions, experiences that strengthened her and tolls that warped her. Not just an abusive brother or a dead father, but something else. Something traumatically sexual.

Anger plunges through my veins, spurring me toward her house and the unknowns that wait there.

I spot her street number on the weathered siding of a narrow shotgun building. The peeling white paint gives way to rotten wood, and the drooping roof over the porch doesn't look safe enough to stand beneath. The houses are too crammed together to accommodate driveways, and there are no cars parked out front. No lights on inside. No movement in the windows. Unless she's sitting in the dark, she's not home.

# DARK
## NOTES

On my way here, I envisioned the worst. But one could argue the house next to hers is much worse, the exterior veneered in scraps of plywood and the entire structure slanting on its foundation. Someone even spray-painted on the neighbor's door: *Home is a fleeting feeling I'm trying to fix.*

As I idle in front of her house, imagining the dilapidated conditions within, a knot of unease forms in my gut. Maybe she doesn't have electricity? If her mother's unemployed, who pays the bills? Her brother?

I don't linger, afraid Ivory will come home and notice my car. A few blocks away, I pull into a crowded parking lot, operating on a hunch and a perverse sense of curiosity.

The bluesy notes of a solo trumpeter vibrate through me as I amble into Willy's Piano Bar. I've never been here, but it's not unlike the other seedy New Orleans bars I've frequented over the years. Grungy and cave-like, the scarce lighting and exposed brick walls give it a basement tavern feel. The kind of tavern men get shot in.

Where did her father die? Near the piano? Or over by high-top tables? Or right here, where I hover between the door and the bar?

This place sees its share of nosy tourists, so I'm not surprised no one spares me a glance. I scan the low-key crowd and zero in on the only other white guy. It's too dark to make out details, but he appears to be close to my age with blond hair and a pale complexion. Matches the Google image I found of a young Willy Westbrook on my way to Ivory's house. Can I be this lucky?

Adjusting the curled brim of my favorite fedora lower on my head, I stroll toward the bar and wave down the bartender. "Is that Willy's son?"

She lifts her eyes to follow the direction of my nod, her white hair forming an ethereal glow around her dark complexion.

"Mm hmm." She returns her attention to the drink she's preparing. "That's him, sugar."

"Thanks." Hooking my thumbs in my front pockets, I wander over to the half-circle booth and tower over his table.

A girl on each arm, he drags his gaze up my relaxed posture and locks on my face. "Do I know you?"

The shadowed corner of the booth obscures his expression, but his delayed movements and slurred speech are hard to miss. High or drunk, he's probably too blitzed to remember me tomorrow.

"Are you Willy's kid?"

"Yyyyup." He reaches for his beer, sloshing it on the table. "What of it?"

I want to tell him the reason I'm here, that *I* am what happens when he hurts his sister. But if I mention Ivory, he might retaliate against her.

Keeping my face angled away from the dim light, I bend over the table and slam my fist into his nose.

The girls fly apart and shoot out of the booth as his head falls back and lolls on his shoulders. The whites of his eyes roll and disappear behind his lids as his body slides down in the seat.

The blood from his nostrils forms twin rivers over his lip and splatters on his shirt. His intoxication probably has more to do with the knock-out than my nonexistent boxing skills. I hoped to see him writhe in agony but take pleasure in knowing he'll wake to the throbbing pain of a broken nose.

The crowd doesn't seem to have any allegiance to Willy's son, because no one makes a move to defend him as I stride toward the door. I know this is a rough neighborhood, but damn, they don't even look my way when I slip out as inconspicuously as I entered.

A couple of minutes later, I find myself parked down the street from Ivory's house with the engine off and my attention glued to her front door. She should've come home by now, but all is dark beyond the front and side windows. Where the fuck is she?

I consider leaving when an orange sportbike pulls up to her curb. The rider removes the helmet, revealing black hair and a dark complexion. Black or Latino? He's too young to be dating Lisa Westbrook. He fucking better not be Ivory's boyfriend.

I pitch forward against the steering wheel, craning my neck as he strolls to the porch and peers in the window. He doesn't knock on the door and instead meanders into the narrow alley between the houses and disappears around back.

My nerves tighten. Is he a family friend? A cousin? A fucking burglar? I type the bike's license plate number in my phone, and a moment later, he emerges from the alley, puffing on a cigarette. A leg goes over the bike, helmet on, engine roars, and he's gone without a glance in my direction.

That was weird.

I should go. I have no business here.

Thirty minutes later, I'm still telling myself that.

With each hoodlum that walks by, with every car that cruises down the street, my impatience multiplies, twisting through me with spastic fits and starts. Eleven o'clock on a school night, and she's out there somewhere doing God knows what. I want to tie her to her bed and belt her for being so reckless. Where the hell is her mother?

This isn't my problem. I reach for the ignition just as my phone beeps with a text message.

*Deb: We still on for tonight?*

When I messaged her between meetings while staring at Ivory's tight body, I was raring to go. But now?

*Me: Another time*

*Deb: I've been such a bad girl today. Spank me!*

My cock doesn't even twitch.

*Deb: I can pretend to be her again.*

By her, she means Joanne. Only Joanne isn't the *her* that's fucking with my head.

*Me: You sound needy. The opposite of sexy.*

*Deb: *pouts**

*Me: Also not sexy*

*Deb: I'm sorry, sir.*

*Me: You can make it up to me by moving forward on that favor I requested.*

*Deb: The GM guy?*

Beverly Rivard's husband, Howard, owns a chain of GM dealerships. I hear his business practices are as sleazy as his wife's, but I've yet to confirm if he cheats on her. If anyone can seduce him, Deb can.

*Me: Yes. Use discretion and pay attention to lighting. His face needs to be clear on the video.*

*Deb: Yes, sir.*

*Deb: I can't change your mind about tonight?*

*Me: Good night, Deb.*

What am I doing? Why am I here? To make sure she arrives home safely?

Fuck me, I just want to see her again. Just a glimpse before I face the emptiness of my house.

Ten minutes later, my wish materializes on the sidewalk up ahead. Even in the faint moonlight, the curve of her breasts, the dip of her waist, and the flare of her hips are distinguishable. Erotic. So goddamn captivating.

With my car tucked behind a truck, my whole body cants against the door panel to keep her within my sight.

Her long legs carry her toward her house, slowly, leisurely, her chin held high and shoulders relaxed. She's not afraid here, not like she is in my classroom. How ironic given the dangerous neighborhood.

In the depraved innards of my soul, I thrill at being the thing she fears. I want to claim her apprehension, dread, and uncertainty. I want to take ownership of all of her emotions and be the sole reason she trembles and cries.

In that moment, I pretend I'm not her teacher. With my hand curled around the steering wheel and my shoulder pressed against the door, I watch a beautiful woman walk toward me. She's strikingly exotic with her enormous eyes and long dark hair, so impossibly stunning I wouldn't be able to stop myself from approaching her. I would pause a few feet away, hold her gaze, and let the malleable silence enfold us in an intimate cocoon. I wouldn't need words, just her awareness of my body, my intent, and my confidence to give her what she craves.

She may not know it but she needs clearly-defined

boundaries, discipline, and a man she can trust to push her beyond her comfort zone. She may not yet recognize me as that man, but she will. Then what?

Parked five houses away, I can't focus on anything but her. What happens tomorrow when I sit beside her on the piano bench, breathing in the scent of her skin? How the fuck will I focus then?

With the engine off, the lack of air is stifling. My shirt is soaked through with sweat, the tie long-ago discarded. I'm burning up, antsy, aching for her. Horny as fuck.

She stops at the front door and unlocks it with a key from her satchel. Reaching in to flick on the interior lights, she doesn't make it over the threshold before an orange cat races out. As it prances around her feet, throwing its body against her ankles, her words come back to me.

*I can't afford running shoes or food for my cat.*

A heavy pressure sinks into my muscles, urging me to storm into her life and fix her problems. I have the money, determination, and desire to improve her situation. As her teacher, she's my responsibility. To nurture. To protect.

All of which is appropriate as long as I don't imagine the grip of her cunt around my cock.

She scoops up the cat and nuzzles it against her neck as she carries it inside. The door closes, and the curtains fall across the window, shutting me out. Time to go.

On the drive back to the Garden District, I resolve to maintain professionalism around Miss Westbrook. If I manage to finish the year without burying myself between her legs, I might find a rather satisfying future at Le Moyne. Of course, keeping my hands off her also means my future won't include a jail cell.

As I walk into my house, I'm greeted with stacks of packed boxes, bare walls, and a total lack of warmth despite the humidity. I moved in three months ago, but haven't really *moved in*. Unpacking feels a lot like acceptance.

Acceptance of a life without Joanne.

I drift through the spacious living room, hearth room, and kitchen, every corner and archway adorned with custom moldings and deep earthy tones. Maybe tomorrow I'll begin filling the rooms with furniture and personal belongings. But tonight, all I need is the brilliant piece of craftsmanship that sits down the hall.

I make my way there, veering into my favorite room, the reason I bought this overpriced estate. The pristine hardwoods shine beneath the chandelier, and the Gothic arched fireplace at the far end conjures images of distant lands and mystical cultures. But the room's centerpiece demands my full attention.

Approaching my grandfather's Fazioli concert grand piano, I run a finger along the curved body. Rare and extremely valuable, it took three years to make, crafted with superb materials, down to the gold-plated hinges and screws. The heart of the piano is carved from the same red spruce trees Stradivari used for his famous violins. But that's not why I cherish this sexy beast.

I take my position behind the keys and let my mood decide the melody. Inhaling deeply, I finger through the slow-building intro of "Toxicity" by System Of A Down. As the metal song changes tempo, growing heavier, more aggressive, every muscle in my body engages. My fingers grab at the notes, my torso sways, and my head rocks in time with the staccato beats, my entire being captured and controlled by the acoustics.

The majestic projection propels me to the top note as I bang my hands along the keys, wrestling every molecule of power the piano offers. The crystalline clarity enchants me, consumes me, and I fall in love with this instrument all over again. I depend on this experience. I've dedicated my entire life to mastering it, and I need it now to carry me through the days and months without Joanne.

Maybe I've reached the pinnacle of my success in the music world. Maybe I'm destined to be a lonely, bitter old man.

Or maybe I haven't found my place yet, my part in it all, and maybe—as Ivory so passionately put it—I'll be there when the music begins.

# EMERIC

It's universally known that the more forbidden something is, the more desirable it becomes. I feel this truth like a fist around my balls as I enter my classroom after lunch and find the forbidden object of my desire waiting for me.

Ivory stands beside my desk, alone and watching me with huge dark eyes. With her arms crossed beneath her breasts and her raised chin radiating attitude, she has no idea how badly I want to restrain her, whip her, and fuck her.

Her black dress hangs like a tarp on her small frame, which only glorifies my memory of her bare body, giving power to the secret we share. Is she thinking about yesterday, when I memorized all the skin she's hiding? The mole on the rib just under her right breast, the delicate patch of freckles on her toned thigh, the decorative ink scrolling across her back—all of it belongs to me now. I crave another peek, more skin, more Ivory.

She straightens her spine, inadvertently pushing out her ample chest, and glares at me as if she's reading my mind and deems it appalling.

I could no more stop my heart from being ripped from my chest—*thank you for that, Joanne*—than I can control the primal way my body reacts to Ivory Westbrook.

Heat floods my muscles as I erase the space between us. My mouth dries as her eyes track my movements around the desk. Gnawing pressure builds behind my abs as I take in the sensual shape of her lips, the vein bulging in her throat, and the wariness in her gaze.

I clasp my hands behind my back, stifling the urge to yank at the strangling tie around my neck.

"Miss Westbrook." I force my attention above her mouth. "You're here early."

She stabs a finger at textbooks stacked on the desk between us. "I found these in my locker."

I glance at the supplies I purchased from the school bookstore this morning. "You're welcome."

"So it *was* you." She closes her eyes, inhales deeply, and her glare returns. "I won't take—"

"You will."

"This?" She snatches the unopened tablet from the stack of books and holds it out to me. "I can't accept this."

"You can." I turn away and begin writing next period's discussion topics on the whiteboard.

Her footsteps approach, pausing beside me. I don't look at her, but I feel her proximity like an electric hum. A cacophony of emotions pulse from her quickening breaths and grinding teeth. She may as well just tell me she's an anxious mess.

Instead, she says, "I don't take handouts, Mr. Marceaux."

Damn her pride. I prefer to not belabor this simple thing, but nothing is easy when it comes to this girl.

I move the marker over the board, the felt tip squeaking through the silence. "You presume too much, Miss

Westbrook. You *will* pay me back."

"That's what I'm afraid of."

She mumbles it so quietly I'm not sure I hear her correctly. I cap the marker and glower down at her. "Repeat that."

"I'm..." She holds her arms at her sides, as if forcing herself not to fidget. "What kind of payment?"

My pulse takes off as alarms blare in my head. She has a wealth of assets most warm-blooded men would value more than money. Whether or not she's aware of her seductive beauty, her question isn't birthed from naivety. Experience has shown her what men want from her, and the thought boils my blood.

"Cash. Personal check." My voice whips through the room, brash and angry. "Something along *those* lines." I soften my tone. "What kind of payment were you expecting I'd want?"

"Oh, I..." She swallows and stares toward the doorway. "I don't know."

The distant din of voices trickle in from the hall, a reminder class will resume in a few minutes.

"The truth, Miss Westbrook."

Her eyes dip to my groin and dart away.

Fuck. I won't make her say it out loud. At this point, I can't bear to hear it.

She's aware of my inappropriate interest in her, and now she knows I know she's aware. But she's misjudged the way I operate. I would *never* coerce a woman into sex, let alone a student. While that infuriates me to a level that has my hands shaking, the ease at which she jumped to sex as a method of payment makes me want to kill someone.

Maybe I'm paranoid. Maybe I've lost my mind, but

goddammit, I'm convinced she's been sexually abused. Someone from her past? Is it happening right now? Who the fuck is hurting her?

I fist my hands on my hips and glare down at her as everything inside me simmers to blow up. "Has another teacher asked for inappropriate favors?"

"No!"

A small relief, but it leaves me with nothing. "Who then?"

She steps back just as several students mill into the classroom, laughing and oblivious. The conversation will have to be postponed, but there's something else that can't wait. I join her at my desk as she gathers the stack of textbooks.

Under the guise of powering up my laptop, I watch her out of the corner of my eye and lower my voice for her ears alone. "I trust your brother didn't touch you last night."

Her grin is reluctant, dimpling the corner of her mouth and crawling across her lips. "Shane stumbled in with a broken nose, whining about a headache until he passed out. Guess that's karma, huh?"

"Yes." My mouth twitches. "Karma."

Arms loaded with books, she turns toward the room full of students, pauses, then pivots back to me.

"Thank you." She stares at my tie, her chin pinning the tablet atop the tower of books in her arms. "I'll reimburse you as soon as I can."

Nodding, I return to the whiteboard.

Maybe I made things more difficult for her. Whatever she does to earn money, she has to do *more* of it to pay me back. But school supplies are a requirement. Besides, I don't intend to accept her reimbursement.

While I know her sense of self-worth arises from paying her own way, from not *taking hand-outs*, I spend the next three hours obsessing over how I can beat that idea out of her without crossing the line.

If her mother's unemployed, how will she pay me back? Performing arts students can't work regular jobs. They don't have time for anything outside of school and practice. Hell, students are required to practice their instruments at least four hours a day, every day, for *years*. If they don't, they fall behind, lose their competitive edge and any hope for a musical career.

Questions about her financial situation marinate in the back of my mind for the next few hours. A beautiful young girl like her, from a neighborhood like Treme, has a slew of undesirable methods to earn fast money. Drugs and prostitution fall on the top of that list, but I refuse to imagine her degrading herself in that way. It's too appalling.

When the final bell rings, the piano students exit the classroom, except Ivory, who sets her belongings on a desk by the door and looks at me expectantly. "Don't the others have private lessons?"

"Sebastian Roth and Lester Thierry have their own tutors at home."

"I know." Her forehead pinches. "But Chris and Sarah always take advantage of the lessons here."

"They opted to study under Mrs. Romero's tutelage."

I planted the suggestion in my meetings with Chris and Sarah yesterday, hinting that the other piano instructor had some openings after school, and her softer approach may be a good match for them. It's partially true. Mrs. Romero teaches the younger grades and already has her hands full. But she works for me, and therefore, I determine her schedule.

Ivory's lips part as she considers the news. "Does that mean I'll have you all to myself from three to seven every day?"

Fuck me, but I love the sound of that.

Her eyes widen. "Oh damn, I didn't mean—"

"I know what you meant, and yes, I'll be mentoring you."

As a general rule, I prefer to groom only one or two students at a time. Though my intentions with Ivory have little to do with her personal development. When it comes to torturing myself, I'm the dean of effort, hell-bent on enduring the entire school year with achingly sore blue balls.

I close the door and make my way around the corner of the *L*-shaped room. Leaning a hip against the Bösendorfer grand piano, I wait for her to join me then rap my knuckles on the sleek black surface. "Four hours every day."

An enormous grin overwhelms her beautiful mouth. "I won't waste your time."

"No, you won't." I could stare at her twenty-four hours a day and feel like the most productive pervert in the world. But if I don't eradicate those thoughts from my head, our time together will be over before it begins. "Did you practice last night?"

"Of course."

She doesn't tense up, change her breathing, or convey vulnerability in any way. She's telling the truth, which might explain her whereabouts last night.

"Where did you practice?" Realizing that implies I know she wasn't home, I rephrase the question. "You own a piano?"

"Not anymore." Her dark brown hair escapes the curve of

her ear and falls over her shoulder. She gathers it at the bend
of her neck and twists it into a rope down her chest. "My
mom sold my dad's piano after he died."

*My dad's*, not Daddy's. I bite the inside of my cheek to hide
my satisfaction.

"There's a music store down the street from my house."
Facing me, she braces an elbow on the edge of the piano and
mirrors my position. "The owner lets me practice on his
Steinway until eleven every night."

Which coincides with the time she came home. So why
can't I shake the feeling she's leaving something out?

Because she's not looking at me. She's toying with the ends
of her hair, and wherever her thoughts just drifted, she's
distracted to silence.

I touch a finger to her chin, lifting it to recapture her
attention. "Time to finish our earlier conversation."

Her lips thin.

"Who asked you for an inappropriate favor?"

She turns away and lowers onto the piano bench. "No
lies?"

"I don't mentor liars, Miss Westbrook."

She nods, her expression grim. "The truth is, I need your
help." Her hands run over the keys without depressing them.
"With *this*. Mastering the piano." She stretches her fingers.
"I'm the best pianist in this school, you know."

"Is that right?"

She peers up at me through her lashes. "I may even be
better than you."

My stomach swoops in the presence of her tantalizing
smile. "Let's not get carried away."

"You're right." She studies her fingers on the keys. "I have a lot to learn. But with the right teacher and enough focus, I'll be out of here at the end of the year. Out of Treme. This is the most honesty I can give you, Mr. Marceaux." She pulls her hands into her lap and stares up at me with pleading eyes. "If you focus on the other stuff in my life, the things not related to my talent, it will hurt my future. And if you involve social services, every opportunity I have here will be taken away."

She's all but admitting I won't like what I find when I poke around in her affairs. I have no intention of involving social services, and she doesn't need to know the extent to which I'm capable of investigating a person.

But I prefer to hear it from her. "Answer the question."

"I can't. *Please.*"

That's all it takes. The seductive sound of her begging in one breathy syllable and she owns every nerve in my body. I want to hear that sound as she kneels to me, releases me from my pants, and guides me toward her mouth.

*Get a grip, asshole.*

It's clear she won't tell me who's taking advantage of her, but I'll find out.

"All right." I flick a hand toward the piano. "Play for me."

She adjusts the bench, slides off her tattered shoes, and positions her toes on the pedals. With her palms on her knees, she gives me her attention. "Baroque? Classical? Jazz?"

"Surprise me."

Eyes on the keyboard, she steadies her breathing. A current of serenity seems to float through her as her posture loosens and her face softens. Then her hands lift, her head bows over the keys, and fucking hell, her fingers fly. The concerto she chose is pure insanity, a high tempo complexity of too many notes. Balakirev's Islamey is one of the most challenging cadenzas in the whole classical piano repertoire, and she plays it like an expert.

She's a tornado of whipping wrists, violent fingers, and rocking hips. Her chin sways, head jerking on the hard-hitting beats, her expression a picture of intense focus. But my critical ear doesn't miss the slips when she hits the chords with too much force, speeds up too fast, and plays all the sixteenth notes like eighth note triplets.

This is why I don't play the piece. I mastered it in college, but it's a goddamn nightmare. The difficulty and awkwardness in positioning the fingers, the left hand hopping over the right, and at the end of eight minutes, it leaves me drenched in sweat. Besides, I'm not a fan of classical interpretation, which is ironic since I hold a seat in the Louisiana Symphony Orchestra.

Despite Ivory's minimal mistakes, she brilliantly manipulates the rhythmic flexibility within the measures while following the rubrics with her own artistic convictions. I find myself exhaling with her at the end of every phrase and bending closer as she falls on strong beats, completely mesmerized by the leap of her hands. She breathes life into the notes, beams, and bar lines, making it the best performance I've heard on this piece.

She finishes with a sweep of her arms and releases a silent sigh. Perspiration dots along her hairline, and her hands tremble in her lap.

A long moment passes before she drags her gaze to mine

and clears her throat. "Well?"

"You hit the notes too hard. Your rubato is rough, too fast. Way too many mistakes."

She nods, her shoulders slumping.

"This is an instrument, Miss Westbrook, not a gun. You're making music, not shooting notes at the audience."

"I know," she says quietly. "Projection is an art, one I'm still...trying to..." Her chin quivers, and tears sheen her eyes before she looks away and whispers under her breath, "Shit."

If she requires an instructor who gives praise just to balance the criticism, she has the wrong guy. I'm a dick, and like I told her yesterday, I respect constructive feedback. I'm also not finished with my appraisal.

I approach the piano bench and move to sit, forcing her to make room. She scoots to the edge, the seat barely holding the two of us. Our shoulders, hips, and thighs touch, and it's not accidental. I want her to feel every contact point and learn to trust it. To trust me.

"What did I say about sniveling?"

Her shoulders snap back, and she stares straight ahead, her voice reedy. "I'm sorry. I don't know why I...I got a little overwhelmed there. I guess I wanted you to—"

"Stop talking."

She presses her lips together.

I shift to face her, and the position pushes the length of my thigh against hers. The heat from her leg seeps into mine, and I fold my hands together in my lap to keep from reaching out and inching up the hem of her dress. "I didn't develop the skill to even attempt Islamey until college, and I couldn't play it all the way through until my final year of graduate school."

Her eyes flash to mine, huge and round and brimmed with moisture.

I cup the delicate curve of her jaw and swipe my thumb to catch a tear. "Very few people can play that piece. In fact, Balakirev admitted there were passages in his composition even *he* couldn't manage."

She leans into my hand, seemingly unaware she's doing it as she clings to my words.

"Your interpretation is extraordinarily passionate and stunning." *Just like you.* "I'm moved."

Her breaths come faster, heaving her chest. "Oh Jesus, for real? I'm—" More tears fall from her eyes, and she pulls away to wipe her face. "Dammit, I'm not sniveling. I swear."

"Why did you choose it?"

"Islamey?"

"Yes."

She gazes up at me with a relieved smile. "The owner of the music store I told you about, the one where I practice? His name is Stogie and—"

"What do you give him in exchange for practicing there?"

Her smile falls as she realizes what I'm implying. "Nothing! He's the kindest man I know." She winces. "No offense."

"We both know I'm not a kind man. Continue."

She bites her lip, but her grin reappears, tugging at the corners. "He's also very old and stubborn and refuses to take his medicine. So he made me a deal. If I learned Islamey, he would take his pills without my nagging." She shrugs. "It took me all summer. All day, every day."

"Dedication."

Her smile lingers. "My hands *still* hurt."

"Get used to it. While you played that piece beautifully, it wasn't perfect. Let's start with Chopin's Etude Op 10 No.5 to get you more comfortable with the appropriate amount of pressure on those black keys."

As she pulls out the music sheet and dives into the etude, I don't move, don't give her space. I'm reluctant to give her any leeway at all.

I sat with Prescott Rivard this morning in an impromptu session with his guitar tutor. Then I made the rounds with other top musicians at Le Moyne. The talent is impressive, but none are as proficient or driven as Ivory Westbrook.

I intend to cultivate, polish, and discipline her, while deriving every twisted ounce of pleasure I can from it. But I can't give her the one thing she desires. I want this job, which means there will be no Leopold in her future.

# IVORY

"I'm going to Leopold." I pause the marker mid-scrawl, the tip pressed against the whiteboard, as the creak of Mr. Marceaux's shoes approaches from behind.

The sheer height of him casts a shadow over my back as his breaths stir my hair, his whisper like a satin ribbon trailing over my shoulder. "Less talking, more writing."

It's only the fifth day of school, and I'm already plotting all the ways to murder him.

I want to poison his coffee for beginning today's private lesson with a punishment. While I forgot all about disrupting his class on the first day, he was happy to remind me by shoving a marker in my hand and leading me to the wall-length whiteboard.

I want to strangle him with his obnoxious yellow-flowered tie for making me write an endless loop of *I will not waste Mr. Marceaux's time.*

With large, angry lines, I scribble another sentence and say, "I'm seventeen, not seven."

*Whack.*

A sharp sting burns across my bicep, and my hand flies up to rub the hurt.

I want to rip that conductor baton from his fingers and

impale it in his throat. Because seriously, where is the orchestra? There isn't one, yet he's twirling the damn thing like Pherekydes of Patrae and slapping it against my arms like a ruler-wielding nun.

"This is wasting time for both of us," I mumble, scrawling another sentence that states the opposite.

*Whack.*

A snap of heat blooms on my back, right above my tailbone. Motherfucker, that hurts. But it's not the worst pain, either. If anyone else raised a baton at me—Lorenzo or Prescott, for example—I'd snarl and throw punches. But this is my mentor, and I want to please him. *While plotting his death.*

I want the teacher back from three days ago. The one who touched my face so tenderly and said my performance moved him. Where did that guy go?

Maybe it's my fault. I've been off-kilter, dreading tonight all week. I can't put off Prescott any longer. His homework is done, and I'm a twisted-up bundle of nerves and anger. And with the weekend starting tomorrow, I'll have two days at home. Two days with Lorenzo and his outrage at not being able to track me down all week.

"What did I say about questioning me?" Mr. Marceaux's footsteps pace behind me, his icy eyes shivering the hairs on my nape.

If I didn't know him better, which I don't, I'd think he's enjoying this. "Telling a student not to question her teacher is the worst rule in the history of rules."

I tense for another swat, but it doesn't come.

He leans a shoulder against the unwritten section of the board beside me, his hands behind his back and a smirk on his too-pretty face. "I'll rephrase. Don't question my methods." His sharp gaze moves to the board. "Erase the last five sentences, and try again with penmanship befitting a seventeen-year-old."

I thrust the eraser over the board with belligerent swipes and begin again. "I can write and talk at the same time, and I want to talk about Leopold."

"You're not good enough for Leopold."

I whirl toward him as the crescendo of my heart crashes past my ears. "You said my interpretation of Islamey was extraordinarily passionate and stunning."

Standing a couple of feet away, he watches me with hooded eyes—*Bored? Sleepy?*—and shrugs half-heartedly. "Those are meaningless superlatives, which I now regret using."

My muscles quiver as a rush of fury slams into me. My hands ball into fists, and before my brain catches up, I rear back the marker and hurl it. Right at his forehead.

It bounces off his scowl lines and rolls across the floor beside his Doc Martens. He glares at it, shocked to terrifying stillness, before flinging the conductor baton across his desk and leveling me with glacial eyes.

Ohshitohshitohshit. My face catches fire as I stumble backward. My shoulder hits the whiteboard, but I keep going, sliding along the wall and toward the door. What the hell is wrong with me? I never lose my temper. Holy fuck, I *never* throw markers at my teachers!

He reaches up, wipes his forehead, and glowers at his fingers. *Yes, Mr. Marceaux, the fat black dot of my shame is now smeared across your furiously creased brow.*

"I'm sorry." I glance at the closed door, wishing I were on

the other side, down the hall, and far away from whatever comes next.

Without removing his eyes from mine, he lifts his chin and loosens the knot of his tie. Fuck, that can't be good.

As his hands slide over the silk, I recall another rumor I heard this morning about the depraved ways he uses his ties, belts, and other miscellaneous accessories. I don't believe gossip, but as I stare into those cruel eyes, I plummet into the chasm of whispered images with a sinking stomach.

With the knot hanging loosely beneath his collar, he crooks his finger. "Come with me."

Three words, spoken without effort, yet they have the power to devastate my future. Fear jolts through my stomach. If he takes me to the dean's office, will it be a suspension? Or is hurling objects at my teacher grounds for expulsion?

But he doesn't walk toward the exit. He strides deeper into the back of the room and around the corner, out of sight. I look through the small window in the door, into the empty hallway, and tremble with indecision.

Running will only make this worse.

I push myself forward on wobbly legs and weave through the rows of desks. Every inch of my body is strung-out, running on a live wire that connects the path of my feet to whatever awaits me around that corner. By the time I reach the piano and find him sitting sideways on the end of the bench, my pulse is a reedy, struggling vibration in my veins.

He points at the floor beneath the space of his spread thighs and flicks his wrist, as if adjusting the position of his heavy watch.

The sleeves of his gray and white pinstriped shirt gather

around his elbows. He's wearing another one of those waistcoat-vest things, this one black with little gray buttons. My attention shifts from the yellow tie to the dark shadow of his jaw, the flat line of his lips, and as I fall into the chilling trap of his eyes, I realize with renewed panic that I'm making him wait.

I hurry forward and stand where he indicated, swaying unsteadily between his spread feet.

There's that crooking finger again, gesturing me closer, closer, and lord help me, when I'm finally in the position he wants, my boobs are right in his face. I curve my spine, attempting to rein them in, but dammit, they're there and there's nothing I can do about it.

Heat tingles across my cheeks as he blatantly stares down the scoop of my shirt. It makes me feel gross, cheap, and really fucking angry.

I grab the neckline to yank it up.

His hand catches my wrist, pulling my arm back to my side. "Stop fidgeting and straighten your back."

I do as he says, even as I'm about to implode with anxiety over the position of our bodies and his silence on the marker incident. "Are you going to report me to the dean?"

"I administer my own punishments." He gestures at his forehead. "Fix this."

"Fix it?" A swallow sticks in my throat. "Like rub it off?"

He glares up at me like I'm the dumbest girl in the world. Yes, well, only a dumb girl puts herself in this situation.

With a trembling hand, I press the pad of my thumb against the ink above his eyebrow. I don't know what I expected—*cold, reptilian scales?*—but his skin is smooth and warm and *human*. As I press harder, my free hand catches the back of his head, and my fingers slide through soft black strands. It feels so...personal, affectionate, *abnormal*.

His face hovers inches beneath mine, the muscles in his cheeks relaxed, lips slightly parted and thick lashes fanning downward. He really is handsome, even if everything about him is potently male. From the woodsy scent of his shampoo and the boxy shape of his jaw to his tapered waist and the way his muscular legs stretch the lean cut of his black slacks, it's all there to remind me my future hinges on the whims of a man.

A man with ink on his forehead.

I rub harder. "It's not coming off."

"Use spit."

My internal ick-meter swivels toward *Eww*, but I'm already up to my tits in trouble, so I lick my thumb and resume scrubbing. "What's my punishment?"

"Is it coming off?"

"Yeah. I'm really sorry, Mr. Marceaux." I wipe away the final traces and drop my arms. "It's gone."

"Put your hands back where they were."

Why would he want my hands in his hair? On his face? It feels so...foreign. Improper. But he asked. No, he ordered. Dammit, why is it so hard to disobey him?

I return my hands exactly where they were, and for some reason, it's easier this time, less awkward. He stares up at me, and the multi-shades of blues in his eyes glimmer beneath the fluorescents. His mouth is kind of pouty, not in a displeasing way. His full lips make him appear softer somehow. I think they're my favorite attribute.

The fact that I have a favorite attribute on any man gives me pause, but I don't remember ever seeing someone as attractive as Mr. Marceaux. Not on TV or in magazines or in person. Certainly, not this close up. I'm acutely aware of the press of his thighs against the outsides of my legs, the crotch of his slacks brushing my knees, and the warmth of his breath whispering across my collarbone. But it's his head in my hands that makes me want to push him away and pull him closer at the same time.

I've never touched a man in this way. The tickle of his hair between my fingers, the brawny lines of his face beneath my palm, the scratch of his barely-there stubble, every sensation beneath my fingertips fills me with fear and excitement and all the chaos in between.

I wonder again about the rumor, about why he left Shreveport. Can the same thing happen here, with me? My fingers clench against his head.

He licks his lips. "Tell me what you're thinking."

I want to yank my hands away, but I don't dare. "I overheard a couple girls whispering about you in first hour."

"Go on."

"They said your first name is Emeric."

"Hardly enough to whisper about." His wrists rest on his thighs, his fingers dangling behind me, and the proximity causes them to graze my legs. "What else?"

"Shreveport."

"Ah." His fingers brush the backs of my knees, and this time I'm certain he's doing it deliberately. "Miss Westbrook, don't make me drag every detail from you."

"They said you were fired." My palm feels too clammy

against his cheek, so I drop my hands to the crisp collar of his shirt. "Because someone walked into a classroom and found you with a woman."

He arches a brow. "Is that all?"

"No." I clear my throat. "Supposedly, her mouth was gagged with your tie."

"And?"

"Her wrists were bound by your belt." I rush forward with the rest. "Her body was bent over the desk while you had sex with her from behind. That's the extent of what I've heard."

His hands close around the backs of my knees. "Wow."

*Wow* is right. The crazy things people say...

A smirk slithers across his lips. "That is surprisingly accurate."

"What?" My chest heaves as I push against his shoulders.

But he anticipates me, his arms hooking around my legs then shifting upward to circle my waist as he stands. He kicks the bench out of the way and spins us toward the closest wall.

My back presses against the bricks with his chest flush with mine, pinning me there. "Deep breaths, Ivory."

*Ivory.* The most intimate word I've heard from his mouth. My skin shivers with bizarre delight.

He touches his lips to my neck. "You're not breathing."

I fill my lungs, but it doesn't help. I feel so small and insubstantial in his strong arms, fastened against his huge body. His chest, biceps, stomach, thighs...my God, he's hard everywhere I'm soft. And hot. Too hot. I think I'm running a fever. I'm definitely going to puke if he removes his tie and belt.

With my hands clenched on his shoulders, I try to shove at

the unmovable muscle. "Please don't do those things to me."

He sighs, stroking his nose along my jaw. "It was consensual. Do you know what that means?"

I shake my head, not sure, but maybe I do know. "Like an agreement?"

"Yes. Only she didn't just agree. She *begged*."

"Why? Why would she want that?"

"Joanne is..." He looks away and stretches his neck to rub his chin against his shoulder. His brows pull in, and his entire demeanor seems suddenly and strangely subdued. When his gaze returns, so does his intensity, and his arms tighten around my waist. "She's like you."

"Me?" I squirm against him. "I don't want those things. You don't even know me."

"Tell me what you feel right now."

"Scared. You're scaring me."

His lips hover a kiss away, the hint of cinnamon gum scenting his breath. "Yes, but there's something else. Describe it."

"My heart's pounding. I'm burning up, and my stomach feels like an ice block."

"Your heart and stomach. Where else? Describe the feeling in your nipples."

A flash of heat sweeps across my neck, through my chest, and builds between my legs. I squeeze my thighs together, humiliated by the reaction, confused by the flush of weird emotions, but I latch onto the feeling I understand. "This is wrong."

"Not *wrong*. It's inappropriate. But we went way past inappropriate the first day. Tell me how your nipples feel. I won't criticize your answer as long as it's the truth."

I suck in a shaky breath and give him what he wants. "Itchy and tight."

"Good girl."

The tingle between my legs grows stronger, heavier, more demanding.

He pushes his hips against mine to stop my squirming, and the hardest part of him, the part I hate most, jabs against my stomach. "Now put a name to all those feelings."

"I don't know." I can't breathe. I can't think. "I can't."

"Dig deep, Ivory."

My throat closes up.

"What do you feel when you haven't eaten."

"Hungry."

His hard eyes are too close, too unsafe. "How about when you see a beautiful piano?"

"Want."

"And when I gave you praise after your performance of Islamey?"

"Desire for more."

"Hunger. Want. Desire. Is that what you're feeling as I hold you against the wall?"

Is it? The aching hunger for something between my legs, my out-of-control heartbeat, and the burning need to express it, talk about it? My head is too mixed-up. Yes, he's a beautiful man, and I hear all the girls talk about wanting to do him. And yes, I crave his appreciation for my talent and his *good-girls* and his warm hand on my face, but this? The length of his body against mine? Holding me immobile?

He's just holding me. Not grabbing my boobs or thrusting

between my legs. He's giving me attention. Asking me about my feelings. Without taking.

Jesus, I do want this, from someone I can trust, from my teacher, and I shouldn't. "I think it's desire. And shame." *Humiliation.*

He presses his lips against my forehead. "Mmm. There's my girl."

"I don't want to be gagged and tied and—"

His finger falls across my mouth then returns to my back. "Not now. But you'll think about it. The idea will consume you. Then we'll talk about it again."

"But you're my teacher!"

"I said we'll *talk* about it." He leans back and rests his hands on my hips. "Where will you get the money to pay me back?"

The subject change gives me whiplash. "I'll have it by Monday, I promise."

"That's not what I asked."

I close my eyes, blocking out his perceptive gaze. He knows my mom is unemployed. I'm here till seven every night and practicing at Stogie's till eleven, so he knows I can't work. There's no way I can tell him I'm doing Prescott's homework and essentially whoring myself out to pay the bills. And I don't know why, but lying to him scares me more than him discovering the truth.

Opening my eyes, I do the only thing I can. I shake my head.

His expression hardens, and his scowl overtakes my entire world. "Let's talk about the punishment for throwing shit at your teacher."

He's only inches from my face, with a frightening glare and a body twice my size. Isn't that punishment enough?

"You have a choice. Tell me where you get your money. Or bare your ass for a spanking."

All the blood drains from my face to my feet. There is no choice.

# EMERIC

I flex my hands against Ivory's waist, my entire body strumming with the thought of reddening her tight ass. But my brain screams for her to make the other choice, to tell me her secrets and steer me away from this dangerous temptation.

With the wall at her back and her gorgeous tits rising and falling against my chest, she lifts her brown eyes and whispers, "The spanking."

Her breathy response hits me in the gut and tunnels to my groin, wrenching a guttural sound from my throat and propelling my hips into a hungry grind against hers. She gasps when she feels me. Fuck, how could she not feel me? I've never been this hard in my life.

This is a mistake. It's Shreveport and Joanne and a goddamn slippery slope to ruination all over again.

I hold my body stock-still against hers, my fingers digging into her waist.

She's not Joanne. This isn't love or attachment. It's not even sex. I'm in control, and her punishment is due.

Releasing her, I step back and calm my breaths.

I gave her the choice, and I'm a man of my word. "Turn around. Hands on the wall."

Her face is a sheet of white as she pivots slowly and follows my order. The slim brown skirt cuts an erotic outline around her pert ass—much better than the black tarp thing she wore a few days ago. The swells of her cheeks are neither too big nor too small, proportioned with her narrow waist and perfect for my hands.

But the frayed hems and roughly faded material of her clothes are reminders that this isn't just about what's under her skirt. Beyond my hunger for discipline and pleasure, I feel this deep aching desire to provide for her in all ways.

"Don't move."

I back up and adjust the bulge behind my zipper. Stepping out of the alcove and into the main part of the classroom, I glance at the door. It's still closed. There's no lock, but the hinges will creak if it opens, giving me about five seconds before an intruder makes it through the room and around the corner.

As I head back to Ivory, my phone vibrates in my pocket. Irritated at the interruption, I consider ignoring it, but maybe it'll distract me away from the mistake I'm about to make. I glance at the screen.

*Joanne: I'm in town this weekend. I need to see you.*

The hollow space around my heart clenches tightly. I pull a stick of gum from my pocket and gnash it between my molars.

The phone buzzes again.

*Joanne: Need your address.*

She's persistent enough to find it, but she won't get it from me.

And now I'm more worked up than I was thirty seconds

ago.

I power the phone off, toss it on the closest desk, and return my attention to Ivory.

Hands flat against the wall and gaze on the floor, she hasn't moved. Except her feet. They're closer together, and her knees visibly shake below the hem of her skirt.

She knows this is improper, that we're doing something we shouldn't be doing. But I doubt she's aware that the thrill in that risk, the chance of getting caught, is currently increasing her brain's transmission of dopamine and heightening the excitement spiraling through her body.

The possibility of getting away with something so wickedly forbidden only feeds my beast and makes me hungrier.

I prowl closer. "Widen your stance."

She slides her feet apart and tilts her head, as if listening for me. I soften my steps, forcing her to concentrate harder to track my approach.

When I reach her, I invade, pressing my arousal against her backside. Not grinding. Just letting her feel how well we fit together as I hold her against me with my hands on her hips. Her shoulders tighten around her ears, and her inhale catches in her throat.

I brush her hair to the side, trailing a finger across her nape, as I slide my cheek along hers. "Last chance to change your mind."

*Don't change your mind.*

Her words rush out on a shredded breath. "Just get it over with."

My heart races as I shift to the right and slam my dominant hand against her ass. It's just a warm-up strike, but she flies up on her toes and lets out a sexy squeak.

My cock swells, pulsing and trapped against my leg. My fingers tingle to touch her, to stroke and welt her flawless body. "Open your mouth."

Her profile pinches. Then her lips part, hesitantly, her chin quivering with apprehension. So damn beautiful.

I remove the softened gum from my mouth and place it inside hers. She jerks back, but I hold her head and set the cinnamon adhesive between her molars with a swipe of my finger.

"Bite down." I stroke her jaw as it flexes. "Good girl. Now hold it there. No screaming."

I glide my hands down her thighs, stretching to reach bare skin. Her breathing quickens as I gather the skirt in my fists, inching it higher, higher, above her gorgeous butt and around her waist.

Goosebumps prickle beneath my hands as I caress the backs of her legs, the crease between her thigh and ass, and the trim of panties where they cut high on her cheeks. Hooking my fingers under the bottoms of the lacy edges, I drag the material upward, pulling the tiny scrap along her crack to expose more flesh.

Her glutes flex and twitch in my hands, and my pulse revs. She's so soft and firm, shivery and warm. So goddamn responsive.

I want to rip her panties off for this, but a glimpse of her pussy would make it impossible to keep my dick in my pants.

Listening for the door, I step back. The sight of her ass trimmed with lace and the pull of the cotton cupping the titillating shape of her cunt threatens to buckle my knees.

"Four strikes," I say gruffly and strengthen my voice. "Two on each cheek."

She stares at the wall, her fingers curling against the bricks as a series of twitches ripples across her buttocks.

With a deep breath, I let my hand fly, applying more force this time, but I still hold back. The slap echoes through the room, and her body responds like a guitar string, stretching, vibrating, her vocal chords humming exquisitely. Then she settles, becoming stable and still.

A pink hand print blooms across her flesh. I massage the heated skin, and she wriggles her ass, only slightly, but it speaks volumes. She's scared, probably terrified, but she's not running or screaming or pushing me away. She's rubbing her ass against my touch, ready for me to take her where I want her to go.

Stepping to the side, I fire off the next three smacks in rapid succession, each one harder than the last while alternating cheeks. She whimpers softly, bows her back, rocks her hips, raises up on her toes. And never lets go of the wall.

She likes it rough, wants to be humiliated, needs to be dominated. If she's aware of this, she would never admit it. Probably because she's never experienced it in the right environment with the right person.

In a classroom with her teacher...still not right. Yet here she is, hanging onto that wall, with her feet spread and ass out, because I gave her an order.

She's made for me, to be instructed and punished and enjoyed. I want inside her with such agonizing intensity my body quakes. I want in her mouth, her cunt, and her soul. I want to rip her apart with my shaft, piece her back together, and do it all over again. Fuck, I need this girl.

And I can't have her.

Her forehead rests against the wall, and with a heavy sigh, the tension drains from her muscles.

I crouch behind her and straighten her panties, gently rubbing the pink skin and thrilling at the way her legs tremble with each of my strokes. I adjust the skirt with the same care, kneading my fingers across her ass and thighs in a soothing motion. When I return to a standing position, I turn her to face me, my hands on her hips to steady her.

She blinks up at me, eyes unfocused, and grooves crease her forehead.

"Where did you go, gorgeous girl?"

"Somewhere deep."

Endorphins, adrenaline, fear, and arousal make a heady cocktail, and she looks absolutely breathtaking in her discovery.

I grip her chin, lifting it higher. "The gum."

She covers her mouth and whispers behind her fingers, "I just swallowed it."

Next time I'll remind her to keep it so she can pass it back to me while my tongue is between her lips.

I scoop her up, hooking arms behind her knees and back. She appears so sturdy and solid with her height, curves, and full tits, but with her cradled against my chest, she's feather-light, barely a buck ten.

Sitting on the piano bench, I hold her sideways on my thighs and drag a finger down her arm.

She shivers and squirms in my lap, wreaking havoc on my throbbing erection. But she doesn't scoot away from it and instead shifts to face me.

"That thing you just did with your finger?" With one arm trapped between us, she glances at the other, where it bends in her lap. "Will you do that again?"

A touch? That's what she wants?

*She wants affection.*

I move my mouth an inch away from hers and steel my gaze. "Beg."

Her chin drops, jaw clenching, but she doesn't look away. After a heartbeat, two, three, her face relaxes, and her lips part. "Please."

A wave of warmth circulates through me. I'm a slave to that word on her breath.

Touching my fingers to her shoulder, I trail them over her short-sleeves, down the satiny skin of her slender arm, and linger on the knuckles of her hand. When she stretches her fingers, I trace the length of them, marveling at how such fragile bones can move so ferociously over piano keys.

Her lashes flutter down, and her nostrils flare with long, deep inhales. She loves this, my hand on hers, giving her pleasure.

When her eyes open, enlarged pupils saturate the brown hues. "What else do you do?"

Christ, this girl is killing me. Her innocence, curiosity, precious submission, it's all putty, begging to be shaped. But it's not just that. Her authenticity and lack of privilege pinches something inside me. It makes me feel protective. Possessive. Maybe even...wishful?

"I can do many things, Ivory." I touch the side of her face and push my hand through her thick hair, dragging fingers over her ear and cupping the back of her head. "But this situation...it's delicate." Sinful. Hazardous. Criminal.

*I want to show you anyway.*

I lean closer, so close our breaths meld.

*I'll show you while I'm buried deep in your throat.*

So close our lips brush together, separate, and hover in anticipation to touch again.

*I'll show you while I'm coming against the walls of your cunt.*

Her thighs clench against mine, and my heart races.

*I'll show you while I'm marking you. Owning you. Cherishing you.*

I want to kiss her. I have to. Just a taste.

Tightening my hand within the tangle of her hair, I draw her to my mouth—

And stop.

Did something stir around the corner? I jerk forward and register the creaking hinges a few seconds too slow.

The petite blonde teacher from the strings department emerges around the corner just as I drop Ivory onto the bench beside me. A bitter tang floods my mouth. Did Ms. Augustin see her in my lap? She definitely saw us pulling apart.

Her beady eyes narrow, ticking back and forth between me and the student I just erotically spanked. I hold my breath.

Here's the thing about erections. They don't deflate just because the rest of the body is freaking the fuck out. The school could be on fire, and the damn thing will stand tall and proud like a flagpole, drawing attention at the worst possible moment.

Thankfully, the piano sits between my flag-waving boner and Ms. Augustin.

"Am I interrupting something?" Suspicion clips her tone. "It's after seven, and I thought..."

She thought she could follow up on all those heated looks she's been giving me in the hall, teacher's lounge, and staff meetings all week. She thought she could swing by on a Friday night and talk her way into my bed.

"No problem," I say casually. Andrea Augustin *is* a problem, one I'm prepared to resolve. "Miss Westbrook was just leaving."

Ivory slips off the bench and walks away without looking at me. No, her attention centers on the other teacher. I can't see her face, but she gives Ms. Augustin a wide berth, her strides stiffening as she vanishes around the corner.

"Have a good weekend, Ivory," Andrea calls after her.

The door to the hall closes with a despondent click.

Every muscle in my body tenses to run after her, but I have to deal with this problem first.

Andrea turns back to me, hands on her hips, her tone shifting from pleasant to snarly. "What were you doing with her?"

In the faculty hierarchy, she's technically beneath me. I'm the Director of Keyboard Studies, and she's just a teacher. I want to use that to my advantage, but she saw what she saw. Enough to report my behavior. Enough to get me fired. Or arrested.

With Ivory, I want nothing between us but the naked truth. But Andrea? All I'll give her is the best-dressed lie. "I've been waiting for you."

Her arms lower to her sides, and she blinks. "You were?" Her eyes return to slits. "Why was Ivory Westbrook on your lap?"

I sigh for effect, and now that my cock has finally calmed down, I stand. "I need to gather my things. Follow me, and I'll explain."

As we walk to the front of the classroom, I shift close to her, closer than socially acceptable, with my arm brushing hers and my neck craned to give her the full impact of my gaze. "You know her father died? He was killed a few years back?"

"Yes. Everyone knows that."

"Well, I didn't." At my desk, I pretend to shut down my laptop, and instead pull up a program and angle the back cover toward her. "She just told me about it, got a little weepy, and I comforted her."

"In your lap?" She crosses her arms.

It's an absurd lie, even on the fly. I'll have to fix this the hard way.

I stalk around the desk, hands behind my back, and let my gaze roam over her body. "I know what you want, Andrea."

She steps back, bumping into the student desk behind her, and her fingers reach up to toy with her earring. "What do you mean?"

"Don't be coy. I've seen you watching me, your flirty smiles, the way you play with your hair and jewelry when *I'm* watching *you*."

Her hand drops, and she breathes, "Emeric..."

In three strides, I close the distance, crowding her against the desk without touching her. I loosen my tie the rest of the way and slide it from my neck. If Ivory's heard the Shreveport details, it's likely Andrea heard as well and is thinking of it now. I wager those rumors are the reason she's here, face blushing and hooded eyes tracking the trail of silk as I wrap it around my hand.

I put my mouth next to her ear. "You want me to tie you up."

She sits back, her ass perching on the desk behind her. Her knees part then spread some more, welcoming the nudge of my hips.

"You want me to feed you my cock." I roughen my voice and quicken my breaths, insinuating I want that, too.

Unfortunately, my unresponsive dick refuses to participate in the ploy, so I maintain a sliver of space between me and the apex of her thighs, where she's covered by the loose material of her skirt.

She grips my biceps and pushes out her tiny tits, but her attention shifts toward the closed door.

I hover my mouth over her neck, exhaling a steam of feigned desire. "Everyone's gone home for the weekend, right?"

"Yes."

"Besides, no one can see us from the window." I recline back. "I'll give you one chance, Andrea. Tell me exactly what you want."

Her gaze lowers to the tie around my hand, and her fingers follow, tracing the silk in my grip. "I—I...want what you said. But we can't. Not here."

She looks back at the door, licking her lips.

"No, not here." I move away and return to the desk, leaning on the edge beside the laptop. "Before I decide to take you home, you have to show me how badly you want me."

Excitement brightens her face. Then her eyebrows dig in. "H–how?

"Show me how wet you are. Go ahead. No one will see."

Her expression contorts as uncertainty battles desire. I know which will win, but she drags out the silence, working herself into a heaving, flushed jumble of anxiety.

Finally, her breathing quiets, and her hands fumble with the folds of her skirt.

"Spread your legs, Andrea."

She does, eyes on the door as she feels around the satin crotch. "How do I–"

"Under the panties. There you go."

She tosses her head and makes some noise.

I'm not really paying attention, but I let her rub around in there for a while. "Now hold up your hand."

She lifts her arm and smiles at her fingers. I don't give a shit if they're wet or not. I have what I need.

I hit a key on the laptop and question the wisdom in telling her what I did.

It's better to be proactive than reactive.

Gripping the screen, I flip the laptop toward her and back up the silent video to the juicy part.

Shock comes first, paling her complexion and paralyzing her body. Then outrage.

"Wha–" She shoves her skirt into place, fists her hands at her sides, and rushes toward me. "What are you–? Oh my God, you recorded that!"

With the camera on the back of the laptop, I caught it all while remaining out of the frame during the incriminating segment.

I snap the lid shut. "Don't fuck with me, Ms. Augustin."

She jerks back, arms wrapping around her mid-section, and stares at me in horror. "Why would you—?" Deep red inflames her cheeks. "Oh God, what are you going to do with it? Is this about Ivory?" She covers her face with her hands, and a sob garbles her words. "I need...job. I can't lose...you can't do this."

"I've done nothing with Ivory. But *you* just masturbated in my classroom." I store the laptop and tie in my bag then turn toward her, wearing an expression that matches my most intimidating tone. "Stay out of my classroom, *out of my business*, and no one will see this video."

She stares back at me, defeated. Betrayed. Yeah, I know the feeling too well. Only I'm not trying to steal Andrea's job. I simply want to keep the one I have.

Hatred soaks her eyes. "What they say about you is true then."

"You don't know the half of it." I shoulder the bag, flash her a charming smile, and stride into the hall. "Good night, Ms. Augustin."

# IVORY

Prescott tangles his hand in my hair, holding my face against his lap.

His penis stabs the back of my throat, and I gag.

*Yellow-flowered tie. Cinnamon gum.*

The buckle of his belt clanks with his thrusts. The console between the front seats digs into my chest.

*Chilling blue eyes. The heat of his palm on my backside.*

A bass-heavy song thumps from the car radio, and I can't find my safe place. I'm not numb enough, not far enough away. I'm trying, trying... I can't gather the notes for Scriabin's Sonata No.9.

*The tick of a mechanical watch. The gentle stroke of his breaths.*

Tears well in my eyes and cling to my lashes. I can't focus. Can't escape.

All I can think about is the spanking and how I wouldn't mind another if it ends with an almost-kiss from Mr. Marceaux.

# EMERIC

Wedged between *Hook 'Em Up* deli and a vintage jewelry shop called *Pawn of the Dead* resides the only music store in Treme. At least, I think this is a music store. Standing on the broken sidewalk, I hang my sunglasses on the collar of my t-shirt and squint against the glare of the sun.

Security bars crisscross the glass front. There's no open sign or any kind of advertisement, and the grime on the windows obscures my view of the dark interior. Since it's Saturday, the store might not be open. Finding Ivory inside is even less likely.

But I'm not here for her. I couldn't sleep last night thinking about where she gets her money and who put those unsettling shadows in her eyes. This Stogie guy might be an avenue to answers, and hopefully, this visit will soothe my nagging need to meet the man she spends her time with.

I check my phone, confirm the address, and try the door.

The jingling bell overhead announces me as I step into a cluttered room of instruments. Voices whisper from the back, guiding my feet through the maze of shelves, drum sets, and miscellaneous junk.

"You need to eat more."

I can't see her around the rows of display racks, but her

sexy lilt speeds my strides and buzzes my body with excitement.

Coming here to meet a man named after a cigar, I expected to walk into a stale cloud of leather and smoke, but instead, the air is remarkably fresh, especially for such an old building.

"Stop nagging," a deep voice says, "and let an old man nap."

"But you have a customer." Her sigh drifts from behind a tall shelf filled with books.

I step into view and find her sitting on the floor, back to the wall, and bare legs stretched out before her. My hands flex as I silently thank the fashion Gods for short-shorts. She's a half-naked fantasy of bronzed skin and devious curves. An *illegal* fantasy.

Lids lifting, her eyes collide with mine and widen. The textbook in her hands tumbles to the floor to join the dozen others surrounding her. "Mr. Marceaux?"

"Miss Westbrook." I'm struck with the wild urge to grin like a jackass, but I manage to maintain a stoic mask.

Her gaze sweeps from my disheveled hair and t-shirt to my dark jeans and Doc Martens. I wish I could read her thoughts as she takes me in for the first time without the pageantry of waistcoats and ties. She makes another head-to-toe pass, nibbling her lip and stirring a torrent of sensations inside me.

The old man beside her sits taller on the metal chair. A frayed baseball cap perches high on his bald head, and horizontal wrinkles crease the broad bridge of his nose, deepening into more lines on his dark-skinned brow. His closed-mouth smile is the kind men wear when they're toothless and...eighty? Ninety? I don't know, but this guy is ancient.

His arm trembles as he reaches for the wall in an attempt to stand.

"Don't get up." I step toward him, offering my hand to shake his. "I'm Emeric. You must be—"

"Stogie." He clasps my hand with a surprisingly strong grip and sits back.

Ivory bends to stand, and her tiny tank top flashes me a sinful view of her full tits. Jesus, fuck, if she doesn't adjust that shirt, I'll be swinging from six to midnight with no way to hide it.

Clutching the low neckline in a subtle tug, she studies me with a bewildered expression. "What are you doing here?"

I meet Stogie's watchful gaze and let him see the questions in mine. *Do you know who I am? How well do you know Ivory?*

He hooks his thumbs under the elastic of his red suspenders and blatantly stares me up and down. His smile fades, and his skeletal frame locks up. Apparently, his cloudy eyes see a lot more than they let on. "Ivory, why don't you go on in the back and warm up one of them frozen meals?"

She crosses her arms, eyes narrowed. "Oh, *now* you want to eat?"

"I'd love a fresh pot of coffee and some of that cobbler you made, too." He grips the seat of the chair and scoots forward. "Don't keep an old man waiting."

She huffs and steps out of the pile of books, pointing a finger at him. "Be nice."

Then she looks at me, her expression vulnerable and hesitant, as if begging me to do the same.

The moment she disappears in the back room, he makes a painfully-slow attempt to climb to his feet while holding my gaze. "I know your kind."

My hackles go up, but the manners my mother ingrained in me has me reaching out to help him stand.

He glares at my hand, scoffs at it, and rises on wobbly legs.

I swallow down my irritation. "Enlighten me on *my kind*."

His hunched frame shuffles past me and toward the front of the store. I follow, glad to be moving out of Ivory's range of hearing.

He circles behind the front counter and settles on a tall stool. Unhurried, he examines my expensive watch, fit physique, wide-stance, and raised chin. I know what he sees. A wealthy, cocksure man in his sexual prime standing in a run-down neighborhood for one reason.

He'd be right.

Finally, he stoops forward and rests weathered forearms on the counter. "That girl has had a rough go of it, and you're the kind of man that'll make it worse."

There's a treasure-trove of answers beneath his words, and I need to discover every one of them. "Explain."

"You're the kind of man that sets his sights on something and doesn't let go till he possesses it."

He's far too shrewd for pretense, so I don't bother playing dumb. "Doesn't matter what I've set my sights on. I'm her teacher."

"Yes." Judgment creases his eyes. "You are."

I measure my breaths, expressionless. "She talks to you. About me."

"She's said nothing incriminating, but she doesn't have to.

She's mentioned you more in the past week than all her other teachers combined in three years." He drums gnarled knuckles on the glass counter. "Whatever you're doing with her, she wants to trust you." His hand quiets, eyes unblinking. "The kind of trust she gives *no one*. But once you have what you want and discard her like your kind do, her distrust in men will be irreparable."

An ice-cold wave of dizziness overtakes me as my mind jumps to sickening images of older men, brutal men, raping her.

I place my palms calmly on the counter and lean in. "Tell me what happened to her."

He looks away, his attention on the back room. "She doesn't talk about the bad things. I'm not sure she even distinguishes between the bad and the not-so bad. What happens to her is *life*. It's all she knows." His overcast eyes return to mine. "She's not just financially poor. She's short of love, affection, and protection. She needs a good example in her life, someone with a *selfless* interest in her."

"You're not that example?"

"I'm just a broke old man with one foot in the grave. I can't buy her textbooks and fancy gadgets. I don't hold her dream of attending a music college in my hands. And I don't have the power to steal her heart."

An overwhelming swell of respect rises in my chest. I can't begrudge this man for caring about her enough to say that shit to my face. I can't even argue with him, because in some ways, he's right. I have nothing to offer her except heartache and disappointment.

"But you give her a place to practice." Glancing behind me,

I spot the only piano in the store and thrust my chin toward the old Steinway. "Is it for sale?"

The strained look in his eyes says *no*, but the splintered floorboards, rickety display racks, and overall dilapidated appearance of the shop tells me he needs the revenue. Desperately.

"She doesn't know I get offers for it." His hands clench on the counter. "I won't sell her piano."

But someday, maybe soon, he'll be forced to accept one of those offers because it's the most valuable merchandise in his inventory.

I pull the wallet from my back pocket and place my credit card on the counter. "Charge it to my card, as well as the cost to have it delivered to her house."

He glares at the black American Express then lifts his glassy eyes to me. "She doesn't want a piano at her house. She's *here* because she doesn't want to be *there*."

My stomach sinks with dread. "Fine. Keep it here. Put the receipt in her name, and don't tell her she owns it or who bought it unless she asks." I slide the card toward his trembling hands and wait for him to look at me. "What is she avoiding at her house? You know her well enough to have a damn good guess."

He picks up the card and swivels to the cash register. "What do you get out of this?" He nods at the piano.

"Peace of mind. Answer my question."

He rings up the purchase, lips pinched between his gums, refusing to talk.

Ivory emerges from the back room with a tray of food and sets a disposable dish of noodles and some kind of bastardized pastry on the counter.

"I...um..." She stares at the charred edges of crust. "Burnt it? Or maybe..." She pokes a finger in the doughy center, and the whole thing caves in. Her cheeks flush. "I should stick with what I'm good at."

Like receiving spankings and playing piano? Or even better, playing piano *while* I spank her.

She looks at Stogie, the card in his hand, and meets my gaze. "What did you buy?"

I harden my eyes in a silent *None of your business*. "Have you eaten lunch?"

She shakes her head.

"Gather your things and join me."

"Oh, I..." At my impatient expression, she rubs the back of her neck. "Okay."

As soon as she walks out of earshot, I turn back to Stogie. "How do her living expenses get paid?"

"I believe she covers the bulk of it." He watches me warily. "I employ her in the summer to help with some of that."

"And when she's in school?"

He sets the receipt and a pen on the counter and scratches his whiskered cheek. "I don't know."

The conflict in his dark eyes affirms she doesn't share these details, but... "She may not tell you, but you *know*."

He offers my card back. I grip it, but he doesn't release it, his focus on the square plastic connecting our hands. Then he lets go and looks up. "You know, too."

Admirers. Stalkers. Creepers. Men with money and needs and the immorality to trap a beautiful young girl?

I feel the muscles pulling and tightening in my neck as

anger burns in my throat. "I didn't buy that piano to—"

"I know. Which is why I sold it to you, and why I will never tell her you bought it, even if she asks." He bends closer, hands braced on the counter. "She owes you *nothing*."

"Whether or not you trust me, I *am* concerned about her well-being, specifically pertaining to her home life." I sign the receipt and scribble my phone number at the top. "Call me if anything suspicious, *anything at all*, arises with her."

Ivory returns to the front with an overstuffed satchel bundled in her arms. I move to take the heavy weight from her, but she shakes her head.

"I'll be back tonight." She stores it behind the front counter and says her goodbyes to Stogie.

Holding the door for her, I glance at the old man. "Nice to meet you."

He nods, his mouth pulling down at the corners.

Yeah, he has every right to not trust me. I don't trust me, either.

# IVORY

"Is the deli next door any good?" Mr. Marceaux holds the door as I follow him out of Stogie's shop.

"Only the best sandwiches in New Orleans." My stomach flutters with butterflies. Because I'm hungry. For food. Not because I'll be eating food with Mr. Marceaux.

Instead of turning toward the deli, he steps to the curb and unlocks the passenger door of a shiny black muscle car. "Stay here while I grab lunch."

I take in the GTO badge on the door panel, the 70's-style woodgrain dash, and the black vinyl interior, wondering why he drives such an old ride. "We're not eating there?"

He removes the aviators from the neck of his t-shirt and slides them on. "No."

Everything inside me melts. From the heat of the blinding sun? Definitely the sun.

I lower into the bucket seat and give him my order while he starts the engine and turns on the A/C.

As he walks with long fluid strides toward the deli, I can't *not* stare at him, because sweet Jesus, I never imagined him in anything except a tie, waistcoat, and buttoned shirt with rolled-up sleeves. But he wears blue jeans like a second skin. The denim was made for his body, cupping his ass and stretching across his thighs as he lengthens his gait. The thin gray t-shirt clings to ridges of muscle in his back and shoulders, the sleeves straining around the bulges of his biceps, just like those models in fitness magazines.

I like the fancy clothes better. They're safer, like a professional barrier to remind me he's my teacher.

When he disappears inside the deli, I shift my attention to his car. The loud rumble of the engine and burnt-oil fume of the exhaust. The scent of warm cinnamon wafting from the pack of gum that bakes in the sun on the dash. The stiff seat beneath me, vibrating with the strength of the motor. The silver knobs of the old radio and Axl Rose crooning through the speakers. It's all so distinctive and different, fascinating and masculine. Like him.

It feels surreal, sitting here. In his personal space. Willingly.

*It's just lunch.*

With my teacher. On a Saturday.

I wipe clammy palms on my thighs, wishing I wore something nicer. And less revealing.

Why is he here? In my neighborhood? No one from Le Moyne ventures into my world, as if the poverty might stain their expensive shoes or something. Yet here he is. What does he want?

By the time he returns, my nerves are twisted to nauseous levels.

"Where are we going?" I ask.

"Down the street." He grips the steering wheel with a strong hand and merges into traffic, slowly, confidently, like this is his road and he has all the time in the world.

A minute later, he pulls into Louis Armstrong Park and
sets his sunglasses in the cup holder. A short walk takes us to
a shaded park bench, where we sit side-by-side and dig into
our *Hook 'Em Up* sandwiches. The thick bread is piled high
with meats and cheeses, requiring two hands to hold it.

Halfway through the sandwich, my stomach aches. I wrap
up the leftovers, wipe my mouth with a napkin, and stare out
over the green-tinged duck pond. "What did you and Stogie
talk about?"

"You."

Maybe I should be surprised by his honesty, but I'm not.
He's always been direct with me, a trait I've come to depend
on. If only I could do the same. I want to tell him everything.
But he would report me. How could he not?

He takes another bite, and I covertly study his jaw flexing
and throat moving as he chews. It's strange watching a man
eat. I've never done that. Not consciously. I feel like I'm
invading his privacy.

When he goes for another bite, I realize he's not going to
elaborate.

"What about me?"

He swallows, grins. "This is really good." Another bite.
Then another.

Two young black men walk along the opposite side of the
pond, but the park is otherwise empty, the sun too high and
hot for a lazy stroll.

"Mr. Marceaux..."

He continues to ignore me as he finishes his lunch between
long draws on his bottled water. Then he sets my uneaten
portion aside, throws the trash away, and lounges against the

back of the bench beside me, hands relaxed on his thighs. "I asked him how your living expenses get paid."

Jesus, he's like a dog with a bone. I twist and untwist the lid on my water. What would Stogie think of me if he knew what I'm doing? And Mr. Marceaux? He'd probably spank me then expel me. My heart gives a heavy thump.

"What else did you talk about?"

He turns to face me. "Tell me why I'm here."

To finish that almost-kiss? Do I want that? My hands shake. "I don't know."

"You do know, and I want to hear you say it."

I look away, eyes on the pond, but every inch of my body focuses on him. On the shift in his breathing, the tick of his watch, the lift of his arm as he touches my chin and forces my head to turn back.

His eyes reflect all the luminous shades of the sky, but they're colder, so terrifying this close up. I refocus on something safer, the ducks on the pond. But his gaze fills my view, his face staying with me, his whole body moving, anticipating my moves. He won't let me escape him. I want to run.

And I want him to catch me.

The fight in my muscles evaporates as he pulls me into his lap. My pulse kicks up when he arranges my legs to straddle him. His thighs are columns of stone beneath me, powerful and supportive.

Sitting on him, against him, isn't a bad feeling. It's much safer than being beneath him, which has been my only experience with other men. But I don't know where to put my hands. After an awkward moment, I let my fingers gravitate to his t-shirt.

His chest twitches against my palms, the ridges and indentations of muscle like bricks in my hands, so unlike anything I've ever felt.

I muster the courage to look up, absorbing the dark shadow on his jawline and the defined curves of his cheekbones. The blue hues in his meteoric eyes fire a voltage of warmth way down deep, below my waist, between my legs. The sensation makes me want to reach up and trace the shape of his lips. But I'm too nervous, too unsure.

It feels like there are invisible strands between us and they're winding tighter, pulling, shrinking, and strumming with tension.

I sway closer. "Is this why you're here?"

He meets me halfway, dipping his head, and his mouth drags a sigh across my neck.

I shiver and heat up. My fingers tighten on his shirt, my hips relax in his lap, and a strife of emotions frantically flap in my brain. The position puts my pussy right up against him, flush with the long rigid evidence of his hunger. It should be enough to make me recoil, to pull away, but I can't. I don't want to.

"Ivory," he breathes along my jaw. His hands clench against my back, pulling my chest to his as he nibbles a trail of pleasure to the corner of my lips. "Yes."

His mouth slides over mine, lips brushing, warm and soft and *nice*. Strong hands move up my neck, cup my jaw, and angle my head. He presses his lips harder, parting them, opening mine, and the first touch of his tongue shoots a thrill of electricity down my back.

My whole body should be shrinking, cringing with disgust, yet the rub of his tongue, the flavor of his mouth, and the pressure of his fingers against my head liquefies my insides into a needy simmer. Instead of jerking away from the strokes of his tongue, I lean in, stretching my mouth and deepening the connection.

A groan vibrates in his chest, and my own moan claws out as his lips move deliciously, firmly, against mine, touching me in a way I've never wanted or enjoyed. Over the past four years, I've been fed pools of drool and gagged by countless probing tongues. But I've never been kissed. Not like this. And I've never kissed back. Never experienced this kind of intimacy with a man while thinking, *Don't stop.*

The hands on my head guide me closer, demanding I stay with him. How crazy is it that I don't want to be anywhere else? I can't even close my eyes for fear he'll disappear.

Thickets of black lashes splay over his cheekbones. The muscles in his face contract with the urgency of his swirling tongue.

"You're so fucking beautiful," he whispers against my lips then attacks my mouth with renewed hunger.

His chest and hips rock against mine. My inhales sharpen, and his exhales pull grunts of satisfaction from his throat.

"I can't stay away." Another drugging kiss. "I want you." He nibbles my lower lip, licks just inside the seam, then rests his forehead against mine. "You make me want things I can't have."

I angle forward to refasten our mouths, but his grip on my jaw holds me still.

"We have to stop." His fingers curl in my hair as his face

draws away, leaving a tingling chill on my cheeks.

I flatten my palms on his sweat-damp chest. "I didn't kiss you to help my chances for Leopold."

"Oh, Ivory." His hands tremble as they glide around my neck, over my shoulders, and down my arms. "So young and straightforward." He grips my thighs, just below the hem of the shorts, and rolls his hips beneath my ass. "So perfect."

The hard length of him pulses against the crotch of my shorts. Why isn't that triggering my gag reflex? Why aren't I curling up and reaching for the safe place in my head?

Why do I want to unzip his jeans and gaze upon that mysterious part of him? Why do I want to hold it in my hands and make his body flex in pleasure?

"This ends now." He clutches my waist and sets me on the bench beside him.

My chest tightens, rejecting those words. No more touches? No more kisses? "What? Why?"

"It's reckless. Dangerous." He bows forward and braces elbows on his spread knees, staring out across the park.

"Because of Ms. Augustin?"

"She's not a concern, but there'll be others." His eyes cut to mine, flinty and unmoving. "There's always someone watching, waiting to ruin the prosperity of a life they don't have."

No one wants my life, and people don't concern themselves with what happens in Treme. "You can come here and kiss me whenever—"

"I'm not a school boy, Ivory. This isn't an innocent make-out session behind the bleachers." In a blur of movement, he's on me, chest against mine and strong fingers wrapped around my neck. "The things I want to do to you would give you nightmares."

He's trying to scare me, but he's not cutting my air. He administers his own punishments, but the sickness inside me craves more of his spankings. He doesn't give me nightmares. He makes me float through the air in a dream.

He releases my neck and perches on the edge of the bench, putting two feet of turmoil between us. My hands shake to reach for him, my entire body aching to climb back in his lap and return to the safety of his arms. For the first time in my life, I want a man to touch me, and he's...casting me away?

"I don't want this to end," I whisper, the backs of my eyes burning.

"I didn't ask for your opinion."

His rejection lands in my stomach like a hot coal, stealing my breath and filling my tear ducts with moisture.

"Shit." He glares at my wet eyes, his expression paling beneath a sheen of sweat. "You *cannot* fall in love with me."

"Cannot...what?" I jerk back, inhaling sharply and swiping at a runaway tear. "Oh my God, of all the cocky, arrogant things to say! I would never."

"I'm offended." He laughs, but it's strained. "High school girls have a way of falling fast and ignorantly in love."

"Well, I'm offended you think I'm that ignorant." I tug at the hem of my shorts. "No worries, Mr. Marceaux. Thoughts of love haven't even crossed my mind."

He stares at the pond. "I know you're not ignorant, Ivory. It's just..."

With a hand resting against his mouth, he bends against his knees and watches the ducks preen and splash in the water. But he's not really watching, not with his gaze turned inward and his expression morphing with whatever he's thinking about.

Why would he even mention love? If his mind went there, does that mean he's feeling something? It was a good kiss. For the love of God, it was a kiss I'll remember for the rest of my life, one I'll compare all future kisses against. But love? What does he even know about that?

I glance over at him, and something clicks painfully in my mind. "You loved her, didn't you? That teacher in Shreveport? Joanne?"

*Please say* no.

He drops his hands, holding them between his knees, forearms braced on his thighs, as he stares at the ground.

"I still love her." He meets my eyes. "As much as I hate her."

Jealousy fires ignorantly through my insides, surging like bile in my throat. I would love to be loved, even if it comes with hatred. It's better than nothing at all. "Will you tell me what happened?"

He reclines and rests an arm along the back of the bench. "I value the honesty between us." His hand sifts through the ends of my hair. "I don't want that to end."

My heart squeezes at the thought of anything ending between us, but I'll never lie to him. At least, not about the stuff that won't get me expelled.

"We were together four years." His fingers move through my hair, softly, hypnotically. "With Shreveport's non-fraternization policy, our relationship was a secret. We owned separate houses, but lived together in one. Drove separately to school. Kept our interactions professional at work. Until..."

He doesn't have to finish that sentence. I'm consumed with images of her mouth gagged with his tie, wrists bound by his belt, and her body bent as he fucked her on a desk. Is she a better musician than me? Smarter? Prettier? Did he tell her she's *so fucking beautiful*, too? I ball my hands into fists. The sexual positions don't affect me nearly as much as the idea of him doing those things with someone else.

With one hand in my hair, he scoots closer and places the other over my fists, prying them open. "We were just playing out a fantasy. Having a little fun after hours."

"Then what happened? How did you lose—? Shit, did she set you up?"

His fingers twitch against mine. "No. But getting caught like that put her in a precarious position. She could admit she violated the non-fraternization policy, that she was willingly tied up, and lose her job in a shroud of shame that would follow her everywhere. Or she could call it what it looked like. Bound and gagged and raped. Either way, I was getting fired."

*Rape.* I turn that word over in my head, examining it from all angles. I think I experience it sometimes, but I never know what to do about it. A girl can say she was forced. A man can claim she wanted it. The police decide who's telling the truth, and if they side with the man? He *will* retaliate against the girl.

But it doesn't sound like Mr. Marceaux struck back.

A crazy surge of protectiveness—*for him*—buzzes through me. "You could've defended yourself. Told them about your relationship. Proved you were living together. At the very least, she would've lost her job and you wouldn't have been charged with forcing her."

"The rape charges didn't stick. The stigma did, but I don't give a shit about that. There are a million things I could've done to ruin her job. Things I can still do."

"But you love her." Oh God, why does my heart hurt so badly?

His expression darkens with a deep scowl. "And she loves her career." He pulls his hands away and sits forward on the bench, his profile etched in pain. "She's Head of School at Shreveport now."

What a bitch. "I'm sorry, but she sounds awful. How can you possibly love her?"

He pinches the bridge of his nose and closes his eyes. "Sometimes you love people you shouldn't, and in the endless space of that love, nothing else matters." When he lifts his head, his entire demeanor changes. The man in the waistcoat and tie returns with a fortified jaw and hard eyes as he rises and clasps his hands behind his back. "No more touching and kissing, Miss Westbrook. I'm your teacher, your mentor, and nothing more."

I jump to my feet. "I would never do that to you. I can't even fathom ruining your career."

He laughs, but it sounds more like a snarl. "If we were caught doing something inappropriate, you would have to choose between my career and your education, between a man you've known for a week and a dream you've chased for three years. What choice would you make?"

*Leopold* shoves itself into my mind, but I fight it back, refusing to admit it. "We'll be careful."

"Exactly. Go home." He thrusts his finger in the direction of my house.

I glance over my shoulder. If it weren't for the trees, I'd be able to see my house from here. How does he know where I live? The address in my file?

When I look back, he's walking away, hands tucked in his front pockets and head down. A bleeding, miserable kind of longing cleaves through my chest. He's done.

I grab the uneaten sandwich from the bench and trudge along the track toward my house, each step heavier and harder to take. Maybe I don't have to obey him this time? Maybe this is one of those rules that are meant to be broken?

Spinning around, I race after him. He pauses at the clapping sound of my ballet flats, his broad shoulders tightening the t-shirt. But he doesn't turn.

I circle the towering pillar of his body, and holy hell, he's so tall and dark and beautiful. And angry. Deep lines fan from the corners of his icy eyes, his lips a slash of displeasure, and the cords in his neck stretched beneath whiskered skin.

Bolstering my spine, I step up to him and wrap my arms around his waist. Every solid inch I touch flexes with muscle.

He holds his hands in his pockets, his chest lifting with a deep breath. "You're disobeying me."

I press my cheek against the ledge of his pecs. "I won't hurt you. I promise."

"*I* will hurt *you*."

"Okay."

His hands grip my shoulders, forcing me back a step, but he doesn't let go. He bends his knees, putting his eyes at the same level as mine. "Tell me who hurt you, and I'll give you anything you want."

My pulse hammers, and my molars crash together. Did he plan this? Did he touch and kiss me until my head spun, only to take it all back so he could dangle it as an incentive to talk?

I back up, shifting out of arm's reach and shaking my head.

His face tightens, and my stomach caves in. I hate disappointing him.

With a hand on his hip and the other pointing toward my house, he stares at the ground.

Good, because I hate his eyes. And I adore them, too. Especially when he touches me and tells me I'm beautiful. And now, he's punishing me by refusing to look at me.

In a fog of shame, I hug the sandwich to my chest and drag my feet home. As I walk, I sneak peeks over my shoulder. He doesn't move. I can't see his eyes, but I know they're following me, watching me, protecting me.

Whatever this is, however inappropriate and risky, he doesn't want it to end. Spending four private hours a day together for the rest of the year, it's only going to become *more*. More punishments, more music, more Mr. Marceaux. I don't care what he says. This isn't over.

# EMERIC

"It's over." I slam the beer bottle down harder than I intended and cringe at the cracking sound on Mom's glass table. Shit. I rub a finger over the chip and glance at her apologetically. "Sorry, Mom."

"I don't care about the damn table. I'm concerned about *you*." She corks a wine bottle on the back counter and crosses the kitchen to sit beside me, a glass of red cupped in her hand. Setting it on the table, she twists the stem and gathers her words. "I know you've been unhappy for a while, but this is different. You've been a hot-tempered, sulky pain-in-the-ass for the past few weeks."

Five weeks, to be exact.

Five weeks since I kissed Ivory. Since I felt her skin beneath my hands. Since I punished her the way we both need. Five agonizing weeks since I sent her home in the park with regret overrunning my nervous system.

"Honey." She places her hand on my forearm and gives it a firm squeeze. "Does Joanne know it's over?"

Joanne is still texting me, but her messages go unanswered. I know what she wants, she knows what I want, and neither of us is willing to compromise.

"She still stubbornly refuses to accept my terms." I shove a hand through the overlong strands touching my forehead. Christ, I need a haircut. "This has nothing to do with her."

"Oh." Mom's persistent blue eyes roam my face, searching for answers. "This isn't about your car, is it?"

"No, I got the car back yesterday."

Though that put me in one helluva mood. After watching Ivory walk away, I made my way back to the parking lot, and the GTO was gone. Stolen. Fucking jacked. I had to call Deb to take me to the police station. When she dropped me off at home, I stood on the doorstep, vibrating with turmoil as I told her, *No, I'm not going to fuck you.* I should've been nicer to her for helping me—with the ride and with Beverly Rivard's husband—but I was too fucking distraught to let her in.

The GTO wasn't the only thing I lost in the park that day.

The cops recovered my car, the interior gutted and body stripped. It took weeks to bring it back to mint condition.

But Ivory... My hand clenches around the bottle. I'm making every effort I can to ensure the thing between us isn't recovered. The attraction remains, stronger than ever, burning like a red-hot ember. It sizzles to be stoked when I sit beside her on the piano bench, hisses with sparks when I slap her wrists for missing a note, and crackles and pops every damn time our eyes connect.

Our first week together moved so fucking fast my nerves are still running wild with hunger. If I hadn't pulled back, she would be in my bed right now, her seventeen-year-young body bowing and flushing beneath my belt and her huge adoring eyes begging me for things I'm unable to give her. Leopold. An open, lawful relationship. My heart...

She's too young to separate sex and love, and I've lost

interest in anything beyond physical pleasure.

*Once you have what you want, her distrust in men will be irreparable.*

Mom watches me in that intuitive way she does, her soft expression framed by black hair that curls above her shoulders. She reaches up to pinch the ends of a loose lock, brushing the tuft back and forth along her jaw as she studies me. I chug the beer and pretend to ignore her.

She drops her hand and tilts her head. "You met someone."

*Here we go.* "No, I—"

"Emeric Michael Marceaux, don't you lie to your mother."

I stand and move to the counter, leaning against it and balancing the bottle on the ledge. "Not talking about this with you, Mom."

I want to, but voicing it makes it real.

Footsteps approach the kitchen doorway.

"Not talking about what?" Dad wanders in, reading glasses perched on the end of his nose, his face buried in his phone.

"Emeric met someone." She smiles over the rim of her wine glass, eyes locked on me.

Without looking up from his phone, he walks past her and glides his fingers along the back of her neck. "Let's hope she's better than the last one."

Better? Joanne is reality. Ivory's an intoxicating dream, the kind that visits a man at night, veiled by the darkness of dusk and safely pursued in the secret corners of the mind. But in daylight, she's a dangerous fantasy, tempting a man to do things with his eyes wide open.

"Who is she?" Mom sips her wine.

"She's off-limits," I say quickly and turn to Dad. "How's that new physician you hired at the clinic?"

"He's...fine." Reservation deepens his voice.

Of course, he knows I'm evading.

He pockets the phone and lowers into the chair across the round table from Mom. "Is this woman married?"

I shake my head and direct my eyes to my Doc Martens.

It's Saturday night. I'm supposed to be in a French Quarter hotel room, trussing up Chloe's huge tits, flogging Deb's ass, and reeking of sex. But the moment I climbed into the GTO, my mind drifted to Ivory. My subconscious took hold of the wheel and a few minutes later, I was sitting in the driveway of my parents' estate in the Garden District.

Because I *need* to talk about this. If there's anyone in this world I trust enough with this conversation, they're in this room. They know about the deal I made with Beverly, as well as every dirty detail of my relationship with Joanne. Not once have they judged me. Hell, they hired the team of lawyers that convinced Joanne to drop the rape charge.

"Is she...?" The question in Mom's tone pitches with alarm. And realization. "Oh no, Emeric."

Before Mom climbed the ranks to Provost of Leopold, she was a high school teacher. When I was younger, Mrs. Laura Marceaux was too pretty for my comfort, with her gaggle of teenage admirers, including the guys I ran around with. Even in her fifties, she still turns heads with her youthful face, warm smile, and gentle eyes.

Those eyes bore into me now, wide and unblinking, because she knows exactly what I'm not saying.

I pivot toward the counter and brace my arms on the

granite surface, my shoulders slumping with the weight of my words. "It's over."

"What, *exactly*, is over?" Her voice floats behind me, full of concern.

"Sit down," Dad says with less tenderness.

I finish my beer, grab another, and sit in the chair between them. "She's a senior at Le Moyne." I let that settle on the table before continuing. "When she walked into my classroom on the first day...swear to God, I thought she was a teacher." I rub a hand down my face and swallow another swig of hops. "She doesn't look like a high school student."

Mom reaches across the table and rests her hand on my wrist.

They don't interrupt as I explain Ivory's financial situation, musical talent, my suspicions of abuse, my visit with Stogie, and her desire to attend Leopold. They share anxious looks when I mention the kiss in the park and the past five weeks of hell. I even admit to driving the streets after her private lessons, trying to track her path to the bus stop. But she never takes the same route, and most often, I don't spot her at all.

I wrestle with the urge to leave out the most implicating part, but my need for full disclosure wins. "I spanked her. In the classroom."

Their faces pale, but neither asks if it was consensual. Their trust in me is infinite, which makes the final piece easier to spit out.

"I was caught with her in my lap afterward. By a colleague." *Fucking Shreveport all over again.* "I blackmailed the teacher."

Mom reaches for her wine and finishes it off.

When I meet Dad's eyes, he sits back, removes his glasses, and cleans them with the folds of his shirt. "Blackmail how?"

"You don't want to know."

"Well." Mom stands and walks to the counter to refill her glass. "You certainly know how to test the limits of social acceptance, but I know where you get it from." She returns to the table, her eyes glimmering at Dad. "Your father loves to spank—"

"Mom," I groan. "Don't make this more awkward."

She lowers into the chair, her expression sobering. "You said she's a gifted pianist? Is she more deserving of Leopold than the one you want me to push through?"

Though retired, Mom still flies out to New York once a month for board meetings. Even after everything I told her, I know she'll guarantee a placement for one of my referrals.

The deal with Beverly has been plaguing me for weeks. Ivory belongs at Leopold. Not because she's beautiful and genuine and in desperate need of saving. She's all those things, but I owe her my referral because she's the best goddamn musician at Le Moyne.

"Without a doubt, she deserves that spot." My chest lifts with passion in my voice. "She's incredible."

"You're in a tough position." Mom's hand finds mine, squeezing my fingers. "I don't envy you, but honey, if you pursue a relationship with her, it won't turn out like Shreveport."

Because I didn't commit a crime with Joanne. Our relationship was consensual, not illegal. But Ivory? Student-teacher misconduct doesn't just get swept under the carpet. It makes headline news. The best lawyers in the world couldn't save me from the charges that would follow if I were caught with her.

"You need to cut your losses, son." Dad sets his glasses on his nose and folds his arms on the table, leaning in. "Quit that damn job, end things once and for all with Joanne, and move out of state if you have to. The shit at Shreveport can only follow you so far."

Mom shakes her head. "Frank, don't tell him that. Our family is finally back together in New Orleans and—"

"No, Mom. He's right." I shove away from the table and empty my unfinished beer in the sink.

I'm already deliriously drunk on Ivory Westbrook, and I don't know how much longer I'll last without giving in.

I can keep the job, try to ignore this forbidden attraction, ultimately fail, and risk going to jail. Or I can quit Le Moyne, remove the temptation from my life, and fuck me, never see her again.

My chest hurts with the agonizing truth. I know... God help me, I know what I need to do.

# IVORY

"This is all your fault!"

My mom's tear-drenched screech cuts through me, but it's the hatred in her dark eyes that makes my insides bleed.

I don't even know what I'm being blamed for. It's the middle of the night, and she stormed in here, flicking on the lights and waking me with her crazy wailing.

Lying on the couch where I sleep, I pull my legs closer to my body, curling smaller on my side and holding Schubert to my chest. "H-how? How is *what* my fault?"

She came home a month ago, crying about the boyfriend who broke up with her. She hasn't stopped crying.

"If it wasn't for your...your..." She paces through the parlor and trips over her own feet, yanking on the cropped strands of her hair. "Fucking selfish bullshit!"

She was pretty once, soft and curvy with contentment glinting in her eyes. But drugs and grief have withered her to bones and rancor. Dad would be as heartbroken as I am.

If I don't get accepted into Leopold, if I never find a way out of Treme, will I end up like that? Whenever my mind flashes forward, I see myself forever chained to Lorenzo and his violent needs. How could I not turn to drugs as an escape from the torment of his touch? That future terrifies me, but it also hardens me. I'll make it out of here, no matter the cost.

My mom stumbles through the room, clawing at her sunken face as if trying to remove imagined objects. She must be coming down from whatever she poisoned herself with, her entire body tweaking with unhappiness.

She blames me for that. Her unhappiness. I'm the reason she uses, the reason she's poor, the reason she can't find a job or keep a boyfriend.

I suppose, in a way, I *am* responsible for her misery. My chest aches to go to her, to hug and comfort her. But she doesn't tolerate those things from me.

Multiple footsteps advance from the back of the house. I bury my nose in the comforting kitty smell of Schubert's hair and steady my breathing.

Lorenzo and Shane push into the parlor, both dressed in jeans and t-shirts. On their way out or just coming home? I glance at my watch on the side table. *3:15 AM.* I rub my eyes. I have to get ready for school in two hours.

Lorenzo gives my mom a wide berth as Shane goes to her, pulling her hands from her face.

"Mom, stop. You're hurting yourself." He adjusts the straps of her nightie on her bony shoulders and glares at me. "Why are you letting her do this?"

Seriously? I sit up, holding Schubert in my lap. "I'm not the one feeding her drugs."

Lorenzo reclines on the opposite end of the couch, watching my mom with amusement. I run a trembling hand through Schubert's fur. *Lorenzo won't try anything. He probably won't even look at me.*

My mom brings a whirlwind of drama when she comes

home, but there's safety in her presence. She and Shane don't believe my accusations about Lorenzo hurting me, but Lorenzo is always on his best behavior when they're in the room. I've evaded the rumble of his motorcycle on my walks to and from school, and he hasn't so much as touched me since my mom came home. Even so, the impatience thrumming from him is palpable.

My mom stares up at Shane, her gaze softening for a calm moment before it slashes through the room and lands on me. "You took everything from me."

My throat tightens and burns.

She steps toward me, scratching at her scrawny arm. "I wish you were never born."

Tears prick my eyes. *It's just the drugs talking.*

Another step, this one stronger, more sober, her eyes hard and clear. "I hate you, you selfish little bitch."

Moisture blurs my vision, and even though she's told me those words a thousand times, I still try. "I love you, Mom."

She launches toward me, screaming, but Shane catches her with the hook of his arm around her waist.

"I hate you. I hate you." She bucks in his hold, trying to get to me, her boobs bouncing and falling out of her flimsy nightie. "You ruined my life!"

"I know, Mom." Shane drags her out of the room. "I'll get you what you need."

She doesn't need the drugs he's about to pump into her. She needs a job, a passion, and a goddamn backbone.

I curl up with Schubert and focus on the tongue and groove ceiling, trying to stop the tears from escaping. Maybe I need a backbone, too.

Her screams echo through the house and eventually ebb into sobs. "He loved her more. He took from us, Shane, and gave it all to her."

My heart shrivels in my chest, and the tears fall, hard and fast. I wait for the couch to bounce beside me, and when it does, Schubert scrambles from my arms.

Lorenzo's hip bumps my feet with his movements. He leans over and forces me on my back, the sinews in his neck rippling the *Destroy* tattoo. "You think you can avoid me forever?"

"That's the plan." I push against his chest as a renewed stream of tears tickle my ears.

His black eyes grow impossibly darker. "So fucking pretty."

He shoves a hand between my legs, but the cocoon of blankets protects me. For a fleeting moment, I imagine the front door opening and Mr. Marceaux standing on the threshold with his terrifying eyes. I bet Lorenzo would be scared of him, maybe enough to leave me alone.

But Mr. Marceaux won't be returning to Treme. Not tonight. Not ever.

In a surge of anger, I kick and shove, hitting Lorenzo's ribs and trying to free the blankets in my attempt to escape. He grabs my knees and holds them immobile. I scratch at his arms, my lungs panting with the race of my pulse.

The heavy thump of Shane's tread sounds his approach, and we both freeze.

Lorenzo removes his hands and faces forward just as Shane enters the room.

"Sitting too close, dickhead." Shane smacks the side of Lorenzo's head. "Move."

I exhale a huge breath and adjust the covers around me.

"I'm heading home anyway." Lorenzo stands and exchanges a palm-slapping, knuckle-tapping handshake with Shane.

When the door closes behind Lorenzo, Shane plops down on the couch beside me and pulls a pack of cigarettes from his pocket.

Adrenaline lingers in my veins, strumming my nerves. "I don't want him here."

"Shut the fuck up, Ivory." He lights the cigarette and lounges against the back of the couch.

I decide to try out a new word. "He *rapes* me, Shane."

His face reddens then turns darker as he stabs the cigarette in the direction of the door. "That guy saved my life in Iraq." His volume grows louder, his arms shaking. "I wouldn't be here, *breathing*, if it weren't for him. So while you're prancing around in your little shorts and teasing him with your fucking tits, remember that. Remember that guy is the reason I'm alive."

I've heard the story, but saving someone's life doesn't give him the right to have sex with their sister. And aren't brothers supposed to defend their sisters? Maybe he doesn't think I'm worthy of that kind of love.

I pull the blankets tighter around me and say quietly, uselessly. "I don't *prance,* and I don't have a lot of clothes. They're Mom's shorts."

"Yet another thing you take from her."

Maybe he'll hit me, and maybe Mr. Marceaux will report the new bruise, but dammit, I can't let this go. "I pay the bills. Not you. Not her. She hasn't once asked me about school or where I get the money. But I'm out there, working my ass off to make sure we don't lose this house."

He takes a drag on the cigarette, his expression tight. "Yeah, I bet you're working your ass. Where *do* you get the money?" He casts me a sidelong glare. "You fucking whoring?"

Shame piles up in my throat. I shake my head. God, if he knew? I don't want to find out what he'd do.

"Fuck this." He stands and flicks his ashes on the floor. "And fuck you." He strides to the front door, opens it, and glances at me over his shoulder. "Mom's right, you know. Dad sold our future to buy yours. He did love you more."

The door slams behind him, jarring more tears from my eyes.

I get it. I do. Their resentment of me runs two-hundred-thousand-dollars deep.

As I flick off the lights and return to the couch, Schubert joins me, purring and nuzzling against my chest in the dark. Sometimes I think Schubert's love is an extension of Dad's. Dad picked him out, surprised me with him, and died the next day. It's like he knew what was coming and wanted to make sure part of his heart was left behind, to console me when I need him most.

But I don't think Dad loved me more than them. He was just trying to do a good thing with my education. I can imagine, though, how they must feel. I can hardly breathe after Mr. Marceaux's rejection, and that wasn't even close to love.

At least, Marceaux didn't take away the private lessons. I should be glad for that, but the last five weeks have only made me angry. Fuming fucking mad. His strictly professional interactions and cold demeanor are daily reminders that I'm not good enough.

Not good enough for Leopold.

Not good enough to risk being with me.

# EMERIC

Despite my misgivings about Ivory's future, I focus on my own. I spend the remainder of the weekend putting out feelers for teaching jobs. By Sunday night, I've applied for a few mid-year openings out of state.

I loathe the idea of leaving Louisiana without resolving one last thing with Joanne. But I have options, and maybe with a little self-control, I'll keep things professional with Ivory until those options pan out.

But it doesn't lessen the intoxicated feeling in my body. As I cross the campus parking lot the next morning, my anticipation in seeing her has me whistling "Patience" with Axl Rose's contagious buoyancy. My blood pumps hotter and my muscles flex tighter with each step toward Crescent Hall.

The mind works in funny ways, making me rationalize all kinds of shit as I enter the building. *If I'm leaving, it won't hurt to touch her today. Just once. Another taste of her lips. That's all. Man, why am I considering quitting? I can't abandon her. How will I fucking breathe? This is bullshit.*

My strides turn away from my classroom and veer toward Campus Center for reasons that can only be described as obsessive.

I run a hand through my hair and slow my gait. I don't

remember feeling this wild and out-of-control with Joanne. But I didn't pursue her, either. Not in the beginning and certainly not after. I've never chased a woman. Never had to. That alone is enough to make me question why I'm craning my neck and scanning the crowd of students, hoping to catch a glimpse of long dark hair. Ivory Westbrook is fucking with my head.

A few halls later, I spot her leaning against a wall of lockers and smiling at Ellie Lai.

The sight of her sends a shot of warm satisfaction through me, locking my legs and paralyzing me twenty feet away. My infatuation might be ridiculous, but it's no less real. I'm completely and thoroughly hypnotized by her.

She stands out among everyone in this school. Not because of the drab style of her white button-up and tattered black skirt, but because she shines above her financial limitations, radiating the kind of beauty that can't be bought. Everything looks lackluster in comparison to the glow of her skin, the brightness of her eyes, and the potency of her aura. I'm so fucking drawn to her I can't see straight.

The flow of students streams between us, but it only takes a moment for her to sense me. When her eyes find mine, her smile slips. Her lips separate, and her hand forms a fist at her side.

She resents me for putting space between us, but she understands why I did it. Even so, we both know that space hasn't accomplished anything. With every passing day, it becomes tauter, thinner, straining to seal up and fall away. Like now.

Her gaze holds mine, piercing me with a vulnerable plea.

*Take the risk. Find a way. I need you.* Maybe those are just reflections of my own thoughts, but I want to grab her wrist, pry her fingers open, and wrap them around mine, while promising to give her anything she wants.

Ellie pokes Ivory's arm, and just like that, Ivory looks away, the trance broken.

I blink and suck in a frustrated breath as Ellie's attention bounces between Ivory and me. *Fuck.*

Relaxing my shoulders, I give them a small chin nod and turn down the hall. Thank Christ, none of the other students seem to have noticed my frozen fixation. I swipe a hand down my face and fight the burning urge to glance back at Ivory.

By the time I reach Crescent Hall, my mind is a mess of disjointed arguments. I can give us both what we want. But can I keep her safe from the fallout? Is she safe now? Without her at my side every damn second, I have no idea who or what is threatening her. I fucking hate it.

I approach an empty intersection in the corridor and pause at the sound of a familiar voice around the corner.

"I don't care what she agreed to do." Sebastian Roth's high-pitched whine grates across my skin.

*She* who? I hover at the bend and remain out of sight.

"Dude, let go of me."

I'd recognize Prescott Rivard's nasally voice anywhere. These two pencil dicks are inseparable friends, which piques my curiosity about their argument.

"I've had an arrangement with her for-fucking-ever," Sebastian whispers, angrily. "She doesn't belong to you."

Paranoia punches behind my ribcage. There's only one girl in this school I would fight over, and I know exactly how they look at her in class every day. I hope, for their sakes, they're arguing about someone else.

Their heavy grunts echo through the hall, followed by the squeak of their shoes. If they fall around the corner, they'll see me, and I'll interrogate. But I wait, listening to them struggle while holding my breath. *Say the girl's name. Say her fucking name.*

"Stop! You're wrinkling my shirt," Prescott says. "We can't do this here. If my mom hears us—"

"I don't give a shit!" Sebastian shouts.

Down the hall, a few girls round the corner and freeze mid-stride. I give them a stern point in the opposite direction, and they turn and rush away.

"You're the one that'll get in trouble." Sebastian lowers his voice, his breaths rushed. "Seeing how you're the only one fucking her anymore. Maybe I'll pay a visit to dear ol' Mom and let her know how you're spending your allowance."

My hands clench and my vision clouds as I connect the motivations of horny rich boys to that of a beautiful girl with an unknown source of income.

Adrenaline shakes my body and shortens my breaths. I want to hit something. My fingers dig into my palms. I want to fucking kill them.

"You wouldn't," Prescott says, his tone venomous.

"Try me," Sebastian growls.

The sound of knuckles smacking flesh reaches my ears right before Sebastian falls into view. He lands at my feet, his plastic-framed glasses hanging lopsided on his forehead.

Cupping his mouth, the scrawny hipster groans and rolls to his side. "You fucking psycho!"

Prescott pounces from around the corner. Neither of them notices me as Prescott crouches over Sebastian and rears back his fist—

"Stand up!"

They freeze at the whip of my voice and lift their eyes, their faces blanching into colorless hues of O*h shit.*

Sebastian recovers first, scrambling out from beneath Prescott and jumping to his feet. He adjusts his glasses and points at the dean's son. "He hit me. You saw that, right?"

The little pussy isn't even bleeding.

Prescott smirks, taking his time straightening his tie without standing. Refusing to acknowledge me. *I can change that.*

I grab his necktie and yank him up. He staggers as I whirl him around. I slam his back against the wall and wrap my hand around his throat. "Her name."

Blond hair falls over his eyes, his lips pulling away from his overbite. "What?"

So help me God, if he stuck his dick in my girl...

*Don't go there, Emeric.*

I put my face in his and let him feel the fury of my breaths. "The girl you're *fucking*. Give me her name."

His throat bobs against the compress of my hand. We're the same height, but I have at least thirty adult pounds on him. Because I *am* the adult, the authority figure who's supposed to be breaking up hallway fights, not engaging in them.

I loosen my grip, but refuse to let go. I want to crush his gangly throat just for infecting my head with images of him with Ivory. "Sexual misconduct will get you expelled, Mr.

Rivard. Who's the girl?"

"Avery," he chokes out. "But just to be clear...we're n-not...having sex."

Avery, not Ivory. The names are too similar, like he was thinking *Ivory* and spit out something else.

I glare at Sebastian. "Who's Avery?"

He stares daggers at Prescott. "Avery Perrault is his girlfriend. She goes to St. Catherine's."

Is he lying? I'm wound too tight to pick up on hints. "Tell me about the arrangement *you* have with her."

Sebastian's eyes flash behind his glasses, his tone low and pungent. "She used to hang out with me, but not anymore."

If *hang out* isn't a euphemism for sex, I don't know what is. And if this is about Ivory, why would they lie? So she can't contradict their story? Is there more to it? Paying her for sex goes beyond expulsion. If caught, all three would be charged as consenting adults for violating prostitution laws. My chest constricts at the thought of Ivory arrested.

I return my attention to the imbecile wheezing in my grip. "How are you spending your allowance?"

"I-I...b-buy Avery things." He paws at my hand. "Because she's my *girlfriend.*"

Every inch of my body twitches with edginess. I release him and hold out my palm. "Unlock your phones and give them to me. Both of you."

They bandy hostile looks and do as I say. A quick scroll through the logs confirms they both communicate with a contact named Avery. Neither phone has Ivory stored in the lists.

Because she doesn't own a phone.

I return their devices and scrutinize their tense postures and indignant expressions, searching for a glimmer of untruth. I want to say Ivory's name, bring her into the conversation somehow, just to study their reactions. But I can't do that without making my own interests glaringly obvious.

However, I *can* write them up for fighting.

Twenty minutes later, I stand beside Beverly Rivard's desk with my hands behind my back. I don't say a word as the boys explain their dispute over Avery Perrault, how it's all just a misunderstanding, and everyone's virtues are still intact, blah, blah, fucking blah.

Prescott cants forward in the chair with his arm waving in my direction. "Then he tried to strangle me!"

The dean shifts her slivered eyes to me. "Mr. Marceaux, are you aware of the no touching policy?"

"Yes." I tilt my head. "Are you aware your son is an asshole?"

"See what I mean?" Prescott throws his hands in the air and slumps in the seat. "He's fucking nuts."

Beverly walks around the desk, stops at the wall of windows, and stares out over the manicured lawns. "Mr. Rivard and Mr. Roth, you'll be written up for language and fighting." She turns, arms folded beneath her chest, and calmly takes in their outraged expressions. "Wait in the hall while I have a word with Mr. Marceaux."

A turbulence of emotions storms through me, and leading the onslaught is a heavy, foreboding kind of urgency. If they're lying about the girlfriend, I won't find the truth in this office. Nor in this school. I need to perform my own investigation of their after-school activities.

When the door shuts behind them, Beverly drops her arms and stands taller, stiffer, her sharp gaze leaping toward mine. "If you ever lay a hand on my son again—"

"*That* is the protégé you want me to send to Leopold?" I thrust a finger at the door. "That little douchebag won't last a month there."

Her head quivers with the force of her shout. "Enough!"

She touches the collar of her blouse and closes her eyes, inhaling deeply.

I amble toward her and stop inches away. Towering over her, I wait for her to look at me.

My insides burn with anxious rage, but I keep my timbre rich, my voice mellow, and my eyes cool. "When he does something I disapprove of, I'll handle it however the fuck I want. If you don't like that, our deal is off."

As I stride toward the door, she says, "I'll fire you."

"No, you won't." No need to tell her I'm considering quitting. "I'm his only way into Leopold."

# IVORY

Something's off today. I feel a weird sort of flux in the air the instant I step into Room 1A. Prescott and Sebastian sit on opposite sides of the classroom. *Odd.* Almost as odd as the hard and resentful way they're staring at me. Mr. Marceaux stands behind his desk, also watching me in a hard way. But there's something else in his expression.

Something I haven't glimpsed in five weeks.

He looks at me like he's visualizing spanking me. It's a subtle smolder contained in his eyes, flickering as if it's been building for a while, growing and strengthening behind his thick eyelashes, and now, perhaps it's become too big, too hungry to suppress.

Maybe I'm imagining it, but the dark and heavy bass-type feeling thumping through my insides is most definitely real.

I study him closely as I find my seat, as he begins the lecture, and as he guides the class through the next hour of discussions. In those countless moments when he meets my eyes, there's a resonance radiating back from his, like he's experiencing something he's aching to share with me.

He holds my gaze. "Every minute you're not in school, you should be practicing your instrument."

Now that it's October, we have a number of events to

prepare for, the biggest one being the Holiday Chamber Music Celebration. As he brushes over the performance calendar, I'm reminded that he hasn't chosen the piano soloist. I know I'm the best, but I don't know if he agrees. His assessment of my skills is so rude and degrading. Even so, his feedback spurs me to try harder, to be better, to please him.

He continues to watch me as he speaks. It's always me who looks away first, his intensity too potent to take in for long and making me feel dizzy. But when I return to him—*and I always do*—I notice his fingers trembling or his tongue wetting his bottom lip, validations that I'm not the only one feeling this deeper presence, this vibe, between us.

What changed? How does a man go from spanking and kissing me to five weeks of rejection to *vibe*-fucking me?

By the time the last bell blares and the classroom empties, I've become so sensitive to the flashes of fire in his eyes he doesn't have to tell me to remain seated. The moment we're alone, he paralyzes me with a single glance. A silent command. *Don't move.*

With strong, measured strides, he approaches my desk, grips the outer edges, and bends over the short distance, invading my space in that predatory way he does.

He looks at me, I look at him, and a woozy tingle sweeps through my limbs.

"Mr. Marceaux?" Jesus, my heart is going to beat right out of my chest. "What are you doing?"

"Tell me about Prescott Rivard."

My heart stops in its tracks. "Sorry?"

He slams a fist on the desk, and the echo bangs in tune with the low *D* of his timbre. "Answer me!"

My shoulders curl forward, and my throat seals shut. Did he find out? I'm supposed to meet Prescott again tonight. What if that fucking prick told on me? But why would he? Prescott would be just as screwed as me.

*Play it cool. Mr. Marceaux doesn't know anything.*

"Prescott's my biggest competitor for Leopold. But I'm better—"

"Not that." His voice evens into a calm tessitura. "Tell me about your relationship with him outside of school."

I open my mouth to form a lie, but the words don't come. I can't be dishonest with him. I don't know why. So I settle on the simple truth. "I hate him."

"Why?"

"He drives around in his fancy car, wearing his too-good-for-everyone smile and being his tampon-ish self."

He lifts an eyebrow. "Tampon-ish?"

"Yes. Like a tampon. A used, gross, sticky...*tampon.*"

He rubs a hand over his mouth, staring at me like I'm speaking another language. Dropping his hand on the desk, he narrows his eyes. "Explain what you mean."

"You really want me to—? Okay, fine. A tampon is repulsive. It bulges and expands with blood. It drips all over the place and smells bad and—"

"Stop. Why is Prescott repulsive?"

"You have to ask?"

He straightens, tucks his fingers in his front pockets, and for the first time in weeks, gives me a half-smile. "No, I guess I don't."

Silence wraps around us, but it's not quiet. The air is so charged and full of heartbeats I get lost in the music that thrums between us. The look in his eyes... My God, it's overwhelmingly sexual. Not in an I-want-to-fuck-you way. He's probably thinking that, but his gaze exudes the kind of sensuality that promises more, like if we spent the rest of eternity just sharing eye contact, it would be intimate and mind-blowing and perfect, with or without sex.

It's a concept I struggle to comprehend. Just thinking about sex with him twists me up in a conflicted heap. But I don't need to understand or analyze it. I *feel* it.

The cadence of our breaths plays a soft song of want and hunger and desire in the background, and while those sexual undertones aren't necessary in our silent communication, they add rhythm and flavor to the heart of our music.

"Mr. Marceaux?" I rub my palms on my thighs, holding his gaze, and whisper, "You're sharing your notes."

Lines form on his forehead as he grips the back of his neck. "What?"

"I feel your notes. Here." I touch my breastbone, my voice shaking. "They're dark and hypnotic, like your breaths and your heartbeats."

He takes a step back, then another step, and another. Distance doesn't matter. I still hear him. Still feel him. He's inside me.

Turning away, he wanders through the front of the room, zigzagging, switching directions, as if he doesn't know where he's going. He ends up at his desk, fumbling with his laptop.

"You're working on Prokofiev's Concerto No.2 today," he says with his back to me. "Go get warmed up."

Damn. That's such an intense piece that requires an incredible amount of focus. Is that why he chose it? To distract me?

Disappointment burrows into my chest as I stand from the desk and follow his order.

For the next four hours, I endure his swatting hands and harsh criticism of my piano performance, all the while regretting telling him about the way he makes me feel. I should've focused first on preparing and nurturing those words before chucking them out, half-formed, into the winds of his volatility, with the ridiculous hope it would snag and hold his affection for me.

He sends me home at seven o'clock, not a minute after, with an immutable and heart-breaking, "Good night, Miss Westbrook."

Only I can't go home. Thirty-minutes later, I'm sitting in the vacant lot in the projects in the back seat of Prescott's Cadillac, watching him roll on a condom for the seventh time since school started.

I can do this. As long as he doesn't fuck my ass—something he's never attempted—I'll endure. I always do.

"I'm not supposed to be here." He reaches under my skirt.

My body is numb, but not numb enough. I feel his fingers yanking down my panties. I smell the greed he exhales onto my face.

"I got grounded today." He drags the underwear down my legs and off my feet. "For two months."

Nothingness rings in my ears. Everything is too quiet, too lifeless in the absence of Mr. Marceaux.

"But I'll find a way to meet up with you." He pushes me onto my back.

I can't do this again. Can't endure his hands, his thrusts,

the sounds of his pleasure. This thing he does with me, it's not rape, but it still feels forced, unwanted, dreaded. If I tell him *no*, he will force it. Maybe I can fight him off this time, but what happens to my bills? My future?

He pries my knees apart, and I jerk them back together.

"What are you doing?" Kneeling over me, he shoves his trousers down his thighs.

The outcomes of my choices are so illogical. If I keep my legs closed, I might lose my house and turn into a crack whore like my mom. If I let Prescott do what he wants, I have a chance at something great. How messed up is that?

I push my hands against him, holding him away. "I don't want this."

But I do. I want *this* in a non-grabby, non-needy, give-and-take way. I want to connect with a man the way I want my music to connect with an audience. Emotionally. Profoundly. Innately.

I want this with someone who cares.

He forces his hips between my legs and wrestles my swinging arms. "What's wrong with you?"

"This." I ram my forearms against his chest. "You."

The throaty rumble of an engine sounds in the distance, growing louder, closer, vibrating my body.

The hairs lift on my arms, and I strain my eyes through the darkness of the back seat, unable to see.

"Is that...?" I grab Prescott's shoulders as he mounts me. I try to push him off, a wasted effort. "Is that a GTO?"

"Fuck if I know." He grips his dick, poking it around my opening. "Hold still."

The rumbling car is close. Close enough to stop on the

street. Close enough that Prescott lifts his head to look out the back window.

"Shit," he whispers. "Someone's here."

Ice fills my veins. *He's looking for me?* I gulp for air and shove against Prescott's frozen chest.

*He can't see me like this. He can't. He can't.*

I kick and buck, trying to straighten my skirt, unable to move Prescott's weight.

"Move!" Oh God, I can't close my legs.

The door behind him swings open, and the sudden overhead light hurts my eyes. An arm reaches in, and in a blink, Prescott is jerked from the car and flying backward, vanishing in the pitch-black of night.

The sounds of pained grunts harmonize with the purr of the idling GTO. I grapple with the skirt, yank it down my legs, my eyes wide and locked on the open door.

Footsteps close in, the crunch of boots on gravel. Black slacks, a waistcoat, then a tie fills the door frame. He bends down, and when his face lowers into view, all I see is murderous blue.

I can't move. Can't breathe. This is it. He might as well kill me, because my life ends now.

No Le Moyne. No Leopold. No future.

No more music with Mr. Marceaux.

He stabs a finger in the direction of the street and bellows, "Get your fucking ass in my car!"

# EMERIC

The fucker is going to die.

I leave Ivory to collect her things from the car as I storm back to the moaning piece of shit on the ground. Despite my cloud of rage, I managed to contain all the punches to Prescott's ribs when I ripped him from the back seat. But as he stares up at me now, arms wrapped around his mid-section, my hands clench to shatter every bone in his contorted face.

The shadows of Central City's projects blanket the empty lot. The decrepit walls of apartment buildings are poorly lit, and the groves of overgrowth and garbage stink of abandonment. Thickly-leaved vines climb light poles and crumbling foundations, forming a protective veil in the absence of moonlight.

Prescott sprawls on his back with his pants bunched around his thighs. One glance at the condom still hanging from his flaccid dick, and my control disintegrates. Madness like I've never known explodes hot and thick inside me, constricting my chest and burning my muscles.

This is the perfect place to kill someone. No one will see. No one will care.

I crouch over him and wrap my fingers around his throat.

"You're dead."

He claws at my hand, sucking for air. "N-not just me. She's a whore and f...f...fucks everyone."

Primal rage smothers me, blinding my vision and fogging my mind. I move on instinct, rearing back and driving my knuckles, hard and fast, into his chest.

A scream coughs from his lungs. "Oh God, please, please..."

"You will never..." I connect with his stomach. "Touch her." Another hit, high on his ribs. "Again."

Then I attack. The sounds of his cries, the pain in my hands, the exertion of my breaths, all of it fades away as I bring the wrath of hell upon him. His arms shoot up, warding me off, but I pummel through it, hitting every exposed inch of his torso.

"Mr. Marceaux!" Ivory's shout comes from behind me.

My insides seethe at her defiance. "Get in the goddamn car!"

Prescott tries to roll away, and I jerk him back, pounding my fists against his chest.

"Mr. Marceaux, stop!" She screams, closer now, inches away.

I'm in a zone, my tunnel vision consumed with blood and vengeance and broken bones. With each smack of my fists, her pleas and shouts no longer register...until her mouth moves so close, her breath brushes my ear.

"Emeric."

I freeze mid-swing, my veins on fire to finish this.

Bending behind me, she snakes her arms over my shoulders, her chest against my back and her fingers digging into my shirt. With her face alongside mine, she whispers, "You won't just lose your job. You'll go to jail. He's not worth it."

I reach up and grip her hand against my heaving chest. "But you are. You're worth it."

She whimpers and squeezes my fingers. "I'm so sorry. I never meant—" She tries to pull me back. "Please. Take me home."

*Please.* King of hell, that word on her lips.

I launch to my feet, knocking her backward with the surge of my body. With a hand on her arm to balance her, I thrust the other in the direction of my car. "I won't tell you again."

Eyes wide and glassy, she hugs the strap of the satchel against her shoulder and drags her feet to the GTO.

The sound of retching draws me back to Prescott. With his pants in place, he rocks on hands and knees and empties his stomach into a snarl of weeds, sobbing between each heave.

As I wait for him to finish, I pull in deep breaths and try to summon some semblance of control. I'm not a murderer. Hell, before Ivory, I hadn't swung my fists since I was a testosterone-fueled teenager.

I glance at her, taking in her defeated posture and horrified expression as she lowers into my car. I shift my attention to my swollen hands, shocked to find them violently shaking. She's turned me into a homicidal animal.

She'll pay for letting this asshole into her body. But the bruises that'll cover his torso for the next couple weeks? That's on me.

"Get up." I grab his hair, relishing his wailing cries as I haul him toward the Cadillac and shove him into the driver's seat.

Tremors twitch along his skinny arms, his face pale and tear-soaked as he stares straight ahead. There's no visible blood or swelling on any part of his exposed skin. If it weren't for his pained expression and dirt-smeared clothes, no one would know I just beat the shit out of him.

With an arm braced on the top of the door, I lean in. "Look at me."

He cowers, and his hands fly up to block his head. "Don't hit me."

My fists flex to strike, to feel his body giving beneath the force of my anguish, but I bury it, saving it. For Ivory.

Once he realizes I'm neither swinging nor going anywhere, he drags bloodshot eyes to mine.

"You have two choices." I enunciate each word, softly, deliberately. "One. Tell no one what happened. Not a word about what you've been doing with Miss Westbrook. Let those bruises heal without revealing them to anyone, and that'll be your only punishment for paying a girl for sex."

His eyes narrow into a scathing glare.

I match his glare with one that makes him wither. "Two. Limp around like a fucking pussy. Tell the dean what you did to earn those injuries, and say goodbye to Leopold. Doesn't matter how powerful my connections, there isn't a conservatory in the world that will accept an applicant facing charges for buying sexual services."

His eyes bulge. "I'm only seventeen!"

"That's old enough to be charged as an adult and young enough to be the belle of the ball in state prison."

"Oh God, oh God, this can't be happening." He wraps an

arm around his stomach and gives me a pleading look. "You won't tell my mom?"

I should've broken him. Should've left him in a bloody pile for the vultures to feed on. "This is between you and me. Keep your mouth shut, stay the fuck away from Miss Westbrook...and when I say stay away, I mean don't think about her. Don't talk to or look at her. Erase her from your fucking mind. Do that, and the dean won't hear of your crime."

"Okay." He grips the steering wheel, nodding, swallowing. "I can do that."

I'm not convinced. If he's half as addicted to Ivory as I am, he won't be able to stay away. But for now, scaring the shit out of him is the best option I have.

I slam the door and stalk toward the GTO.

Did she enjoy fucking him? Will she hate me for breaking them up?

No way. She compared him to a bloody tampon.

But what about other boys? Other *customers?*

Deep in my gut, I know she didn't want to be here. She didn't even understand the concept of sexual desire until she met me. But finding her with someone else is a crushing hit to my pride. Christ, I can't even bring myself to look at another woman, yet here she is...with him.

Jealous rage claws its way through my chest, stealing my air and speeding up my gait.

She should've come to me, confided in me, asked me to help her. Instead, she chose this. *Him.*

Flashbacks of the back seat crash through my mind, tormenting me with images of her spread legs, his bare ass, the condom.

My legs tense to turn around, my fists tingling to pulverize his throat until he stops breathing. But I keep walking, focused on her, on what I intend to do.

Of all my passions, disciplining a woman is the most exhilarating. The most arousing. The reason I work and fuck and breathe. I can do this without destroying her. If I keep my temper in check, I'll be able to open something inside her she has no idea exists. Pain and pleasure. Fear and arousal. Give and take. Once she understands how these things work together, it will change her, strengthen her, and tie her to me irrevocably.

The rational part of my brain demands I take her home, quit my job, and end this dangerous infatuation. But I've reached the point of no return.

It's no longer a matter of *if* or *when*.

Tonight, she'll bend for my punishment, tremble for my touch, and I'll risk it all to show her exactly what she means to me.

# EMERIC

The tension in the GTO is as stifling and disorienting as my anger. I welcome Ivory's silence, but the secrecy of her thoughts winds me tighter and tighter with each passing street.

When I speed past the turn off for Treme, she twists in the seat and points.

"My house is..." Her gaze flies to mine. "You're not taking me home?"

Pulling up to a stop light, I turn toward her. "Will anyone notice if you don't return home tonight? Your mother? Brother?"

I thought her eyes were dark before, but now they're the color of nightmares. Even in the passing headlights, they coax me in and chill me to the bone.

She looks at her lap, shakes her head, her voice a soft shivering pianissimo. "What are you going to do to me?"

She's thinking the worst. I hear it in the serrated gusts of her breaths, and it infuriates me. But I can't blame her. She watched me lose my shit with Prescott, and as sure as I can feel her fear, she can sense my vibrating need for atonement.

I reach over and grip the hand in her lap. "Listen very carefully, Ivory." I squeeze her trembling fingers. "I would never hit you in anger. When I welt your ass, you'll love it as much as you hate it. Tell me you understand."

Her breath catches, and a sob hangs on the edge of her voice. "You won't hurt me in anger." She touches the broken skin on my knuckles. "How did you find me?"

"Sebastian Roth was all too willing to give up his friend's favorite parking spot." A torrent of animosity invades my throat, and I'm unable to stop it. "You're fucking him and Prescott? How many others?"

She attempts to pull her hand away, but I hold tight. Her fingers fall limp while mine continue to shake from the lingering adrenaline.

It's probably best that she doesn't answer while I'm driving. Seconds from detonating, I'm liable to jerk the damn car off a bridge.

Lasalle Street, fifteen blocks, two turns, and a high-security gate later, here I am, sitting in my driveway, about to make the biggest mistake of my life.

A nearby gas lamp illuminates the interior of the car, but we're parked around back, shrouded by massive oaks and hidden from the street.

When I turn in the seat to face her, she's not staring at my enormous estate with envy in her eyes. She's not surveying the million-dollar landscape with parted lips. She's looking at me. Like I'm the only thing that exists in the world. Like I'm more important than all the wealth surrounding her.

I fall helplessly into her gaze, lost in the shadows of tragedy and fear and neglect. But there's a glint of light in the dark depths. As she sways closer, seeking, my heart kicks with realization. That tiny glimmer in her eyes is trust.

That's when I hear it.

The tempo of our breaths. The drum of our heartbeats. The crackle in the air.

The exquisite cadence pulses through me, awakening sensations I've never felt, composing a melody I've never heard.

Our hypnotic, dark notes.

This is so much more than punishment or forbidden pleasure.

She could never be a mistake.

"Are we going to..." She tilts her head and searches my face. "Do the vibe thing all night? I'm okay with that, but not knowing what comes next has me...um, a little jumpy."

I trail a finger across her cheek and along her bottom lip. "Tell me you trust me."

She nibbles the corner of her mouth. "You've given me every reason not to."

I drop my hand, but she catches it and lifts it back to her face.

"You've also shown me every reason I should." She holds our hands tightly against her cheek. "Thank you for finding me." Her fingers trace the cuts on my knuckles, and her eyes shimmer with tears. "For protecting me."

Christ, this girl... She's my music, my place in this life, my part in it all.

I move in and touch my lips to hers. "You're going to follow me inside." I slide a hand into her thick hair. "You're going to tell me everything I want to know." I tighten my grip and yank her head back. "Then I'm going to test the depth of your trust. Say *yes*."

Her eyes flicker with vulnerability and desperation. Then she blinks, breathes, and relaxes in my hold. "Yes, Mr. Marceaux."

# IVORY

I follow Mr. Marceaux through the wide, echoing passages of his monstrosity of a mansion. Between the questions I'll have to answer and whatever punishment that will follow, my legs threaten to buckle with each step.

He touches my lower back and steers me forward. Oddly, the tremors in his hand give me strength. Like maybe he's as freaked out as I am.

His fingers have been shaking since he climbed into the GTO, his breaths fluctuating in volume and tempo all the way here. I'm well-acquainted with the indicators of a man in need, but this feels different, safer somehow. Maybe it's because he's not attacking me like the other men I've encountered. Or perhaps it's because the hand on my back is *guiding* me, not forcing me.

We pass a living room filled with plush leather furniture, a hearth room with more couches, and a massive kitchen gleaming with stainless steel. Compared to the gloomy Victorian Gothic exterior of stone and steeples, the inside is warm and bright, flaunting the kind of luxuries I'm not sure a teacher's salary can afford.

Wrought iron chandeliers, long heavy draperies, shiny wood floors, black damask wallpaper, it's all so old-world-ish yet modern at the same time. Such a profound reflection of his personality. He seems like such an old noble soul in the sense that he loves knowledge and truth—those pursuits interest him far more than the latest gossip or high-tech car. But after two months of lectures, I've learned he also appreciates the transience of life, the fleeting trends, and the way people and music change over time.

After countless rooms, a spiraling staircase that wraps around the atrium, and a maze of corridors, I've lost my bearings. Why would a single man need so much space?

I really don't care how much money he has or where it comes from. I'm more interested in the man himself, what he has planned, and where he's taking me.

"Mr. Marceaux?"

"It's Emeric." He stops, turns me to face him, and strokes the pad of his thumb across my cheek. "I'm Mr. Marceaux when I'm your teacher."

His touch races a shiver across my skin and electrifies my heart. "If you're not my teacher right now, what are you?"

The mechanisms in his watch tick beside my ear as he slides his fingers through my hair and holds my head in the frame of his hands. "I don't think you're ready to hear that."

Maybe not, but I think he's showing me. As I stare into the stormy blue of his gaze, the wall sconces, arched doorways, and dark woods in the hallway all melt into oblivion. He's wearing his dead serious face, the one that says *I want to fuck you* and so much more.

That look in his eyes turns my insides upside down, pulling my breaths through a diaphanous haze of happiness and confusion. He doesn't temper the hunger in his expression, but doesn't act on it, either. It's as if he's letting it build naturally while keeping it contained. As if he's enjoying the way it makes him feel without thrusting it against me.

I could stand here and stare at him all night, at his model-perfect features, the barely-there stubble on his sculpted jaw, and the heat dancing in his eyes. My fingertips tingle to run through his hair again. Softly, though, unlike the way he stabs his hands through the black strands when he's angry.

He's just...so...damn gorgeous. Way too hot to be a teacher. But it's his self-control I'm attracted to the most. Funny that, since he showed zero restraint with Prescott. Or maybe he did? Prescott *is* still breathing.

When it comes to me, though, his control is evident in his tight expression and even tighter breaths. He wants, but he doesn't take. That alone makes me feel more drawn to him.

I grip the gathered sleeves at his elbows and glide my fingers along his sinewy forearms. "Can I bandage your hands?"

"Later." His face moves an inch closer.

"I don't get you, Mr. Mar— *Emeric*. You went from spankings to five weeks of nothing to swinging fists to..." I hesitantly reach up and touch his warm, chiseled cheek. "To looking at me like this. Why?"

"Well, something happened recently." He gives me a half-smile. "About ten minutes ago." He turns his face toward my hand and presses his lips to my wrist. "I had an epiphany."

In the car? My heart rate jumps. "What do you mean?"

"I realized I've been in denial since..." His gaze lowers to my mouth momentarily then returns to my eyes. "For a while."

"Denial about what?"

He steps closer, strokes his hands through my hair, and holds my cheek against his chest. "Let's not give it a name yet."

*Love* pops into my mind, unbidden, quickly followed by *hug*. Instinctively, my arms wrap around his torso. My hands grip the back of his wool waistcoat, and muscle by muscle, I relax against him. His fingers trail down my spine, shooting shivers from my head to my toes. The circle of his arms tightens, and every molecule inside me becomes hyper-aware of every inch of his body.

His towering height and hard physique feels intimidating and protective, immovable and warm, strange and wonderfully right.

My dad used to hug me, and I miss that love with excruciating heartache. Stogie loves me in a non-huggy, protective-uncle way. But that's the extent of my experience with the concept.

Exploring something like love with Emeric is terrifyingly reckless. He's too volatile, unpredictable, and insanely intense. Would he give it one day and take it back the next? Would he taunt me with it, make me beg for it, and use it against me?

Even so, I'd rather receive it in rations than never have it at all.

Except he's my teacher. He specifically told me I cannot fall in love with him. And he loves another woman.

What exactly am I to him? My stomach boils with jealousy and trepidation, but it doesn't hurt as much with his arms holding me close and his mouth resting on the top of my head.

Whatever this is...this thing he's been in denial about, it seems to be making his heart race. Or maybe it's the hug causing those heavy beats against my ear. Maybe it's all the same.

I tilt my head and look up at him. "Are you afraid?"

He releases me and steps back, his focus on his hand as he smooths down the black and white striped tie.

I grit my teeth. Dammit, I want him to own his feelings, not pull them back and brush them away. I open my mouth to say just that, but his eyes ensnare mine, and I forget to breathe.

That moment...my God, it feels like a lifetime in the making. His hands curl around my neck, wrenching me into a kiss so consuming it touches me everywhere. Seconds pass like hours. The caress of his mouth robs the strength from my knees. The instant he offers his tongue, a chill of electricity runs wild across my skin. His soft groan vibrates against my lips, eliciting a warm throb between my legs. And his answer...

"Yes." His hands collar my throat, snugly, possessively, as he kisses a shivery path to my ear and rasps, "I'm afraid."

My fingers find his hair and pull his mouth back to mine. "Afraid of?"

"Getting caught." He turns us, presses my back against the wall, and whispers between drugging licks along my lips. "Going to jail."

I want to argue, but I have no voice, no breath, only his sinful mouth and the support of his strong chest against mine.

He angles his head, twining our tongues, deeper, faster, and I float on the thermal currents writhing between us. The crotch of my panties feels wet, my body temperature dialed to feverish levels. The cotton of my shirt and the elastic of my bra itch and squeeze my skin. I want them off.

"I'm afraid of hurting you." He tilts his head in the opposite direction, a new angle, eating at my mouth as if he can't reach deep enough. "But I'm not stopping, Ivory." Another hungry kiss. "You're mine."

A sense of belonging swells in my chest. It feels so big and full and too good to be true. I don't know if I can trust it. As I waver, his heat and strength vanish, leaving me swaying against the wall.

He grips my wrist and yanks me ahead of him in the hall, steering me forward. I attempt a wobbly step, but he's behind me, his strong fingers sliding from my waist, over my hips, and curling around my thighs.

His mouth traces the line of my shoulder and nibbles along my neck. He pauses at my ear, his tone husky. "Last room on the right."

With a staggering inhale, I walk ahead. His footfalls trail a few steps behind, and I can't help but crane my neck to hold his heated gaze. When I reach the doorway, I pivot and back in, my attention paralyzed by all the unnamed emotions hardening his fierce expression.

I should be anxious. I should be fucking terrified. But he's not Lorenzo or Prescott or the countless others who make me want to die. Emeric has made me feel more alive tonight than I have in seventeen years.

The periphery of my vision catches a bed, some furniture, lots of grays and blacks. His bedroom? I don't glance around, don't avert my eyes from the man who is jeopardizing his career, his freedom, to be with me.

He prowls closer, his overwhelming proximity chasing me backward, slowly, breathlessly, deeper into the room. Will he ask his questions now? Will the truth disgust him to the point of hatred? There have been so few people in my life who believe in me. I can't bear the thought of losing that protective look on his face.

He catches my waist and pulls me against him, his voice low and guttural. "You have no idea what that does to me."

"What?"

"The way you stare at me like I'm worth more to you than"—he glances around the room—"a big fancy house."

A burning flush sweeps across my cheeks. What is he saying? That because I'm poor, I should be star-struck and gaping at his stuff? I care more about him than all the money in the world. But maybe I shouldn't. Maybe he thinks I'm a lovesick high school girl.

I narrow my eyes. "The molding in this place... It's everywhere. Scalloped designs on the living room ceiling, square panels on the walls, chair rails run the length of the hall. I could peel it all off and hock it while you're—"

"Brat." His beautiful face splits into a smile as he shuffles me backward and sets me on the edge of the mattress.

He leaves me there and strides to the dresser. As he empties his pockets, I'm hit with a heavy dose of reality. I'm in Mr. Marceaux's bedroom. Sitting on his bed. Watching him do things, personal things in his private space, that no one else at school has witnessed.

With his back to me, he places his wallet and keys in a wooden dish. His phone and mechanical watch go next. His waistcoat falls over the back of a stiff leather chair. His necktie follows.

When his hands fall to his belt, my breath catches.

He shifts to face me, his fingers slowly unclasping the buckle. "It's time to address the issue we've been avoiding."

My stomach sinks, and a wave of vertigo shivers through me.

He slides the belt free, winds it into a coil, and sets it on the nightstand beside the bed.

"No lies." He clasps his hands behind his back, squared shoulders stretch the white button-up across his chest, and his glare hardens. "Omitting is the same as lying."

*Shit!* I squeeze my eyes shut. Shit, fucking shit.

"Ivory."

I open my eyes and find him studying me. Of course, he is. Always watching. Always seeing too much. I bite my lip. This isn't going to end well.

"I'm probably going to lose my cool again." He glances at his shoes, smirking to himself. "Since I can't seem to control my temper where you're concerned." He looks up beneath a veil of thick lashes. "Remember what I said about that."

My eyebrows pull in as I think back. "You never hit a woman in anger?"

"Good girl."

My lungs expand, inhaling those words.

He kneels before me, his chest touching my closed knees and his hands on my hips. "I know you need money. I've deduced that Prescott and Sebastian pay you." His eyes spark with anger. "Tell me how and when the arrangement began."

I want to caress his face, but the angles of his bone

structure suddenly appear too sharp, too untouchable. So I place my palm on the warm skin of his forearm, where it rests alongside my thigh. "I'll tell you. I promise. But what will happen to my education and Leo—?"

"Leopold is neither here nor there. This isn't a student-teacher conference." He shifts, grips the hem of my skirt, and shoves it up my thighs until it sits just below my panties.

I keep my knees together, but I don't fight him.

"This is you and me, Ivory." His fingers slide beneath the gathered fabric, tracing the hidden bend between my legs and hips. "We're just a man and a woman, sharing an intimate moment of honesty."

I like the sound of that almost as much as the soothing touch of his fingers. A silent caesura stretches between us, during which time isn't counted or weighed. Eventually, his caresses calm me enough to speak.

"Freshman year, I was desperate for friends, desperate to fit in, and offered to help some of the kids with their homework." Sweat slicks my hands, and I clasp them over the crease of my clenched bare thighs. "Only the boys took me up on the help. Prescott and his friends. At some point in that first year, my tutoring turned into me doing their homework for them."

"And what I saw in the car?"

"They touched and kissed and took things I didn't want to give."

Emeric rises, his hands raking through his hair as a violent symphony clashes and vibrates in his eyes.

"They *took* things..." He drops his arms and flexes his fists at his sides. "Explain that."

I tell him how I threatened to stop helping them, how they offered to pay me if I continued, and how badly I needed the income to keep my house. By the time I get to the part about them taking more than the homework, Emeric is pacing a furious track through the room.

If he's going to burn off steam, he has the space to do it. I mean, it's the biggest bedroom I've ever seen, with nothing on the floor to trip him up. For a guy, he's surprisingly tidy.

And for a girl who's in a cage with a pacing lion, I feel strangely detached. Liberated even.

Finally voicing these things is freeing, and he absorbs every word like he's living it, feeling it. Yes, he's angry, but he hasn't once directed it at me. He cares enough to be angry *for* me.

He stops before me, his face as red as his swollen knuckles. "You told them *no*?"

Directing my eyes to his Doc Martens, I nod. "For a while."

"Define *a while*."

"The first couple of years."

"They raped you. For *years*." His scathing voice rolls into bellow. "Look at me!"

My gaze jumps to his. The horror etching his face makes my heart pound so hard it hurts.

How do I explain these embarrassing things when I'm not even sure about any of it? "I don't know."

"There's no *I-don't-know*'s about it, Ivory." He grips the back of his neck with both hands and paces in a tight circle. "You were either willing or you weren't. Which is it?"

"Sometimes, I feel trapped by circumstance. Sometimes, I'm held down. Other times, I just let it happen."

"You just let it happen," he echoes with venom. "Bullshit!"

The roar of his shout hitches my shoulders. He spins and slams his fist into the wall, wrenching a gasp from my throat.

I leap from the bed, shoving my skirt down as I cautiously approach his back. "Emeric."

He punches another hole, and another, his arms flexing and contracting with the impact as dust and sheet rock explode around him.

"Emeric, stop!"

Breathing heavily, he braces a forearm on the wall, rests his brow on his arm, and angles his head to look at me. "Which one of those fuckers took your virginity?"

"No one at Le Moyne." I step closer, within arm's reach. "I was already..." *Used. Ruined.*

He reaches out and drags me against him, pinning me between his heaving chest and the wall.

Blood and dust cover the knuckles of the hand he lifts to gently caress my cheek. "There's more you haven't told me."

More men who take. More truth to share. I'll tell him everything, because he hasn't pushed me away, hasn't once looked at me with repulsion.

He drops his forehead to mine, fingers resting against my cheek, and says quietly, "I want to whip you for being so damn uninformed about rape."

But I'm learning the differences, as well as who to trust and when to ask for help. I always thought the safest place to go was in my head, that no one could hurt me there. But standing between a busted wall and the fuming man who destroyed it, I've never felt safer.

I hold his hand against my face and meet his passionate

gaze. "I trust you."

All my disgusting secrets have finally caught up with me. But for the first time in my life, I don't have to face them alone.

# EMERIC

My self-control is a goddamn joke, and the unflappable part of my brain is lost beneath chilling images of Ivory cornered, hurt, and alone. My hands shake as I teeter on the verge of manic brutality, consumed with the kind of throbbing headache that can only be comforted by bloodshed.

I knew there was sexual abuse, but part of me believed it was in the past, like it had been a single horrifying moment in her life. I never envisioned years of rape.

How many motherfuckers will I have to kill? And while I'm murdering my way through her nightmares, how will I stop myself from becoming the worst of them all?

Ivory's view of sex is most likely damaged all to hell. How will she respond to sex with me? Will she freeze up? Am I pushing her too fast? What the fuck do I do now, if anything, regarding our relationship?

My heart thunders louder, faster, my muscles expanding with the direction of my thoughts.

"Hey." She holds my sore hand against her cheek. "You're getting all tense again."

I think she may be crazier than I am. She doesn't cringe or try to put a safe distance between us. Instead, she gives me a gentle smile and stares up at me with huge brown eyes full of trust.

Yes, I brought her home to keep her safe, but she has no idea how close I am to snapping. My entire body shakes to bend her over and fuck her so hard all she remembers is me. And that will destroy her.

I step back and stab a shaky finger toward the bed. "Sit."

She smooths down her skirt and follows my order, glancing nervously at the belt on the nightstand.

My palm feels hot and achy, my arm tensing to swing that strap. Less because of anger and more because I'm desperate to put all this shit behind us and spend the rest of the night welting her into orgasmic bliss.

But it's not like I can just go at her with a belt in hand. That would sabotage her trust. I have to teach her that there's a better, more meaningful kind of pain than what she's experienced. The *willing* kind.

To do that, I have to pull myself together.

With measured breaths, I take a moment to indulge in her beauty, absorbing her perfect turned-up nose, tawny complexion, and dark shiny hair. But it's the boldness in her eyes, the strength in her smile, and the potency of her aura that calms me. It's impossible not to gravitate toward her, to not be captivated by the grace and tenacity she emanates.

As I stare at her, I realize with startling clarity she doesn't need me to slay her past. She's already lived it and came out the other side with more fortitude than any person I know.

But she does need me to listen, to support her without losing my head, and most of all, to protect her from future harm.

With a steadier pulse and the headache subsiding, I join

her on the edge of the bed, my feet beside hers on the floor. Bending over her lap, I reach for her ankles. I've despised her glued-together shoes since the first day when I slid them onto her feet. They're not good enough for her, and watching her walk around in them week after week makes me want to give her every penny I have.

I push the little black flats off her heels and let them drop to the floor. If she only knew how many size-seven replacements I've bought her. The whole damn closet behind me is filled, not just with shoes, but clothes and bags and... Jesus, I sound like a psychopath, even in my head.

I'm not even a shopper. Fucking hate it. But for the past five weeks, it was the most benign way I found to channel my inappropriate obsession with her.

Gathering her sideways in my lap, I scoot up the mattress and recline against the headboard.

With my arms wrapped around her delicate frame, I caress her back. "Tell me about your first time. How old were you?"

She rests her cheek on my shoulder, her voice tentative. "You go first."

An outraged *Answer me* builds in my throat, but I swallow it, reminding myself that honesty goes both ways.

I kiss her temple. "I was sixteen. So was she. A summer girlfriend. It was..." *Sweet. Awkward. Vanilla.* "Uneventful. We broke up shortly after."

She fidgets with my shirt button beneath her chin. "Is it crazy that I want to hunt her down and scratch her eyes out for getting that *uneventful* first with you?"

A laugh bursts from my chest as I flex my swollen hand in her lap. "If that's crazy, I should probably be committed." *For being uncontrollably, insanely, violently protective of this girl.*

She chuckles softly, her fingers tracing circles around the pulpy mess on my knuckles. "I want to clean your hands."

"When we're finished."

In her sideways position on my lap, she leans against my chest and hooks an arm around my lower back, pressing her face in my neck, as if to keep me close.

I'm not going anywhere.

"I was thirteen my first time."

I close my eyes and remember to breathe.

"My brother's friend did it, behind my house, on the stairs."

I seethe. Goddammit, I seethe from every pore in my body. Her brother is nine-years older than her. If the friend is the same age, that sick filthy molester was twenty-two when he fucked her thirteen-year-old body.

It's all I can do to just sit there, hold her against me, and not blow up in a roaring, ballistic fit of fury. "His age?"

She shifts up my chest and loops her arms around my shoulders, resting her forehead against the side of mine. "Same age as you."

I know I'm squeezing her too hard when she squeaks and digs her nails into my neck. Questions pile up amid the growling vibrations in my throat, but there's no way I can form sophisticated sounds right now, let alone words.

She pets my shoulder like she's comforting a damn rabid dog. "I told him *no*, fought him, *hated* it. I know what that means now, but I didn't understand it then."

"Ivory—"

"Just let me finish." She tilts away from my chest, staring at the doorway to the master bathroom as her fingers toy with the buttons on my shirt. "After it happened, I was pretty screwed up in my head. I let anyone and everyone have sex with me, like I was trying to prove to myself that I wasn't weak. I didn't want to cry through it. I wanted to own it, like 'I've got this. *I* am doing it.' And him and him and—"

"How many?" I ground out through clenched teeth.

She blinks and shakes her head. When she blinks again, her eyes shine with tears. "It didn't work out the way I wanted."

"Stop sniveling and tell me how many *him*'s there have been."

Her jaw sets, and she levels me with a tear-sodden glare. "I don't know, okay? Sixty? Eighty? More? I don't keep track because I don't want to know!"

My stomach hardens. Fuck me, I'm ten years older than her, and sixty is twice as many partners as I've had. And that's her low number.

Her attention returns to the bathroom. "Go ahead and say it. I'm a slut. A disgusting whore."

I capture her chin in a hard grip and jerk her face to mine, my tone coarse. "Don't ever put words in my mouth."

When I let go, she pulls her knees up between our chests, her firm ass digging into my thighs where she sits sideways on my lap. Her legs twitch to close impossibly tighter as she stares at the bathroom again. My first thought is she needs to pee. But given the conversation, I know there's something else going on.

I tuck her hair behind her ear and trail my fingers down her neck. "Did Prescott...touch you or have sex with you before I arrived tonight?"

She hugs her knees, her expression darkening. "No."

I didn't think so, but being caught in that position is probably doing a number on her head. "Tell me why you're staring at the bathroom."

Her lashes sweep down. "I would really like to...to take a shower."

"Because?"

"I'm dirty," she whispers.

My teeth clench. It's going to take a fuckton of time and patience to repair her dignity, and I'm starting right fucking now.

"You know what happened the moment I ripped Prescott out of that car? I asserted ownership over you. I know you don't understand the significance of that, so I'll make it simple." I grip her throat and hold her gaze. "You're mine. That means every inch of your gorgeous body, every thought in your head, and every word out of your mouth impacts me. Calling yourself dirty or any other offensive adjective is an insult to *my* girl, something I will not tolerate. Tell me you understand."

Her throat relaxes against my palm, her eyes round and searching. "I understand."

Fucking beautiful.

I release her neck and touch the juncture of her closed knees. "Part your legs."

The slim fit of the skirt won't allow for much, but I only need enough space for my hand.

She stares at my fingers, and her wide eyes flash to mine. Whatever she sees in my face smooths the worry lines on hers.

Her arms fall to her sides, and breath by breath, she opens her knees.

Fucking hell, I ache to strip her bare and taste every glorious curve and dip of her body. We're going to be so fucking wild together, grappling and reckless, messy and drunk on pleasure. I feel the promise of that churning in the air between us, shaking my legs beneath her ass, and slicking my palm as I glide my fingers along the inside of her thigh.

The deeper I reach beneath her skirt, the warmer and damper her skin. I watch her expression for signs of panic and inch closer to her pussy.

An inch from my target, I caress her thigh, teasing her. "I'm not going to erase your self-hating comment with flowery words like *You're pretty and sexy and perfect*, because I suspect you've heard it all, most likely uttered on heavy breaths that haunt you when you sleep."

Her bottom lip quivers, the rest of her stock-still and rigid.

"Instead, I'm going to show you exactly how *not dirty* you are." I touch the crotch of her panties.

Damp satin meets my fingers, and my cock jerks against her hip. Christ, I want her. It's this swelling, constricting feeling at the base of my spine, making my thighs clench and my balls tighten. I don't know how I'll stop myself from taking her like every other barbaric asshole once I remove the barriers between us.

Her eyes lock on mine as she grips my forearm, not pushing me away but sliding her fingers along the muscle as if feeling the way it moves.

I twist my wrist and hook a finger beneath the edge of satin between her leg and pussy. With a long, slow stroke, I slide my touch from her opening to her clit, parting her flesh and relishing the feel of soft short hairs. As I make another sweep, and another, she's grows wetter and wetter. Her pussy swells, her legs tremble, and I fucking thrill at the idea of giving her pleasure in a way no one has before.

She plants her feet on the mattress, clinging to my arm with both hands. Her full tits rise and fall as the alluring sound of her breaths chases the silence from the room.

Her parted lips, the flex of her ass against my quads, and the feel of her arousal coating my fingers turn me on in ways I've never known. This reaches so much deeper than the rigid pressure between my legs. She's in my veins, fiery and weightless. She's in my head, like a whisper of promises. She's in my heart, softening it, mending it, and making it pump again.

I remove my hand and lift it to my mouth. Holding her gaze, I suck each finger clean, slowly, deliberately. "You taste dirty, Ivory. In the most agreeable, delicious, addictive sense of the word."

Her jaw drops in a soundless gasp. She closes her mouth, opens it again, but I cut her off with a kiss. My hands slip over her face and hair, holding her to me as I hunt down her tongue, catch it, and tangle it with mine. She follows me, hands on my head, moaning into my mouth and licking her taste from my lips.

Need coils low and tight in my body. The bed frame creaks as I kiss her deeper, pull her closer, pursuing her with fingers and teeth, silently demanding she take everything I give her, because it's all hers. I'm hers.

She moves her lips over mine, her voice husky. "Damn,

you...you really know how to kiss."

Her sultry exhale carves a space in my lungs, and with each of her little breaths, that space grows fuller and fuller. When she clears her throat, I hear her question in the inhale that follows. *What now?*

I have my own questions, more than there are minutes left in the night. But she hasn't eaten, exhaustion weighs heavily on her eyelids, and we're not leaving this room until she's learned a crucial lesson.

With great reluctance, I shift her off my lap and settle her on the bed. Her gaze instantly falls to the tent in my slacks. She may as well get used to that.

I stand and grab my rigid length, forcing it sideways in my pants. "Many weeks ago, you said you didn't want to be gagged, tied, and whatever else you think accompanies those things." I reach for the belt and loop it in half, holding tight to the ends. "But you've thought about it."

She stares at the leather strap and rubs her hands over her lap. "I...I didn't mind the spanking."

"That's a half-truth. Try again."

Frustration crinkles her brow. "Okay, I liked it. But that doesn't even make sense. It was humiliating and painful."

"Define the pain."

"It was...I don't know. It should've scared me. Instead, it just made me feel warm and fuzzy all over. Maybe because *you* don't scare me. Because I...I like..." She drops her gaze to her hands.

"Look at me."

She does, her teeth sawing along her lip. "I like you. You make me want things I've never..." She looks away and quickly returns to me. "I want your spankings and kisses and...*more*."

"Good girl." Standing over her bent position, I cup her chin with my free hand and kiss her mouth.

The moment our tongues connect, I'm lost to the aimless, sensual slide of our lips. She's fantasia in the flesh, unbound to convention, vibrating beneath my hands and begging to be directed.

I straighten and step back. "The pain you experienced with other men... That was unacceptable, Ivory, because it was non-consensual." I punctuate each syllable with a stern tone. "You are not at fault. You will never blame yourself. Say *yes* if you understand."

She sits taller, her chin lifting higher. "Yes."

That glimmer of confidence in her posture does wonders for my ego. We're making progress, and damn if that doesn't harden me like a rock.

I widen my stance, the looped belt hanging at my side. "Just like the spanking, I'm going to show you good pain. The kind of pain *you* control. You'll have all the power here, because the moment you say *no*—"

Her shoulders tighten, a reminder that in her experience that word is a useless son of a bitch.

A renewed blaze of anger hits my blood. I spear a hand through my hair and draw a deep breath. "Scratch that. Give me a word you would naturally use in place of *no*. Something that—"

"Scriabin."

The speed in which she spits that out shocks me. And why a Russian composer? As I stare into the shadows of her muddy brown eyes, I decide that Scriabin is rather fitting given the conflicted, dissonant quality of his music.

I flex my hand, my heart pumping wildly. "When you say *Scriabin*, I stop."

She scans my face, my shoulders, and the belt in my hand. A frown pulls on her mouth.

"I need your trust, Ivory."

She looks up, her lips parting. "You have it."

"Show me." The ache in my cock magnifies. "Feet on the floor and chest on the mattress."

When she obeys, the tightness inside my ribs loosens.

I step behind her and trail the loop of leather up her leg and over her round ass. My hands continue upward, holding on to the belt as I extend her arms above her head. "Tell me why you're being punished."

With her fingers curling into the quilt, she rests her cheek against the bed and meets my eyes. "For selling my body."

"That's not—" I feel the tremor of my outrage all the way to my feet. "Listen to me. You were in a desperate situation, and those fuckers took more than you offered. I'm punishing you because you put yourself in that car instead of coming to me."

She starts to rise, but I hold her down with my weight, my chest on her back and my hungry cock against her ass.

"But you're my teacher," she says, quietly. "I didn't know what you would—"

"You also had Stogie. And the police, social services... You had options."

Her muscles deflate beneath me. "You're right."

"Right and pissed. You refused my help with the textbooks, yet you accepted money from those assholes. You didn't trust me enough to confide in me, but you trusted those boys with a dangerous arrangement."

She nods, her mouth soft in agreement. But I know her mind must be racing into the future, searching for new solutions to lingering problems.

I trace my lips across her jaw. "You're mine, Ivory. That means your problems are mine. Your bills, your worries, your safety..." I kiss the corner of her mouth. "All of it belongs to me."

She releases a heavy sigh.

Shifting downward, I roam my hands over her clothes. Her slender shoulder, the curvature of her spine, the rise of her ass, there's so much femininity to touch, devour, and welt.

I crouch behind her, my muscles buzzing with excitement. With the belt in my hand, I let her feel the scrape of leather as I slide the skirt to her waist. Toned thighs and freckles, pert ass and creamy skin, goosebumps and pink satin...it's all mine. But the panties have to go.

As I yank them to her feet and step back, everything inside me narrows to one basic instinct. Jesus, fuck, I want inside her with blinding ferocity, but I manage to keep my feet on the floor and my hand off my dick. "What's your safe word?"

"Scriabin," she breathes, clutching the quilt.

The sight of her bent over for me has my cock jerking painfully in my slacks, damn near tearing through the zipper. Does she touch herself when she's alone? Has a man ever pleasured her? I doubt it, but I need confirmation, even if it tempts me to strap her down and fuck her until I break her.

"One more question." I stroke a finger up her thigh and slide it through the soft, wet flesh between her legs. "Have you ever had an orgasm?"

# IVORY

I press my face into the manly scent of Emeric's bedding and force my trembling legs to keep me from sliding to the floor. Cool air brushes against my bare backside, and his fingers... Holy hell, his fingers slide back and forth between my thighs, producing the strangest, most invigorating kind of warmth down there.

I can't focus on anything but the path of his strokes, my entire body singing for him to keep doing that...that...exactly what he's doing. Please, don't stop, don't—

He stops, cupping me in his huge palm. "I won't repeat the question."

I press my teeth into my lip, hating his gruff, impatient tone. Or maybe I love it.

"I don't know. I...I touch myself sometimes." I've tried to create the toe-curling *Oh yeah, right there!* the women in my neighborhood go on about, but it never feels as good as they claim. "Can it happen when I don't enjoy it?"

His hand flexes against my pussy. "All those motherfuckers, and not one of them got you off." He relaxes his fingers, caressing lazily. "It'll be different from now on."

The next stroke curls all the way inside, thrusting me into a whole new world of different. Air shoots from my lungs, and my body clenches around the invasion. Oh my God, it's so...painless. Not dry or searing or too tight.

With slippery drives of his finger, he plunges again and again. A molten, coma-inducing pleasure courses through my body. My nipples tighten, and my pulse goes crazy. I dig my toes into the carpet as the slurping sounds of his rhythm saturate the room.

Heat rushes to my face. I know this is desire, and he's found that mysterious trigger to release my natural lubrication, to show me how to want this. But I'm leaking all over his hand. Is it normal to be *this* messy?

He crouches, burying his finger inside me as his other hand drags the belt along my thigh. The leather shakes against me, like his exhales. And his voice. "So fucking wet."

"I'm sorry. I don't know why—"

"Don't," he growls, dipping his finger in and out, massaging and rubbing with so much control. "This is what it feels like to be taken care of, to receive pleasure from someone who wants to give it desperately." His lips graze my inner thigh. "I know how to touch my girl."

He knows how to be both languorous and *male* and how to coax my surrender with only the strength of his words. I've never been with someone so powerful and confident, who can also remain calm enough to touch me like this.

His fingers leave my body, and his heat slips away. I turn my neck and catch a glimpse of deep navy eyes as he straightens and swipes his wet hand over his mouth.

That's the second time he's tasted me. It's obscene yet fascinating at the same time.

He steps to the side. "Don't move your hands."

I twist my fingers in the bedding above my head just as the air whistles behind me. A fiery thwack lands across my ass, and I can't stop my hand from jerking back to rub the pain.

But his mouth is already there, sealed over the stabbing heat, sucking and licking. He grabs my wrist, pinning it to the mattress as his lips transform the hurt into something else completely. The sweep of his tongue chases away the sting, leaving a drugging kind of tingle across my skin.

Maybe it's because he spent so much time touching me first, suspending me in a state of over-stimulation, but I don't cower as he stands to swing again. My body is already buzzing like an addict. I want more.

Except he doesn't strike. He moves away from the bed with determined strides and disappears within the closet. What the hell?

A second later, he emerges with a black duffel bag and unzips it on the bed beside my head. Leather cuffs drop on the mattress, followed by nylon straps.

My heart bangs so loudly it could drown out an orchestra. "Wh—what is that for?"

He unwinds the straps, squatting as he attaches them to the bed frame. "If you had moved your hand a second sooner, the belt would've sliced your fingers. Maybe even broken them. We're going to do this without endangering your piano career."

Says the man who punches walls.

I lift up on elbows and point at his damaged knuckles. "When is your next symphony performance?"

"Two weeks." He stretches his swollen hand then pats the edge of the bed. "Arms here."

"You're going to tie me down?"

"I'm going to protect you." He opens the first leather cuff. "This or your safe word. Make a decision."

I imagine myself in those restraints, trapped and unable to escape as he belts my ass, kisses it better, and makes me the center of his universe. He's not forcing me. He's empowering me with a choice, an offer to take me somewhere exciting when no one else has ever bothered to care.

I rest my cheek against the mattress and extend my arms above my head.

"Your trust is intoxicating." His hands are suddenly on my face, angling my head as his mouth crashes against mine.

I melt beneath the demand of his lips. This kiss is harder than its predecessors, more hungry and lethal, his tongue looping with mine and his strong jaw scratching my skin in a delicious burn.

He breaks the kiss and returns to the cuffs, connecting them to the straps and locking them around my wrists. His fingers move expertly over the buckles and latches.

How many times has he done this? With how many women?

With my history, I'm in no position to be jealous, but it doesn't stop the clawing ache in my gut.

The touch of his hands pulls me from my thoughts. He's here with *me*, trailing goosebumps across my arms as he secures them in the restraints.

That done, he moves to stand behind me, hands on my hips and tugging my ass against his thighs. The straps strain with the movement, the manacles holding my arms above my head.

But I don't feel trapped or held down. I feel anchored. To him.

The folded belt swings in my periphery right before a new sting inflames the underside of my ass. He teases the welt with feathery touches, and his lips join in, kissing and soothing the lingering pain. Then he swings again.

Thwack, massage, kiss. I don't know how many times he repeats those steps. At some point, I slip into a blissful trance, lost in some floaty place where there's only him and me and the harmony of our breaths.

This is what it's supposed to feel like when two people come together, willingly, wantonly. What would sex be like with him? I can't even fathom it. The emotional connection alone might explode my brain.

He covers my heated backside in caresses and kisses, kindling such a big feeling inside me. The swollen throb between my legs rallies and flares, energizing my nerve-endings and expanding into parts of my body I didn't know existed. Something's coming, something wonderful, but before the sensation reaches a breaking point, he steps back to swing again.

Over and over, he brings me closer to the edge, burning me hotter with need, and teasing me one stroke at a time.

When the hot lashes and affectionate touches stop completely, I moan into the quilt. "You're done?"

His groaning laughter follows him around the bed where he bends to release the cuffs. I'm too limp and weightless to move. But my pussy pulsates with emptiness, clenching and soaked beyond embarrassment.

I don't care. I need...need... "Please."

Climbing onto the bed, he rolls me to my back and straddles my hips. His erection is right there, trying to stab a hole through his pants. But he doesn't free it or look at it.

He weighs enough to crush me, but his quads contract at my sides, bearing his bulk. His gaze lowers to my button-up, and he grips the collar, ripping it open. My nicest blouse. But the look on his face makes me forget why I care.

His lips separate with the force of his breaths, and his eyes drift over me like a vast ocean, heavy and deep, drowning me in wonder.

Men have sat on me like this before, but only during a struggle when my arms are swinging and my hips are bucking. No one has ever straddled me in such a vulnerable position without thrusting and taking. *With his pants still on.*

He takes in the white satin of my mom's bra, the material too small to fully cover my chest. With a groan, he tugs the cups beneath my breasts, exposing them. "If you knew how many times I've imagined these the past couple months, what they would feel like, taste like, how they would look trussed up in rope..."

"I've imagined you, too." I lift my hand to reach for the hard length straining his slacks.

He catches my wrist and lunges forward, his chest on mine and his voice guttural. "If you touch me, it's all over. I'm barely hanging on."

Part of me wants to see what he looks like when he lets go. But I'd rather give in to my curiosity about where he's taking this and let him lead.

With a shaky hand, he traces the outer edge of my breast. His other hand tangles in my hair as he leans in and tastes my lips.

I love the cinnamon flavor of his tongue. It's so unique to him, just one of the thousand things that separates him from all the others. When I'm with him, the bruises inside me tuck themselves away. Or maybe they fade. I can't feel them or the fear they ignite. Why? Because he's viciously protective? Because he's achingly tender even when he's punishing me?

He's a deep well of discovery, and I hope he gives me the time and permission to learn everything about him.

He slides off my hips to lie against my side, facing me. The hand in my hair clenches tighter, and his lips stay with mine, each bite and roll of his tongue delivering an electric shudder up my spine.

His free hand travels down my throat, trails a path between my breasts, over my stomach, and dives between my legs. I gasp against his mouth, my fingers grasping at his shoulder.

The placement of his thumb stuns me, and my clit throbs against the diabolical pressure he rubs against it. He sinks one then two fingers inside me, and I writhe against his hand, my skin hot and exposed beneath his gaze.

I must look ridiculous with my skirt bunched around my waist, and my too-small bra shoved beneath my boobs. But he doesn't seem to care.

He steals glances at my bared breasts, even as his mouth feasts on my lips. I despise my chest, but I love how he stares at me like he appreciates what he sees, like he's never wanted another woman the way he wants me. My body pleases him. *I* please him.

The length of his frame trembles against mine, all sharp edges and contracting muscles. I don't know when he slipped off his shoes, but his socked feet brush against my toes. The shirt and slacks he's still wearing doesn't diminish the heat seeping from him. His intensity smothers me, and his gravely noises shiver my skin. He's a starving, growly man in need, and I want to feed him.

His hand grips my hair, holding my lips against his as our tongues lap and twine together, hot and wet, ravenous and unguarded. His erection grinds against my thigh in maddening circles, and a combustion of sensations lick across my skin, hardening my nipples into painful points.

He tears his mouth away to devour my breasts with a hot tongue. Sucking and laving, he pulls a bud deeper into his mouth as his fingers and thumb continue their wicked assault.

I'm going to explode. I feel it simmering deep in my core, rising faster, hotter, robbing my air. When his lips return to mine, he swallows my moans. His kiss, his scent, the feel of his strength surrounding me... My muscles shake with the overwhelming pleasure of it all.

A tremor skips down his arm, spurring his fingers faster and his hips harder.

"Come, Ivory," he pants against my lips. "Come all over my hand."

My mouth slackens, my chin tilting upward as I reach for it. I fall into his smoldering gaze and feel the expanding pressure, right there, like a brewing storm inside me, collecting and strengthening. But I don't know how to make it happen. "I—I'm trying. I don't know..."

"Get out of your head." He rotates his thumb and trails his tongue across my pliable lips. "Let it all go."

My earlier confessions had been shockingly freeing. It

should've relaxed me enough to do this with him. And I *am* relaxed, but also nervous about what's happening and what it all means.

He shakes with the urgency of his arousal, rubbing himself wildly against my thigh as he fingers me into insanity. With each circle of his thumb and pump of his hand, my release hovers on the ledge, galvanized with determination yet teetering with uncertainty.

"Stop thinking, dammit, and feel me." He drives his cock against my leg, his breath catching in his throat. "Feel how much I want you. How much I want you with me. I'm not finishing without you."

An invisible wall crashes down inside me, and an outpour of quivering, overwhelming heat spills from my spine, detonates through my womb, and shatters every neuron in my body. The shock of it steals my breath, my back bowing against the force of so many new and frenzied sensations.

"Ah God, there you go. So beautiful," he rasps. "So fucking mine." His fingers, hips, and breathy groans work in tandem, shoving me deeper into tingling bliss and shredding his voice. "Fuck, I'm gonna—"

He comes with a strangled shout, his body jerking as he rolls halfway on top of me and captures my mouth in a breathless kiss. His weight slouches against me, and the rocking of his hips ebbs into a lazy roll. His hand slips from between my legs, his chest heaving hard against mine. But his movements are slow, reverently gentle as he cups my jaw and kisses me into a languid, dreamy cosmos.

I died somewhere between my release and his. And now I know how it feels to be alive.

I can't seem to move the muscles in my face to kiss him back. My skin is hot and slippery with perspiration, but who cares? Every inch of me is luxuriously numb, listless, and happy.

He holds my gaze, his eyes wide and mesmerizing as he chokes a jagged sound against my lips. "Now I know why you're illegal."

# EMERIC

I lift Ivory's beautifully exhausted limbs, molding my hands around her flexuous curves and touching more than required to slip the shirt off her arms. "Still with me, sleepy girl?"

Her hooded brown eyes make a sluggish climb over my mouth before meeting my gaze. "Mm."

My smile is so deep, I feel it in my lungs like a nourishing breath. There's no limit to what I would do to put that look on her face every night. But what are *her* limits? What is she willing to gamble? Her education? Her future?

If she's caught in my house, I'm the one at risk. I'm the adult, taking advantage of a student, a victim. While I might end up fighting a legal battle, she would be safe from all blame.

When I pull my head together, I'll figure out a plan. But right now, her safety far outweighs the consequences I might endure.

I remove the rest of her clothes. When I toss the final scrap to the floor, I'm left with a view so fucking tantalizing I couldn't have dreamed it—and hell knows I tried for weeks.

Sprawled in my bed, her nude hourglass figure beckons every masculine nerve, organ, and connective tissue in my body. From her wet mouth and the slackness in her muscles to her abundant chest and flushed clit, she draws me in and holds me in mindless fascination.

She hasn't said a word since she came on my fingers. She seems to be in shock. Or soaring in bliss. Definitely in awe, given the widening of her eyes as she slides a hand between her legs and feels the swollen flesh of her pussy.

Christ almighty, she's innocence wrapped in sin.

The innocent part rattles me the most. Not only have I crossed the line as her teacher, there's a ten-year age difference between us. Add to that her abusive past and the ruthless dominating way I fuck, and we're navigating a land mine. If I move too fast or make the wrong step, the consequences will be devastating.

I run my fingers over hers, brushing the dark curls on her cunt. "Don't shave this."

She glances at our hands and returns to my face. "Why not?"

"I don't want to feel like I'm—" *Touching a little girl.* "You're young, Ivory. I don't need any more reminders."

"I've been with a lot of guys older than you." Her cheeks bloom with heat, and she pulls her hand away. "I shouldn't have said that."

The impulse to demand she never mention other men burns in my throat, but I bite it back. "If you need to talk about it, about *them*, I want to be the person you turn to." I kiss her lips and trail my finger over her pussy. "Okay?"

"Okay." She grips my wrist and squeezes. "Thank you."

I slip off the bed and swat her thigh. "Up."

Ten minutes later, steam drenches the bathroom, fogging my reflection in the mirror as well as the shower door behind me. The splash of water against tiles broadcasts her movements as the woodsy scent of my shampoo infuses my inhales. There's something deeply satisfying about her using my things, smelling like me, and making herself at home in my space.

While she showers, I wash my dick at the sink, both appalled and riveted by the fact that I jizzed in my briefs. I haven't done that since high school. But it shouldn't surprise me. I've been jacking off like a fucking fiend for weeks.

It takes every ounce of restraint I have left to not join her in the shower. I want to fuck her thoroughly, completely, and in every way imaginable, but I have to prove to her I'm not like the others. Every step with her is a risk, and there are still so many unanswered questions.

I clean my knuckles and lather them in antibiotic cream from the supplies beneath the sink. "Are you on birth control?"

Her misty silhouette freezes behind the shower door. "No."

I turn to face her, straining to make out the shape of her body in the curl of steam. "Do you use condoms?"

She presses a palm against the glass door, as if to steady herself. "When I can."

My fist clenches, but the next thing I punch should be my own stupid mouth. Could I be anymore heartless? Of course, she doesn't always use condoms. If a man doesn't stop at *no*, he's certainly not pausing to wrap up.

I manage to hold my temper in, but the rapid-fire of my pulse and the rage scorching up my spine propels me out of the bathroom.

"I'll set out something for you to wear," I shout from the

bedroom. "Meet me in the kitchen."

Tossing one of my t-shirts on the bed for her, I strip my clothes and drag on a pair of flannel pants.

On my way out, I grab my phone and make a call to my dad's clinic. As expected, it goes to voice mail. My bare feet pad down the carpeted stairs and into the kitchen as I tell the recorder who I am and what I require.

I could've called my dad to schedule her appointment, but I don't want to field his questions tonight. Not when I still don't have all the answers.

By the time she emerges in the kitchen doorway, I have two plates of heated linguine carbonara set out on the island.

She hovers on the threshold, her deep brown eyes darting between the food and my bare chest. Her expression creases with every emotion in existence before softening with a smile. "You cooked?"

"My catering service did." I grab two glasses and a pitcher of sweet tea. "The oven warmed it up."

She approaches the island, tugging the mid-thigh shirt down her tanned legs. Her long wet hair soaks the white cotton against her chest, revealing taut nipples and delicate shoulders. I find it impossible to look away. It's as if every fiber of my being is tied to hers, and every movement she makes moves me, pulling me closer, deeper.

I never stood a chance.

"Thank you." She sits on the bar stool, tucking the hem of the shirt between her legs. "This smells incredible."

I settle on the stool beside her, twisting to face her, and stab a fork into the noodles.

Her eyes return to my chest.

I arch a brow. "What?"

She holds a finger in front of me, tapping the air as her concentration travels from my shoulders to my waist.

Is she counting?

Fuck me, my pecs bounce. All she has to do is look at me and my body reacts.

She drops her hand and turns to her dinner, mumbling, "Twelve indentations and ten muscly bumps."

I glance down, trying to make sense of her numbers. I spend two hours a day, seven days a week in my home gym, honing my physique into tiptop shape for the same reason every other guy works out. To get laid. But now I want to hit the weights just to watch her count my muscles again.

She sucks a noodle off her fork, grinning. "You don't look like a teacher."

"You don't look like a student."

Her smile disintegrates.

I wipe a hand down my face, wishing I could call back those words. How many times have her looks attracted the wrong kind of attention? *She attracted me.*

She waves her fork up and down the length of my body. "You'd make more money modeling than teaching."

"Do I look like I need money?"

"Good point." She scans the kitchen, taking in the high-end appliances that never get used. She doesn't ask about the source of my wealth, but I know she's wondering.

I swallow a buttery bite of pasta and twirl more noodles around my fork. "My family holds the patent on the wooden bracings in pianos."

"Wow. Really?"

"Really. So money is not my incentive for working."

"Why work at all? You could live on a yacht, drink rum, and grow a smelly beard." Her eyebrows lift. "Like a pirate."

"A pirate." My lips twitch. "As appealing as that sounds, boredom doesn't suit me." I would lose my fucking mind. "I need challenge and self-earned success, and I find those things playing piano, teaching..." I give her a narrowed look. "And disciplining."

Her eyes flicker. "You're very good at that last one."

"But not the others?"

A sly grin pulls at the corner of her mouth. "I've never heard you play."

"I play every night." Except I won't be able to tonight.

I glance at my throbbing hand with no regrets.

She scrapes a forkful of linguine. "I know this is a big place, but I haven't seen a piano."

"I'll give you a tour another time. Finish your dinner."

She inhales the remainder of the pasta and follows it with gulps of sweet tea.

I finish mine soon after and slide the dish away. "I made a doctor's appointment for you."

Her fork clanks against the plate, her voice quiet. "I don't have insurance or the money to pay for that."

My hand flexes. I want to hurt her mother and every other person who's never been there for her. "It's covered."

"I can't—"

I slam my fist against the counter, rattling the china. "You will go to that appointment and get a full examination, for the sake of your health and for my peace of fucking mind."

Jaw clenched, she pitches me a stubborn glare.

She can scowl all she wants. I'm not finished. "From this point forward, the words *I can't* are no longer in your vocabulary." I angle forward until all she can see is my eyes. "Do I make myself clear?"

"Oh, you're clear." She holds my gaze. "And abrasive and surly. You have a terrible temper."

A playful kind of youth twinkles in her eyes, but there's something else there, too. Her lips separate to allow for the climb in her breaths, and she's not blinking, like she's forcing a mask of toughness and bravery.

Deep down, she's scared. To stand up to me? To disappoint me? To put faith in what's happening between us?

I close the inches between us and kiss her mercilessly on the mouth. Cupping her head in both hands, I work my tongue against hers, fusing us together, licking and biting and flooding her with every last drop of fervor I feel for her. I love her strength in the face of fear, her determination despite all her roadblocks, and fuck me, I love her mouth. The way the hot, wet suction of her lips wraps around my tongue and hardens my cock.

She tips back in the frame of my hands and searches my eyes. We stare at each other, chests heaving, suspended in the energy pulsing between us.

After an endless stretch of heartbeats, she blinks. "I have the money to pay you for the textbooks...but...I can see..." She cringes at the heat rising in my face. "Now is a bad time to bring that up."

I stack the dishes and carry them to the sink. "By tomorrow night, I want a list of your bills and all the things you need." I throw her a hard look over my shoulder. "Things I won't know to buy."

She joins me at the sink, her expression pinched in frustration.

I rinse a plate and hand it to her. "I know you're strong enough and brave enough to stand on your own. Hell, you've been doing it for years." I brush my fingers over her stiff jaw. "But now you have help. I'm here to make your hardships a little less hard. You *will* lean on me."

She stares at the rack in the dishwasher, sets the plate in the wrong way, studies it for a moment, then turns it. "Like this?"

I nod. The realization that she's never loaded a dishwasher makes me appreciate a lot of things in life, putting her at the top of that list.

With a stoic expression, she helps me finish the dishes in silence. I give her the time to think, to weigh her pride against mine. When the cleanup is completed and the counters are wiped down, I turn to her.

She stands just out of arm's reach, her small frame swallowed by the t-shirt as she stares at her bare feet. "The thing I value most doesn't cost a dime, yet it seems to be the hardest for people to give."

Friendship? Protection? Love? My head swims, searching for the answer. "Name it, and it's yours."

Her eyes find mine, and she steps forward. Another step, and her arms encircle my waist. She presses her cheek against my chest, skin-to-skin, and releases a heavy sigh.

A hug. That's the thing she values most.

My ribs tighten as I embrace her, crushing her as close as possible without bruising her soft skin. She's a head shorter, too short to feel her heart pounding against mine. So I catch her beneath her knees and back, swoop her up, and hoist her against my chest.

I flick the light switch with my elbow and head for the stairs.

She snuggles against me, hands snaking over my shoulders and sliding into my hair. Her entire body relaxes in my arms as she nuzzles her face against my cheek, touching, breathing, feeling me. "I should tell you to put me down, but I like this too much."

Good thing, because I'm not letting go.

As we reach the bedroom, she murmurs against my neck. "I need to go home in the morning to get clothes and feed Schubert."

I bite down on my smile. "Do you feed him brains?"

"What?" Her startled expression eases into a glimmering smile. "Not the dead Schubert. My cat."

"We'll swing by your house before school, but you don't need clothes."

I enter the closet and set her on her feet. Stepping back, I lounge against the door jamb and block her exit. When she realizes just how fucking crazy I am, there's no telling how fast she'll run.

She circles the island in the center, rubbing the back of her neck. "Your closet is bigger than my house."

I slide my hands in the pockets of my flannel pants and wait.

Her gaze snags on the far wall, and her hesitant strides carry her toward it. She trails a hand over the long shelf of high-heels, flats, sandals, and tennis shoes. Tilting her head, she stares up at the racks of dresses, shirts, and trousers. The entire wall is hers.

Her shoulder blades tighten, her hands falling to her sides as she speaks with her back to me. "Do you have an alternative lifestyle I don't know about? A fetish with women's clothing?"

"Something like that."

She snatches a beige Louboutin pump from the shelf and checks the size. "How did you—" She sighs, returning it carefully to its place. "The first day, when you slid my shoes back on."

My blood pumps thick and hot in my veins. Separated by the island and the length of the room, I watch her peruse the clothes, anticipating her next words.

"I ca—" She whirls toward me, her eyes shimmering with unshed tears. "I know. No *I can'ts*. No sniveling. No questioning your methods." She hooks an arm around her waist and presses a fist to her mouth, staring at me from beneath her lashes. "It's a lot to take in, but I'm trying." She stands straighter, glancing at the clothes behind her. "It's just...this is all too much, too fast, and—"

"Come here." I remove my hands from my pockets, my posture open, welcoming.

She crosses the room in a vision of dark skin, thin cotton, and allure.

When she reaches me, I lift her and carry her to the bed. "What's mine is yours, Ivory. The sooner you accept that, the easier this will be."

Shifting under the blankets, she stares up at me. "If I don't accept it?"

I slip in beside her, pull her to my chest, and entwine our legs together. "Then you get to endure more of my... What did you call it?" I lean in and kiss her bottom lip. "Abrasive and surly temper."

"There's medication for that."

"You're the only drug I need." Reaching back, I switch off the light and rest my head on her pillow, our faces inches apart.

The illumination of gas lamps and moonlight filters in through the nearby window, blanketing us in pale silence. Her eyes glisten with wonder, worry, and unspoken words, reflecting all the emotions I openly express in mine.

I brush her hair behind her ear. "I don't share. That means no more high school or neighborhood boys. You're in my bed and no one else's."

She opens her mouth.

I tap it with a finger then trace the soft curve of her lips. "I'll protect you from those who don't respond to *no*."

"What about you?" Her leg twitches in the bend of mine, her tone low and suspicious. "Are there other women?"

"You're the only one."

I've turned down every goddamn woman since I met her. First time in my adult life I've gone this long without sex.

Vertical lines form between her brows. "What about your love-hate thing with Joanne?"

"She's complicated. But I haven't seen her in six months."

I haven't told Ivory everything, but I need to make a decision about that mess before I expose her to it. And there's a second secret I've kept from her, a more urgent one that I need to address now. "I have something to tell you about

Prescott Rivard."

Her gaze shatters into rippling pools of brown. "Will he get you fired? Or press charges?"

"I scared him enough to keep him silent for a while, but that fear will eventually sour and grow resentful. Then...I don't know."

"I'll go to the cops and explain what happened."

"No, you will not." I hook an arm around her back, preparing for her to jerk away. "I promised his mother a spot for him at Leopold."

A frozen moment passes before she tenses against my hold. "How? Why?"

"She gave me a career at Le Moyne in exchange for my connections. To get Prescott into Leopold."

"Connections? Leopold admits their students on talent alone."

"My mother holds a seat on the Board of Trustees. She'll slide him through without a formal audition."

She studies my expression, curling her hand against her chest between us. "This affects my chances, doesn't it?"

"If I refer you, their recruiters will come. They'll attend a school-wide performance and..."

Her breath hiccups in her throat. "They'll see Prescott play and potentially reject his application."

"And accept yours instead." I comb a hand through her hair and rest my lips against her forehead. "You have more talent than anyone at Le Moyne, but if I ask my mother to sneak two applications through—"

"No way." She yanks her head back. "*When* I'm accepted into Leopold, it will be on merit and talent alone."

I cuddle her against me as pain pounds behind my breastbone. I can't bear the thought of fucking her over. "I'll make this right."

"How? You took that deal for a reason, right? Because of Shreveport?"

"Yes, but I can get an out-of-state job." I tilt her chin up and kiss her, smiling against her lips. "Or I can become a pirate."

After the shit with Prescott tonight, however, my resignation brings new complications for Ivory.

She caresses my jaw. "The dean will just replace you with another deal. She hired you under wrongful terms and wiped Mrs. McCracken's recommendations from my file, so clearly, she's on a devil's mission. Why does she want her son to go there so badly?"

"It's the best school with the wealthiest endowments. Prescott's admittance is her shoe in to elevate Le Moyne's power and status. Or who knows? Maybe she aspires to sit on the board there someday."

She nods, her face furrowed in contemplation. "If you quit, Prescott won't have enough incentive to keep his mouth shut about me. After tonight, he can give his mother all the leverage she needs to get rid of me."

Exactly where my head is at. Just like that, I know with absolute certainty I won't leave Le Moyne or Ivory. I'm smarter and meaner than Beverly Rivard, and I have a few months to decide the method and level of cruelty I'll use to beat her.

"I understand why you did it. Why you took that deal." Ivory trails her fingers across my chest, watching the movement. "Even after what Joanne did, it's hard to let go. To move away."

My breath catches at the accuracy of her statement. She's right, but she doesn't know the real problem, the one I'm working to resolve with Joanne. And my feelings for Joanne? Those have dulled enough that they no longer drive my actions.

Ivory's eyelids flutter heavily, her limbs slackening around me, as she mutters under her breath, "Everything is possible."

"Such as?"

"I'm going to Leopold."

Her stubbornness is inconvenient. And painfully admirable. Unfortunately, I have no idea what I'm going to do about it.

I hate to postpone her sleep, but there's one more thing I need to know. "Where is your brother's friend?"

Her eyes flash open, and her voice catches in her throat. "What?"

"Did he disappear after he raped you? Or is he still around?"

Her complexion turns bloodless in the dim light, her cheekbones pressing against her tightening skin.

Everything inside me goes still, strangling my throat and thickening my voice. "Tell me."

She throws back the covers, rolls on top of me, and rests her forehead against mine. "No more punching tonight."

I grip her firm ass beneath the shirt and try to focus my energy on her body and not what's been done to her body. "When was the last time he touched you?"

She drops her knees to my sides, straddling me, as she

holds my face in her hands. "He hasn't raped me since August."

*August?* I jackknife to a sitting position, my vision blurred by red fog. "This *past* August, as in two months ago?"

She clings to my chest, holding on to my head as she mashes her mouth against mine. The moment her tongue seeks entry, I kiss her back, angrily, possessively, tangling my hand in her hair and yanking her hips against mine.

I bite her lip. "His name."

She rocks her pussy against my cock, thrusting her tongue and, goddammit, distracting me.

I rip my mouth away. "His name."

She slumps, her whisper hollow. "Lorenzo Gandara."

Latino? The same motherfucker lurking around her house that night?

"Does he ride an orange sportbike?"

Her fingernails dig into the back of my neck. "How do you know that?"

# IVORY

"Go to sleep."

That's the only response Emeric gives to my endless questions about Lorenzo. Eventually, my worries dissolve beneath the weight of fatigue.

I tuck close against the rigid wall of his chest, sheltered by the bulk of his arm around my back, and guarded by his vigilant gaze. I fall fast into sleep, lost in a great timeless space where forever isn't long enough.

I've never felt this weightless, like a strange airy sensation has replaced my bones and skin, and there's nothing left but my breath. Soft, floaty breaths of ether. Each exhale forms a cloud that joins the others drifting around me in a vast blue sky.

I'm dreaming. I try to hold onto the enchantment. It's so safe and gentle here I don't want to leave. *Don't wake up.*

I blink against flashes of sapphire haloed by lamp light.

"Good morning." Emeric's blue eyes fill my horizon, so deep and majestic, glimmering with all the colors and stars of heaven.

I stretch my arms over my head, delighting in the softness of his bed. "I'm dreaming."

He stands over me, biceps bunching as he plants his hands

on the edge of the mattress. "Still dreaming?"

"Well...I was in heaven." I reach up and caress the day-old scruff on his jaw. "Until the devil showed up."

His lips crook up in a territorial grin, his complexion rosier than usual. His skin is damp beneath my fingers, his hair dark and drippy against his forehead.

"You already showered?" I drag my focus from his face, down his wet t-shirt, and pause on the gym shorts. "Oh. You worked out. What time is it?"

I shift to my side and find the clock on the nightstand. *5:15 AM.* School doesn't start for two hours.

He straightens, rolling his shoulders. "How long do you need to get ready?"

I sit up, the room wobbling around me as I recall the conversation we didn't finish last night. "Depends. You haven't told me how you know Lorenzo."

"He's no longer your concern." He turns toward the bathroom.

"You can't just go beat him up." I slide off the bed and adjust the shirt over my thighs. "He's an ex-Marine, a thug, maybe even a criminal. And you're a—"

He shoots me a scalding glare that shrivels the rest of my words in my throat. His fist opens and closes at his side, his lacerated knuckles glowing red. Okay, maybe he could get a few punches in, but...

"It's too risky." I slump on the edge of the mattress, trembling against the idea of him fighting another one of my monsters.

Lorenzo rarely comes to my house without Shane, so it would be them against my teacher. Nothing good would come from that.

I meet his eyes. "The cops might get called. You could go to jail. Or worse, if you keep hitting stuff, you could break your hands and lose your ability to play piano."

He strides back to me, his expression marbleized with shadowy lines of intensity. "Despite what you've seen, I usually don't confront problems with my fists." He raises one of those fists and strokes it across my jaw. "I prefer subtle and deceptive planning. Lorenzo Gandara won't see me coming."

Okaaay. So he's going to...what? Go ninja on his ass?

He returns to the bathroom, his voice rumbling over his shoulder. "I'm taking a shower. Then the bathroom is yours."

The door shuts behind him, followed by the hollow click of the lock.

I flop back on the bed, the shirt lifting to my waist and exposing me to the cool air. I don't know what he did with my panties. I don't even care. He's seen me naked and put his fingers inside me. Yet all he's let me see is his bare chest.

Why did he lock the door? What is he hiding? My pulse elevates as ridiculous theories fill my head. Is his dick malformed? Or maybe he doesn't want me near it until the doctor checks me for diseases?

My emotions overflow, but the sharpest feeling is the one deep in my core. Just thinking about him naked sends a quiver up my thighs and a jolt between my legs.

Sensations that have never been there before surge like a fever. I feel so damn hot and needy. *For my teacher.*

It's wrong. Being here is wrong. Sliding my hand over my pussy feels wrong, too, but I do it anyway, stroking the way he stroked, dipping and circling exactly how he did it. My fingers are his fingers, caressing, giving, and building that wonderful energy inside me.

Soon, my body takes over, my hand moving the way *I* want it to move, coaxing shivers across my skin and producing an unimaginable amount of wet heat beneath my touch.

My legs fall open, and my head tips back, my neck stretching as I rub my clit and sink two fingers inside, out and up, down and back in.

He's right behind that door, lathering soap along his shaft, stroking it, caring for it. God bless it, I want to do that. I bet his nude body is a legendary sight to behold.

The pressure inside me snaps, cutting my air as pleasure rolls over me in warm electric waves. I shudder and jerk, gasping with throaty groans. Holy hell, maybe I can do that again. After I catch my breath. How many of those can I have back-to-back?

I glide my fingers into my slick opening. Maybe just one more before he—

It's too quiet. Is the shower off?

The bathroom door swings open, and he steps out in a fog of steam.

I yank my hand away and shove the shirt down.

He grips the towel at his waist as his arctic eyes lock on mine.

Neither of us breathes. Or moves.

He knows.

"You touched yourself."

My face heats to nuclear levels.

He clutches the door frame, squeezing so hard the wood creaks. His eyes cloud with pain, harden with resolve, then he jerks backward and slams the door between us.

I groan, embarrassed beyond belief.

A thump hits the wood on the other side. The lock clicks, followed by the sound of the shower turning back on.

What the hell just happened? What should I do? As soon as he comes out, I'll have to face him.

Dammit, I refuse to be ashamed about this.

Darting across the room, I knock on the door. "Emeric?"

"Five minutes!" His muffled shout sounds too close to be in the shower.

"Are you mad?"

"No, Ivory," he grunts.

"Then what?"

He makes a deep growly noise. "Fuck, you're killing me here."

I back away from the door and sit on the bed. He hasn't tried to have sex with me, but all his kissing and touching and staring tells me he wants to. Given my unsavory sex life, I can guess why he won't.

One thing I can depend on, though, is his directness. So rather than making myself sick over assumptions, I wander toward the lunacy that's in his closet.

Clothes and shoes line a wall that's three times longer than my height. The quality of the fabrics and seams is unlike anything I've ever touched. I open the built-in drawers along the side and find heaps of lace, satin, and oh my God, leather lingerie. The tags have been removed, but everything looks new and exactly my size. I mold the cups of a red lacy bra around my boobs. Perfect fit. How the hell does he know my bra size?

Five minutes later, the bathroom door opens. I slip out of the closet, still wearing his t-shirt, and return to the bed to sit on the edge.

His black hair is partially dry, and the earlier tension in his muscles is gone. My attention falls to the bulge beneath his towel. It's not tenting. I bet he touched himself, but why behind a closed door with the shower running? Emeric Marceaux does not get embarrassed.

He sits beside me on the bed, drops his bruised hand in my lap, and loops our fingers together. "To clarify my earlier reaction... I do not, in any way, object to you masturbating."

Just hearing him say that naughty word sparks a firestorm inside me. "That's good, because I'm definitely doing it again." I lift a daring brow. "Whether you approve or not."

"Killing me," he mutters beneath his breath.

"Why?" Why not just touch me instead?

He pulls our laced hands between his spread knees and braces our elbows on the towel covering his thighs. "I love that you want to pleasure yourself." He slides me a sexy grin. "I love it a little too much."

"I hear a *but* coming."

"But..." He flashes me another heart-racing smile. "I won't show you how much I *really* love it until you're ready."

"You won't show me your erection, you mean?"

He closes his eyes. "I'm not a gentle lover, Ivory." He looks up, and his gaze lands on my lips. "I'm confident that, with time, you'll discover you don't want gentle. Until then, I'll wait."

"Behind a locked door?"

He nods.

I nibble my lip. "With an erection?"

The corner of his mouth bounces.

I glance at the outline of his cock beneath the towel. "You made yourself come?"

The potency of his stare riles my nerves as he rubs a hand over his jaw, rubbing, glaring hard, rubbing harder.

I really shouldn't poke the beast, but... *Deep breath. Strong voice.* "Next time you jerk off, I want to watch."

His inhale cuts off right before he launches. His chest collides with mine, hurdling me backward against the mattress. An *oomph* escapes my lips, but his mouth is there, devouring my voice, my air, and my sanity.

The weight of his body sinks mine into the bedding, his strength contracting around me as his hand slides up my ribs, taking the shirt with it. My fingers latch onto his hair, curling through the damp strands as he kisses me with firm lips and a devastatingly urgent tongue.

Held down by his size, my mouth controlled by his, I close my eyes and simply enjoy his feral affection. He catches my nipple and gives it a painful tug. When I gasp, he groans. I rock my hips, and he grinds his, pinning me to the bed and pressing his hard length against my core. A little more of that and his towel will fall off. Maybe I could help it along?

I reach behind him and glide a hand down the flexing ridges of his back. When my fingers bump the towel, I slip beneath it and meet the rise of hard firm muscle. My God, how can a man's ass be so irresistible? I want to feel it with both hands, but his body's too long to get a good grasp. I stretch my arms, reaching—

He grabs my throat and squeezes. The force of his grip

shoves my chin up, and my hands lose precious inches on his backside.

The angle of my mouth gives him deeper access, his tongue curling around mine and his wet exhales heating my face. "I'm a raging fucking animal around you."

I want to tell him to use me in whatever manner feeds his hunger, but as his fingers clench tighter around my throat, it's too much. My lungs burn for oxygen, and black spots invade my vision. Panic rises, my jaw working against his. Not kissing. *Fighting.*

I can't breathe. My hands flail against his back, my body bucking to escape. *Let go. Let go.*

The fist around my throat disappears, followed by his weight. I clutch my neck and wheeze for air as fear ices my veins and tears blur my eyes.

He stands beside the bed, righting the towel over the hard, jutting length I've yet to see.

Raking a hand through his hair, he glares down at me. "You're not ready."

I let go of my aching throat and sit up, shaking against a full-body tremor. "Ready for what? Sex?"

"For me!" He strides to the dresser and pulls out checkered socks and black briefs. "Keep that in mind the next time you ask to watch me jack off."

My stomach sinks. "I don't understand. Why did you strangle me? To scare me?"

If so, it worked. My heart is still pounding.

"To show you." He crosses the room, stops at the foot of the bed, and scowls at his erection beneath the towel. Then his gaze bores into mine. "I get off on watching your body bow in anguish, on knowing I put those tears in your eyes. But only when you give me that pleasure freely and with absolute trust."

Did I give it freely? Did I even have a choice? "If you care about me, why can't we do this without...tears?"

His rumpled black hair and thick eyelashes give him a softer look, but the sharpness in his blue eyes reminds me that if there's any gentleness inside him, it's easily choked by his meteoric temper.

He glances at the clock and looks back at me. "I have a deep sexual need to push a woman beyond her comfort zone. When you're ready to let me take you there, you'll fight every instinct in your body, but I promise...the result is far more fulfilling than an orgasm."

What could be better than an orgasm? Is it something deeper, like that warm feeling that fills my chest when I know he's enjoying me? Giving him pleasure heightens mine to euphoric levels. So yeah, maybe there's more to intimacy than just lying on my back while he ruts on top of me. But I have no idea what it could be.

I swallow. I don't know how I feel about the choking. Does it go beyond my comfort zone? What will he try next? "Why do you want to push me like that?"

"It's the ultimate trust, and the power in that is unparalleled."

Despite the unease gurgling inside me, I manage to keep my voice steady. "I don't want anyone to have power over—"

"No, Ivory. You're the one with the power. *You* set the limits and decide when it stops." He frowns down at me as a twitch skates across his hairless chest. "You didn't use your safe word."

Fuck, I forgot. "I couldn't talk with your hand—"

"Bullshit. You didn't try."

I adjust the shirt over my thighs. "That's the lesson, isn't it?"

"Yes." Without another word, he steps inside the closet, leaving me in a flushed heap of turmoil.

A few minutes later, he emerges fully clothed and tells me to come to the kitchen when I'm ready to go.

The purpose of his lesson consumes me as I shower, brush my hair and teeth, and dress alone in his bedroom. I know my perceptions of sex and men are jaded, but the pressure of his hand on my throat was nothing compared to the past four years of pain and fear. Doesn't make his methods acceptable, but the shockingly harsh way he does things might actually be effective.

The next time he makes me uncomfortable, I'm positive I'll be thinking about that safe word. And he'll heed it. Since I've known him, he hasn't taken a single thing I wasn't willing to give. My God, there *is* power in that. Knowing he'll stop when I say the word makes me feel taller, steadier...lighter.

I tread down the stairs in the soft leather of new shoes. The adorable flats have little silver spikes and black mesh around the toes. They add a trendy touch to the red woven dress. The three-quarter sleeves will keep me warm in the autumn evenings. The straight hem goes past my knees, and the bodice has this cool sash that crisscrosses from back to front and ties at my waist.

The whole outfit makes me feel elegant and...cherished. A niggling voice in my head reminds me that I didn't earn these clothes. Except Emeric gave them to me under the very clear understanding that I belong to him and, in turn, everything he possesses is mine. Hard to wrap my mind around that. But for now, I'll wear the clothes because his gift means more to me than my damnable pride.

I find him sitting at the island in the kitchen, picking through a plate of pastries topped with eggs, cheese, and bacon. His attention jumps to me, and he freezes. Only his eyes move, heating beneath dark brows as he makes an unhurried tour up and down my body.

It's obvious he bought these clothes because my current wardrobe is lacking. But when he continues his head-to-toe perusal, I realize he went shopping because he was thinking about me, maybe imagining how I would look dressed in the things he likes.

On the final pass, his rock-hard facial features soften with satisfaction. Something inside me catches and holds. I put that look on his face by accepting his gift. I don't know what it is, but knowing I please him meshes so well with all the new feelings he stirs in me.

He meets my eyes. "Luckiest dress on the planet."

My heart trundles into a cadenza of heavy beats. "Can't believe how well it fits."

He glances at my lips. "Sit down and eat."

His brown paisley necktie, off-white button-up, and brown slacks would look old-fashioned on another man. But on him, it's a statement in designer metro-sexy. Hell, he could wear a popped collar and bedazzled cutoffs, and women would drop their panties as he walks by.

The robust scent of coffee swirls around me as I sit beside

him. "No waistcoat today?"

"Jacket weather."

I glance at the brown suede jacket draped over the back of his seat. The long sleeves might help hide the cuts on his knuckles.

He loads up my plate, pours my juice, and rests a hand on my thigh. I haven't been cared for this way since my dad was alive. Sitting here in nice clothes, putting food in my belly, I study him as a fatherless girl would her protector, as a student with her teacher, but more than that, I look at him as a woman opening her heart to a man.

He fills so many voids in my life, and my desire for him only knits me closer, tighter to a world I've only dreamed about. A world where I interact with a man because I want to, because he cares about me as much as I care about him.

Except he says I'm not ready.

Before I met him, gentleness was all I wanted, but now?

When I began formal musical studies, I gained an acute appreciation for Bach's kickass usage of counterpoint. Those who don't know how to listen to his music only hear a mess of noisy lines. But what he composed was multiple melodies, with each hand playing a different version of the same song.

Emeric applies counterpoint in everything he does. With one hand, he taps with tenderness and self-control while his other bangs with intensity and dominance. His methods may be contradictory, but he executes them in perfect harmony.

I set down the fork and grip his fingers on my thigh. "How will I know when I'm ready?"

He lifts my hand and presses a kiss on my palm. "*I* will know."

I search his face, lingering on his sculptured lips, freshly-shaved jaw, and ultramarine eyes. "Then what?"

Promises dance like sinister notes in his gaze. "Then you'll be grateful for that safe word."

A shiver licks my spine, and an ache flares between my legs. I want what he's offering as much as I don't want it. Or maybe I want to *not* want it.

I rub the back of my neck then dig into breakfast.

He scrapes his plate clean and pushes it away. "When you're not at school or here, you won't leave my side."

I choke, mumbling around the cheesy bite. "How does that work?"

"Don't talk with your mouth full."

Chewing quickly, I swallow. "When I go home—"

"You live with me now."

I stiffen as his words penetrate my eardrums. I hear them, but their meaning isn't syncing with my brain.

He sips his coffee, glances at his phone, and looks up at me like he told me to come for dinner, not fucking *move in*.

I stare at him with my mouth hanging open. "You're fucking with me."

Lifting his mug to his lips, he stares right back, not a hint of a smile in his eyes.

He's serious.

Did I miss an entire conversation where he asked me to move in? Oh wait. He doesn't *ask* for anything.

I slouch against the back of the stool. "This is because of Lorenzo."

"It's a convenient reason." He refills his mug with the carafe on the island and returns to his phone.

Damn his anti-*I can't* rule, because I want to scream those words repeatedly. "It's against the law. You're my teacher!"

"You're my girl." He lazily swipes the screen on his phone. "That's the only law you need to worry about."

What? My head hammers. "You're insane."

"You're mine."

"What if someone finds out?"

He scrolls through his email, not a care in the world. "My problem."

"But Schubert—"

He drops the phone and crashes his lips against mine with a kiss that says *Shut up and trust me*. Then he leans back and returns to his email. "We're picking up the cat after school."

# EMERIC

Three lots away from Ivory's house, I idle the GTO on the street while she feeds the cat. The orange motorcycle isn't here, but I don't know if anyone else is home.

If I had a legal explanation for arriving with her at six-thirty in the morning, I'd be in that house with her right now. Instead, I'm forced to monitor her from afar, through the connection between our phones, ready to do whatever is needed to be her anchor point of protection.

The first light of dawn illuminates the patchy shingles on the surrounding homes. I hold my phone in a tight grip, hating that I can't see her moving around inside. But I hear her through the speaker. Every rasp of her breath through the ear piece draws my own.

Before we left my house, I gave her the phone I bought for her weeks ago. She cradled it in her hands as if it were the priceless Vieuxtemps violin, her pale expression suffused with reluctant acceptance. I look forward to her reaction when I give her a car.

"Is your mom or brother there?" I ask though the phone.

"Both," she whispers. "Asleep."

If I hear a gasp or a single troubling sound, I'll be on that doorstep in under ten seconds.

I flex my hand on the steering wheel, the bruised knuckles peering out from beneath the overlong sleeve. Ivory probably knows the real reason I'm wearing the jacket is to hide the cuts. I don't want her worrying about what people assume or don't assume. That's *my* job.

As I focus on the rustle of her movements through the phone, my mind wanders back to the bedroom this morning and the erotic way her neck felt in the collar of my grip. She trusts me, yet she panicked, fighting with her body and begging me with her eyes, just as she would with any other man. That's unacceptable.

Asphyxiation, whipping, deriving pleasure from any kind of pain and humiliation isn't for the faint of heart. If I had any doubt about what arouses her, my approach would be different. If she were too timid to hold my gaze, she probably wouldn't have caught my eye in the first place.

If she was anyone else, I wouldn't be sitting here, one-hundred-percent invested and risking my neck to be with her.

Ivory Westbrook isn't fragile. She's built for my brand of protection and appetite for dominance. Treating her with kid gloves would do a great disservice to her.

Her emotional strength is one of the many reasons I'm so wildly attracted to her. Yes, she's the most beautiful creature I've ever seen, but I'm spellbound by the entire package. She stands up to me when she thinks I'm wrong, yet grows wet beneath the force of my voice and the heat of my belt. I bet my grandfather's Fazioli that normal monotonous sex with an unassertive man would stifle her.

Whether those qualities stem from her submissive nature or her abusive past, it's my responsibility as her first real sexual partner to make her aware of the many facets of pleasure. Sex doesn't have to conform to society's standards to be sane. It doesn't have to be slow and tender to be safe. And it doesn't have to be free of leather cuffs to be consensual.

She's learning, but how aware is aware enough? This is the hard part.

I want her, and that need is an endless throbbing beat inside me, like an unwritten song banging against my ribcage to get out. Moving her into my home and sleeping beside her while *not* fucking her is pure torture. But I know she's aware of my restraint, and I also know how much she appreciates and respects it.

The fact that I ache to truss her up, sink my teeth into her tits, and strangle her gasps isn't the issue. The very circumstance of her abuse combined with my role as her teacher makes even the gentlest intimacy with her tricky. I could coax her legs open with eloquent words, fuck her sweetly, and she'd let it happen because it's the only way she knows how to respond to a man.

Well, fuck that. Before I enter her body, she'll be with me mentally and emotionally, on her terms, making a conscious choice between stopping me or surrendering to me. Unlike this morning when my hand was around her throat. She neither yielded nor used her safe word. Because she doesn't yet understand what it really means to be willing.

A few minutes later, she returns to the car and latches the seat belt.

I hit the gas, taking in her relaxed posture in the edge of my periphery. "They didn't wake up?"

"Nope." A soft smile touches her lips. "Schubert misses me." She turns in the seat to face me. "Emeric, we need to talk—"

"If this is about moving in, it's non-negotiable."

"I have a say in where I live."

"Not when it comes to your safety." I veer onto Rampart Street and head toward Le Moyne. "With Shane and Lorenzo in that house, I don't need to tell you how un-fucking-safe it is to live there."

She purses her lips into a frown.

I rest my hand on her thigh. "Stop fighting this."

"I'm your student. If someone figures out I'm living with—"

"*I* will be arrested, and you will be free and clear of any consequences."

"Exactly. I don't want that!"

"The risk is *mine*." I infuse my voice with authority, a tone that reminds her I'm the solution for her situation simply because I'm in charge, in control, and it is my purpose, above all else, to keep her safe. "This is *my* decision, and you will not question me about it again."

As I slow at a stoplight, she unlatches her seat belt and leans over the console.

Her hand makes a familiar sweep through my hair, her eyes smiling up at me. "You're sort of charming when you get all serious and bossy." She lowers her chin and deepens her voice. "Like *I'm the man, laying down the law, and this is how it's going to be.*"

Cute. I shake my head, fighting back a grin.

She tightens her fingers against my scalp and moves her mouth a hair's width away. "But I have my own mind and voice, and you're going to hear it whenever and however *I* want."

I stare at her lips, amused and aroused. "I expect nothing less, Miss Westbrook."

Just as she expects me to shut her down when she questions me.

"Good." A glimmer flickers in her gaze. "You should also expect that I won't be giving up on Leopold."

Of course, she won't, which means I need to figure out how to make it work.

She slides her fingers to my jaw, cupping my face as she kisses me. No one from Le Moyne would venture into this part of town, so passing motorists can gawk all they want.

I lick her lips and press forward to join our tongues. Just a nuzzling stroke, a suggestive movement, but that's all it takes. She moans, angling her head for a deeper connection, her chest shifting closer, heaving for air. Christ, her desire is as staggering as my own.

The traffic light is going to change any second. I don't give a shit. I take over the kiss, gripping her hips and wrenching us together against the console. With my foot firmly pressed on the brake, I give her a thorough teasing with my tongue, stabbing and lashing between her lips, as my hand shifts lower to grab her ass in a bruising grip.

A honk sounds behind us. We pull apart, laughing through heavy breaths like school kids.

I propel the car forward, my attention darting between her and the road. "Every time I see you today, I'm going to think about that kiss."

She tucks her hair behind her ear and gives me a sultry

look. "Me, too."

As blocks of buildings blur by, we settle into a vibrating nexus, a wordless bond strengthened with an exchange of lingering glances and smiles. It's such a comfortable thing, this energy between us, like we're in our own private world, where past mistakes, college dreams, and student-teacher laws don't exist. Here, in this secluded suspension of time and space, nothing can break us apart.

I weave our fingers together in her lap. "Tell me what you're thinking."

She rolls her tongue against the inside of her cheek. "It's weird sitting in your car, dressed in nice clothes, feeling stuffed from a huge breakfast. My stomach's happy." She closes her eyes then opens them, locking on mine. "I'm happy. And scared. I guess I'm scared a lot, but happiness... That doesn't come around very often, and I'm so afraid to lose it."

She's probably thinking of her father and the security she lost when he died.

I want to command her to leave all the worrying to me, but it doesn't work that way, so I offer her a different perspective. "When we're together, Ivory, when it's just you and me like this, happiness can only be limited by us. We make the rules and decide how this is going to go. *Our* world is as boundless and real as our feelings for each other."

She lifts my hand and places a kiss on my fingers. "Thank you."

"For?"

"For always knowing what to say." She holds my hand beneath her chin. "For feeding me. For letting me feed Schubert. For the phone, the clothes, and—"

"You're welcome."

I swear her heart is wrapped around mine, stretching and purring and rubbing against the walls of my chest. It's exhilarating and terrifying, the way she sneaked inside me so swiftly.

A few blocks from school, I pull over on a quiet side street. "I'm not happy about this."

She opens the door and tosses me an easy smile. "I walk to school every day."

"I don't like the secrecy."

Been there, did this dance with Joanne. Ivory deserves better.

But if I'm caught, she goes back to Treme, Lorenzo Gandara, and financial desperation. I'm the one responsible for protecting her *everything*.

I grip the back of her neck and pull her in for a kiss. "It won't always be this way."

When she graduates, I won't be her teacher. Our relationship will be legal and... She'll go to college, wherever that may be. Then what? Will I follow her? Will she want me to? She won't have a fucking choice.

She rests her forehead against mine. "Don't make promises you can't keep."

My face inflames as conviction hardens my gut. "I'll do whatever—"

She presses her soft lips against mine and instantly abates my rising temper, kissing me until my dick swells.

Too soon, she pulls back. "We can discuss the future after I absorb everything that's happening right now."

With that, she slips out of the car, her killer body, fuckable ass, and long legs all back lit by the sun. Fucking stunning.

Shouldering her new satchel, she bends down to poke her head in. The neckline of her red dress drops open, giving me an unholy view of her firm young tits heaving against the red silk bra.

She catches me staring and raises an eyebrow.

How can I not look? It's genetic programming, and Ivory has great fucking tits.

One corner of her mouth lifts in a seductive smirk. "See you in class, Mr. Marceaux."

She walks away, leaving me with no fucking oxygen in the car. I roll down the window and rev the engine a few times to get her attention.

Glancing over her shoulder, she tucks her grin between nibbling teeth. "Are you trying to race me or impress me?"

I just wanted to see her smile one more time. Now I can breathe again.

# EMERIC

I spend the day listening for whispers and paying close attention to subtle expressions. Beverly Rivard greets me in the faculty lounge wearing a tight-lipped scowl of disdain. Nothing new there. Andrea Augustin watches me from a distance, wary and bruised. She'll get over it. Prescott stays out of my way in the halls and slinks in his seat during class. He's the one who concerns me the most. I humiliated him in front of Ivory last night, a horrendous blow to his boy ego. But if he opens his mouth, he has more to lose than his dignity.

In the classroom, Ivory maintains her demeanor as a student. She doesn't hold my gaze too long. Doesn't flirt or show affection. But the sexual tension between us hovers like an electric storm. If someone knew what to look for, they'd pick up on it. Prescott should have some inkling after the way I defended her, but he doesn't dare look at her or me. For now, all I can do is keep him under my scrutinizing watch.

After Ivory's private lessons, we return to her house. The starless sky and absence of light casts her street in a smudge of shadows.

Tucking the GTO into the same spot I used this morning, I take in the blackness beyond her windows. "No one's home."

"Guess not." She opens the car door. "I'll be quick."

I turn off the engine and join her on the street.

She shakes her head and points back at the car. "Stay here. Someone might come home."

It's risky, but she's not going into a dark house alone at night. Nor is she going to carry out a cat and all her belongings by herself. But in case her brother shows up, I need to prepare her for an unpleasant reintroduction.

I grab her hand and lead her to the front porch. "I met Shane a while back."

"What?" She stops on the sidewalk and stares up at me with wide eyes. "When?"

I pull on her squeezing fingers, forcing her feet to follow me up the stairs. "He doesn't know who I am, and sadly, he doesn't know why I broke his nose."

She gasps, her steps faltering, but I keep her moving.

"That was you?" Her brow draws down as she unlocks the door. A sigh billows past her lips. "Because of the cut on my lip."

"No one hurts my girl."

"I love when you say that," she whispers softly.

With gentle hands, she straightens my tie, her fingers drifting down the silk before she turns away.

When she opens the door, the scent of stale cigarette smoke floods my nose.

A second later, an orange tabby races out of the dark depths and slows at her feet, purring like a motor and rubbing against her ankles.

She scoops him up, nuzzling his round head against her neck like he's the most vital thing in the world.

I tuck my hands in my pockets and try to restrain my jealousy over a damn cat. "Are you going to let me in sometime tonight?"

"So impatient." She flicks the wall switch and floods the small room with light. Then she holds the cat out to me and drops him in my arms, forcing me to take him. "I just need to grab his stuff."

As she races through the line of doorways toward the back of the house, the fur ball in my hands sheds no less than a thousand orange hairs all over my suede jacket.

I step inside, glaring down at him. "Are you going to piss on my rugs?"

Round gold eyes blink lazily. Then he drags his hairy cheek across my chest, burrowing in.

I've never lived with a pet, but he seems friendly enough. The shedding, though...

"Can we shave this thing?" I shout toward the back room.

The creak of her footsteps pauses. "I thought you didn't like shaved pussies."

A grin stretches my face. *Touché, my beautiful girl.*

I carry Schubert through a tidy living room. It's clean because there's not a damn thing here but a cardboard box of clothes in the corner, a small end table, and a couch with sagging cushions. Continuing toward the back, I pass a bedroom, then another bedroom, both barely big enough to accommodate the mattresses on the floor and the mess of laundry and ashtrays.

Neither bedroom offers a hint of the girl I know. Ivory is organized, her clothes are simple and few, and she doesn't smoke. Realization tightens my chest and quickens my steps.

I reach the last room, the kitchen, and find her lifting a pan of litter by the back door. "Where do you sleep?"

She grabs a few cans of cat food from the cluttered counter and walks past me into the closest bedroom. "This is my mom's room."

I trail behind her, stroking the cat and stirring up more loose hairs. My heart slams against my chest as I absorb the impoverished conditions she's lived in. When she reaches the second bedroom, I know what she's going to say, and I don't want to hear it.

"Shane's room." She stares blankly at the piles of dirty clothes. "It used to be mine, but when my dad died, Shane moved back in. So..."

She continues forward, returning to the front room. My stomach caves in as I glare at the droopy sofa with new eyes.

"This is where I sleep." She looks up at me expectedly. "Ready to go?"

I swallow down my anger with the reminder that she will never sleep on a goddamn couch again.

"That's all you're bringing?" I nod at the litter pan and cans of chow in her arms.

Her eyes lower to the cat purring against my chest, and she smiles warmly. "He's all I have left here."

As I drive out of her neighborhood, the tension in my muscles loosens with each block I put between her and that house. I've never felt more right about a decision than I do about this one.

With the cat crouched and mewing in the back seat, there's only one thing left that will bring her back to Treme.

I make an unplanned stop, pulling up to the curb along the

barred windows of the store.

She twists in the seat and searches my face. "What are we doing here?"

"The old man hasn't seen you in a couple days. Go in there, give him your phone number, and tell him you're safe."

That wins me a huge smile before she leaps out and dashes inside.

An hour later, while dining in my kitchen over a spread of catered quesadillas, Ivory gives me her written list of bills. Just like I specified, it includes items she needs to buy, such as miscellaneous school supplies, deodorant, and tampons. I grin when I see birth control on the list.

She tries to tell me what I will and won't do with her bills, but I shut her up with my lips fused to hers and my fingers in her cunt. Her back bows over the kitchen island, our empty plates rattling with the thrust of my hand. Two orgasms later, she stumbles into the living room to work on her homework, argument forgotten.

My bruised knuckles are still too tender to play piano, so I run on my treadmill, shower, and jack off to memories of her head tilted back, throat exposed, legs spread, writhing and vulnerable in my arms. Vulnerable to all the dirty, depraved things I fantasize about doing to every hole in her body. Christ, if she only knew what I have planned for her.

Before exiting the shower, I rub out another orgasm because fucking hell, I'll be sleeping beside her tonight.

I tell myself she's not ready for the kinky, savage way I fuck, but in the back of my mind, there's an expiration date on my self-control. A date that's attached to her doctor's appointment on Saturday—only four days away. I have this strong coiling need to be with her without anything between us, including condoms. Once her test results confirm I can do that, all bets are off.

She moves to the bedroom to finish her homework with Schubert curled up beside her. I slip into my office and set up the payments to cover her family's measly expenses. I consider paying off their mortgage. It would be easier, but fuck them. I'll fund their bills until Ivory graduates, only because I don't want to give them a reason to go looking for her. After that, they can sleep under a fucking bridge.

I reach out to my catering service and have them add Stogie to their daily route. He might refuse the food. Or maybe he'll see it for what it is: my gratitude for offering Ivory a safe place to go all these years.

With that finished, I place a few more phone calls, find a reliable PI, and make contact. Ending the conversation, the investigator has very little to go on. A name. A license plate number. But he ensures me it's enough.

By the end of the week, the PI proves his worth by providing everything I need to move forward.

I know exactly how I'll deal with Lorenzo Gandara.

# IVORY

Friday afternoon, I head toward my locker in Campus Center. Ellie hurries alongside me, going on about how I have a fast skip in my step. Rather than pointing out that her legs are shorter than mine, I slow my gait and playfully hip-check her.

"You seem different." She smiles up at me, blinking angular brown eyes. "That's all I'm saying."

She hasn't mentioned my new clothes. No, she's too busy trying to find hidden meaning in the way I walk.

"You're...lighter. You know, like easy breezy." She springs ahead of me and bounces backward toward our lockers, her black ponytail whipping around her neck. "You have a boyfriend, don't you?"

I don't know what Emeric is, but it definitely doesn't begin with *boy*. "So you think a guy is some magical remedy for weight loss? Or maybe you're saying I'm gassy?"

She laughs and spins around to dial in her combination. "You're so weird."

I open my locker and find a small folded paper on top of the textbooks. With a huge smile, I reach in and touch it. Stroke it.

Emeric's been leaving me notes all week. Just imagining

him scrawling each one in his eloquent script and walking out of his way to slip it through the vent on my locker door sends a flutter through my chest.

Ellie stands a few feet away, distracted by her phone.

I hold the note inside the locker and unfold it.

*I want you.*
*I wait for you.*
*You have me.*

He makes my soul ache. I read it again, and my whole body aches. When I close my eyes, I hear his deep voice, feel his bruising touch, and taste the cinnamon on his breath. He's with me, always surrounding me, lifting me. Damn, maybe I am more light-footed.

The click of heels approaches behind me. I wad up the note in my fist and glance over my shoulder.

Ann leans against the locker between Ellie and me and gives me a once-over. "The girls have been talking."

Uh huh. She's here, on behalf of the female population, to remind me that she's prettier, smarter, and more popular.

I slide my hand into the satchel and drop the balled-up note. Then I shift to face her head-on, wearing the smile my dad always said was my greatest weapon.

Her sneer warps her smooth black skin and perfect features. "That's a Dolce & Gabbana dress."

I glance down at the yellow and white daisy print, loving how the A-line silhouette fits my body. "Okay."

"Yesterday you wore Valentino. Day before that was Oscar de la Renta. For reals, Ivory. You're a shoplifter now?"

Why couldn't Emeric have just picked up some clothes from Wal-Mart? I wouldn't have known the damn difference.

*Because he doesn't do anything unless it's over-the-top.*

Ellie steps beside me, hitching her humongous backpack over her shoulder. "Leave her alone, Ann."

"It's fine." I nod in the direction of Crescent Hall. "I'll catch up with you, okay?"

She gives me a sympathetic smile and heads toward our next class.

I turn back to Ann and contemplate a repulsive response, because it's so much fun watching her squirm. I could tell her I fucked the store manager at Neiman Marcus. Is that where people go to buy these clothes? I don't know, but that suggestion hits too close to my prior arrangements. Oh, I know... "I started selling my eggs."

Her brown eyes bulge. "Your...what?"

"Eggs." I shrug. "Who knew ovulation could be so lucrative? With my good looks and excellent SAT scores, the fertility center pays me double the going rate."

She makes a gagging noise. "That's disgusting."

"So is your attitude." I shut the locker and step around her. "But I'm deeply touched by how closely you pay attention to me. Brings new light on our friendship. Maybe we can go shopping and have sleepovers." I'd rather be crushed by a twelve-hundred-pound piano. "We could get BFF necklaces—"

"You're such a bitch."

"—or not." I pat her bony shoulder as I pass. "Thanks for keeping it real."

Several hours later, I'm sitting behind the Steinway on the campus theater stage. Emeric moved my private lessons here a few days ago to get me comfortable with the acoustics. The Holiday Chamber Music Celebration is only a couple months away. As one of Le Moyne's biggest performances, the ballet is open to the public and showcases the academy's top musicians and dancers.

Piano is only a small piece of the production, but I would love to finally be part of it. Emeric still hasn't announced who will fill that seat. He takes his job so seriously he's not giving me any advantages just because we're together. I have to earn it, and there isn't an ounce of me that begrudges him that.

Even so, he has a frustrating way of making me wait for things.

When he joined me in the kitchen this morning, he told me it's beautiful to see me waiting.

I will gladly go to exhaustion waiting for him. Waiting for his discipline. Waiting for his affection. Waiting for the unknown.

"Begin again." His voice booms from the shadows of the tiered seats.

We have the theater to ourselves. He's somewhere in the front row, but I can't see him beyond the blinding stage lights.

Bending over the keyboard, I dive into Tchaikovsky's Nutcracker suite. My hands fly through the bursting tremolos, wrists snapping over the quickly-changing keys. I've played this piece so many times I know it by rote, my fingers moving of their own volition, seamlessly adapted with the notes.

As the dial on my watch reaches seven o'clock, perspiration licks my skin, and spasms twinge the joints in my shoulders and hands. Emeric has only interrupted me a few times to point out slip-ups. Hell, he's been so quiet for the last hour I wonder if he left.

I pivot on the piano bench and squint against the lights. "Did you fall asleep out there?"

"No." He clears his throat. "That was exquisite, Miss Westbrook." His dark, deep-toned voice echoes through the theater. "This stage isn't big enough for you."

Tendrils of warmth unfurl inside me, spiraling along my arms, between my breasts, and around my spine.

"How about the stage at Leopold?" I tilt my head, blinking against the lights. "You know, since that's where I'm going."

"Leopold is just an idea stuck in your head. Think bigger. Better."

Better than the best conservatory? I purse my lips. "Like what?"

"There's not an audience in the world big enough to contain you. But you need one passionate enough to hold you."

Wow. I've never thought of it like that before.

"Come here."

It's a command he would give to any of his students, like *sit down, stop talking, answer the question.* But to me, it holds a deeper meaning, one that doesn't belong within the walls of a school.

My thighs quake as I stand from the bench. My breaths tighten as I move toward him, down the stage steps and into the darkness of the empty seats.

He sits off to the side in the front row, just beyond the edge of light. With an ankle propped on his knee and forearms draped over the arm rests, he's a picture of calm self-possession. But his eyes are steely and focused, drilling into mine.

I stop within arm's reach, and my attention drops to the long, hard length rising in his slacks.

"Ivory." His sultry tone snaps my head up.

I rub the back of my neck. "You're...um, hard. Because of my performance?"

"Everything you do turns me on," he whispers. "Especially the feminine motion of your body when you play. I want you naked, sitting at my piano and rolling your hips like you're fucking the notes."

A thunderbolt of heat shoots between my legs, lighting up every inch of me. I want to free him from his pants and feel the weight of his cock in my hands. In my mouth.

He strokes a finger over his bottom lip. "The soloist position in the ballet is yours."

A sigh of happiness tingles through my limbs. "Thank you."

"I love when you're grateful." He licks his bottom lip. "But you earned this, Ivory. You're going to steal the show."

His words commend my talent, but the smoldering flicker in his eyes appreciates all of me as his gaze traces the lines of my body and probes beneath my skin. He knows me on a deeper level, better than anyone, and he likes what he sees inside me.

A sudden and very specific need resonates through my chest, sparked from the marrow of my being. A need to satisfy him, to feel the power in giving him that gift.

I tug at the foot propped on his knee until he lowers it to the floor. He shifts to stand, but I stop him with my hands on his rock-hard thighs. Then I kneel between his spread legs.

He grabs my hair, his tone stern with warning. "Ivory."

With a surge of bravery, I grip his cock through the trousers, touching him for the first time. "I want to taste this."

"Fuck." His exhale ricochets through the vast room. The hand in my hair pulls, pinching pain across my scalp. "Not here."

If we go back to his house, I'll lose my nerve on the way. I've loathed the feeling of a man in my mouth since the first time Lorenzo took me there. The gagging, loss of air, and utter humiliation of something so vile squirting across my tongue...

I want it to be different with Emeric. I need him to show me how to do this willingly.

Surrounded by the stiff muscle groups of his chest and legs, I stroke my hand over the pulsing swell of his erection. "I will crawl to you. Bow to you. Whatever you want, I want. Just...give me this."

A thick, hoarse noise escapes his lips. "Christ in hell. How the fuck do I say *no* to that?"

He wraps my hair around his fist, his gaze cutting through the theater and pausing on the closed doors.

Is he thinking about Joanne and the time they were caught?

It's after seven on a Friday night. We're probably the only two people in Crescent Hall, and no one comes into the theater after school hours. But if those doors open, I'll be on my feet before we're spotted. Besides, only my back is illuminated by the dim edge of the lights. No one can see him in the shadows.

I know he considers all of this before he whispers gruffly, "Take me out."

Excitement shivers through me as I loosen his belt and slide down his zipper. My hands shake, and my mouth floods with moisture.

The fist in my hair clamps down as tension ripples from his body. He lifts his hips, ripping at the trousers with his free hand. As the zipper shifts below his heavy sac, my gut quivers with anticipation to touch him.

In the dim space between us, the largeness of him juts up, long and beautiful and throbbing with veins. My hands gravitate toward it, fingers curling around the thick base.

He wrenches me backward by my hair and studies my face, his blue eyes a faint glow in the darkness. "The moment you want this to stop, raise your hand in the air."

Because I won't be able to use my voice? Fear trickles in, but I shove it away. I have the strength to be vulnerable with him. "I will."

He releases my hair and grips the arm rests with both hands. "Now suck me."

Kneeling to him, with my fingers trembling against the dark short hairs on his groin, I lower my head and slide my cheek along his shaft, nuzzling, kissing, and savoring the feel of steel sheathed in silky flesh.

His entire body melts into the seat.

I drag my nose along his length, inhaling the scent of a man I trust, pulling his woody musk deep into my lungs.

A groan notches his breaths, and his legs widen, stretching the seams around his fly. "Stop playing with it, and suck it."

Smiling, I swirl my tongue around the tip, shredding a gasp

from his throat. The sight of his blanching fists around the arm rests produces a throb between my legs. The jerk of his cock against my lips rushes wet heat to my core. His pleasure is my pleasure.

As I suckle and lick the crown, I reach into his briefs to tease his balls with kneading fingers. Then I close my eyes and draw him into my mouth.

"Ah fuck." He grunts. "That's it. Deeper. Flatten your tongue. There you go." His legs shake. "Jesus, Ivory. Just like that."

I thrill at his praise and bob my head faster, tightening the suction of my mouth. When he's not turning his neck to glance at the door, I know he's watching me, absorbing the contentment on my face as I give and give. Imagining the desire hooding his eyes charges me up, almost as much as the way he bosses me every step of the way. *Spit on it. Lick under the head. Twist your wrist. Take it deep.*

Holy hell, this man. He can't just sit there and enjoy a blow job. His harsh whispers demand I do it the way he likes it, ordering the exact motions to make. *Suck faster. Stroke harder. Make it wet.*

He's a control freak through and through, but I knew he'd respond exactly this way. I love him like this. His filthy fucking mouth and the coarseness of his timbre makes my lips tingle and my nipples harden.

When he loses the last of his restraint, there's no warning. In a blur, he grabs my hair and slams my head down. I gag, slobbering atrociously and sucking for air. A pained moan escapes him as he bucks his hips and drives harder, deeper. I choke so violently my eyes water against the pressure, and my fingers scramble for purchase in the folds of his slacks.

Both hands tangle in my hair as he holds my face against his groin, his cock digging against my throat, his voice hoarse. "Raise your hand, dammit, and I'll stop."

My hands are free. I can lift them anytime. Then he'll release me, and the discomfort will end. The power in that breaks something open inside me.

I want this. I feel it at gut level, this need for him to fuck my mouth savagely, carelessly, and without thought. Maybe because he's held back for so long, restraining himself *for me*, and I ache to give this back to him. Or maybe because I want his hurt so hard and deep inside me that he's all I feel.

With the broad head pounding the back of my throat and taunting my airway, it already hurts. My tonsils feel like painful masses of swollen tissue. He's doing this because he wants to, and I love that, crave it, like no decent woman ever would.

I've never been decent. I'm dirty—Emeric's kind of dirty that leaves a claiming painful pleasure in my throat. He tries to fuck me as deeply as he can because he's my master, the man I hunger for in the darkest, most terribly beautiful way possible.

"Raise...your...fucking...hand." He punctuates each word with jabbing strokes in my mouth.

I bury my nails into his thighs, a silent plea. *Don't stop.*

He stabs his hips and pulls my hair, legs shaking, and breaths wheezing out of control. Just when I think I can't take any more, the balance shifts. He goes quiet, slowing his thrusts, stroking my hair, and filling my mouth with his release.

# DARK
## NOTES

My name reverberates through the theater as his body convulses and sighs.

The power is mine. I bask in it. His hands tremble, and I grab them, hold them, our fingers intertwined. I have him.

# IVORY

The next morning, I shield my eyes against the glaring sun and step toward an unfamiliar car in Emeric's driveway. "What is that?"

He follows me out of the house and walks ahead of me. "A Porsche Cayenne."

"Okaaay. Why is it here?" I thought he was driving me to my doctor's appointment in his muscle car. "Where did it come from?"

His strong legs carry him toward the white sporty SUV, his gorgeous ass flexing in low-waist jeans. With the chirp of a key fob, he unlocks and opens the driver's door then faces me with a wide stance, arms crossed over his chest.

The t-shirt stretches around defined biceps and formidable shoulders, and creases of denim outline the impressive bulge between his legs. I stare without apology, a smile hitching my lips as I recall the way his swollen length pounded against my throat last night.

"Look at me." Censure hardens his tone. When I lift my gaze, he says, "I had it delivered this morning."

I grit my teeth. This car better not be for me. "I thought you preferred loud American gas guzzlers."

The blue in his eyes glows magnetically in the sunlight.

"True. But this is one of the safest SUVs on the market."

Yep, it's for me, dammit. Another gift I don't need. Now I know why he asked me earlier in the week if I had a driver's license. "Thank you, but no—"

"We're not arguing about this."

"Uh, yeah, we are. It's hard enough explaining my wardrobe at school. But a car? No way." I anchor my hands on my hips. "Return it."

"No." He tosses the fob in my direction.

I let it thunk to the driveway at my feet and give him my best glare.

His mouth sets in a thin, severe line.

Oh shit. My pulse trips.

He clasps his hands behind his back and prowls toward me, slowly, methodically, his eyes boring into mine.

Double shit. I lower my arms to my sides and scan the yard. We're behind the estate, hidden from the street. The towering oaks form a living wall of privacy between the lots. Not that I'm afraid to be alone with him when he's like this. Or maybe I am, but any fear I have is smothered by the heady mix of give and take that melds us together so beautifully.

Doesn't mean I have to accept a car, though. I glare down at the key fob.

"Eyes on me!"

My focus flies to the sculpted lines of his face and the pulsing vein in his brow. It's been a few days since I riled him up, but I know that look. As he circles me, I'm both dancing and cringing inside, anticipating a strangling hand on my throat or a hard smack on the ass. Maybe he'll finally have sex with me, right here in broad daylight. I'd welcome any or all of it. I've been in such a heightened state of arousal since I moved in, I might just strip off my clothes and make the decision for him.

He stops behind me, not touching, but close enough to stir my hair with his breaths. "I've had my fingers in your cunt, my cock in your mouth, and your taste on my lips. I'm the only person on the planet who knows how beautiful you look when you come. All those freckles on your thighs, the sounds you make when you sleep, the passion you evoke with a piano, everything about you is priceless and irreplaceable. So I'm going to wrap you in nice things and protect you in a safe car. And you are going to thank me with those gorgeous lips around my dick when you get home."

My heart rises and dips with each word, my breaths stuttering noisily.

"This is who I am, Ivory, and you are the essential and most important part of me." He steps back. "Now bend over."

My knees wobble at his words. I reach for the black Chucks on my feet, and the fancy designer denim cuts into my thighs. The downside of low-rise jeans? He's getting an ungodly view of my butt cleavage right about now.

His palm slams against my ass with a force that steals my breath and topples me forward. But his arm catches me around the waist, and the hand on my back keeps me in a doubled-over position. Sweet Jesus, my butt cheek is on fire. The heat fans outward, circulating through my blood and gathering between my legs.

He rubs the sore spot, limited by the heavily-stitched pocket of my jeans. "Pick up the keyring."

Hanging over the brace of his arm, I snatch the fob from

the brick pavestones.

He grips my bicep and walks me toward the car. "I would redden your fucking ass if you weren't about to show it to the doctor." He stops at the driver's door. "Hands on the roof."

Shit. What now? I drop the fob on the seat and place my palms on the shiny white top, smudging the pristine paint job with sweat.

His fingers slide around my hips and release the button of my jeans. My heart kicks into a feverish crescendo. He unzips the fly and, in one shove, yanks everything to my feet.

Standing outside in the daylight, nude from the waist down... This is a first for me. I can't decide if I'm shaking from the thrill of someone seeing, from the fear of inevitable pain, or from the burning anticipation of him touching me again. Probably all of the above.

"Bend down and grip the seat."

As I follow his command, a sense of peace washes over me. Whatever he does next will make me feel a little less lost. Every time he takes me in hand, he opens another door that shows me more about myself. The person he reveals isn't ashamed or weak. I'm finally figuring out what I want.

His Doc Martens scuff against the bricks as he lowers behind me. His hands wrap around my thighs, and in the next heartbeat, he buries his nose in my pussy.

A slap of embarrassment flushes my face. But it quickly transforms into a torrent of desire as his exhale brushes against my flesh. A deep inhale follows, and his fingers tighten against my legs.

He's smelling me. Down there. Deeply and repeatedly. I never would've imagined being so wildly turned on by this,

but I'm shaking and panting against the strange and
incredible sensation. He's shaking, too, and... Oh fuck, he's
licking me, kissing my pussy the way he kisses my mouth.
Another—*holy fucking shit*—first.

I bite my lip to silence my cry as he stabs his tongue
between my legs. He laves my folds, brutally bites sensitive
skin, and scratches me with his stubble. It's pain and pleasure,
soprano and bass, and every octave in between. I'm going to
come. I feel the pull, and I reach for that wondrous place,
grinding my pussy against his face and digging my fingers
into the leather seat. Almost there. Almost—

He steps back.

I straighten and twist around to grab him, but he's right
there, catching me in the tangle of my jeans with his hands on
my hips and his tongue in my mouth. He slides his lips over
mine in slippery strokes, spreading the tangy taste of my
arousal between us.

He breaks the kiss and drags my panties up my trembling
legs.

My insides throb, aching to finish what he started. "I didn't
come."

"I know." He pulls up my jeans and fastens them. Then he
grabs my hand and presses it against the erection behind his
zipper. "I'll wait for you."

"You're not going to the appointment with me?"

Regret etches his face, and he releases my hand.

Of course, he can't go. Someone might see us together. I
mentally slap myself. "That's why you gave me the car."

He cups my face and kisses me.

"I'm sorry." I lean back and peer up at him through my

lashes. "I was kind of a brat about it."

"The brattiest."

"Why didn't you just tell me?"

A smile stretches his gorgeous face. "Where would the fun be in that?"

He likes me to act out so he can discipline me for it? Today's lesson: the worst punishment is a denied orgasm.

When I'm settled in the driver's seat, he leans into the open window and gives me a flinty glare. "Don't argue with the doctor."

"I won't."

"Get the blood work."

"I will."

"And the birth control he prescribes."

My pulse leaps. "Of course."

Those hard eyes soften into a look I've never seen on him before. "Come back to me."

I reach up and stroke his shadowed jaw. "Count on it."

# IVORY

Unease buzzes through me as I turn out of Emeric's driveway. Maybe because I'm wearing designer clothes, driving an expensive car, and obsessing about a man with no idea where I'm headed. I know my way to the clinic, but after that? Months down the road? After I graduate? Where am I going and how will I get there?

I know Emeric intends to keep me around. That both delights me and troubles me. Part of the reason I want to go to Leopold is to get out of Treme. Well, I did, and here I am with an address even Ann would envy. But I yearn to continue practicing piano, and not just under any instructor. The very best instructors Leopold has to offer. How could I throw away my dream for a man and forgive myself? How could Emeric respect me if I did that?

He wouldn't. Of all the lessons he's taught me in and out of the classroom, the most profound is how to recognize my own strength and go after what I want.

Amid my churning thoughts, I wonder about Mom and Shane. Do they question where I am? Emeric keeps the bills current, so maybe they don't care. Or maybe they're too strung out to even notice my absence. I try not to dwell on that. The things I want from them, their interest and concern, died with my dad. My family is broken, a harrowing truth I accepted a long time ago.

A couple of minutes from his house, I park the Porsche in front of Southern Family Health. Tucking the phone in my back pocket, I head inside the modern one-story building.

A few people fill the waiting room, but none of them look up from their phones when I enter. I check in, fill out the forms, and return them to the middle-aged woman behind the counter.

"Take a seat." She brushes her frizzy brown hair behind her ear. "Dr. Marceaux will see you shortly."

I stiffen, my attention darting over the rack of pamphlets, searching for something to validate what I just heard. "Did you say Marceaux?"

"Is that not..." She glances at the computer monitor. "Says here you requested Marceaux."

My veins turn to ice. Emeric mentioned his father's a physician, but I assumed the man worked at a fancy hospital or something. For fuck's sake, why would he send me to his dad to have my vagina examined? Maybe this doctor is a different Marceaux? Is it a common last name?

"Does he..." Is it too risky to ask this? Fuck it. "Does Dr. Marceaux have a son? A teacher?"

"Oh, yes." The woman cracks a huge smile and leans back in the chair, regarding me. "From the look on your face, I'm guessing he's got you under his spell, too."

"No. I..." My cheeks burn. "What do you mean?"

"Every time that fine-looking man comes in here, he gets all the girls in a tizzy." She laughs. "Take a number, honey. There's a long line of women waiting for a piece of that."

Did she seriously just say that? Grinding my teeth, I find a seat and pull out the phone. I have two names in my contact list. Stogie and LordandMaster. The latter was Emeric's attempt at humor when he set up the phone. I haven't had the heart to change it.

I launch a text window.

*Me: U sent me to ur dad??? To get birth control? R u crazy?*

The front door opens, and a very pregnant woman sashays toward the counter. She's all belly. Skinny and petite everywhere else. How the hell does she walk so gracefully in those sky-high heels?

The vibration of an incoming text draws my attention back to the phone.

*LordandMaster: He'll do everything but the Pap test. Don't question me.*

But he'll see me in a thin gown and check me for STDs? I feel sick.

*Me: Does he know about us?*

*LordandMaster: Yes*

Yes? That's all he's going to say?

I pinch the bridge of my nose, debating the wisdom in storming out.

"I need to see him right now." The pregnant woman's rising voice brings my eyes up.

She gathers her long blonde hair and holds it away from her pale complexion, her tense posture screaming with frustration.

"Ma'am," the receptionist says sternly, "if you give me your information, I'll set up—"

"Go back there and tell him Joanne is here."

My stomach drops as my entire world narrows to her belly. She can't be his Joanne. This...this woman is pregnant. *A lot* pregnant. Like easily seven or eight months along.

Emeric said he hasn't seen her in six months.

My chest clenches. *No. No, no, no.* Emeric would've told me.

The receptionist stands. "Is Dr. Marceaux expecting you?"

"I'm expecting his grandson." She points at her stomach. "VIP pass. I need to see him. Now."

Nausea barrels through my gut, doubling me over. *It's not true. I must've misheard.*

The receptionist widens her eyes then slips down the hall toward the back.

Relaxing against the counter, Joanne rests her phone on the ledge of her baby belly. *Emeric's baby.*

My insides roil with bile. I scan the waiting room for a bathroom, and my gaze catches and locks on hers. She gives me a tight smile and moves on, taking in the people sitting near me.

Her small nose, smooth flat features, and close-set eyes give her a tiny pixie look, one that works well for her. Really well. She's painfully beautiful, like a perfect mix of Kristen Bell and Keira Knightley.

No wonder he loves her.

*The mother of his child.*

I ball my hands to stop the trembling. Why didn't he tell me? Is he trying to resolve things with her? So they can be a happy family?

Tears sneak up, burning my eyes, and a horrible ache seals my throat. I spring from the seat and walk as calmly as I can into the single-person bathroom. As soon as the door shuts, I drag in loud, ragged breaths and hit the last call dialed on my phone.

Emeric's gravelly voice scrapes against my eardrum. "Ivory."

"Your *pregnant* girlfriend is here."

*Please tell me I'm mistaken.* My chest hurts so badly I can't breathe.

The line goes silent for a weighted moment. Then a flurry of sounds rushes through. His exhales, the slam of a door, the roar of a motor. "I'll be there in three minutes."

So it's true. The gravity of that steals the strength from my legs. I slide down the door, drop to the floor, and try to keep the tears from wobbling my voice. "You lied to me."

"Bull—"

"Omitting is the same as lying." I squeeze the phone. "Your words."

His heavy breaths rasp through the receiver. "Tell me you didn't talk to her."

"Why?" My chin quivers. "Because I'm your dirty secret? Your side piece while you work on your relationship—"

"So help me God..." His voice is so cold it lifts the hairs on my neck. "I'm going to break my fucking belt on your ass."

I lower the phone, take a huge calming breath, then lift it back to my ear. "You're a bastard."

"Keep going, Ivory. You're not going to walk for a week."

"Why didn't you tell me?"

A loud thump vibrates through the phone, at odds with the silkiness in his tone. "This is my problem, one that's going to go away very soon."

"What?" Outrage pitches my volume. "You don't just make

a baby go away!"

"Lower your fucking voice. Where are you?"

"In hell."

"Melodrama doesn't suit you."

I punch a pathetic fist against the tiled wall. "Fuck you."

"Fuck *you* for making assumptions about shit you know nothing about!" he roars.

"Is the baby yours?"

"I asked you a question!" he shouts then reins in his tone. "You're making me wait."

"Good." Sitting against the door on the bathroom floor, I kick my legs out in front me. "You can go fuck yourself while you wait."

"I'm outside." The grating of his breaths strains the silence, followed by the bang of a car door. "Listen closely. I know you're hurt, and I caused that. But you're going to get the fuck over it and trust me."

He can't be serious. I don't bother responding.

"I'll deal with Joanne," he says, "and you will get that fucking check-up."

He ends the call, and I stare at the screen in disbelief. I remain on the floor, grinding my molars and cursing the creation of the opposite sex.

Men who praise and promise are the ones who hurt the most. They coerce and bribe and fuck with my head. Then they fuck my body and leave the kind of scarring fear that no one can see.

I thought he was different. Now I'm not sure.

But I do know he's not the type to get a woman pregnant and bail. He's too controlling and obsessive to not be fully invested in his child's life.

That's why he took the deal with the dean rather than moving out-of-state.

I love that about him. But I hate it, too. Because I'm jealous and selfish. I hug the pain twisting in my mid-section. God, this fucking hurts.

A fist knocks on the door. "Ivory Westbrook?"

The unfamiliar voice is deeply masculine. Probably the nurse or Emeric's dad. So what do I do? I dread seeing Emeric with Joanne, but I can't stay in here forever.

I climb to my feet, wipe away stray tears, and open the door.

The man on the other side stands a foot taller than me. *Frank Marceaux, M.D.* is embroidered on his white coat, but there's nothing familiar in his handsome features. Wrinkles line his brow, though not many. He's probably in his fifties? Reddish-brown hair combs back from a severe widow's peak. Thick eyebrows curve over green eyes, and a small gold ring cuffs his earlobe.

But it's his presence that denotes the family resemblance. Hands behind his back, feet planted in a wide stance, he studies me with too much focus. A shiver trills up my spine.

He raises an auburn brow. "Are you ready?"

No, definitely not. I slide the phone in my back pocket. "Yeah."

As I follow him through the waiting room, my gaze locks on the wall of windows and the scene playing out in the parking lot. My shoes stick to the floor, and every cell in my body zeroes in on Emeric.

He paces a circle around Joanne. His mouth moves, his

eyes blaze, but his overall posture conveys calm confidence.

She stares at her hands where they rub her belly, head lowered, and lips in a thin line. Probably the way I look when he's teaching me a lesson.

Jealousy burns hot and fierce in my chest.

"Ivory," Dr. Marceaux says.

I step forward to follow then pause.

Emeric stops just behind Joanne, breathing down her neck. With his fists on his hips, no part of him touches her, but he's so close. The kind of closeness two people share when they've spent a lot of time together. When they're familiar and intimate.

My heart squeezes and shrivels. She knows him better than I do. He's been inside her, put a baby in her, and I'm... I don't know what I am to him. We haven't even had sex.

"Ivory." Dr. Marceaux steps in front of me, blocking my view. "Follow me."

I can't seem to make my feet move, but my eyes work just fine, burning images of Emeric and Joanne into my brain and leaking tears all over my damn face.

Dr. Marceaux gently grips my elbow and leads me to an exam room. The moment he shuts the door, he stabs a finger toward the exam table. "Sit."

I jump at the command in his voice and hurry to the table, crinkling the paper against the vinyl as I hop up.

He sets a box of tissues beside my hip, which makes me feel like an emotional little girl. I grab one anyway and wipe my face.

Lowering onto the stool, he rolls it across the floor until he's sitting right in front of me. "He didn't tell you about her?"

I wad the tissue in my fist and square my shoulders. "Not about the pregnancy."

A muscle tics in his jaw, and his hard eyes crease, fanning wrinkles from the corners.

"Is it his?" I ask.

"He doesn't know."

My breath hitches. "He doesn't...? She was with someone else? Did she cheat on him?"

"He has no proof of that."

"Oh." My chest deflates. "She told the receptionist she's carrying your grandson."

He swivels toward the drawers behind him and removes equipment and supplies, giving me a momentary reprieve from his stony gaze.

"I know you're living with him." He rips open packages of instruments. "I'm not going to lecture you on the risks you and he are taking. I gave him my opinion on the phone last night." He turns back to me, his expression pensive. "Emeric is hardheaded and unstoppable when his passion is provoked."

I disagree with the unstoppable part. At least when it comes to my limits. Where his passion is concerned, I've been on the receiving end of that for two months. I guess that's why this secret he's kept from me feels like a blade in my chest.

Dr. Marceaux slides on reading glasses and grabs the blood pressure monitor. Without asking me to change clothes, he begins an above-the-waist exam. For the next ten minutes, he pokes, prods, and draws blood while I answer his medical questions, including the embarrassing ones about my sexual history and mishaps with protection.

He maintains a professional demeanor, but I wonder if he thinks I'm just a money-grubbing whore.

While he makes notations on his tablet, the door opens.

Emeric slips in, shuts the door, and his frosty eyes find and imprison mine.

Chills sweep over me, and I find it difficult to look away.

Dr. Marceaux stands, his voice clipped. "What are you doing in here?"

Emeric doesn't break eye contact with me. There are so many emotions seeping from him, I don't know how to sort them. Anger is the easiest to recognize, locking his jaw and engorging the veins in his tense forearms. But there's an undercurrent of something more vulnerable. His fingers twitch at his sides, and tendons stand out in his neck. Is he scared? Afraid I'll leave? Or is that my wishful thinking?

Dr. Marceaux moves toward the door, his voice low and harsh. "Emeric, there are five nurses here today, watching your every move. I won't be able to contain the gossip."

Emeric holds my eyes as he speaks to his dad. "After the scene Joanne just made, they'll think I came in here to talk to you."

"Is she still here?" I relax my hands in my lap and try to look brave and mature. "What did you talk about?"

"You can discuss it at home." Dr. Marceaux pulls a gown from the drawer and sets it beside me. "Dr. Hill will be in any second to do the pelvic exam."

"I'm staying." Emeric leans against the counter, hands in his pockets, settling in.

"No, you're not." I grab the gown, turning it every which

way to make sense of it. "This is awkward enough. Besides, I'm pissed at you."

He snatches the smock from my hands and holds it open. "It goes on like this."

Dr. Marceaux grips the doorknob. "Let's go, son."

In a flash, Emeric closes the distance between us, grips the hair at my scalp, and puts his mouth at my ear. "We're not finished."

Then he follows his dad out of the room, leaving me breathless and even more confused than I was before.

In a daze, I pee in a cup in the bathroom and change into the weird gown in the exam room. The elderly Dr. Hill arrives with news that I'm not pregnant. Then he hands me a package of birth control pills, does a breast exam, and sticks his hand and other invasive things in my vagina.

By the time I climb into the Porsche, my head is pounding with a barrage of questions. Where do I go? What should I do?

I grip the steering wheel and search my gut for the right decision. Going to his house doesn't mean I'm desperate or needy. I can always go back home and return to the way things were before.

But I've never been the girl who runs from an argument. I need answers, and there's only one place to find them.

A few minutes later, I punch in my code at the security gate, a code Emeric let me come up with on my own. Then I park beside the GTO and enter the house through the unlocked back door.

Schubert greets me in the mud room with a purring leg rub. As I scoop him up, I'm distracted by the muffled melody of a piano. He's playing?

I give the kitty a nuzzle, set him down, and follow the notes through the winding corridors.

I've peeked into his music room several times, admired his Fazioli from afar, but I've never gone in. I had this idea that he would lead me there when his hands were healed. Then he would sit behind the keyboard and play something crazy amazing, like Ravel's Gaspard de la Nuit.

As I draw closer, I don't hear Ravel or Brhams or Liszt. He's playing *Metallica*.

I freeze in the doorway, held in paralyzing captivation as the familiar tune of "Nothing Else Matters" wraps around me. Twenty feet away, he rocks on the bench, eyes closed, profile relaxed, and forearms flexing as he hammers the keys.

He's conservatory trained but plays metal on the piano? Without a music sheet. Only virtuosos can so smoothly replicate pieces they've heard. I'm completely and totally awestruck.

When I remember to breathe, my lungs expand, inhaling the sight of him, the poignant arrangement of notes, and the energy in the air.

Head down, black hair hanging over his brow, he sways his jaw side-to-side in a slow tempo with the music. The melody is a desperate plea infused with longing, and he opens it up with expert strokes, tapping his bare foot softly, his posture a powerhouse of contracting muscle beneath the white t-shirt.

The face of his watch glints in the light as he leaps between octaves. With each snap of his wrist, I imagine that hand whipping across my skin. The spread and flex of his fingers makes me wish they were curled around my throat with the same passion and intensity. His hips roll, and I tremble to straddle his lap and ride the wave of his body as he plays.

In the right hands, the piano can steal the soul. Clearly, his hands are made for the keys, because I don't just feel the notes inside me. They devour me like a dark, voracious flame.

He's so sexy and talented I don't know what to do with the dangerous feelings he stirs in me. I'm supposed to be mad at him and demanding answers. I should feel lost, uncertain.

Instead, I feel claimed, as if he's caressing each key with me on his mind. *We're not finished.* He wants me here, even though he hasn't acknowledged my presence.

It takes me several seconds to realize the lid is closed on the Fazioli. Did he forget to open it? Looking closer, I see something that doesn't belong.

Familiar black straps hook underneath the piano, stretch across the black top, and attach to leather cuffs near the keyboard.

My pulse skyrockets, and my gaze flicks back to his face.

His eyes are still closed. I could slip into the hall and... What then? I'm not going anywhere until I talk to him.

Am I afraid of what he has planned for me? Well, my lips are numb, and my heartbeat is raging out of control. But I'm certain those cuffs will lead to answers about Joanne as well as myself. If the truth is too painful, he'll release me with one word.

I stand taller, but not quite confident enough to step into the room.

The song winds to a close, and he rests his hands in his lap.

Lifting his head, he turns his glacial eyes on me. "Leave all of your clothes at the door."

# EMERIC

"Metallica." Ivory tucks her hands in the back pockets of her jeans and gives me a tentative smile. "That was good."

I was trained by the best, graduated from Leopold, and hold a seat in the Louisiana Symphony Orchestra. Not once in my musical career have I cared what anyone thinks of my talent.

Until now.

She's been frozen in the doorway for five minutes, and *good* is the only compliment her gorgeous lips utter?

When we met, I was afraid the balance between us would be heavily tipped, that I would overpower her and take advantage of her. I weigh almost twice what she does. I'm twenty-seven, and she's seventeen. I'm a Dominant, and she's my high school student. Christ, I had so many doubts.

But no more.

As I sit here, aching for her brilliant pianist's mind to spout poetry about my music, I realize she doesn't just hold the power in the bedroom. She commands my emotions, tests my confidence, and haunts my every thought. She could destroy me, not just my livelihood, but the very fiber of who I am, and she doesn't even know it.

It's my responsibility to balance the harmony between us

and manage our roles. Right now, she's disobeying, and I'm going to remind her what it means to be mine.

"Your clothes. Now."

Flinching at my hard tone, she glances at the restraints on the Fazioli. Her chest heaves once, twice. Then she closes her eyes and lifts the t-shirt over her head, dropping the material to the floor.

Her tits swell over lacy pink cups, her toned abs encased in dark golden skin. Those sexy legs... I clench my hands. She's making me wait, her fingers frozen on the button of her jeans.

I rise from the piano bench, the Dom in me taking over. I straighten my spine, roll back my shoulders, and even my breaths. She watches me with hooded eyes, parted lips, her hands dropping to curl against her thighs.

Knowing her trust in me was fractured at the clinic, it's incredibly satisfying to see her standing here, let alone considering my order. But for us to work, it's vital I push her to the edge, to that place where she both fears and respects me, but not so far that she can't breathe.

I force myself to ease back a notch, to use less growl and more finesse.

Approaching her slowly, I hold her gaze with assertive focus. As I crowd her space, her chin lowers, breath hitching, but those huge brown eyes stay with me, refusing to look away. So brave. So fucking intoxicating.

I lower into a crouch and, with painfully slow movements, unzip the fly of her jeans. Hovering my lips an inch from her panties, I drag the denim down her legs. She trembles as I gaze up at her and take my time kissing the skin around the pink satin.

With my fingers on the backs of her calves, I trail them up her legs, speaking softly yet firmly. "Remove your shoes."

As she toes them off, her swift obedience builds a hungry pressure in my groin. My hands trace the rise of her ass, and my lips follow the dip of her naval. She gasps and rolls her hips, her fingers plunging into my hair, clinging to me for balance.

Fuck, I want her on my cock, clenching and spasming and giving herself to me in every way.

I kick the sneakers to the side and guide her feet out of the jeans and socks. With featherlight touches, I tickle the serpentine line of her spine and toy with the clasp of her bra while rising up her body and kissing a sensual path between her breasts.

Her head falls back, and her slender frame rocks in my arms. She smells like jasmine soap, sultry with arousal, and exquisitely Ivory.

My cock jerks in my jeans, trapped and demanding. *Not yet.*

I tease the clasp of the bra, my mouth gliding across her delicate collar bone. Moving higher, I kiss the slender column of her neck and nibble along her jaw.

Our foreheads touch as I unlatch the bra and flatten my palm against her spine. Our breaths rush out, melding together, our lips gravitating closer, closer. When our mouths finally connect, she melts against me.

My hands lift to her face, thumbs stroking her cheekbones as I devour her seductive moans. I kiss her aggressively, ordering her without words to trust me. I whip my tongue against hers, a promise of impending pain and ecstasy. Her mouth parts in acceptance, and her hands clutch my waist, pulling me against her.

I break the kiss and let my fingers linger on the straps on her shoulders. My eyes never leaving hers, I gently slip the bra down her arms. Her nipples are so hard the lace catches on them. I slowly ease the material away, exposing her delicious flesh. She exhales sharply as the bra falls to the floor.

Jesus, she's perfection. I need to bury myself inside her and struggle to think past my raging hard-on.

Taking a step back, I let my gaze roam her long, lean body, worshiping every flexure, twitch, and fragile bone as she regards me with round eyes. Full perky tits rise with her breaths, narrow hips shift with anxiousness, and a wet spot darkens the satin of her pink panties.

Her body loves my touch, but her mind hasn't forgiven me. If I don't let her take the next step on her own, she'll only feel worse afterward.

I nod at the panties. "Take them off or say your word."

Biting her lip, she hooks her thumbs under the satin, glides it down her legs, and kicks it away. Her gaze never leaves my face, watching me with wariness, curiosity, and undeniable desire.

I prowl around her, reveling in her stunning nudity and the way her breaths stop and start with each of my steps. My finger traces the scrollwork pattern inked from her waist to the opposite shoulder.

She shudders against the sensation, panting and craning her neck to see me.

I press my chest flush with her back, fingers teasing her hipbones. "You're going to tell me about that tattoo. Not now." I rest my mouth in the juncture between her neck and shoulder and lick. "Maybe not today or this week." Sliding my hands around her pelvis, I dip between her legs and slip through her wet folds. "But you'll tell me soon."

She releases a heavy sigh and arches her neck, tipping her head to the side to give me easier access.

I set my teeth on her shoulder and bite down. She whimpers and writhes against me, her arms lifting and fingers seeking my hair.

Kissing the hurt, I step back. "Follow me." I lead her to the Fazioli and point to the ledge above the keyboard. "Sit on the edge. Legs spread. Right foot on the lowest keys, left foot on the highest."

Her expression pinches with uncertainty, but she climbs into position, filling the silence with random notes.

Nylon straps snake from beneath the piano and over the lid, two on each side and all four connected to leather cuffs. I attach two to her wrists and cinch them behind her with a hard yank. She gasps.

With her arms restrained at her back, her eyes track my movements, lips separated and shoulders lifting. She seems to be fighting her posture, battling the fear that's pulling her body in on itself.

As I cross in front of her, I caress the backs of my fingers along the inside of her outstretched leg. "What is the word that makes this stop?"

"Scriabin," she breathes, watching me cautiously.

"Will you use it?"

She nods with a flutter of fear in her eyes. "If I need to."

"Good girl."

With the other two cuffs, I lock her ankles against the molding that brackets the keyboard. Then I stand back and absorb the erotic view before me.

Perched on the edge of the lid, thighs spread wide enough to hold the entire keyboard between her feet, and arms restrained behind her, she's a picture of lust and torment, strength and trust. Her pussy is open, pink and drenched, begging for my cock. Her tongue peeks out and touches the underside of her bottom lip.

I've never wanted anyone the way I want her. Not just her body. I want her everything. *She* is the strongest emotion I've ever felt.

I adjust the throbbing ache in my jeans. "I'm so fucking aroused I want to roll over and die."

"Dead is one way to get rid of that erection."

The playful glint in her eyes makes me impossibly harder.

"Or." She bites her lip. "There's...you know, the other way."

I hold her in a suspended moment of eye contact as my hand strokes along my trapped cock. "Is that what you want, Ivory? Your cunt is soaked and ready for me. I could slide right in and fuck you so hard you'll feel me for days."

She averts her gaze, nostrils flaring and muscles straining in the shackles. She might've been ready to surrender this morning, but not now. Not after seeing my ex.

"Look at me." I wait for her eyes then reach for my belt. "You get two strikes for referring to anyone but yourself as my girlfriend."

"But Jo—"

"Don't say her fucking name." Heat courses through my

veins. "We'll get to that, but right here, right now, this is *us*. You and me and no one else."

Grooves form in her forehead then smooth away. "Fine. Two strikes." The corner of her mouth lifts. "Do your worst."

She's smiling now, completely clueless about *where* I'll be doing my worst.

I cock my head. "As for the attitude you gave me on the phone..." I yank the belt free from my jeans and fold it in half. "Six orgasms for your six bratty comments."

"Orgasms, huh?" She laughs, relaxing in her restraints. "Gee, that sounds like torture."

My lips twitch. *Oh, it will be.*

# IVORY

The edge of the piano lid digs into my ass, and the muscles in my inner thighs strain in the locked and spread position. But it's the heated blue gaze tracing every line of my body that holds me captive. I straighten as tall as possible, my heart banging and body aching for Emeric's hurt and affection.

Since I'm sitting on his usual target, where will he hit me? My thighs? My back? I look down the expanse of my torso, and a chill tingles across my neck. With my legs extended wide and arms bound behind me, my tits and pussy are front and center. Surely, that's not...

My gaze flies up, but he's not looking at my eyes. His attention is glued to my chest, his fist clenched around the ends of the belt. *No, he wouldn't. Not somewhere so vulnerable.* My nipples throb at the thought.

Stalking toward me on silent feet, he slides the bench to the side and puts his face in mine, studying my expression, watching me breathe, peering into the darkest, most depraved parts of me.

I swallow. "Where are you going to—"

He crashes his mouth against mine, licking and sucking and spinning my brain off its axis. Gliding his lips along my neck, up and down, slowly, achingly, he covers my throat in whispers of pleasure. My head drops back on a gasp. His mouth is so gentle and safe it's like he's kissing my soul. *Please, don't stop.*

His hand joins in, lightly stroking up my side and over my breast. Those four fingers, four tiny points of contact, charge my veins with electricity and strum my body through multiple arpeggios in a matter of seconds.

"I need you." The words rush past my lips, breathy and unbidden.

"You have me," he says softly, lowers his head, and bites my nipple.

I yelp, consumed with pain, jerking against the manacles and going nowhere.

He laughs and bites again, pulling on the nub with his teeth until it throbs and stretches out of shape.

When he moves to the other one, I hold my breath and shake my head.

His lips graze my nipple, teasing, and his eyes flicker to mine with so much need swirling in the deep blue depths. "Breathe."

The moment I do, he sinks his teeth. I shriek in agony and buck my hips, slipping off the edge. He catches me, sliding my ass back in place as his teeth tear into my sensitive flesh, sucking hard and setting me on fire.

"Stop!" I sob, twisting my wrists in the shackles. "Please, stop."

Rolling his tongue, he licks the godawful burn, his voice a razored rasp. "I don't hear your word."

Tears flood my eyes, and my entire body quivers like a harp string.

He leans into my face and bares his teeth. "Say it."

I suck on my bottom lip and look down. Fucking hell, it feels like he sliced my nipples off, but they're still there, huge, hard, and angry red. Not a drop of blood.

He steps to the side and taps the folded belt against his leg. "Where's the cocky little brat from just a moment ago?"

"You bit my boobs!"

"You just increased your orgasm count to seven. Are you finished?"

If he's trying to provoke me to say the word, he'll have to try harder.

I twist my wrist behind my back and flip him off. *Too bad he can't see it.* "I'm good."

He raises the belt and touches the loop of leather to my nipple. A torrent of tremors ripple through me.

His eyes meet mine, lower to my chest, then return to my face.

I harden my expression and lift my chin.

Time stands still as his head tilts, and his mouth opens slightly. Then he swings.

Leather whips across my swollen nipple in a fiery flash. A gasp lodges in my throat, and tears blind my vision. He doesn't give me a second to regroup before he strikes the other breast.

My back bows, and I swallow my scream as my mind scrambles to make sense of the pain. How did I get here? Why am I letting this happen? What in the holy fuck am I doing?

The belt hits the floor, making me jump. He reaches behind his neck and drags the t-shirt over his head. Denim hangs low on his tapered waist, his bare chest flexing and bunching with dips and ridges.

In the next breath, he's on me, hands in my hair and lips chasing the tracks of tears across my cheeks.

"So beautiful when you cry for me." He sprinkles kisses across my eyes, nose, and mouth as his fingers stroke my hair. "Oh, Ivory. You have no idea what you do to me."

The rumble of his voice and the tenderness of his touch soothes the fire in my nipples and stokes a new flame deep in my core.

"Tell me," I say, my voice reedy.

He drops his forehead to mine. "I'll show you."

Dragging the piano bench closer, he sits. The position puts his mouth inches from my pussy. Fingers spread over the keys, he dives into a raucously violent song. Another metal cover, but I can't place it. I'm lost in the banging notes, shivering against the pain in my breasts, and wondering if those seven orgasms will be his or mine.

I test the bindings on my ankles, my legs twinging in the extended stretch. "What song is this?"

His eyes dart between my lips and my pussy, his hands pounding the keys. "'Symphony Of Destruction.' Megadeth."

Never heard of it, but sweet hell, it sounds ominous.

He leans forward and presses his mouth against my inner thigh. My entire body stills in anticipation as he slides his lips toward my center. His hands move manically over the keys, and when he reaches the crease in my thigh, he changes direction without a slip in the melody. He licks a path to my knee, nibbling and sucking my skin, then shifts back once again toward my cunt.

With his lips hovering above my clit, the song changes to

one I immediately recognize.

I burst into groaning laughter. "You've got to be kidding me."

He flashes me a grin before he buries his face between my legs. As he curves his tongue through my folds, the piano vibrates to the tune of "Smells Like Teen Spirit" by Nirvana.

The swarming sensations beneath his lips plunge me into a panting mess of desire. He probes deeply with stabbing strokes, and when he finds my clit, it doesn't take long. I'm already primed with all the touching and kissing, and hell, even the whips on my breasts made me wet.

I come with a loud, gasping moan, rocking my hips against his relentless mouth as my limbs jerk in the restraints.

His hands fumble over the keys, losing the rhythm before picking it back up again.

"That's one," he says in a husky voice.

I meet his eyes, panting and shaking. "There's no way. I—"

Can't say *I can't*. But seriously? Six more? He's way too diabolical with his punishments. I'm going to die.

He presses a kiss to my clit then attacks it with lips and teeth. I scream through orgasms two and three. After that, I no longer hear the music or feel the vibrations through my limbs or see the room around me. Every sense narrows on the tongue inside me and the deluge of climbing and falling sensations attacking my body.

After the fourth release, I reach a strange floaty kind of catatonic state. My pussy tingles with over-stimulation, the nerve-endings in my clit stinging against the lightest stroke of his tongue. But he doesn't stop. Not when I tell him to go to hell or call him a sadistic bastard.

He silences me by clamping his teeth around my bundle of nerves.

He's not playing the piano anymore, because those talented fingers are inside me, banging me into a torturous hell of pleasure.

"You have to stop." I sway in the restraints, my spread legs shaking with exhaustion. "Please. I'm done."

His soaking wet lips burrow in, kissing and licking, his groan thrumming a different kind of song through my core. A moment later, he curls three fingers inside me and wrings another agonizing orgasm from my body.

"Six." He leans back and wipes his mouth on the back of his hand. "The last one will be with me."

"No more." My head is so heavy my chin drops against my chest as I suck for air. "Please."

He lifts my chin with his finger, his gaze burning against my lips, his voice a ragged whisper. "I love when you beg."

He stands, and with a few flicks of his wrists, he releases my hands and legs from the straps.

I slump against him, my muscles like water, pouring out and falling over. But he has me, my limp body held in strong arms and supported against a damn fine chest.

The heat of his forearms disappears from my back, replaced with the hard surface of the piano lid. He lays me face up, feet pointing away from the keyboard, shoulders on the edge where I'd been sitting. My head dangles upside-down, bumping against the keys.

My already hypersensitive skin flushes hotter, and blood rushes to my brain with the pull of gravity. "What are you doing?"

He circles the piano, inspecting my body as if memorizing every inch. His fingers tickle along my skin as he moves, starting at my throat, gliding along my sternum, veering around my belly button, and lingering between my legs.

My pelvis lifts toward his touch, straining to maintain that point of contact. Despite the fact he just finished biting and welting my breasts and torturing me with orgasms, I want more. He must have short-wired my brain.

Locking the cuffs around my ankles and wrists, he effectively pins me like an *X* on his Fazioli. When he returns to my head, he gives me an upside-down view of the steel rod pushing against his zipper.

He opens his fly. "You know how hard to suck." Shoving down his jeans, he releases his sizeable cock, the pink skin taut over the wide girth. "You know how fast or slow to move that wicked tongue."

Heat pools and throbs between my thighs with every word.

Touching the crown to my inverted mouth, he fists his length and smears salty pre-come across my lips. "Tap your right hand against the piano if you want this to stop. Tell me you understand."

"I—" My pussy clenches, empty and needy. Such a foreign feeling to experience. "I'll tap if I need to."

He wraps a hand beneath my dangling head, his fingers serving as a buffer between my skull and the wood casing. With his eyes half-mast and steadily watching mine, he grips his erection, rubs the shaft across my cheeks, and thumps the tip against my lips.

I open my mouth, instinctively, eagerly. *Do it already*.

His gaze flicks down the length of my body as he presses

himself against my tongue. His exhale shudders out, and he thrusts.

He doesn't ease in. He ruthlessly and repeatedly plows. Over and over, he stabs his cock past my lips, fucking my mouth as if he were plunging between my legs.

His thighs flex against my forehead as he clamps his fingers against my scalp, tangling in my hair, and holding my head immovable. I can only lie there, hands and legs tied down, throat relaxed, and jaw stretched for his pleasure.

Bending over my chest, he squeezes my breast with his free hand, pinching the nipple and tormenting it with his hot mouth.

I surrender in drugged wonderment as his length drives deeper against my throat, his hips grinding and rolling with his urgency. This is what he would look like if he was filling my pussy. The strain of his muscles, flex of his ass, and ram of his cock compose a seductive dance of intensity. He gives as much as he takes, his hunger spreading over my skin, garbling my moans around his pounding length, overtaking me.

Holding my head against his thrusts, he slides the other hand over my stomach and hooks two fingers inside me, sparking a needy clench through my inner muscles.

"Not gonna last long." His sharp breaths husk the air. "We're doing this together."

He shifts his touch to my tender clit and applies a solid, rolling pressure. My hips reach for it, grinding and rocking against his fingers. *Right there, right there.*

A spasm of tingling heat explodes beneath his diabolical caress.

He jerks against my tongue, his forehead falling against my chest as he strokes us into a moaning, trembling orgasmic duet.

I greedily swallow his release, panting beneath the wave of my own. His cock twitches against my lips, and my inner thighs quiver through the remnant aftershocks of orgasm number seven.

He tucks himself away and frees the shackles, lifting and moving me, limb by melted limb. I hang like a rag doll in his arms as he carries me to the piano bench and arranges my legs in a straddling position around his waist.

I slump against him, chest to chest, skin on skin, and hug his broad shoulders. "That was the worst torture ever."

Chuckling, he kisses my cheek and reaches behind me, fingers on the keyboard. With a deep breath, he envelops us in a gentle song, tranquilizing my hammering heart with Pink Floyd's "Comfortably Numb."

I curl up against him, soaking in the flex and sway of his body as he plays. The tempo of his breaths synchronizes with the melody, pacing my own. His skin, so soft and warm, smells woodsy and masculine and safe. I bury my nose against his neck and fill my lungs.

With my arms and legs hooked around him, I cling to the pillar of his torso. This brutal man is my home. His hell is my heaven.

I'm his Ivory, and he's my darkest note.

No matter what happens, I will never resent this. I'll never regret *him*.

He closes the song on a low, deep key and slides his strong hands across my back, massaging my spine.

Hugging me tighter against his chest, he lowers his lips to my shoulder, his tone quiet, gentle. "I didn't know she was pregnant until after..."

After Shreveport. After her betrayal.

I kiss his neck and run my fingers through his hair as bitterness flares inside me.

"She's seven months along." He breathes in, out. "The baby could be mine. Or not."

I lift my head and find his stark eyes. "Do you think...?"

He blinks, his expression conflicted. "I don't know. There was never an indication of cheating, and I'm pretty fucking observant."

Hard to argue that. "Then why do you question it?"

He tucks my hair behind my ear, his fingers lingering on my jaw. "I never thought she would betray me the way she did. If she can do that..."

"She could cheat."

He lowers his hand to stroke my hip, his eyes following the movement. "When I took over Shreveport, I worked long hours. Day and night. I was rarely home."

She could've been doing anything during that time. With anyone. Maybe he wasn't so observant back then?

I swallow around the ache in my throat. "Why was she at the clinic today?"

His gaze lifts to mine. "I've been ignoring her messages. Only way she knows how to find me is through my dad."

"What does she want?" My voice shakes with fragile nerves. "To reunite with you? Pick up where you left off?"

"Yes." He grips the back of my neck when I start to pull away. "She wants my money, Ivory."

I find that hard to believe. Anyone with half a brain must know that any love this man offers is more valuable than all the wealth in the world.

Leaning forward, I comb my fingers over the short hairs on the back of his head. "How much money are we talking?"

"Half of my inheritance. Millions. I would gladly give it if I knew the child was mine." He folds his arms around my back, holding me against him. "I gave blood months ago in my demand for a paternity test. She's yet to provide the results."

"That doesn't bode well for her. I mean, if the child is yours..."

"This would be a done deal, and she would be a very wealthy woman." He looks down at me, his eyes swirling in thought. "She knows my terms. I want those test results. If the baby isn't mine, she doesn't get a penny, and I'll never have to see her or think about her again. If it is mine, I'll be a father in every sense of the word."

And Joanne will be fully embedded in his life. My heart stutters and breaks.

He cups my neck, searching my face. "There is no *Joanne and me*. I'm yours. Tell me you understand."

I close my eyes against the intensity in his. "You said you love her."

"I also said I hate her." With a deep sigh, he lowers his forehead to mine. "Then I found something more meaningful than love and hate."

I stop breathing, my eyes fluttering open. "What?"
"You."

My pulse jolts with the rapid rush of my breaths. How can he shred my trust and stitch it back up so thoroughly in the span of such a short time?

"I'm sorry, Ivory. I should've told you." He rubs my back. "You have enough to worry about, and I just... I trust my instinct, and it tells me she's lying."

"I forgive you." Deeply. Endlessly. I rest my head on his shoulder. "What happens now?"

"I never wanted to threaten her career. I don't get off on leaving her jobless with a baby. But I *need* to know if that child is mine." The muscles beneath me harden with tension, and his tone sharpens. "She has until next weekend to prove paternity. If she doesn't meet the deadline, the Shreveport Board will receive damning photos of their dirty, deceitful Head of School."

# EMERIC

The following week passes in a blur of restlessness. With Lorenzo Gandara still on the loose and my constant paranoia about my living situation with Ivory, I'm on edge, irritable, and fucking exhausted. Adding to my stress is my orchestra performance this weekend.

Between nightly meetings and dress rehearsals for the symphony and Ivory's private lessons and homework, there's little down time. We spend half of our waking hours together, but we're focused on school, piano practice, and the necessary chores of everyday life.

The few times I've been able to pin her down with my fingers in her cunt, we're either rushed or exhausted. Not fucking her is torment worse than death, but the timing and my focus needs to be perfect.

I want to *date* her, and I'm frustrated by my inability to do that. She's never been treated to a romantic dinner or spun across a dance floor, all dressed up for a night out and appreciated by a man who simply enjoys her company. I ache to give her those things, without the expectation of sex. But venturing out in public with her has to wait.

The reminder that she's only seventeen tempers some of my impatience. She has an entire life yet to experience, and I intend to be a part of it.

In the meantime, I cherish our brief moments before sleep, those small spaces of time when she curls her body around mine. With the shedding fur ball nestled between our feet, we share stories about our lives, random pieces of ourselves, until she drifts into dreamland. Without fail, I lie awake for long hours after, holding her tightly as the looming news of three pivotal things monopolize my mind.

One, it's Thursday, and I still haven't heard from Joanne. Not a call or a text. Logic tells me if the baby is mine, she would've provided the evidence months ago. But she gets off on mind games and making me wait as a means to control me.

Two, my dad expedited the blood work from Ivory's exam, and the results are due any day. Once I have her clean bill of health, I won't be able to stop myself from fucking her into next week. I know she thinks she's ready, but she's yet to use her safe word. When I fuck her, will she lie beneath me—like she's done for every other dickhead—and silently will me to stop? Or will she be with me, making a conscious choice to surrender completely?

I need to find at least one of her hard limits and force her to confront it. Then I'll know.

The final thing occupying my mind is Lorenzo Gandara. After implementing my plan to remove him as a threat to Ivory, I'm stuck in a holding pattern, burning to see it come to fruition. The wait is maddening, making me question the sagacity in my approach. Maybe I should've handled him more directly, legal risks be damned.

Doesn't help that Ivory asks about him every fucking day.

I've been honest with her about the current proceedings, but if it doesn't pan out, I haven't enlightened her on my intent to straight-up murder that motherfucker.

I doubt she would care as long as it doesn't interfere with her dream. Ivory's nothing if not ambitious. She lives by the motto, *Everything is possible,* and her everything is the ivory tower of Leopold. I'm not in a hurry to upset the tenuous balance between her and me and the dean, but when the time comes, Ivory and I will have some decisions to make.

On a positive note, Prescott Rivard appears to be cooperating. I assigned his activity to my PI, his phone calls and movements all monitored discreetly and reported back to me. There's been no indication of retaliation.

On Friday, everything changes.

The afternoon arrives in a rapid succession of phone calls and messages. The explosion of disruptions makes it impossible to lecture so I give the students some busy work and bury my head in my phone. Ivory watches me curiously from her desk, her brow lifting in a *What the hell are you up to?* arch of suspicion.

I give her a hard glare, but on the inside, I'm barely holding myself together. By the time the final bell rings, I'm unable to keep my rabid fucking emotions at bay.

When the last student exits the classroom, I slam the door shut, yank Ivory from her desk, and crash her against the nearest wall.

She yelps, stretching her toes to reach the floor. "What are you—?"

I attack her mouth and devour her lips, starving and possessed, my hands flying over every inch of her I can reach, stroking, grabbing, holding. My cock hardens, and my pulse detonates. No more waiting. I fucking need her.

"Someone...will...see," she pants between kisses, both pushing and pulling against my chest, her attention straining toward the window in the door.

I bite her lips, thrilling in the soft feel of her body along the length of mine. "No lessons tonight. Go home. I'll meet you there."

With a stupendous amount of will power, I release her and storm toward my desk.

"What happened?" She stares at me, eyes wide and frozen where I left her. "Is this about—?"

"I gave you an order," I say quietly, harshly.

Turning my back on her, I stuff my belongings in the satchel, my blood roaring with heavy, urgent need. If she doesn't leave right this second, I'm going to fuck her against the whiteboard.

The instant her footfalls fade down the hall, I straighten my swelling cock, making it less visible with the tip pinned beneath my belt. Then I trail behind her at an unassuming distance. Outside, I watch from the main entrance as she crosses the parking lot and safely climbs inside the Porsche. Same thing I do every night. Except tonight is different.

Tonight, the wait is over.

The three-minute drive feels like three hours. I race through the house and find her in the kitchen with Schubert burrowed against her neck.

She nibbles her bottom lip, her huge brown eyes round and watchful. "You got the test results?"

The paternity test? Her blood work? Whichever one she

means, I'm too worked up to draw this out.

Separated by the length of the kitchen, I take a step toward her. "The baby isn't mine."

She buries her expression against Schubert's furry head.

"Don't do that." I inch closer, ten feet away, and take in her quickening breaths. "Never hide from me."

Setting the cat on the floor, she gives him a pat on the rump. Then she straightens and faces me head-on. Her lips thin, but the smile in her eyes is blinding. "Are you...happy about it? Or did you want..." Her gaze dims, her voice barely a whisper. "That baby?"

Two months ago, I would've been devastated by the proof that Joanne so callously cheated and pissed away our life together. But now? I'm floating on a cloud of liberated emotions, and the chief of those is gratitude. I want to thank her for being a traitorous cunt. If she hadn't betrayed me, I would still be with her, completely oblivious that the deepest, strongest love shines from brown eyes and a selfless, seventeen-year-old heart.

Another couple of steps, and I stop. Six feet away. I need to tell Ivory the rest before she's within arm's reach. Before I lose the grip on my control. "I want a child. Several, in fact. Someday. In the very distant future. With you."

She touches her parted lips as a ragged inhale shakes her chest.

I take another step toward her and tap anxious fingers on the island. "Lorenzo has been detained."

She gasps and places her hands on the back counter, breathing deeply.

With a rap sheet a mile long, he's wanted on suspicion of

robbery, drug possession, and assault with a deadly weapon. My PI identified his routine and hangouts, turned the information over to NOPD, and leaned hard on the police sergeant until priorities were adjusted and the arrest was made.

Tears well up in Ivory's eyes, her hands shaking against the granite surface. "How long?"

"He's looking at years for multiple offenses. The bail is set at two-hundred-thousand."

She nods as a trembling smile unfolds across her lips. "Thank you."

When she moves to come closer, I stop her with a strained expression. I want her. Too much.

She tilts her head and licks her lips. "You believed me when my own family called me a whore and a liar. I've been running from him for four years, and in one week, you removed him from my life." She stares at me in awe. "Emeric, you've done something no one has done for me in a really long time."

She doesn't clarify what that is, but I can fill in the blanks. I've made her feel safe.

"I wish it was more." I flex my hand on the island, holding her gaze. "I want him punished for rape, Ivory. If you change your mind about pressing charges, I'll be with you every step of the way."

"No." Her jaw sets. "I want to move on."

She's worried he'll come after her, and frankly, I am, too. I don't want her connected to his demise in any way. He won't be locked up forever, and I'll have to deal with his inevitable freedom when that day comes. But there's less risk for Ivory if he's not blaming her for the next however many years he's rotting in a cell.

As for the best piece of news I received this afternoon... I close the final few feet between us and prowl around her, lightly gliding my knuckles up her arm.

She shivers, turning her neck to maintain eye contact.

I pause behind her and grip her wrists. With her body facing the counter, I flatten her palms on the cabinet door above her head. "Don't move your hands."

She smiles at me over her shoulder. "If I do?"

*Brat.* I slam a hand against her gorgeous ass.

She flies up on tiptoes, head dropping back with a squeak of surprise. But her hands remain where I put them.

"Such a good girl," I whisper at her ear, causing her entire body to tremble.

Her responsiveness is such a fucking turn on. I've been hard since the day I met her, but I'm finally, *finally*, going to slacken this long-suffering ache between us.

Unless she uses her word.

I cover her hands with mine, pressing them against the cabinet, a silent reminder. Then I move down her bare arms, fingers stroking skin, then shifting to caress around the outer curves of her breasts.

She holds still for me, but there's a subtle sway in her posture as she lifts and leans toward my touch, her head tipping and eyes alert, following my every movement.

I roam my hands over the stiff material of her black dress, tracing the outline of her muscles and hipbones beneath. When I reach the hem at her knees, I gather the dress up her thighs, over her supple ass, and let it cling around her waist.

With her eyes turned to watch me, her lashes lower as I slide my mouth down the back of her dress. She sighs, bowing against the counter and dropping her head between her raised arms.

Crouching behind her, I fill my hands with her high round cheeks. The black lace panties look so damn sinful on her. Too bad this is the last time she'll wear them.

I grip the tiny straps around her hips and yank.

The sound of ripping lace brings her head around. "I liked those."

"I'll buy you a hundred more and rip every fucking one of them off your gorgeous ass."

As I stand, I reach around the front of her legs and drag the tips of my fingers up her inner thighs. Her trembling limbs and husky moans scorch heat through my cock, engorging it to painful steel.

When my hand encounters the soft hair on her pussy, I tug hard on the short strands. She bites down on her lip, muffling a gasp.

My heart pumps faster, harder. I press my chest against her back, kick her feet apart, and slide my finger along her slit.

Her head falls back on my shoulder, and her mouth chases mine. I dodge her, tickling my lips along her jaw, down her neck, blanketing her skin with my breaths.

"God, Emeric. I've never felt like this."

"Shhh." I nibble on her shoulder, let her feel my teeth, my tongue, and the heat burning me up inside.

Her head rolls, exposing her neck to my kisses. I suck on her ear lobe, circling my tongue as I plunge my fingers into her slippery cunt. Fuck, she's so warm and wet and tight.

She whimpers and rubs her ass against my cock, propelling my teasing touches into a panting, grinding imperative. Our bodies roll together, fucking without penetration. My cock is lined up, but my slacks are in the way.

I thrust my fingers in her soaking pussy, savoring the clench of her inner walls. "You're clean, Ivory."

Her hands twitch against the cabinet door. "Clean?"

"Your test results." I slide my touch toward her anal rim. "We're both clean."

She clenches her ass. "Are we going to—?" Her glutes squeeze against my probing finger. "No! Not there." She pants. "What are you doing?"

"I'm going to fuck you, Ivory. Tonight. Right now." I grind against her hip, rubbing my finger between her crack, teasing that tight ring of muscle. I ache to take her there, to fuck every hole in her body.

Holding her hip in a bruising grip, I reach deeper between her legs, pressing my finger against the tiny pucker of skin.

A pained keening noise tears from her throat, and her hands fall from the cabinet. "Scriabin."

I jolt backward, my pulse racing and hands in the air. "Ivory?"

*Fucking hell, she used her word. She used her fucking word.*

She shakes against a full-body tremor, torso curved over the counter, thighs clenched together, and arms wrapped around her chest. "I c-c-can't."

Frustration pummels through me, angry and vicious. *And irrational.* I force it back, breathing tightly, then deeply, desperate to understand.

Relaxing my arms at my sides, I try to soften my voice. "Be

PAM GODWIN

specific."

"Not my..." She shoves her dress down her legs and turns toward me, eyes glassy and terrified. "Not back there."

"Have you ever been touched there?"

Her face falls, and she curls in on herself.

Molten rage pours through my veins like lava. I haven't examined her closely enough to see scarring, but it's obvious someone sodomized her. Possibly several someones.

Horrific images cleave through my brain, kicking my heartbeat into a macabre orchestra of violence.

"No anal." I clench my shaking hands and take a cautious step forward. "That's your limit?"

"I can't, Emeric." She backs up and bumps against the counter, her expression pinched in torment. "Please, don't do this."

My stomach drops. She thinks I'd force her?

"Ivory." Another step, my voice gravelly with heartache. "I won't touch you there. I promise."

She stares at the doorway, chin quivering and knees twitching. She looks like she's going to run.

"Eyes on me," I say gently and wait for her to obey. "Is that your only limit?"

*Please say yes.* I thought for sure she was willing to have sex. How the fuck did I misjudge this?

"I-I don't know."

My lungs tighten, laboring for air. I stand just out of arm's reach, respecting her safe zone. But I'm not ready to back down. I'm sure as fuck not giving up.

She has all the power here, and goddammit, I'll do whatever is needed to make sure she knows it.

I keep my voice level but firm. "You have two choices. One. Walk down the hall, sit behind the piano, and wait for me to begin your lesson. Two. Head upstairs to the bedroom, remove your clothes, and wait for me to fuck you." I steel my gaze. "No anal, Ivory. You have my word."

Arms wrapped around her chest, she rubs her biceps, still not looking at me.

I infuse my tone with conviction. "Whatever you choose, there will be no disappointment or shame. Not from me *or* you. Understand?"

"Yes." A shaky whisper.

"Go."

The second she's out of sight, I spin toward the counter and grind my fist against the granite. *Fuck, fuck, fuck.* I should've known she didn't want to be touched there. I shouldn't have pushed her.

No, that's bullshit. If I could just think past my aching cock for a goddamn minute... *Deep breath.*

We just made a huge fucking step forward. She used her word and showed me one of her limits. Now I can trust her to use it again. I'll wait for her for an eternity if I have to.

The pad of tiny feet draws my attention to the floor. Schubert prances around me and leans his body against my leg, covering my black slacks in orange hair.

I reach down and scoop him up.

"She's going to shut down on me, isn't she?" I press my lips against his head, holding him against my chest. "Fuck, I want to kill every fucking prick that's ever touched her."

He purrs like a motor and arches his neck for a scratch. Curling my fingers beneath his chin, I oblige. Soon, my pulse evens out, and my muscles loosen.

"Let's go find our girl."

I place him on the floor and follow him out of the kitchen, through the hearth room, and into the living room. He veers off toward the couches and stretches out on one of the cushions.

Straight ahead and down the hall is the music room. To the left and toward the—

A delicate black shoe sits on the rug in the foyer. My pulse jumps.

I head toward it, loosening the tie around my neck as I gaze up the staircase. The second shoe perches on the curve in the steps.

*She chose the bedroom.*

My cock twitches, and my breaths speed up. I launch forward, racing up the stairs and around the corner.

The sight of her black dress on the floor in the hallway spurs me faster, building a hungry pressure at the base of my spine. When I reach the bedroom door, I find it shut, the handle adorned with her black lacy bra.

Christ, she's turning me inside out. I adjust the rigid ache in my slacks and drag in several calming breaths. Then I open the door.

# IVORY

The bedroom door swings open, and I release a sigh of relief.

I perch on the side of the bed, nude and vulnerable, as we stare at one another. Seeing him framed in the doorway and watching me with those stony eyes sweeps my breath away.

I'm so damn conflicted about why I used my word. How did I let one paralyzing moment of terror override every ounce of trust I have in him?

Not only did Emeric stop, he didn't explode into a fit of anger. His patient reaction and dependable control proves my fear of him was unwarranted and weak. Am I so dysfunctional that I can't have an intimate relationship with a man who would rather die than endanger me?

His light blue button-up hangs open at the collar, the cobalt tie unknotted and dangling around his neck. The waistcoat is a multi-colored plaid of blue, gray, and black. It would look drab on a clothes rack, but with his sapphire eyes, chiseled jaw, and grungy mess of black hair, he sells it like a trend-setting catalog model.

Jesus, he's painfully handsome. But it's the synergy of his commanding aura and unwavering devotion that makes him particularly effective in stealing my heart.

Instead of forcing himself in my ass or kicking me out of

his life, he gave me a choice. There wasn't a millisecond of debate in my mind. I won't ever willingly accept anal sex, but he will *never* force me. My faith in that made it easy to leave him a trail of clothes.

Now that he's here, I don't know what to say or how to steer us back to the way things were. But I don't have to do anything.

He crosses the room with effortless strides, frames my face in his strong hands, and brushes his lips against mine. "Are you okay?"

"Yes." My breath hiccups. "I'm so sorry."

"Never apologize for using your word." He kisses my mouth and eases back to look into my eyes. "Everyone has limits."

I jerk my head. "You? What are they?"

He lowers, squatting between my legs and glides his hands down my neck. "Defecation."

"Defe—what?"

"Scat. Feces. That's a big fat *no*."

"Oh my God, people do that?"

"Yes." He fights a twitchy smile and wins, flattening his lips. "And bestiality. Also my limit."

My throat convulses. "How does your mind even go there?"

"You have to ask?"

I grin. He's a perverted, kinky man, and damn if I don't love that about him. "Good to know you won't be taking advantage of poor Schubert."

He makes a disgusted face. "That was *your* mind going *there*."

"You started it."

He molds his hands around my waist, his thumbs tracing my hipbones. "No sharing. Ever. You're mine. I'm yours. *That* is my hardest limit."

"You'd rather I shit on you than have sex with someone else?"

"Yes." His gaze flies to mine, the hardening blue depths cemented with a biting tone. "If another man so much as touches you, my reaction will be murderous. Remember that."

"Okay," I whisper.

He rises to his feet, his fingers making a descent down the front of his waistcoat, slowly releasing each button as his eyes rake over my body. "Touch yourself."

Parting my legs, I slide a hand between my thighs. His vest drops to the floor, and my nipples tighten against the sudden flutter of excitement.

He removes the tie and unbuttons the shirt in the same unhurried fashion, seemingly content with his view of me. His head tips minutely, lips parting as his gaze follows the roll of my fingers against my clit.

I stroke softly, watching him watch me, my pulse slurring a smooth legato rhythm through my veins.

He shrugs out of the shirt sleeves, exposing curved biceps and defined pecs and abs. Then he crouches to remove his shoes and socks, never looking away. "Lie back. Widen your legs."

I scoot toward the center, lying sideways on the mattress, and swirl my fingers over my wet folds. The sensitivity of my touch and his uninterrupted attention on me fuels a blazing fire in my core. I'm so attuned to him, to the harmony of his breaths and the subtle twitches in his hands. It comes from a habit of sexual enjoyment of his presence, and it's solidified in the knowledge that he will never let me down.

With an economy of movement, he loosens the belt, opens his slacks, and shoves the last of his clothes to the floor. I've seen his rock-strong body parts in bits and pieces, but never all of him at once, fully in the buff. Sweet heaven, he gives new meaning to *buff*.

His cock rises up, jutting above the columns of his powerful thighs. He doesn't touch it, doesn't even acknowledge it as he approaches, eyes locked on mine and expression intense.

He grips my ankle and circles the mattress, dragging my legs and rotating my position until my head is near the headboard. He stops with my feet at the foot of the bed and leans forward.

The indentation of his knee on the mattress jump-starts my heart. The predatory look in his eyes stops my breath. He crawls over me, legs on the outsides of mine, prowling on hands and knees and straddling my thighs.

I expected him to wrench my legs open and shove between them, but he's proved repeatedly he's not like the others.

Hovering over me, he fuses his mouth to mine while his hand roves my body, stroking and fondling my chest, thighs, and pussy. His feverish tongue, heavy exhales, and devilish touches drive me breathlessly insane.

I tug at his shoulder, attempting to bring him closer. "Will you...lie on top of me? Let me feel your weight?"

He's pinned me against a wall, tied me to a piano, and

fingered me against the kitchen island, but I've never been in this position with him. No matter how many times I've imagined it, I know it'll be unlike anything I've experienced.

With my thighs squeezed together between his, he cups the back of my head in both hands and lowers his long frame on top of me. His eyes search my face as his weight sinks me into the mattress, his chest covering mine in heat and muscle.

My mouth falls open on a blissful gasp, and he catches it, his tongue sliding and claiming, his lips firm, aggressive, and all mine. The bulky size of him smothers me in security, his strength a shield of protection, and his hands supporting my head as if in supplication.

We kiss through an endless sonata of heartbeats and moans, our foreheads rolling together and hips grinding greedily. Our bodies rock in a synchronized wave, trapping the steely length of him between us.

I'm scared out of my ever-loving mind thinking about his wide girth being rammed up inside of me. But I'm ready. I've never been so ready for this.

I flex my quads, trying to open my thighs. Why hasn't he spread my legs already?

"Don't test me, Ivory." He reaches between us and rubs his fingers along the slippery seam of my pussy. "Where my head's at right now, I'll split you in half."

In the next breath, he flips us, rolling me on top and folding my legs to straddle his hips.

"I'm giving this to you. Just this once." He reaches over his head and grips the laddered rungs of the headboard. "My hands won't move. I'm going to lie here and hold still while *you* fuck *me*."

Oh.

Wow.

Okay, that's...different. And really nice.

Until I gaze down at the huge, long cock rising up in front of me. How does this work? He wants me to...sit on that thing?

I meet his eyes, shaking my head. "I've never..."

His fingers blanch around the rungs, his expression pained. Is that anger?

"Never been on top?" he growls.

"Never." Nervous energy trickles through me. I grip his shaft with both hands, stroking up and down, reacquainting myself with his size. "I don't know, Emeric. Can I even fit...?"

His breath rushes out. "Dammit, Ivory. It'll fit." The sinews in his forearms strain with his hold on the headboard. "You're fucking tormenting me here."

Flexing his thighs beneath me, he pins me with a look that is so integral to who he is. The almighty confidence in his eyes tells me to shut up and pay attention because he's about to share a mind-blowing experience with me. It's his most powerful expression, one that's probably gotten him laid, without a single spoken word, more times than I care to think about.

"That look you're giving me..." I squeeze my fingers around his cock, enjoying the sound of his strangled breath. "Do you do that when you're performing on stage?"

His hips shift beneath me, his voice tortured. "What?"

"Do you eye fuck women in the audience?"

"Ivory, get on my dick before I lose my fucking mind."

I bend down and place a kiss on the bulbous crown in an

affectionate greeting. The next kiss is a plea to be gentle.

Then I rise on my knees and position him between my legs.

True to his word, he doesn't thrust or move his hands. His eyes glow like blue flames as he waits for me to draw him inside.

I lower onto him, inch by inch, marveling at the stretching sensation, the easy slide, the perfect fit. It's never this wet, this careful. Fuck, I feel so full. Hungry. *Relieved.*

The sound of his guttural groan spurs me faster. When he's all the way in, I squeeze my inner muscles around him.

His eyes clamp shut, muscles flexing in his jaw, his body shaking beneath me. I don't think he's breathing.

"Emeric?"

A throaty grunt is the only response he gives, charging my already overloaded senses with giddiness. And I haven't even moved yet.

I lean forward and press my lips to the ridge of his tense chest. "This is it. We're doing it."

His eyes fly open, and he releases a pained laugh. "We're not *doing* anything." His hands tighten around the headboard, his glare hard and demanding. "Fuck my cock, Ivory."

I roll my hips, testing the feel of him sliding against my insides and filling me with jolts of static.

His entire body trembles beneath me. "Faster."

With my palms on his chest, I rotate along his shaft, lifting and rocking. The dragging, tickling strokes are unreal. The little shocks of electricity, the panting sounds of our breaths, everything centers around where we're joined.

He raises his head, watching me intensely. "Ride it."

I do, willingly and with abandon.

"Fucking grind it." His hand slips from the headboard, but just as quickly, he adjusts his grip. "Harder, Ivory. Deeper."

I let loose, lifting my arms behind my head, closing my eyes, and circling my hips. When I bounce, my breasts sway and the bed frame creaks. When I bear down and rock, my clit catches fire.

I could come like this. A bona-fide orgasm. With a cock inside me. Mr. Marceaux's cock. Hard to ignore the significance of that.

"Ah, fuck." The headboard groans in his grip. "Look at you."

I open my eyes and collide with his, a smile pulling at my cheeks. "I'm fucking my teacher."

"Jesus Christ, Ivory." His biceps flex above his head, his thighs hardening beneath me. "Give me your mouth."

I slide up his chest and thrust my hips, delighting in the feeling of the new angle. When I reach his lips, his tongue seeks mine, twirling and tasting.

He snaps his teeth at me, his muscles bunching and twitching. "Your sloppy cunt is dripping all over me."

His filthy mouth strengthens the brewing tide inside me. I sweep my hands over his biceps and cup his face, the scratch of his stubble scraping my palms. He deepens the kiss, the strong stretch of his jaw as erotic as the sinful way he glides his tongue.

I miss his hands on me, though, and the bite of his belt, his painful pleasure. I don't like his silence, either. I ache for his growly orders commanding my every move. But he seems incapable of talking all of a sudden. With his body so rigid and hard, I suspect it's taking a heavy dose of concentration to not move his hips or let go of the rungs.

No more torturing.

With my hands on his face, I kiss him fiercely, passionately, while working my pussy up and down his length, searching for the spot. When I find it, all of my nerves, cells, and thoughts rush to my womb, gathering, pressurizing, and exploding through my body in a pounding series of percussions.

My mouth opens in a soundless scream, my gaze locked on his eyes. His lips part with me, his pupils dilate, and his hands fly to the back of my head. Then he's kissing me mercilessly, hammering his hips, and spiraling me through another orgasm.

He rolls us, hands on my face, his mouth and breaths consuming mine. Our tongues battle, licking and lashing as his weight crushes my chest and his cock fills me up. Over and over, he slams his hips with wicked-hard thrusts. I reach down, put my hands on the hard muscle of his ass for the first time, and hold on.

My God, it's a perfect ass. He's perfect everywhere. The cinnamon on his tongue. The dark bass notes in his voice. The musical talent in his hands. The sight of him in jeans and t-shirts, ties and waistcoats, and nothing at all. I'll never get enough.

His plunging pace jumps and jerks, falling into an abrupt staccato. He tears his mouth away, his hand dropping to the mattress to support the bow of his back as he roars through his orgasm. His eyes stay with me through every gasping shout, telling me I'm the reason for his pleasure, the heart of it.

Lowering his head to my shoulder, he seems to be winding down, trying to steady his heaving breaths. But the press of his teeth against my skin holds me on a heightened edge of arousal.

A moment later, he pins my arms above my head, hips rocking, cock throbbing inside me. "Remember your word."

My eyes widen. "We're not done?"

He makes a tsking sound, closes a strong hand around my breast, and bites my nipple.

Then he fucks me.

For hours.

His rhythms span between gentle and wild, his tempo quickly changing with countless alternating positions. He arranges me on hands and knees and smacks my ass while he thrusts from behind. He tosses me on my back, collars my throat with his fingers, and fucks me with my thighs pinched together between his. The choreography gets a little foggy after that as my body surrenders to the floaty, perverted world of Emeric Marceaux.

Much of the evening slides past my heavy-lidded eyes in a blanket of sweat-slick skin, tender caresses, and passionate kisses. But as this is Emeric, and his way is infused with domination, it requires an emotional and mental subtlety that goes far beyond the technical act of sex. He tells me when, where, and how hard, and I roll with it, yearn for it, my need to satisfy him outweighing all else.

In turn, he pleasures me. Right into a coma.

"Ivory?" He bites my thigh.

I can't even move. Why do I need to? He'll just move me himself.

Having just come from the shower, where he banged me against the tiled wall, I lie face down on the bed. Naked, flushed, sated, I try to talk myself into lifting my hand to remove the dripping hair from my face. *I'll do it in a minute.*

He moves up my limp body and brushes the wet strands behind my ear. "You're ten years younger than me. Don't tell me an old man wore you out."

I snort—the extent of the energy I can muster. But in my defense, he works out two hours every day.

The mattress bounces as he shifts around me, kissing every inch of my body from my head to my toes. Doesn't take long before I fall blissfully asleep beneath the affection.

When I wake, he's stretched out beside me with a towel wrapped around his waist, trailing a finger along my spine.

"How long was I out?"

"Fifteen minutes."

I fold my arms beneath my cheek and meet his hooded eyes. "I've never done this."

He reaches behind him, grabs a glass of water from the nightstand, and holds it out to me. "What?"

After a long refreshing drink, I hand it back and change the subject. "You didn't eat dinner."

He returns the glass then lies on his side, resting his head on the bend of his arm. "Neither of us ate. Finish what you were going to say."

I reach out and trace the curve of his upper lip. "The *after* stuff. This. It's always been sex and run, usually followed by crying and hiding." I give him a soft smile. "I like this. A lot."

He pulls me against his chest and kisses my temple. The hush of our breaths envelopes us, and he hugs me like that for so long I wonder if he fell asleep.

Eventually, his whisper breaks the silence. "I like it, too, Ivory. So much so I'm terrified it'll be taken from us."

I wrap an arm around his wide back. "We'll be careful."

"We need to tone it down at school."

I scratch my fingernail across his nipple. "You need to stop giving me those eyes."

"What eyes?" A smile teases his lips.

"The ones that say..." I deepen my voice. *"Come here, Miss Westbrook. Look at me, Miss Westbrook. On your knees–"*

He surges up with a roguish grin on his face.

I roll out of reach, my mocking tone tumbling into laughter. *"Suck my cock, Miss Westbrook."*

He flashes his teeth and crawls after me, losing his towel in the process.

My gaze dips down his chest and lands on his dick. It's...*soft?* Holy shit, it looks weird. I tilt my head, trying to get a better view.

He sits back on his ankles and narrows his eyes. "You're going to give me a complex."

"I haven't ever..." I lean over his lap and wrap my hand around it. It's still heavy, just... "So soft."

He stares at me curiously. "Keep touching it, and it won't be."

Sure enough, within seconds, it begins to stiffen. I'm familiar with this part, and he's the biggest and baddest of them all. Ironically, he's also the safest.

He swings his arm around and slaps my ass. "I'm not finished with you, but we need to eat."

We make it through half a gourmet pepperoni pizza before

he bends me over the kitchen island and proves exactly how he's not finished with me.

I hope he never is.

# EMERIC

The following evening, I stretch behind the piano during the intermission of Mahler's Ninth Symphony and tug at the strangling bow tie. The tux is one of many from my private collection, tailored and designed with quality workmanship. Doesn't matter how fucking expensive it is. The restricting fabrics make me itchy and overheated. The whole pretentious look just doesn't suit me.

Neither does the music.

Joanne never attended my performances, claiming boredom in hearing the same masterpieces on concert programs year in and year out. Can I blame her?

While I appreciate the classics, I doubt Gustav Mahler intended for his symphonies to become commercialized affairs of mindless repetition. In his fifty-one years, he only conducted his second symphony ten times.

I scan the Beaux-Arts style of the philharmonic theater, surrounded by an orchestra of pompous old farts and full-time musicians, most of which have their own resident halls. Rather than composing passionate modern music, they seem to be content wasting their extraordinary talents on routine recycling of classical repertoire.

But *I* am not content. Not even a little.

So why am I here, wallowing in this jeremiad?

Securing a seat in the symphony was a natural progression in my musical career, a highly notable one. It was a means of self-justification, a validation of all my hard work and talent. It wasn't until the goal was achieved that I realized it was the wrong aspiration for me.

I want to create my own music, tap into my imagination, and transform classical piano into something fresh and wild. And I want to share that passion, teach it, and open eager minds to new ideas.

Sitting behind the strings section, I take in the shadowed silhouettes of concert-goers in the balcony seats. A grin twitches my lips as Ivory's question teases my mind.

*Do you eye fuck women in the audience?*

There were several months after Joanne when the highlight of my concerts was finding my next fuck. Now?

My gaze connects with the most attractive feature in the theater, the only reason I'm smiling tonight.

She sits in the front row, glowing like a bright aria surrounded by dark instrumentals. Her red Versace dress follows the sinuous lines of her body from tits to toes, the thigh-high slit bordered with Swarovski rhinestones.

I know every detail because I handpicked it myself—just like I did all her clothes. But I chose this particular dress for a night just like this one, imagining her wearing it while watching me perform.

Despite my misgivings about her attending the concert, seeing her in that evening gown almost makes the risk worth it. Almost.

The parents of Le Moyne Academy students frequent these

DARK
NOTES

venues, and though Ivory drove separately with Stogie in tow, I worry about the wrong people making the right connections about our relationship. But she begged to be here, seducing me with *Please* on her lips. So I secured two front row seats and lined up her date.

Seated beside her, Stogie reluctantly wears the tux I bought for him, his big hand repeatedly rubbing his bald head, as if lamenting the absence of his beloved baseball cap. What a pair they make. Two musicians passionate about classical interpretation, and this is their first philharmonic performance?

I wonder if it meets their expectations. I'll pay close attention to Ivory's reaction after the show, as well as her responses to the other things I have planned for her in the coming months. She claims she wants to attend Leopold, that her ultimate dream is to sit where I'm sitting now, *in a sold-out venue, shivering under the stage lights.*

But what does she really know about the music world and the opportunities available to her? I intend to enlighten her. Then, if she still wants to go to Leopold, I have a plan to make that happen.

Two sections away, my parents occupy their season-ticket seats, heads bowed together in conversation. I asked them not to approach Ivory tonight, in order to maintain her disassociation from me outside of school.

Ivory and I willingly accept the risks of our entanglement. But it also puts my parents' livelihoods in jeopardy. If I'm caught with her, no one would go to a doctor whose son is a convicted sex offender. And my mom? Leopold would burn her at the stake. So I've been holding Mom off from introductions.

The concert ends, and the next three weeks float by in a blissful fog of Ivory.

When Thanksgiving arrives, I finally give in to Mom's demands to meet her.

As I drive my seventeen-year-old student to my parents' house for turkey dinner, I'm on tenterhooks, not feeling any easier about the secrecy of our relationship.

The moment my mom opens the door and stares at my hand where it grips tightly to Ivory's, my hackles go up.

Yes, I'm her teacher. Yes, I shove my cock in her, rigorously and with unadulterated depravity, morning and night. But the depth of my feelings for her goes so far beyond bullshit laws I really don't give a fuck what anyone thinks.

But my parents worry. They're also overly supportive and devoted to my happiness. That's why I brought her here. She had a parent like mine once.

I want her to experience that kind of love again.

# IVORY

After dinner, I lean back in the couch, shifting the waistband
of my skirt to ease my aching belly. I don't know if it's from
my overindulgence of turkey, mashed potatoes, and buttery
bread, or if I'm riddled with plain old nerves about being
alone with Laura Marceaux.

"I see why he's so taken with you." She smiles at me
warmly and reclines in the chair beside the couch.

My gaze wanders through the doorway of the kitchen and
lands on the white t-shirt stretching across Emeric's back.
Sitting at the table with his dad, he straddles the back of a
chair, deep in conversation. I can't see his face or hear his
words, but the deep notes in his voice vibrate through me,
soothing me like a sensual lullaby.

He doesn't wear briefs beneath his jeans, and right now,
the denim hangs dangerously low on his hips, barely covering
the hard muscles of his ass. If he leans over just a little more,
my view will become a whole lot more distracting.

I clear my throat. "I'm taken with him, too."

She swirls the red wine in her glass, studying me intently.
It's so strange to see Emeric's blue eyes set in such a soft
expression. She's intimidatingly beautiful. Not a wisp of gray
in her shoulder-length black hair. But there's decades of

wisdom in the way she looks at me, like she can read my thoughts and make sense of them.

She sips her wine. "You both seem happy. Maybe a little on edge, understandably, but happy. You've only been living together for...a month?"

"Five weeks."

Does she think that's insufficient? That five weeks isn't long enough to measure the seriousness of a relationship?

I want to point out that we've been emotionally wrapped up in each for three months and the actual sex part didn't happen until three weeks ago, but that's TMI. Besides, on the way here, Emeric forbade me to act weird about us. *No shame. Be yourself. They won't judge us.*

As it turns out, he was right. Laura carries on like the most important thing on her mind is her stories about Emeric's ornery childhood. Her kindness eventually opens me up enough to share memories of my dad. We steer clear of discussions about Leopold, the conflict of interest too sensitive. But it doesn't hinder us from settling into a comfortable exchange, as if I'm just a normal girlfriend, getting to know the family.

An hour later, I'm completely enraptured with her. Her disposition is so weightless and refreshing. Her gentle eyes and sincere smile radiates the kind of serenity that only comes from deep-seated happiness.

She's the embodiment of maternal warmth and affection. Such a devastating contrast to my own mother. She makes me feel accepted and nurtured and...young, but only in the best way.

In the kitchen, Dr. Marceaux stands from the table,

squeezes Emeric's shoulder, and disappears down the hall that leads deeper into the estate.

"If you don't mind..." Laura rises from the chair. "I'm going to go see where Frank went off to." As she passes the couch, she reaches down and grips my hand. "It's so good to finally meet you, Ivory."

I let the tenderness of her words sink in. "You, too."

Emeric hasn't moved from his seat in the kitchen, his forearms folded on the back of the chair.

Standing, I brush down the flirty mid-thigh skirt. I feel pretty, but not flashy, my sleeveless green blouse a fitted button-up over a thin camisole. If I did my own shopping, the outfit is something I would've chosen.

I approach his back and zoom in on the peek of skin above his low-hanging jeans. No ass crack. He's too cool for that. But a shadow teases the valley between his brawny cheeks. It's too inviting to ignore.

I dip a finger beneath the denim and trace that sexy cleft.

He draws in a long, deep breath, his voice husky. "Ivory."

Stroking the top of his crack, I put my mouth next to his ear and whisper, "I love your ass."

His hips rock, and his forehead lowers to his bent arms. "My ass loves you."

My breath falters. His ass loves me or *he* loves me? I want him to mean both.

I place my palms over the lean muscles along his spine and caress in slow circles. I still find it startling that I'm able to touch him like this. To just walk up to him when we're alone and show him affection. How crazy is it that I actually *want* to put my hands on him?

The last five weeks have drastically changed my perceptions about myself and my ability to do normal things *with a man.*

Leaning in, I loop my arms around his shoulders and press my upper body against his.

With his head tipped down, he wraps a large hand around both of my wrists, shackling them against his chest. "One of the most erotic things a woman can do is brush her tits against a man's back, and Ivory, your tits are sinful."

Jesus, his parents could hear. I try to lift my chest away, but he holds me still with his grip on my arms. My attention flicks toward the empty hallway.

"Even sexier, you're not even trying to turn me on." He shifts his head and bites my bicep.

My mouth parts on a soundless gasp, my breath held in anticipation. What am I going to do with this naughty man? If he touches me in a more provocative manner, I won't care where we are or who's watching.

He slides his lips up my arm, and I melt against his back.

His free hand drifts behind me, latching onto the bare skin of my thigh beneath the skirt. "Did my mom give you the third degree?"

I kiss his neck, savoring his warm smell. "I've become impervious to the methods of Marceaux interrogation."

"Is that right?"

The tightening pressure of his fingers around my hands kicks up my pulse. His thumb strokes the underside of my wrist, and I know he can feel the thudding palpation of my heartbeat there.

I bury my nose in the soft hair behind his ear, inhaling the scent of wood from his shampoo. "What did you talk about with your dad?"

"You. Us."

With the manacle of his hand around my wrist, he hauls me to his side. Then he rises from the chair, snags his gray fedora from the table, and sets it on his head with a tilt so subtle it could be accidental.

I'm not fooled. Everything he does is insidiously calculated. Like pairing his jeans and white t-shirt with a fedora? Seemingly harmless, as if he just threw something on. But dammit, he knew that sexy look would work me into a lusty froth.

It's his steady stare, though, the deep oceans of his eyes beneath the brim of the hat, that makes me never want to look away.

The room dims around us until I'm only aware of him and the pulsing beats between us. I sink into the luring waves of desire, into that deliciously dark abyss that craves his punishing grip, growly voice, and vicious thrusts.

*Not here.*

With great effort, I pull myself back to the surface and take a deep breath. "You talked to your dad about us? What did he say?"

Does his dad condemn our relationship? Is Emeric having second thoughts?

The fingers around my wrist tighten, and he wrenches my arm behind my back. The movement shoves me right up against his swelling erection.

His eyes ensnare mine. "He wanted to make sure I have all my bases covered, that I've thought through everything."

With my arm pinned behind my back, he cradles my face with his free hand. "I'm working through a few cautionary measures to keep us safe until you graduate."

"Like what?" I hate this constant looming threat of someone hurting us.

He brushes his mouth against mine. "Trust me?"

"Deeply."

His teeth catch my bottom lip. "Let's go home and take care of your pussy."

I grin into the kiss. "Schubert?"

"Him, too."

We say our goodbyes to his parents, climb into the car, and drive to his house without attacking one another. But the second the garage door closes behind the GTO, he gives me a look that liquefies every bone in my body.

In a fluidity of motion, he tosses his hat, releases our safety belts, and flings his seat backward away from the steering wheel.

His hands fly to his zipper, yanking it down and freeing his hard cock. "Straddle me."

One gravelly command, and I'm instantly wet.

I launch at him, banging a knee on the console as I tumble into his lap. He wrenches my legs around him, my ass bumping the wheel and honking the horn. We laugh with our mouths melded together, his hands under my skirt and my fingers tangled in his sexy-as-hell hair.

Yanking the crotch of my panties to the side, he plunges a finger inside me. "So fucking ready."

Then he slams me down on his cock.

I moan through the bursting sensations, clenching my

inner muscles and arching my back. He grips my ass with one hand and the back of my head with the other, thrusting vigorously and holding me so tightly he's the only thing that exists.

He bucks beneath me with hard-hitting drives as the hand on my head directs the angle and depth of the kiss. His tongue fucks my mouth the way his cock fills my pussy. Deeply, urgently, and completely unrestrained.

His muscles shake and contract. His hoarse groans harden my nipples, and the sensual, hungry roll of his hips reduces me to a trembling puddle of surrender.

I dissolve in the steel bands of his arms as he kisses me senseless, drags me up and down his length, and jacks himself off in the clutch of my body.

I come hard and long, my nails scratching his scalp and his name howling from my throat. He shoves inside me in a ruthless grind, drops his head on my shoulder, and chases his release with a deep, throaty groan.

When he lifts his head, we stare at each other, panting, clinging tightly together, lips touching and releasing. He trails his nose along mine, his eyes so close, never looking away. I'm so lost in this man, so over my head, heart wide open, and soul quaking.

We aren't just a teacher and student, a Dom and submissive, a man and woman.

"We're a timeless concerto." I kiss his lips. "A musical masterpiece."

He drags his mouth across my jaw, his cock jerking inside me. "Like Scriabin's 'Black Mass?'"

Too dissonant.

I arch my neck for his lips. "I was thinking along the lines of Beethoven's 'Ode to Joy.'"

"Lame." He bites the skin beneath my ear. "We're more like Van Halen's 'Hot For Teacher.'"

Oh my God. I stifle my grin. "You're ruining my analogy. That's not even a concerto."

"We'll compose our own masterpiece." His mouth glides down my neck, kissing and licking. "A song that will never end."

I *love* the sound of that.

# IVORY

Two weeks later, I trudge across the school parking lot, digging through my satchel for the car keys. The sun's long gone, and the time is ticking somewhere south of sleep-thirty. Man, my ass is dragging.

At school, Emeric's been working me hard behind the piano in preparation for the holiday performance this weekend. At home, he works me hard against the wall, strapped to his headboard, and kneeling beneath the heat of his belt. He's an endless, high-intensity, cardiovascular workout. For the life of me, I don't know where he finds his energy.

There's only a few cars scattered in the lot, the Porsche on one end and the GTO on the other. The surrounding darkness cools the air, chilling my skin beneath the light sweater. The scarce lighting doesn't help my search for the keys. I root around the text books in my bag, head lowered, cursing under my breath.

*Found them.* I punch the unlock button and wince at the loud chirp.

When I look up, I come face to face with the last person I expected to see.

Six feet away and leaning against the Porsche, my brother

gives me a no-good smile. "Where've you been, Ivory?"

My muscles freeze up. How does he know that's my car? Has he been following me? Does he know where I live? *Who* I'm living with?

I fidget with the key fob. No use hiding it. I already made the damn car light up. "It took you two months to come looking for me? Wow, Shane. I guess I should feel special you noticed me missing at all."

He straightens and plucks a cigarette from the pack in his pocket. His buzzed blond hairline recedes from his broad pale forehead, his cheeks sunken beneath dark eyes. He looks as tired as I feel. And thinner. His jeans and flannel shirt hang on his tall, gaunt frame.

What the hell happened to him? Does this have anything to do with Lorenzo's arrest? My chest tightens.

"Nice ride." He lights the smoke and glides a hand over the white hood. "How'd you score it? Turning tricks?"

My trembling fingers curl around the strap of my satchel. Emeric will be right behind me, and Shane will recognize him from the night he broke Shane's nose. If I run back inside, maybe I can circumvent him.

I pivot in the direction of Crescent Hall. Too late. Emeric's halfway across the lot, his long strides eating up the pavement and heading right toward me. I can't see his face from this distance, but I know exactly what I'd find in his eyes. The hairs lift on my arms.

How can I warn him that the shadowy line behind me is my brother? Anything I do will make Shane suspicious. He's blocking my path to the car, but I could walk in the opposite direction, head down the road or something. Emeric would chase me down.

Shane would, too. He came here for a reason, and he's not going to leave until he gets it.

There's nothing I can do to stop this impending confrontation.

I spin back to Shane, my stomach rolling. "What do you want?"

He exhales a stream of smoke. "Mom's gone."

"So? She's always—"

"No, she packed up her shit a month ago and fucking dis..." His eyes shift over my shoulder, tapering into slits. His mouth drops open in disbelief. "I fucking know that guy."

Shit. My pulse leaps to my throat. Why couldn't Emeric just let me handle this?

"Is there a problem here?" His chilling voice is right behind me, tingling up my spine.

Emeric steps in front of me, hands clasped behind his rigid back, his expensive suit pervading the air with authority.

Shane might've lost weight, but his frame is wider and taller than Emeric's. If this turns into a physical throw down, Emeric might never be able to play piano again.

I move to Emeric's side. He shifts with me, as if to block me again, then stops, planting his feet in a wide stance. He knows as well as I do the importance of maintaining a neutral demeanor in front of my brother. He's here to investigate a trespasser, not to protect his girlfriend.

Shane takes him in from head to toe, flicking his ashes into the six-foot distance between them. "You work at Ivory's school? Like a teacher or something?"

Emeric cocks his head, eyes on Shane. "Miss Westbrook, is

this man bothering you?"

I need to choose my words carefully. The intensity in the way Shane's gaze darts between Emeric and me tells me he's trying to figure out why a teacher at my uppity school walked into a bar and punched him four months ago.

I gaze up at the stone-hard angles of Emeric's profile and return to Shane. "This is my brother, and he was just leaving."

Shane smirks. "Need some answers, little sis. Like, I don't know... Who are you living with? And why did this frat boy"—he waves the cigarette at Emeric—"break my fucking nose?"

With his attention bolted on Shane, Emeric doesn't move, not a twitch. His silence is somewhat shocking, but there's a purpose to everything he does. A spoken word reveals things. Muteness gives less away. But Shane's not going to let this go, so I open my mouth.

"I'm staying with a friend from school." I arrange my lips into a display of wonderment. "She has this huge house and has all these spare cars." I gesture at the Porsche. "Can you blame me for moving out of our dump to live in a mansion? A mansion, Shane. For real."

He studies me with skepticism. "Didn't realize you gave a shit about that stuff."

I don't, dammit, but I can't exactly tell him the truth. "Where did Mom go?"

He drops the cigarette and smashes it with his boot. "Don't know." His eyebrows pull together, his focus flitting to Emeric and back to me. "Her phone's shut off. No note. No calls. Not even a *Fuck you. Have a nice life.*"

Even in her frequent absences, she always kept in touch

with Shane.

I rub my arms. "Do you think she's in trouble?"

"Nah." He shrugs, stares at the pavement. "She found something better is all."

Something better than family. In a way, I guess I did, too.

We exchange a suspended look, and in that tiniest sliver of a heartbeat, I see the boy I knew before he enlisted in the Marines. The brother who used to walk me to school, put gum in my hair, and draw penises in my music books. The son who loved his father as much as I did. As we stare at one another, we share a raw moment of loss, for our dad, our mom, and the love we once had for each other.

He blinks, breaking the connection, and grips the back of his neck. "Someone is still paying the bills."

I wait for Emeric to react, but he stands still and silent like a watchtower, no doubt weighing every spoken word and preparing to expose his relationship with me if Shane does something stupid.

"I won't leave you homeless." *For now.* I send a silent thank you to the man at my side for covering the expenses and making this easier.

"I'm going away for a while." Shane steps toward us, slowly, arms at his sides, expression sullen. "But I don't want to lose Dad's house."

My head swims. "Where are you going?"

He stops within arm's reach of Emeric and boldly plucks something from the lapel of Emeric's jacket.

Tension seeps into Emeric's posture, his lips flattening in a line. I stop breathing.

Shane holds up one of Schubert's orange hairs between his

pinched fingers.

A smirk twists his lips. "I used to live with a cat. Damn thing shed all over my clothes." He flicks the hair and levels me with a knowing look. "I miss him."

Dread swells in the back of my throat, and my skin breaks out in a sickly sweat. He knows. Oh God, he fucking knows.

His gaze touches mine, his tone bitterly soft. "Fuck you." Shoving his hands in his pockets, he walks away. "Have a nice life."

I hold my breath as his dark silhouette crosses the parking lot and melts into the shadows of the street. The road that will take him to the bus stop. To wherever he's going. Hopefully to a place where he forgets all about me and the man at my side.

Emeric's sharp whisper jolts me out of my breathless stasis. "Get in the car."

# EMERIC

I stretch my gait, running harder, faster, letting the burn sink deep into my muscles. The digital display on the treadmill reads *8.07 miles*. I have two more miles to go, but I might cut it short this morning. It's Saturday, and I'm anxious to crawl back into bed with Ivory.

I'd still be with her if my internal alarm clock hadn't woken me. Or maybe it was a nightmare. Awake or asleep, I can't shake this chronic feeling of dread.

It's been five days since Shane Westbrook disappeared. He walked out of the parking lot, and *poof*. Gone. After I put Ivory in her car, I drove the streets, looking for him. Then I turned the hunt over to my PI.

There hasn't been a sign of him at the house—his or mine, at the bars in Treme, or anywhere in New Orleans.

Of all the ways he could expose my relationship with Ivory, I repeatedly ask myself, *Why would he?* He has nothing to gain from it—except my retaliation. Why bite the hand that pays his bills? Doing so would only cause him to lose his father's house, which seemed to be the purpose of his surprise visit. That, and to say goodbye to Ivory.

Good fucking riddance.

The pound of my sneakers paces my breaths as my

thoughts race ahead to tonight. The Holiday Chamber Music Celebration will be a sold-out event. Ivory is years ahead of her peers and too damn talented for the concertos she plays.

But I look forward to being there. I want to be at her side tonight and every night after, with an up-close view of every moment she shivers beneath the lights of her dreams.

Midway through my cool down, the doorbell rings. I hit the stop button and grab a towel, my pulse sprinting.

The security gate doesn't encompass the front entry, so anyone can walk right up to the door from the street. Who the hell would be here at seven in the morning?

I jog through the house, toweling sweat from my bare chest and neck.

Ivory stands beside the open front door with her back to me, her silhouette haloed by the flush of dawn.

What the fuck is she doing? She's blocking my view of whoever is on the porch. If it's someone from school...

"I'm a friend of Emeric's," says a familiar feline voice.

In three strides, I reach the door and meet Deb's vivid hazel eyes. She spent some time styling her light brown bob this morning, her full tits and shapely legs on display in the skimpy dress.

I suspect this visit is a mix of business and pleasure. "You should've called."

"I thought..." Her smirk reveals her dirty thoughts. It slips when she meets Ivory's glare. "I didn't know you had company."

It's none of her business who I spend my time with. But she's good people, and I have no reason to be a dick.

Ivory crosses her arms beneath her chest, her boobs

threatening to spill out of her tiny camisole. Then she turns her glare on me. "You know her?"

"Yes." I grip the muscle on the back of her arm and apply a warning pressure. "This is Deb."

Ivory sets her jaw and widens her stance in cheeky sleep shorts that reveal more ass than they cover. My dick twitches.

"Ivory." I wait for her to look at me. "Deb and I have a few things to discuss. Go start the coffee."

She presses her lips flat, studying Deb from beneath her lashes, then storms off toward the kitchen.

I'm tempted to yank those sexy little shorts down and stripe her fucking ass.

The moment she disappears around the corner, Deb steps inside and caresses her hands over my pecs. "God, I've missed you."

I clutch her wrist and guide her back, hardening my expression with a look that makes her posture wither.

She twists her arm until I release her, disappointment creasing her face. "Who is she?"

I close the front door. "*She* is serious."

"I see that. She's also a bit territorial, don't you think? Where'd you find her?"

"*Where* isn't important. What matters is she's not going anywhere."

She scans my face, and her shoulders slump. "Jesus. You love her?"

Also none of her business. I turn away and head toward the kitchen, expecting her to follow. "Did you get the recording?"

She catches up with me, dips a hand into her purse, and holds up a flash drive.

I take it from her, hoping to hell I'll never have to use it.

In the kitchen, Ivory bends over my multi-thousand-dollar Astra coffee machine, squinting at all the switches. When she looks up, her attention locks on Deb, and a muscle bounces in her cheek.

She refocuses on me, her finger blindly, sassily, stabbing at buttons. "This thing doesn't work."

I feel my grin all the way to my cock. "Did you put the beans in?"

"Beans?" She stares at the funnel on top. "This?"

Adorable. With my hands on her hips, I scoot her to the side.

Deb settles in at the island behind us. "Nice place."

The confirmation that she's never been here should soothe some of Ivory's bratty jealousy. I sneak a peek at her.

Nope. Ivory's arms return to a crossed position beneath her heaving tits.

Focusing on the coffee, I level the beans in the scoop, discarding the ones that rise above the rim. It's an impractical habit, one I enjoy for the pure trivia of it.

"Sixty beans?" Ivory asks.

"Yes." I share a smile with her, marveling at the richness of her mind. "If I fill the scoop right to the rim."

Deb watches us from the island. "Why sixty?"

Ivory leans against the counter. "Beethoven counted out sixty beans every time he brewed coffee. He claimed that made the perfect cup." She raises her eyebrow at me. "He was rigidly meticulous."

She's trying to insult me, but I know she loves my attention to detail.

"So...Ivory?" Deb perches her chin on her hand. "Are you a musician, like Emeric?"

"Yes." Ivory smiles, sweetly. "Emeric and I went to Leopold together."

What is she up to?

Her grin doesn't look as sweet when she glares in my direction. "He still has a hard time accepting that I graduated with higher honors than he did."

I bite down on the inside of my cheek. I'm going to welt her so raw she sees triple.

With the coffee brewed and poured, Deb spends the next twenty minutes outlining her adulterous affair with the dean's husband, Howard Rivard. She's been fucking Mr. Rivard for weeks, without his knowledge of the recordings or suspicion of blackmail. It's more than enough.

Ivory refuses to join us at the island, maintaining her stubborn position against the back counter. During Deb's accounts, Ivory's expression morphs between shock and disgust, all while maintaining a heavy glare of antagonism.

Deb seems oblivious, her attention completely focused on me. "For an old guy, he's really quite virile." She winks at me. "But he's got nothing on you, Sir."

"That's it." Ivory charges toward the island and slams a hand on the surface, the other pointing shakily at Deb. "Who is she to you?"

Glancing at my wrist, I realize I'm not wearing my watch. But I know it's still early. I'll have plenty of time before her performance to draw out an appropriate punishment.

Pretending to ignore Ivory's outburst, I stand. "Thank you, Deb, for seeing this through."

She rises, glancing at Ivory and back to me, her lips turned down. "This is it, then."

"It is." There's only one woman in my future, and she's due for a spanking. "I'll walk you out."

Ivory's fuming glare follows me into the hall until I turn the corner. I wish Deb well at the door, close it with a relieved sigh of finality, and return to the kitchen.

Ivory paces along the counter, hands balled at her sides. "You've had sex with that woman. That much is obvious. But what else is going on? Why does she do things for you?" Her tone rises to a maniacal pitch, her strides quickening as she circles the island. "Oh, right. Because she wants you. She's so fucking hot for you I'm surprised she didn't pull your dick out and suck—"

"Ivory."

The strike of my voice brings her pacing to a full stop.

Lacing my fingers behind my back, I give her a list of short, specific commands and punctuate it with a stern, "Go."

A flush spreads from her neck to her chest, and I bet it travels further down and licks her sweet pussy like a hot, wet kiss. She wants what I offer more than she dreads it.

She stomps out of the kitchen. I pour another cup of coffee.

Her needs, desires, and fears run deep. So deep she could easily lose her way in the darkness. She needs a rope, not one that tethers her to her horrific past, but a strong, unbreakable line to guide her forward. The bindings might hold her down, but I'm pulling the other end.

I'll never let go.

With Schubert at my feet, I make him a plate of leftover chicken, grinning at the memory of Ivory's stern tone when she moved in. *No table scraps, Emeric!*

Sitting the cat in my lap, I let him lap at the dish of chicken on the island. It's a harmless secret between Schubert and me.

I scratch his neck while he eats and enjoy my coffee. When he's finished, I take a shower and throw on a pair of jeans. Then I grab my favorite belt, a length of rope, and find her waiting for me in the music room.

Naked and bent over the keyboard of the piano, she rests her palms on the lid beside the cuffs. Exactly as I instructed. Her feistiness might be my fuel, but her obedience is my fucking fire.

Without speaking, I lock her wrists in the shackles and use the rope to tie a simple breast harness around her chest, making sure the vertical sections press against her nipples. She watches me with huge brown eyes, her curiosity momentarily outweighing her anger.

Once her full tits are trussed up, I tighten the straps, cinching her against the piano until her chest brushes the keyboard.

When I take my position behind her, the erotic view poises my arousal on the cusp of detonation.

In teasing strokes, I trace the belt across the perfect rise of her ass. "What are the first rules I taught you?"

With her cheek pressed to the surface of the piano, her lips push out in a heavy sigh. "No lies. Don't question your methods. Never look away." She cranes her neck to glare at me. "And always call you out for being a dick."

I swing the belt, my cock throbbing painfully at the sound of her yelp. "Apologize."

"Fuck off. That's *my* rule, and it stays. Whatever you're

doing with that woman..." Her chin quivers, her voice a pissed-off snarl. "You're a dick."

I stifle my grin and give her another hard whack. "You just doubled your strikes. Tell me what was going through your stubborn fucking head when you answered the door."

"I checked through the window first. I've never seen her before. Not at school or—"

"Are you sure about that? Can you identify every parent of every student?"

She squeezes her eyes shut and groans. "No."

"You fucked up."

"Yeah."

"No unnecessary risks, Ivory."

"Okay." She rocks her hips.

I let the belt fly, tapping, whipping, and pounding her ass like a drum, every strike filling the room with her musical moans.

When her backside glows hot and red, I bend over the curve of her spine, tightly embrace her slender torso, and let her feel me breathing with her. My lips touch her shoulder, and her inhale stutters. I cup her breast, pinching the rope around her nipple, and she grinds her fevered ass against my trapped cock.

I hold her there, caressing and kissing, until her breaths fall into rhythm with mine. "When I met Deb over the summer, she had some financial problems. I paid off her debt, and she did a few favors for me. Our relationship was physical, practical, and convenient." I lick the soft skin on her neck, stroking her ear with a murmuring tone. "We haven't been intimate since school began."

She nods, her entire body lifting toward my voice, shivering beneath my lips, and purring for my touch. "Imagining you with her makes me feel really twisted up."

Welcome to my world. With the belt in my grip, I tease her with it, dragging the leather up and down the *V* of her inner thighs. "You'll never see her again."

"Thank God."

I release her abruptly and step back. "I, on the other hand, have to spend hours every day with Prescott, Sebastian, and all the other pricks who have touched you."

"Shit." She closes her eyes. "I never thought of that."

I swing the belt again, over and over without pause. She tenses, whimpers, and jerks in the restraints. My cock throbs with the sound of every hard blow, my focus locked on the wriggle of her beautiful ass as I alternate between her cheeks, thighs, and the sides of her legs.

Within minutes, she sinks into the pain, her muscles relaxing, all that smooth golden skin a canvas of pink stripes.

Each snap of welting heat is a reminder she's not the only one who feels jealous, possessive, and twisted up. But there's a deeper purpose for the pain. It gives her the power to open her mind. To mend emotional injuries inflicted by men who used her. To put all her fears in my hands, trusting me to protect her.

"Please, Emeric." She bends her neck to see me, her eyes half-mast and clouded in a fog of agony and pleasure.

Her pleading look and the hungry rush of her breaths jolts a primal current through me. I love fucking her, but nothing compares to this moment as she begs with a hooded expression, her fingers curling against the shackles, and her arousal leaking down her thighs.

I grip the rope at her back and tighten the harness over her nipples, stimulating her until she releases a husky moan. Then I flog her again, harder, faster, relishing the bond in our eye contact.

She's mine, and her gaze tells me she knows this, her body trembling for me to take her and push her. To punish her so painfully she cries only for me, knowing I'll keep her safe from anyone who wishes to harm her.

When the tears finally come, she slumps over the keyboard and drops her head on the piano lid. Her skin flushes and shudders, her hips rolling with mindless need. She's so fucking captivating I drop the belt, unable to slow my urgent frenzy to remove my jeans.

I wrestle the denim down my legs and off my feet. Then I launch at her, dipping fingers inside her tight wet cunt and spreading her open. She moans and grinds against my hand, making me so goddamn hard I don't have the patience to slow this down.

I fist my cock with shaking fingers, line up our bodies, and bury myself in one, long thrust. We groan in concert, our hips crashing together and deepening the connection. Christ, she feels so fucking good. I drive harder, sinking and retreating, obsessed and enthralled with the snug clasp of her pussy.

Sliding my hands over her arms, I hook my thumbs beneath the shackles and lace our fingers together. She clutches at my grip and clamps down around my cock, her breaths a musical motif of desire.

Her reactions, her emotions, every movement she makes belongs to me. Entirely under my command to bend at my will. She possesses me, as well, in all the same ways. I'm hers.

Leaning over her back, I show her through the twitching heat of my body that she owns me. As I pound inside her, lost in her warmth, she rests her cheek on the piano and gasps with her eyes closed. Her soft mouth, the feel of her body against mine, and the bliss of her clenching muscles around me propel me toward release.

"We're going to come, Ivory." I kick my hips and tighten my fingers around hers as the pressure in my cock builds, threatening to burst. "Now."

With her mind and body under my charge, she leaps off the cliff with me, moaning and panting as we plunge together into an exploding, body-trembling harmony of pleasure.

I slide my lips over her spine, coating her skin with the heave of my breaths. She's so sensitive, shivering against my touch. Fuck, I love that, almost as much as the way she strains in the restraints to arch into the brush of my mouth. I stay there, holding her in sated relief, mesmerized by the lyrical language of our heartbeats.

Eventually, we pull ourselves from the state of exhausted bliss. After I untie her, we eat breakfast and return to bed in an entwined knot of limbs. There, I make love to her without fight or urgency. My hips rock lazily between her thighs, her ankles cross at my back, and my mind revels in the erogenous sensation of tenderness. I can fuck her gently or violently, missionary or upside down. Doesn't matter as long as I'm inside her, with her, connected to her on every level.

Too soon, the sun slants through the window and dips behind the horizon. I don't want to leave the cocoon of her body, but it's time to get ready.

Showered, shaved, and groomed, I stand at the dresser in my tux, fucking with the bow tie around my neck. The sound of her footsteps exiting the closet brings my head around.

The first glimpse stops my heart. As I absorb the view, my pulse restarts, ticking higher, faster, and striking the chime of complete and utter adoration.

Ushered in ivory lace, the Louis Vuitton gown sheathes her knockout figure from the bateau neckline to the crystal pumps on her feet. I bought the dress after the first time I heard her play, knowing without a doubt she would wear it for tonight's performance in a sold-out theater.

"Turn—" My voice cracks. I cough behind my fist. "Turn around."

A coy smile lifts her lips as she pivots. Her long dark hair wraps in an elegantly messy knot on the back of her head, with wayward tendrils trailing down her neck. Slim ivory straps loop around her shoulders, leaving the expanse of her back on gorgeous display.

Black curlicues of ink draw a graceful, meandering vine from her waist to her nape, swirling flourishes over her spine and around her shoulder blades. She's so damn arresting, my chest burns with the reminder to breathe.

Crossing the room until I'm right up on her, I brush my lips along her shoulder. "So beautiful I'm shaking."

I let her feel the tremors in my fingers as I trace the delicate artwork on her spine.

She hums softly, her head tipping. "The tat was my first *arrangement*."

I freeze then resume my caress, my stomach twisting. "You were thirteen."

404

"Yeah. I got it after my dad died." Her hand reaches back and finds the one at my side, bringing it forward to rest on her hip. "Right after Lorenzo..."

Just the mention of his name makes me want to pound my fists into his face until he chokes on his blood.

Her shoulders tense, relax. "The tattoo artist refused me because of my age. Until I suggested a different kind of payment."

I continue to trace the whorls of ink, letting the softness of her skin calm my rising anger. "You offered him sex."

She nods. "I needed this tattoo."

With her back to me, I can't see her eyes, but the emotion in her voice squeezes my chest.

"My dad claimed he didn't just hear the notes when he played. He could see them curling through the air like scrollwork. Every song was a graphical image in his mind, and he drew those embellishments in the margins of his music sheets."

When I was thirteen, I played with my dick while daydreaming about a girl—any girl—touching it.

When she was thirteen, she sold her body to a tattoo artist for a permanent keepsake of her dead father.

I glance down the curve of her back, my finger following the curls of ink with new appreciation. "Which song is this one?"

She gives me a watery smile over her shoulder. "His favorite Herbie Hancock, 'Someday My Prince Will Come.'"

I'm no prince, but when I'm buried inside Ivory, I will always *come*.

Stepping around her, I remove a platinum bracelet from

my pocket and clasp it around her wrist.

She studies it with wide eyes, holding the tiny frog charm between her fingers. "Edvard Grieg kept a frog figurine in his pocket at all times."

I curve a hand around her waist, fingers stroking her naked back. "And he would rub it before concerts for good luck."

She nods and kisses me, breathing against my lips, "Thank you."

That night, she plays with more passion and skill than all of her peers combined. Stogie watches from the audience, his face stretched in a huge smile. I watch from the stage wings, my heart beating in time with her fingers.

Everything is good.

Joanne, Shane, and Lorenzo are gone. Prescott and Ms. Augustin are contained. The dean has nothing on me, while I have enough blackmail to ruin her career. I've been so careful.

Everything is perfect.

Too perfect. Like life has handed me a song filled with soul-deep joy and told me to savor every note.

Because eventually, the song will end.

# IVORY

Christmas comes and goes in a blur of extravagant presents and warm smiles at his parents' house. Emeric and I spend the rest of our two-week break at home, in bed, tucked in an indestructible bubble of whispering, touching, kissing bliss. Every second with him feels like a dream, like any moment, someone's going to cruelly shake my shoulder and force me to wake up.

Since I moved in, our trips outside of the house have been limited to school, weekly visits to Stogie's, and weekend dinners at the Marceaux's. There are no date nights at the movies, romantic dinners in the French Quarter, or hand-holding strolls along the Mississippi River. We do *normal* in the privacy of our own world, such as binging on a TV series starring bearded pirates with perfect teeth.

Doesn't really matter what we do as long as I have him to do it with.

When I graduate, we'll be free of the student-teacher restriction. No more hiding and living in fear. Then...?

He says Leopold is mine if I want it. I don't know how. If he breaks his deal with the dean, our entire world will come crashing down. I intend to pursue a spot there on my own. Maybe it'll take me years. Maybe I'll move there and knock on the recruiters' doors every day until they get sick of seeing me.

He says he'll move to New York with me while I work on my degree. That makes my heart soar, but I can't ask him to leave his job and his family.

He says I can do whatever I set my mind on. I believe him.

December ends a discordant passage in my life, a coda to Treme and my broken family.

January is the prelude of a new song, promising a year of hard decisions.

February glides by in a glissando of homework, piano lessons, and quiet evenings with Emeric.

March kicks off with a countdown to spring break, unseasonably warm weather, and...

A bladder infection.

Squatting on the toilet, I hunch over in pain. I haven't moved for thirty minutes, every teeny trickle of pee burning fire between my legs. "I'm going to be late for school."

Emeric crouches in front of me and rests the back of his hand on my forehead, concern darkening his blue eyes. "Still no fever, but you're staying home, and that's final." He shoves a glass of water in my hand. "Drink."

More water means more urinating, which means more burning. "No more."

He arranges my fingers around the glass, forcing me to hold it. "Dehydration is the reason you're sitting here."

"And too much sex." I manage a grin and take a sip.

"No such thing." His palms slide up my bare thighs, stroking tenderly. "Keep drinking."

I force down the fluid with a glare. The black hair on top of his head is a finger-raked rebellion of sexiness, while the trimmed sides scream clean-cut Mr. Professor. With his freshly shaved jawline, potently masculine scent, and swank gray waistcoat and jacket, he's ready to take on the world. Or at least, a school full of privileged teenagers.

My dirty ponytail hangs down the front of the only thing I'm wearing—his Guns N' Roses t-shirt. I won't be ready to go anytime soon. My stomach sinks. For the first time in four years, I'm going to miss a day of school.

"I know it hurts." He takes the glass, sets it on the floor, and brushes his thumb over my bottom lip. "My dad's bringing medicine."

My body clenches against a sharp wave of pain, releasing another stream of pee. I groan, my eyes watering through the godawful burn.

"Fuck this." He reaches for the knot on his tie. "I'm staying here."

"What for?" I grab his hand, stopping his attack on the shirt collar. "What would you do? Sit in here and watch me pee all day?"

His eyes flash. "Yes."

"Terrible idea." I tangle our fingers together and hold them between my knees. "How will it look if we're both gone? Neither of us ever miss school. People will notice."

He drags his free hand down his face, his expression pained. The secrecy of our relationship, seeing me sick, leaving me alone, all of it torments him.

I lean in and kiss his mouth, wishing my teeth were clean. "This is embarrassing enough without your hawk eyes all up in my business."

It's really not that bad. I'm well-adjusted to his invasiveness. Whether I'm on my period or using the bathroom, he has no concept of personal boundaries, always hovering, interrogating, and examining me inside and out. I get it, though. Because I'm just as obsessed with him.

Straightening my back, I use one of his favorite commands. "Go."

I expect his jaw to harden and his voice to crack the walls in his outrage. But what I find in his eyes is something wholly different. Something that's been expanding between us for months, doubling in size when we're together, and growing in strength when we're apart. As if finally bold enough, everything we've ever felt for one another gathers into one monumental sentiment and shines from his gaze.

He wraps his hands around my hips. "I love you."

There it is. Spoken without fireworks, received without weepy tears, and absorbed without the ricochet of distant thunder.

It's simple, real, and right there in the open.

In a bathroom.

I grip his face, eyes connected, hearts beating in sync. "You waited until *now* to tell me that?"

The corner of his mouth lifts. "It's not like you didn't already know."

"Yeah, but a girl doesn't forget the first time her crush says those words." I fight a grin. "I'll always remember this moment with the image of a toilet seat imprinting a ring on my ass."

He rests his forehead against mine. "Did you say *crush?*"

"Not just any crush." I touch our lips together. "A crush on my hot teacher, who also happens to be my cocky Master. And the man I love."

Doesn't matter if I'm sitting on a toilet, splayed on his piano, or straddling his lap. This is *our* secret world, and it's more meaningful than every aspiration I've ever set for myself. Our relationship isn't practical or convenient. And it's not just physical. We need each other, not because our bodies fit so well together, but because our hearts beat the same tune, for the same reason.

"Say it," he breathes.

"I love you." I'm not the first woman who's said those words to him, but I'll make damn sure I'm the last. I comb my fingers through his hair. "The kind of love that doesn't end in betrayal."

His hands clench against my hips. "It won't end at all. *Ever.*"

He kisses me passionately, achingly, his mouth molding against mine as if trying to convey the depth of his words. He kisses me until my bladder howls again.

Lingering longer than he should, he tucks me into bed and piles the nightstand with food and water. Then he leaves the room and returns a few minutes later with Schubert bundled in his arms.

I curl on my side, grinning despite the discomfort. "You thought of everything."

"Not everything." Settling Schubert beside me, he pets the kitty into a lazy purr of contentment. "I haven't figured out a way to stay home with you."

"You're late, Mr. Marceaux. Get out of here."

He presses a longing kiss to my lips. "Dad has his own code

to get in, so stay up here. Get some sleep. He'll be by soon."

I close my eyes and stroke Schubert, trying to ignore the irritating urge to pee again. I sense Emeric hovering in the doorway for a silent moment before his footsteps fade down the hall.

The beep of the alarm tells me he armed it. The slam of the door punctuates his frustration about leaving.

Sleep pulls me under within minutes. It's a disorienting, uncomfortable kind of slumber that bounces me between awareness and dreamland. Minutes pass, or maybe hours, as my mind replays Emeric's tenderness while my body begs me to release my bladder.

At some point, the alarm system sounds its thirty-second entry delay, snapping my eyes open. I force myself up and make a mad dash to the toilet. After a great amount of trickling relief and scorching pain, I debate hunting down a pair of shorts. At the very least, I should put on underwear.

Fuck it. I'm sick, he's a doctor, and the closet is too damn far away. Stretching the t-shirt down my thighs, I roll beneath the covers and wait for the blessed delivery of medicine.

I must've fallen asleep. Schubert leaps off the bed, startling me into a blinking state of grogginess as I try to make sense of the silhouette in the doorway.

Blue jeans. Black *V*-neck t-shirt. Dark skin. Beefed-up arms... I stare at the *Destroy* tattoo on his neck and choke.

Am I dreaming? Having a nightmare? This can't be real. Inwardly, I give myself a once-over. My heart is pounding, lungs panting, throat tight. This is really happening. A spasm convulses through my body.

Lorenzo stares right back with wide eyes. "You're supposed

to be at school."

Ice saturates my veins as I scramble backward, dragging the sheet with me. "You're supposed to be in jail!"

He cocks his head and takes a step into the room. "How do you know about that?"

"Why are you here? What do you want?" With rasping breaths, I shove a hand beneath the covers and dig around. Where's my phone? Fuck, I know Emeric left it right next to me. Where is it? Where is it?

He slinks into the room and pauses in front of the closet. The bed sits in the center with the bathroom on the other side of the door. There's a lock on that door. I inch my way across the mattress in that direction.

Keeping his body angled toward me, he glances inside the closet, his vile gaze staining everything he looks at. "Shane and I have been casing the place."

Shane...? Casing...? My head spins as I covertly pick through the blankets. Where is the goddamn phone?

His eyes latch onto my trembling hands, and I freeze. I don't want to give him any reason to attack me.

Is Shane in the house? Are they here to rob Emeric? Lorenzo was arrested for burglary, but... "How did you get in?"

I slowly shift my legs beneath the covers, hoping to bump into the phone while subtly moving closer to the edge nearest to the bathroom.

Lorenzo crosses his arms over his chest and studies me. "I know these alarm systems. There's a master code, as well as codes assigned to each user. Shane guessed yours on the third try."

*The date my dad died.* My heart caves in.

He tsks. "The weakest link in security is always the human."

Sweltering pain grips my chest. Why is this happening? I can't bear it if he touches me again. What the hell am I going to do?

My eyes blur with tears. "You have to leave. I'm expecting a delivery any second."

He prowls closer. "Your brother is outside on lookout."

And Shane doesn't know I'm home? *Fuck. Fuck. Fuck.*

I scoot closer to the edge, untangling my legs from the blankets.

Lorenzo stops ten feet from the bed, watching me. "Don't do anything stupid, Ivory. I know the suit you're shacked up with is at school. We have *hours* before he comes home." His smile forms a vicious fissure across in his face. "You owe me months."

Changing course, he veers toward the foot of the bed. Anticipating my escape to the bathroom? He's faster, stronger. If I run, he'll beat me there.

"Where's the safe?" he asks as he circles the mattress.

It's in Emeric's office, and I know the damn combination. But he won't just take money. Not now that he's seen me. I jerk my attention at the closet.

He follows my gaze, his body turning, distracted.

I waste a half-second scanning the sheets for the phone before shoving off the bed and running like hell into the bathroom. Heart racing, I skid through the doorway as he chases, screaming, "Ivory!"

I'm hyperventilating by the time the door slams. I hit the

lock. Punch it again. And again. Then I step back, dizzy, nauseous, struggling to breathe. Will the door frame hold? The molding looks thick and sturdy. But will it keep out Lorenzo?

Not for long.

His fist pounds on the door. "Ivory! Open it the fuck up!"

I spin, scanning the bathroom for escape, self-defense, a weapon. The half-moon window is too high, too small, too unbreakable. I rip open drawers and cabinets, digging for something, anything.

Oh God, this can't be happening. How did he get out of jail? Why did he target *this* fucking house?

*Shane.*

That selfish motherfucker knew I lived with Emeric. He's been gone for three months. More than enough time to find out where I live. Or maybe he's known all along.

The heavy banging on the door hardens my stomach. "Ivory, if you don't open the goddamn door, we'll have to do this the hard way."

A chill sweeps down my spine. The banging stops.

I hold up a toothbrush and discard it for a hairbrush. What the fuck am I going to do with this?

"Here, kitty kitty," Lorenzo calls, softly.

The hairbrush thumps to the floor as all the blood in my body rushes to my feet. *No no no.*

"Come on out, Schubert."

His sickening sweet voice and gentle coaxing sounds twist my gut and flood my eyes with tears. Then he whistles, using the same cat call he's heard me use for years.

Everything inside me curls up in horror. I fly at the door

and press my palms against it. *Run, Schubert. Oh God, please run.*

My heartbeat thrashes past my ears as silence draws tightly on the other side. I stare down at the handle. Emeric would whip my ass just for thinking about turning it. But Schubert...

His long, pained howl penetrates the door and rattles me to the bone.

A sob rips from my throat, and violent tremors wobble my legs. "Let him go!" My hand falls to the door handle, squeezing it in a death grip. "Let's talk about this. Just...please, let him go."

Schubert lets out another keening scream, this one louder, more frenzied.

I yank open the door and stumble out, eyes frantically searching.

Lorenzo leans a shoulder against the wall beside the bathroom, his hand around Schubert's neck as the cat's body flails and contorts in pain.

"Stop!" I launch at him, screaming and shaking with hysterics. "You're hurting him!"

He kicks me in the stomach, knocking the wind out of me and sending me sprawling across the floor. His hand clenches around that tiny neck so hard Schubert's back arches, legs spread out and thrashing against the restraint.

I scramble to my feet, fear tearing me apart as I throw myself at him again.

"Please, let go. Please," I wail uncontrollably, clawing at his arm, unable to remove his torturous hold. "He can't breathe. Oh God, stop!"

"Get on your hands and knees, ass in the air."

Every muscle in my body locks up in terror as the

vulnerable hole in my backside clenches in remembered anguish. *I can't. Not there. I can't. I can't.*

"Do it!" he roars.

My head shakes on its own, taking control of my response. I want to be strong enough to do whatever is needed to free Schubert. But my jaw is glued shut, my legs so frozen I can't feel them.

His entire demeanor changes, twisting and tightening, his expression transforming from rotten and ugly to horrifyingly evil. I see his intent coming a fraction of a second before it happens. But I move too slowly, too fucking weak to remove his hand from around Schubert's neck, to stop his arm from swinging, to prevent my beloved kitty from slamming into the wall.

Schubert's limp body drops to the floor, and something inside me breaks, detaches, and shrivels away. My ears hear him thump against the wood floor. My eyes trace the awkward, unmoving bend in his spine. But my mind refuses to accept it. *He's not dead. He's not. He can't die.*

The floor rises up and slams against my knees. I'm screaming, but there's a palm over my mouth. I'm crawling and reaching, but the heavy weight on my back pins me down. I'm sobbing, but I don't feel the tears. Determination drives me, my arms straining for my little broken kitty, aching to hold him. He needs me to comfort him, to fix him.

But his head's at the wrong angle. Eyes open. Not moving. Looking but not seeing. Oh God, why won't he move?

The sane part of my brain knows. But I bury it, focusing all of my strength on reaching him, desperate to shake him awake, to hear his purr, to see him shift those unblinking eyes.

Until the press of hard flesh probes between my legs.

Dead, chilling darkness sits on my senses. Numbing the hand on my hip. Lightening the chest on my back. Muting the sound of hungry breaths.

"Scriabin," I sob, fingers stretching and bumping against the soft pad of a kitty paw. "Scriabin."

Just a few more inches, and I'll be able to pull Schubert into my arms.

The forceful pressure against my core adjusts, realigning with the ring of muscle in my ass. I squeeze my eyes shut. Paying attention to my body will bring agonizing pain, so I concentrate on the notes in my head, the dissonant sonata, the deadening dark where I can hold my kitty.

*Fight, Ivory.* Emeric's voice shatters through my mind. *Fight and fucking win.*

The erection pushes against my barrier, searing my nerve-endings. I twist my neck and sink my teeth into the flesh of Lorenzo's bicep. Hard.

He bellows and rears back his arm.

Just as his fist flies toward me, Shane's frantic voice echoes from somewhere downstairs. "Lorenzo! Man, where are you?"

The punch connects with my face.

# EMERIC

I idle the GTO at the gate and punch in my code. With all the neighbors at work, the street is deserted and quiet. I don't like quiet. It makes my instincts prickle with paranoia.

No doubt my nerves are related to the gamble in canceling my afternoon classes. But since my dad's delayed at the clinic, I claimed a family emergency, consequences be damn, and picked up her prescriptions on the way home.

When the gate opens, I follow the driveway around the back of the estate, wondering if Ivory hears the rumble of the engine.

I slam on the brakes. What the—?

An old black Honda is parked near the back door. Unfamiliar. Unoccupied. No tags.

My stomach hardens into ice. *Ivory.*

I don't breathe until I'm in the house. *The alarm isn't armed.*

The next breath doesn't come until I reach the kitchen. *Footsteps on the second floor.*

I race through the living room, every cell in my body hyperalert. *Who the fuck is here?*

"Lorenzo, he's in the driveway!" A man's voice echoes upstairs. "Where are you?"

*Shane.* My blood runs cold as I sprint toward the foyer. Did he say *Lorenzo*? How is that possible?

Lorenzo's in my fucking house.

With Ivory.

Rage propels me up the stairs, every step an opponent between me and her. I climb faster, taking two...three stairs at a time.

"The fuck?" Shane roars from the direction of my bedroom. "Get the fuck off her!"

No! Oh, Jesus, fuck, no! Urgency fuses into my muscles, pushing me faster, harder, locking my jaw. I can't hear her. Why can't I hear her?

I hurdle the last stair, but the remaining distance feels like it's forcing my heart to explode out of my chest. The landing is too big, the hall too long. I'm too far away. I never should've left. I failed her, and I'm fucking fuming in my regret. Goddamn shaking in my desperation to reach her.

I follow the sounds of rising shouts. Almost there. A few more steps. I rush through the doorway, my focus zooming in on the far side of the bedroom.

Ivory stands motionless in my t-shirt. Blood on her lips. Expression empty. Schubert in her arms. Dead.

Shane's balled fists. Wounds on Lorenzo's face and arm. His zipper open.

Each millisecond snapshot sears into me with a viciousness that staggers my steps.

No one notices me.

I'm outnumbered, unarmed, and over-fucking-wrought with fury. Everything inside me pulls toward Ivory, but I fight it, refusing to look at her or think about her. If I do, I'll lose my fucking shit.

Sticking to the edge of the room, I close the distance. Ivory stands a few feet away from the face-off between Shane and Lorenzo.

"Did you rape her, motherfucker?" Shane throws a punch at Lorenzo and misses his dodging head. "She was telling the truth all this time?"

Cold lethal intent spreads through me, hiking my breaths. My fists flex for destruction. My heart hardens for permanent, irrevocable death. I will end this.

My impulses take over, my hands dropping to my belt and yanking it free as venom simmers through my veins.

Lorenzo widens his stance. "Dude. Look what she did to my face."

"You were on top of her!" Shane attacks him, arms swinging.

Lorenzo ducks, hooks him around the waist, and takes him to the floor in a series of punches.

I approach on swift silent feet, sliding the end of the belt through the buckle. A foot away, I stand behind Lorenzo. Shane sprawls on his back with Lorenzo kneeling over him. I'm certain Shane sees me, but they're both throwing punches, blocking, grunting.

I shove the belt loop over Lorenzo's head and hold my madness together with both fists.

Shane's eyes, red and outraged, collide with mine. Lorenzo turns his neck.

I cinch the belt around Lorenzo's throat, wrenching the end with the full strength of my wrath.

His body flings backward with the ruthlessness of my pull, thrashing across the floor, hands scrabbling at the noose. I hang on, yanking harder, fueled with malicious purpose.

Shane crawls toward Lorenzo's bucking body and glares up at me with feral eyes. How am I going to fight him off while holding on to the belt?

With a bellow of rage, he slams a knee onto his friend's chest, his fists pummeling Lorenzo's face. I falter, stunned, and readjust my grip, pulling the belt with a vengeance.

Shane's weight holds Lorenzo to the floor as I stand over them and wring the garrote tighter, tighter, the brutal imperative for this to end slicing through my wavering breaths.

Fingers clenched around the leather, I meet Ivory's shattered brown gaze. I'm killing a man in front of her, coldly, consciously, and without apology. There's no going back from this.

Her legs support her unmoving posture. Her hands hold Schubert's dead body. Her eyes stay with mine, but she's not here. She's not with me.

Probably for the best, because I'm not stopping until this son of a bitch can't hurt her anymore.

The phone in my pocket vibrates with an incoming call. The school? My parents? The fucking cops following up on suspicious activity? Fuck!

Lorenzo's jaw gapes in a silent scream. Blood smears his face, eyes swollen, his complexion waning from red to blue.

I stand on one side, hands numbing around the belt. On Lorenzo's other side, Shane presses him against the floor as his body writhes, legs kicking, fingers clawing at the leather around his throat.

Strangulation is an excruciatingly slow way to go. In those

harrowing minutes, the enormity of what I'm doing has time to slither beneath my skin and suffocate my vital organs. I hold strong with the reminder that my responsibility to protect Ivory overrides everything else.

Lorenzo's fingers fall away from his throat, and with a jerk of his leg, he loses the fight.

It's finished.

Shane collapses on his ass, hands flying to the back of his head, his mouth hanging open with exertion. Horror. Shock.

Adrenaline tingles through my limbs as I drop the belt and press my shaking fingers against the swollen *Destroy* on Lorenzo's throat. No pulse. There's irony in that, something I'll contemplate when our wounds are no longer raw.

I step back and shrug out of my jacket, sweating against conflicting bouts of relief and reality.

I just killed a man.

A man who broke into my house.

Who killed our cat.

Who attempted and maybe succeeded in raping Ivory *again*.

Because I wasn't here.

My chest burns, my entire world rotating and spinning toward her. "Ivory?"

For the first time since I came in, she moves. Just her eyes, shifting them to mine. Blood rims her nostrils, stains her lips, and dots the front of her t-shirt.

My stomach twists. I need to take the cat, hug her, obliterate the distance between us. I reach for her.

She jerks back, her arms tightening around Schubert's dangling body.

Not ready to let him go? Not ready for me to touch her?

I understand, but dammit, I feel her rejection like a fist to the heart.

A glance at Shane confirms he's still dazed, staring at the body with unblinking, glassy eyes.

My pocket vibrates with a text alert. Goddammit. Whoever is trying to reach me has terrible timing.

I loosen my tie and toss it. Then I step in front of Ivory and brush my fingers across her jaw. She doesn't react, her gaze distant, unfocused. When I lower my caress to the arm around Schubert, she releases an anguished cry and stumbles back.

Okay. I won't separate her from the cat. "I just need to know you're okay."

Her demeanor goes cold, detached, except her arms, which hold Schubert tighter.

"I fought him." Her voice is a hollow metronome. "Bit him. Scratched his face."

"Good girl." I want to pull her against me so badly, but if I do, I'll unravel. I have to keep my shit together until this mess is contained. "Did he rape—?"

"No." A flicker of life stirs in the muddy brown depths of her eyes. "Shane stopped him."

Did her brother have a stroke of guilt? A sudden heart transplant? A hidden agenda? Hell knows why he stepped in, but fuck, I'm breathing a little easier knowing he did.

Shane's wheezing grows louder, more frantic, his bloodshot eyes on the waste of life that was Lorenzo. Maybe Shane isn't a threat at the moment, but he will be if he runs. Honestly, he looks like he's seconds from a meltdown.

Another text comes in. I pull the phone from my pocket, but Shane's guttural cry draws my attention.

He covers his face with his hands, wailing like a fucking pansy. "He was my best friend." His body rocks. "Oh God, he saved my life, and we killed him."

I maintain a towering stance above him, a position of power. "We killed the sack of shit who's been raping your sister for four years."

Snapping his jaw shut, he looks away.

Ivory stares at the floor, her expression blank. She's in shock. But she's strong as hell. There isn't a doubt in my mind she'll be sassing me again in no time.

I refocus on Shane and steel my voice with authority. "You're in deeper shit than I am."

His eyes lift, tears falling down his face. "How's that? We both—"

"Castle law. In the state of Louisiana, I have the right to defend myself and others on my property. That includes the use of deadly force against intruders. Justifiable homicide." I point at Ivory. "I was fucking justified."

Problem is, if I call the cops, I'll be arrested for a different crime. My high school student wasn't just visiting my house while I was at work. She *lives* here. I won't be able to hide that. Not with Shane involved. If I turn him in, he'll return the favor.

I have two choices. Call the authorities and face a publicized student-teacher trial that would destroy not only my future, but Ivory's. Or deal with the body and make all of this go away.

The second option only works with Shane's cooperation.

As much as I want to bury his worthless ass with Lorenzo, we're in this together.

I glance at my phone. A missed call and two texts from my PI.

*Smith: Gandara is free.*

No shit. I look up at Schubert in Ivory's arms, his neck hanging awkwardly, likely broken. A renewed wave of anger funnels through me.

*Smith: Released yesterday. My CI just contacted me. Lawyer argued PTSD as grounds for an insanity defense. Got an appeal. Reduced sentence. I'll be in touch as soon as I locate Gandara's whereabouts.*

Lorenzo had a year left on his sentence. At least now I don't have to worry about dealing with his release.

I type out an acknowledgment since that's what I would do if I weren't standing over a dead body. I'll let the PI look for Lorenzo. It's a risk, but I need to see if his investigation leads him back to me.

Shane's gaze bounces between the phone in my hand and the door, as if considering escape. "You can't call the cops, man. I stopped him from raping her!" His voice rises. "I killed my best friend. For *her*."

"Shut the fuck up." I hit send on the text and drill my gaze into his. "You broke into my house. You're an accomplice to murder. If you run, I'll make the call. If you give me what I want, this stays between the three of us."

He swallows. "What do you want?"

"Answers. Cooperation." I flick a hand at the body. No way in hell can I lift that big motherfucker by myself. "Then you'll crawl back into whatever hole you've been in for the past three months and never come back."

"Okay." He nods, his throat bobbing and eyes shifty. "I can do that."

I don't fucking trust him. In a perfect world, I would've killed Lorenzo without another soul knowing about it. Two witnesses are two risks too many. Ivory won't betray me, but whatever knowledge she has about my next steps could incriminate her. I need to distance her from it.

I also need to disentangle her from Schubert.

"Ivory." As I wait for her to look at me, I remember the reason I rushed home. "Do you need to use the bathroom?"

"I—" She hugs the cat against her neck, looks down at her bare legs, at the floor by the bathroom door, and back at her legs. "I might've..." Her chin quivers. "I'm sorry."

Sorry for what? Releasing her bladder while fighting off a rapist?

I capture her arm and pull her to me. "I hope you fucking pissed all over him."

Her hand strokes the cat's fur. "I hope so, too."

I slide my arm around her waist, shifting her against me with Schubert between us. I move my other hand over his eyes, brushing them closed, petting his soft fur, letting myself mourn his death.

He was a gift from her father, her comfort when she was scared, her friend when she had no one. He was all she had the last time she lost someone she loved. Now she has me.

I hold her until her tears fall and caress her back while she silently sobs. Her trembling makes me ache. Her grief magnifies my own.

Shane watches us from a few feet away, eyes wet and turbid, noises strangling in his throat as if he's trying to contain his sniveling. Maybe it's guilt. I hope he chokes on it.

I reluctantly lean back. "It's time to say goodbye."

The look of devastation on her beautiful face threatens to bring me to my knees.

I strengthen my stance and gesture Shane over. "Your brother's going to take Schubert."

Her arms tighten around the cat as a sob climbs up from deep in her chest.

I cradle her face. "I'm so sorry, Ivory. I would give anything to make this easier." I press a kiss to her forehead. "We'll bury him in the backyard. I'll build a memorial there, whatever you want, okay?"

Tears drip down her cheeks, mixing with the blood on her lips as she stares at the cat.

I nod at Shane.

After a few cries of protest, she releases her hold. Shane bundles the body against his chest, his face falling.

I turn her away, guide her into the bathroom, and draw the bath. "I'll be right back."

Grabbing a towel, I step out, close the door behind me, and meet Shane's eyes. "Who knows you're here?"

He flinches. "No one. I swear."

His promise means nothing to me.

"Go out the back door and get the medicine from my GTO. Park the Honda in the garage. You'll find a tarp and duct tape in there." I drop the towel beside the body. "Grab whatever else we might need."

If he's going to run, he would've done it by now. If he changes his mind, I won't be able to stop him. So I leave him there with the cat in his arms and hope he's smarter than he looks.

In the bathroom, I give Ivory some sleeping pills, roll up my sleeves, and silently, soothingly, bathe her into drowsiness. I hate sedating her, but I don't want to leave her awake and grieving by herself. She needs to be comatose for however many hours it takes to deal with the body.

The urge to call my parents itches at me. Mom could stay with her while I'm gone. But making them accessories to disposing of a body is not an option.

When a fist knocks on the bathroom door, some of the tension eases from my shoulders.

I gaze down at Ivory, her skin pink from the heat of the water and her eyes hooded with fatigue. "If I leave you here for a few minutes, are you going to drown?"

Her lashes lift, and a hint of a small smile touches her lips. "If you don't stop hovering, I might drown *you*."

There's my girl. I press a kiss to her brow, her nose, her mouth. Then I head toward the door.

"Emeric?"

I turn, my pulse singing at the sound of her voice.

She leans her head back on the ledge. "Thank you."

I doubt she's thanking me for a specific thing. Her gratefulness is always all-encompassing. Christ, I love this girl.

"I'll be right back." I slip out and shut the door.

Shane already has the body wrapped in tarp and duct tape. He sweeps the towel over the wood floors, clearing away any urine or blood, his expression colorless and etched in torment.

I step beside him. "You look like you've done this before."

"Never."

Fear, shock, revulsion...there are so many overpowering emotions in that whisper, I believe him.

With the body bagged, we haul it down the hall. I leave him at the stairs and return to Ivory.

By the time I dress her, give her the medicine, and tuck her into bed, she's deep asleep beneath the weight of sedation.

I spot check the wood floors for blood with each pass I make through the room. I'll do a thorough cleaning later, but to the unassuming eye, there's no indication a crime was committed here.

I change into a Henley and jeans and find Shane sitting on the top step, staring into space.

"Let's finish this." My voice makes him jump.

A few minutes later, the body is loaded in the Honda in the garage.

I hand Shane a shovel. "Where's Schubert?"

He takes it, his glare digging into the closed trunk of the car. "Shouldn't we deal with that first?"

"At dusk." I head toward the hall that leads to the back yard. "We need to talk."

Outside, the sun slips behind the monolithic tower of my estate, fading the sky into streaks of violet.

Surrounded by oaks and blooming bushes, I set Schubert's body on the ground and direct Shane to a spot beside the concrete bench in the garden. "Where have you been for the past three months?"

He stabs the shovel through the mulch and starts the hole. "Not in New Orleans."

If I press, he'll likely lie about his location. He said he flew in. Maybe that will help the PI track him this time.

I sit on the bench and take in his receding blond hair, pale complexion, and the stupidity emanating from his dull eyes. Hard to believe he's related to Ivory.

With a deep breath, I rest my elbows on my spread knees. "Tell me how this came about."

Working the shovel through the dirt, he says quietly, tiredly, "Lorenzo called me yesterday, said he was released—" He stops, glances up at me, hesitating. "He was in jail for burglary."

He's either fucking with me or he doesn't know my involvement in Lorenzo's arrest. As dumb as he is, I'm leaning toward the latter. That means he didn't want to mention the burglary conviction for another reason. I can guess why.

He returns to his task. "He called me when he got out, said he lost his apartment and needed fast money." He shovels more dirt, avoiding my eyes. "I owed him my life, so I offered him a solution and flew home to help him."

I look up at my estate as the pieces slowly click together. Shane must've been following Ivory before he approached her in the parking lot. If so, he already knew where she lives. When he saw me that night and recognized me as the guy who punched him, he figured out our relationship and *who* she lives with. Our schedule is obvious, so he bet on the assumption we would be at school.

"You came here to rob me." My hands clench. "How did you get in?"

He pauses then resumes digging. "I guessed her code."

Fuck. That's a huge goddamn oversight on my part.

So then what? Lorenzo went in alone while Shane kept

431

watch? She fought him. Somehow the cat was pulled into it. I won't demand those details from Shane. She'll give me an honest account when she's ready.

He stares at the ground, voice tight. "She wasn't supposed to be here."

"Except she was. What do you think Lorenzo intended to do to her after he raped her? Would he have left her alive to point him out in a line up after he robbed the place?"

"Oh God." His head lowers, his fingers wrapped so tightly around the handle of the shovel it has to be cutting circulation.

"Do you know why I punched you that night?"

He glares at the dirt, nostrils flaring.

"She came to school with a busted lip." I let my disgust clip the words.

His eyes close, face pinched in pain.

I find a sick sort of comfort in his guilt. "A brother is supposed to protect his sister. Stand up to bullies for her. Walk through fucking fire for her."

He leans on the shovel like a crutch, his entire body shaking. "I fucked up, okay?" He lets go of the handle and scrubs his hands over his head, his eyes stark with anguish. "She tried to tell me for years, but I didn't listen. I was just so...*angry* with her. About the school thing and her relationship with Dad. Then here she is, living in this huge mansion..."

I don't think he's talking for my benefit, and I don't give a shit what his justifications are. I just need to know if he's going to be a continuing threat to Ivory.

Rising from the bench, I grab the shovel and dig. "So

Lorenzo's call gave you the idea to take from her. With his robbery experience, you jumped on the opportunity to steal some of her happiness for yourself."

He drops his arms to his sides and stares at the house, his voice a croaked whisper. "Yeah."

I settle the cat in the hole, swallow a knot of sadness, and return the dirt. "I should be burying you instead of Schubert."

A frown contorts his face, his ignorant eyes backlit with conviction. "I promise I won't cause her any more trouble. Fuck, I'll spend the rest of my fucking life staying the hell out of hers. It's the only thing I can offer her."

I'll have a PI on my payroll for the rest of her life to make sure of it. "It's time to deal with the other thing."

"Yeah." He lifts his chin, gazing out toward the darkening sky over the eastern horizon. "I know a place."

# IVORY

The moment I wake, my muscles tighten in memory of the day's events. A dim lamp glows in the gloom of the bedroom, casting shadows over my brother's dour expression where he slouches in a chair beside the bed. It's disturbing to see him in this house, in a place that's always represented safety, happiness, and love. But I'm not scared. Emeric would kill him before allowing him to be alone with me again.

I shift my attention down the length of the mattress and find watchful devotion in eyes of shimmering blue. My heart hums.

Emeric told me once if anyone touched me, his response would be murderous. He's a man of his word. Lorenzo is gone. Dead. No longer able to hurt me. I still feel heavily weighted by shock, my insides aching with the loss of Schubert and coiling with worry over Emeric taking such a drastic gamble with his future to protect me. But we'll get through this together, no matter what.

Sitting on the bed beside my feet, he traces a hand along the outline of my leg in the blankets. His chiseled face is smoothed into a calm mien framed in exhaustion. His black hair spikes in a chaos of perfection, and a steel gray Henley stretches across his shoulders, accentuating the strength of his neck. He risks that neck for me repeatedly, and today was no different.

My grateful smile comes easily. "How long have I been out?"

His jaw shifts, mashing the gum in his mouth. "Six hours."

I'm aware he spent that time dealing with Lorenzo's body. What did he do with it? The flicker in his gaze tells me he anticipates the question, but there's a hard glare there, too. He's not going to tell me.

I don't want him to carry this burden alone, but it would be important to him to keep me isolated from the details. Pushing him on it would only make him frustrated and conflicted.

I can be rational on this one thing.

His hand moves over the bend of my knee, his thumb stroking against the covers. "Your brother is leaving." He looks at Shane and steels his voice. "For good this time."

Blowing out a breath, I check what I'm wearing—another one of Emeric's t-shirts. No panties. I shift to sit against the headboard, dragging the covers with me, and meet Shane's eyes.

He scoots to the edge of the chair and rubs his palms over his jeans, watching the movement. "It's a little late, but I'm saying it anyway." He glances at me. "I'm sorry."

Two words don't erase years of abuse and bullshit. However, his actions today, his choosing *me* over Lorenzo, hit hard and true, fracturing the ugly barrier between us.

A fracture doesn't bring down a wall. But it does leave behind a precious weak point, one that will always be there. Whenever I think of him, I'll feel that fracture and remember it fondly.

Emeric studies our interaction, his expression neutral, his caresses lingering on my ankle.

Shane lifts a hand and reaches for mine, making an awkward hesitation in the space that separates us before hooking our fingers together.

He smiles sadly, squeezes my hand, and whispers, "Fuck you, Ivory."

I squeeze back. "Have a nice life, Shane."

He pulls his hand away, then his gaze, and walks out the door without looking back.

A pang of loss tightens my chest. The urge to stop him tenses my legs.

But he broke into Emeric's house. He beat me for years. I'm no longer a victim. With those reminders, I let him go.

Emeric follows him out. When he returns a few minutes later, he strips naked, slides into bed behind me, and curves his body around mine. I revel in the warmth of his skin and twine our legs together, melting against his chest with a sigh.

Instead of demanding I talk or eat or take my medicine, he touches his mouth to my shoulder then my neck and jaw. When I turn in his arms, he teases my lips apart and sinks his tongue in to slide against mine. The scruff on his chin rubs softly. Cinnamon flavors his breaths, his lips a firm pressure of sensuality.

His mouth is the best place to get lost in.

With my hand on those sexy indentations in his waist, I nip, lick, and taste, taking my time, following his lead. It's a kiss without expectation, a melding of lips simply for the comfort in the connection.

We maintain that gentle mood for the remainder of the evening.

The next morning begins with a fight.

He says we're not going to school. He can do what he wants. I'm going. He thinks I need rest and refuses to leave me home alone. It's Friday. I can rest over the weekend. If we both miss another day, we might as well announce our relationship over the intercom.

We argue for an hour. I win. It turns out to be an uneventful day. And fruitless. My concentration is shit. Emeric might've been right about one thing. I need rest—the mental kind.

By Saturday afternoon, the sore spot on my stomach where Lorenzo kicked me turns a violent shade of purple. Emeric's horror at seeing it is the impetus for our inevitable conversation.

We soak in the tub, my back against his chest and his legs bracketing mine. As I walk him through what happened, he swirls soap over my skin, his fingers massaging and soothing. I give him every gritty detail, my voice strong at the beginning. When I tell him about my brainless attempt to use my safe word, his body turns to stone beneath me. My voice wavers from there. By the time I recall those final moments with Schubert's body in my arms, I crumble against him.

It hurts. That little fur ball was such an essential part of my life, and I ache in his absence. But I'm not broken. Not like I was when I lost my dad. It's easier this time. I feel it in every touch and glance Emeric gives me, that much-needed support of another person holding me up during those times when I struggle to stand on my own.

# DARK
## NOTES

That night, he snores softly behind me, his chest pressed to my back, our limbs entangled, bodies aligned. I can't join him in sleep, my mind too restless, thinking about his reaction to using my word with Lorenzo.

Nothing has changed between Emeric and me. We haven't had sex since that day, but I've had a bladder infection. His lingering glances still make me purr. His kisses curl my toes. What I don't know is how I'll respond when he straps me down, grips my throat, or raises that belt. I trust him, unequivocally. But do I trust a word—any word—enough to use it again?

Before I met him, Scriabin's sonata was a black mass in my mind, the place I went to when terrible things happened to my body.

Over the past five months, those dark notes have become synonymous with Emeric and the safety he gives me. Did I ruin it by using it with the wrong man?

I play the sonata in my head, but I don't feel it. I need to hear it.

Sneaking out from beneath the heavy weight of his arms, I listen for his even breaths then tiptoe to the music room.

With the door shut, the room is supposed to be soundproof. I sit behind the piano, soaking in the silence and clearing my head. After a few calming breaths, I run my fingers over the keys and ease into Scriabin's Sonata No.9.

It's rough at first, the melody banging through the room in a disjointed rhythm. But I keep at it, transforming my interpretation from eerie and neurotic to something more nebular and meditative. The sonata drifts around me in a cloud of notes. My mind absorbs it, reflects it.

It feels safe. The kind of safe that enwraps me during my darkest times. It's doing that now, melting away the room, fogging my headspace, and immersing me in dissonance.

Except I suddenly don't feel like playing it. I rest my hands in my lap. The sonata is a place to go to, a word to speak, when I've reached my limit. But do I enjoy it? Not really. It doesn't...thrill me.

I want to try something different. Something beyond Chopin, Rachmaninov, and Debussy.

My attention shifts toward the door, and I startle.

Emeric leans against the frame, arms relaxed at his sides, his phone in one hand. He's been in constant communication with his PI over the past couple days. Probably tracking Shane. Maybe something involving Lorenzo, as well. He doesn't tell me, and I don't ask.

Black pajama pants sit seductively low on his trim hips, the *V* of his abs pointing like an arrow to the soft bulge beneath the cotton.

I raise a brow. "How long have you been there?"

"I followed you." His brows lower, his eyes dark, haunted. "You played Scriabin."

"Yeah. I needed to know." I glance at the keyboard. "I won't be afraid to say *no*. With the word." I return to him. "Trust me to use it."

He straightens, studying me intently. "Be sure, Ivory."

"I'm sure. It's safe." I wrinkle my nose. "And kind of boring."

His eyes light up. "I'm intrigued." He prowls toward me. "Name a song that's not boring."

*The tick of your watch. The harmony of your breaths. The tempo of your heart. The notes I feel whenever you're near.* "'I Will Follow You Into The Dark.'"

He stops behind me and places his phone on the bench beside my hip. "Death Cab for Cutie?"

I nod.

"Interesting choice." He moves my hair aside and traces his knuckles along the line of my neck. "Play it."

"I don't have the music sheet."

"You don't need it." His lips touch the path of his finger, his breath stroking my ear. "You have the world's greatest teacher."

I shiver. "So cocky."

He gives my neck a warning bite and steps back. "Raise your arms."

I do, recalling his words the night I sucked his cock in Le Moyne's theater.

*I want you naked, sitting at my piano and rolling your hips like you're fucking the notes.*

He pulls the t-shirt over my head and drops it, leaving me completely bare beneath his gaze. With his hands on my waist, he lifts me, takes my seat, and positions me on his lap, facing the keyboard.

This is different. I'm up a little higher, but as his arms come around me and his hands guide mine to the keys, I relax my weight on his powerful thighs. Knees together between his, I tremble in anticipation.

He cues up the song on his phone and sets it on the bench. In the next breath, the inspiring arrangement of music and lyrics trickle from the speaker. His hands move beneath mine and guide me through the simple complexity of chords.

I spread my fingers through the spaces between his. My hands are smaller, bonier, and darker-skinned, but they mold around his exquisitely, like our hands are meant to be joined this way, for holding each other, for creating music together.

Fumbling along, I become frustrated by my inability to catch on. I can recreate classical pieces without sheet music, only the ones I've played a gazillion times. How does he just pluck mysterious notes out of the air without visual guidance? It's insane. And brilliant.

"Listen." He brushes his mouth across my nape. "Feel it."

I close my eyes and focus on the beats, the glide of his fingers, and the sway and flex of his tensile muscles around me. His breaths on my neck and the twitches in his legs make it easier to predict his movements and rhythms. I don't just feel the music. I feel *him* as the vocals lead us through each measure, painting passionate imagery about fear being the heart of love.

I don't know how many times he replays the song. I'm lost in his arms and the meaning of the lyrics. Our love is risky, adventurous, and real. Is it founded in fear? Maybe, but it's a respectful fear, because our love is almighty and powerful.

The taut skin on his chest rubs against my bare back, the friction erotically pleasurable, his body a conductor of sensual heat and sound. I roll my hips against his, liberated by my nudity, rocking to the music and *fucking the notes*.

He groans, a seductive rumble, and one of his hands slides out from beneath mine. I carry the tune, missing keys but keeping up as he trails his fingers across my thigh, along my ribs, and around my nipple.

I sigh as his cock swells beneath my ass.

His other hand slips from the keyboard to join the first, and my pulse speeds up. His fingers rove hungrily around my breasts, up and down my legs, over my arms, always returning to my chest. When his lips fall to my throat, my hands falter, ruining the melody, but I don't care. He's strumming a better song, *our* song, set to the tempo of our breaths and beating hearts.

Besides, his erection is all kinds of distracting, pinned beneath me and pumping with blood. I want to take him out of his pants and slide down that hard length as I continue to play.

I spread my legs, hooking them over his, my hands bungling two measures of the song. "Emeric."

His tongue traces the shell of my ear, his fingers dipping between my thighs, probing, rolling my clit, and sinking into my pussy. "So wet for me."

Gasping, I give up on the keyboard and grip his thighs where they flex between mine. The diabolical thrusts of his fingers arch my back, make me whimper, and propel me into a boiling crescendo of lust.

I tug at his pajama bottoms. "Take these off. I need you."

The recording on the phone ends, the sudden silence amplifying the chorus of our heavy breaths.

He pinches my clit with a wicked amount of pressure, shooting painful pleasure through my core. Working both hands between my legs, he slaps and strokes, flicks and dips inside. Whether it's ruthless or gentle, giving or taking, every touch is a declaration of utter commitment.

With an arm around my waist, he lifts my hips and shoves his pants to the floor, kicking them away. I shiver as he lowers me onto his cock and pushes inside. He's hard and persistent, thick and aggressive, his fingers digging against my hips and controlling the up and down glide of my body with powerful confidence.

I clutch his strong forearms and hang on, my head dropping back to his shoulder and my inner muscles spasming around every thrust. The deep slide of hot steel stretches my pussy and fills me up. My body sings for him with each pulsing beat between my legs, pulling him in, clamping down, and holding him there. He belongs in me, with me.

"So fucking tight." He kicks his hips. "Leaking all over me." He grunts, his fingers tightening against my hips. "Love your hot little cunt."

I love his dirty fucking mouth.

He grinds against me in tight circles, his timbre low and rough. "Play the song."

Now? Without the recording? Even if I had total concentration, I would struggle. But while he's fucking me? No way.

I turn my neck to look at him. His hand plunges into my hair, wrenching my head forward and angling it to the side. The graze of his teeth on my shoulder makes me shudder. The fucking bite that follows rips a scream from my throat.

The stinging burn seeps into my muscles, charging and rolling like liquid electricity. Holy shit, that's going to leave a mark.

I stab my fingernails against his rock-hard forearms. "You're an animal."

He laughs, lifts me all the way off of his cock, and slams his hand against my ass. With a yelp, I fall forward and catch myself on the piano, fingers splayed over the keys.

The man knows exactly how to get what he wants.

He pulls me back down, shoving inside me with a force that brings tears to my eyes. It's blissful, overpowering pain, the kind that stimulates the mind, arouses the body, and trembles the soul.

He heightens the sensation by rolling into tender thrusting, ensuring I feel every thick inch of him dragging along my sensitive walls.

"Play the song, Ivory." He nips at my shoulder, his hand lifting to knead my breast.

With focused strokes, I launch into the parts I remember, mentally looping through chords and letting my fingers follow along.

He kisses my neck, tasting my skin, our bodies rocking and shuddering together as the music coaxes us into a languorous dance. He fucks me slowly, sensually. The motion of our hips wave in sync with my fingers on the keys as the sounds of our love-making hum a passionate rhythm.

*We* are the ultimate love song.

The tip of his tongue circles my earlobe. "Come."

My body obeys instantly, and I moan through the vigorous ripple of pleasure, clenching around his length, my fingers depressing aimless keys.

"Ivory." He groans, holding my hips against him as the hot pulse of his cock swells inside me, marking me, claiming me.

I twist my neck to watch him in the throes of his pleasure.

The air rushes from my lungs at the sight of his dilated pupils encircled by intensely beautiful swirls of blue fire. I used to hate his eyes, unable to imagine gentleness or safety in those crystalline depths. I was so very wrong. This is the only view I want, when I wake, when I go to sleep, and all the seconds in between.

I rise off of him and quickly spin to straddle his lap, sliding back onto his cock. The kiss that follows is a mutual seeking of lips, met in the space between us and prompted by a shared need to connect in every way.

He's it for me. The zenith of my happiness. All roads, however perilous and winding, lead to this man, my teacher, the music of my soul.

I want to go to Leopold to learn from the best of the best, yet here I am, sitting on the cock of one of their most brilliant alumni. Whether it's dumb luck or some kind of magical destiny that brought me here, I won't squander it.

Leaning back, I frame his sculpted face with my hands. "Teach me how to play."

"Miss Westbrook." His lips form a firm line. "I *am* teaching—"

"No." I kiss that hard mouth, because seriously, it's too sexy to ignore. "Teach me the way you did tonight. Without classical music theory and technical books. I want to play...whatever I want to play."

A very male smile breaches his lips, his cock jerking inside me. "Turn around. Hands on the keys."

And so it goes. For the next few weeks, he teaches me how to play whatever rock or pop song that suits my mood while holding, touching, kissing, and fucking me.

Some songs are harder than others. All of them challenge me. I don't use music sheets, but I don't need them. Not with his fingers beneath mine, showing me, and his voice at my ear, instructing me.

Mastering modern music won't help me get into Leopold, but man oh man, it exposes me to a whole world of composers outside of classrooms and textbooks. I discover a passion for blending classical masterpieces with top forty hits. There's something about the originality and distinction in putting my own twist on the music. It strikes a glowing, breathing note inside me.

Of course, Emeric's enthusiasm in teaching and disciplining me isn't a surprise. He gets off on it, especially when I slip up. God, that man loves to spank my ass. But it's his endless encouragement that reminds me why I'm so fiercely, deeply, crazy in love with him.

My eighteenth birthday falls on the last Friday in April. That morning, I wake with him straddling my hips, hands planted on either side of my head, and blue eyes filling my horizon. *Perfect.*

He puts his face in mine, his expression serious. "I'm going to ask you some questions, but before you answer... Take me out of the equation. I go where you go. We stay together no matter what."

Okaaay. I nod.

He searches my face. "Do you want to go to Leopold?"

"Of course." I raise my eyebrows. "What else would I do with my life?"

"Anything you want." He kisses me, his voice a silken tempo of notes. "What does Ivory Westbrook want?"

Well, that's easy. "I want to play piano, with you at center stage beside me."

He grins, evidently liking that answer. "How will you get there?"

Hmmm. Is this a trick question? I've always believed rigorous training, persistence, and prestige will help me reach my dream. Isn't Leopold the best way to obtain those things?

I purse my lips. "I don't know."

He reaches for something above my head and hands me...an airline ticket? "Let's find out."

# EMERIC

Saturday morning, we don't fly out of New Orleans. I drive Ivory an hour and a half away to catch a plane from Baton Rouge. A city where I know no one. But as we walk through the airport—not touching—I'm suspicious as fuck of every person who casts their eyes in our direction. Do they know me? Are they affiliated with Le Moyne? I could explain our trip as business travel for the school, but that doesn't stop my skin from crawling with paranoia.

When we step off the plane at our destination, I finally let myself relax.

Ivory sits beside me in the limo, her eyes darting everywhere, her expression a mesmerizing depiction of wonderment. The wide grin, sparkling eyes, and bouncing hyperactivity has been ongoing since I gave her the first-class ticket last night. She's never been out of New Orleans. Never been on an airplane or in a limo or hotel.

I'll show her every corner of the world if it keeps that smile on her face.

It's been two months since Schubert died, and her happiness hasn't fully snapped back. Until now. Fuck if that doesn't make all my earlier nervousness worth it.

For the first time since we left Baton Rouge, I touch her,

not as a teacher but as the man who loves her. In the privacy
of the limo, I wrap an arm around her lower back and pull
her against my side. Resting my lips against her temple, I
stroke the crease of her thigh and hip.

She sighs, her body melting in my hold. "A limo, Emeric.
It's...unnecessary, but wow." She leans forward, gaze locked
on the side window and jaw hanging open as she takes in the
surrounding glass metropolis of skyscrapers. "I can't believe
I'm in New York."

I capture a strand of her hair and pull. "Can't?"

She slides me a sexy grin, twists in the seat, and throws a
leg across my lap, straddling me chest to chest.

With her hands on my face, she touches her smile to mine.
"I can't. I can't. I can't."

I would bend her over my lap and spank her perfect ass,
but we're five minutes away from our first stop. So instead, I
pinch her nipple through the dress and hang on.

She grips my wrist and tries to jerk back, but the
movement tightens my fingers and elongates the pebble of
flesh.

Grabbing my necktie, she yanks hard. That only brings our
lips closer together. I take advantage, kissing her greedily
while squeezing the hell out of her nipple.

Her body bucks, a devious curve of flesh wrapped in black
silk, as she exhales heavy huffs. "I'll never say *can't* again. Just
please...my boob!"

Blood rushes to my cock, making it rise.

I release her. "Good girl."

She rubs her breast. "So mean."

I spy the smile pushing through her pout. "You love it."

She slides off my lap but stays close, leaning across my thighs to peer out my window. "Are we going to Leopold first?"

Familiar streets and sights pass by. We're a block away.

She thinks we're dressed up for a fancy dinner reservation and that the purpose of the trip is to open her eyes to Leopold campus life.

What she doesn't know is that I brought her here to open doors.

When the limo stops, she looks at the front of the building and gasps. Her elbow swings an inch from my face in her scramble across my lap to exit on the side closest to the shiny front doors.

I meet the driver's eyes in the rear view mirror. "We'll be a couple hours."

As I join her on the sidewalk, the brisk wind chills the back of my neck. But I barely feel it in the warmth of her blinding smile as she takes in the campus where I spent five years of my life, earning my undergrad and master's.

"Holy shit." She hooks an arm around mine, hugging tightly. "This is really happening. I'm really here."

As much as I loathe our secrecy, I force the warning tone past my lips. "Miss Westbrook."

"Shit." She drops her arm, steps an appropriate distance away, and stares straight ahead. "Sorry." The corner of her mouth twitches. "Mr. Marceaux."

*Smart ass.* "Follow me." I lead her inside and through the halls.

I haven't been here since I graduated four years ago. Nostalgia pulls at me, but I don't take the time to look around. We have an appointment.

She walks quickly to keep up with my long strides, her heels clicking against the cement floor. "You're not a very good tour guide. Slow down."

"We'll explore later." I stop at a closed door in Richter Hall and shift to face her.

She studies me, glances at the door, and looks back. Her hands rub down the front of her dress. "What are we doing?" She narrows her eyes, suspicion lashing through her tone. "What did you do?"

"You're here for an audition."

Her mouth falls open, working to form words. "Now?" She clutches the frog charm on her bracelet, rubbing with anxious fingers, her voice a harsh whisper. "Why didn't you tell me?"

"Because of this." I touch her fidgeting hands and drop my arm. "Your excitement about this trip would've been ruined by nerves."

She nods jerkily, her eyes wide and terrified.

The hallway is empty, but I won't risk a kiss. Instead, I let her see the depths of my support and love in my gaze. "Remember, your sound is the first thing the panel members will judge you on, and they'll do that in the first thirty seconds."

"Oh God." She inhales deeply. "Which pieces do I play?"

"Play what you identify most with, what you feel you play well, and what fits your style and aspirations. Let them see the exquisite heart of Ivory Westbrook."

I check my watch. It's time. Turning away, I open the door.

The stadium-style classroom hasn't changed since all those semesters I spent taking notes right up there in the bleacher seats. The same Steinway grand piano sits in front near the door. It's like walking into a time warp.

With Ivory at my side, I head toward the middle-aged woman and two lanky old men in the front row. I've never met them, but I've been in contact with the woman, Gail Gatlin, who stands and crosses the room to greet us.

Her stern gray eyes peer up at me from behind spectacles rimmed in gold. Sandy brown hair combs back from a complexion that probably sees little to no sunshine. Her stature is short and pudgy, yet she radiates confident authority.

She holds out her hand, shaking mine. "Welcome back, Mr. Marceaux."

"Thanks for seeing us today." I gesture to Ivory. "This is my protégé, Ivory Westbrook."

"I'm Mrs. Gatlin." Gail shakes Ivory's outstretched hand. "You must be quite something for Mr. Marceaux to bring you all the way here himself. His appraisal of your talent was convincing enough to gather a panel of judges on a Saturday."

In other words, don't waste their time. I wouldn't have brought her here if I thought she would.

Gail gestures at the two men waiting in the front row. "We don't usually interact with the candidates, but since this is an unusual audition, it will be somewhat free-form. Begin when you're ready." She nods at the piano and takes her seat.

Ivory settles behind the Steinway, her fingers rubbing the frog charm. I find a chair off to the side where I have a direct view of her face as she stares at the keyboard.

My leg bounces, and I tense it to stillness. What will she play?

Right now, her smile reminds me of Queensryche's "Silent Lucidity." The corners of her lips lift in self-possession, the curved peaks arching into luminous competence as she looks her dream straight in the eye. A dream that has only just begun.

But Queensryche won't be in her repertoire. She's researched Leopold for years and knows the audition requires standard pieces from 19th-century concertos, contrasting movements from an unaccompanied Bach partita, and arpeggios in three octaves with double stops.

Whatever she chooses to play, she can nail it with her eyes closed.

Leaning over the keys, she moves her fingers and sways into a slow-burning prelude. I don't immediately recognize the piece. It's not baroque or classical... My breath catches. It's an Irish pop band.

My entire body locks up, my hands curling around the arm rests. What the hell is she doing?

The despairing chords of Kodaline's "All I Want" fill the room with heavy undercurrents of sadness and positivity. The unspoken lyrics scrawl across my mind, a message that can only be interpreted as, *It's over, but I'll find somebody. Life will go on.*

It's a breakup song.

My heart stops, sinking into the snarling pit of denial as the piano notes pound in my head. Why is she playing this? Is it a message to me?

*Look at me, Ivory.*

Her eyes flicker to mine and return to the keyboard, the fleeting glimpse too quick to read. I ache for her to glance up again, to give me something that will pull me out of this nebulous mindfuck.

I told her I'd follow her anywhere. I brought her here knowing she would get in. I'm fully committed to move back to New York with her. So what the fuck is she trying to tell me? And why is she ruining her audition to do it?

The judges shift uncomfortably in their seats. Any second, they're going to shut her down.

This is going all wrong. No, not wrong. There's so much passion and depth in the way she hits those keys. Her execution is perfect. But the song doesn't show off her technical talents. It most definitely doesn't meet the audition requirements.

Gail holds up a hand in a stopping motion, annoyance biting through her tone. "Miss Westbrook."

Ivory pauses, peering at the woman expectantly.

With a bothered sigh, Gail gestures at the surrounding walls. "This is Leopold. Not School of Pop."

Subtly, slowly, Ivory's eyes shift and connect with mine. In that fragment of a second, I see the heart of the woman I love, and it's smiling at me with radiant resolve. It's merely a moment of eye contact, but I feel her as if she were right beside me, assuring me that all is right in our world. My pulse thrums through my veins.

She knows exactly what she wants, and she's not just telling me. She's showing me in the most earthshaking way possible. In an audition for her dream. Through a song she identifies most with.

I maintain an expression of indifference and calmly fold my hands in my lap. But inside, I'm shaking beneath the shock of realization. She's not breaking up with me. She's saying goodbye to Leopold. What I don't understand is *why?* What changed?

Gail leans back in the chair. "Why do you want to attend this school?"

Shoulders back and spine straight, Ivory lifts her chin. "To learn from the best of the best."

"I see." Gail adjusts her glasses. "What are you looking for in an instructor?"

Ivory smiles, her eyes alight. "Expertise, of course. A firm hand to push me. An untraditional mind to expand my own. And discipline." Her gaze flicks to me and back to the judge. "When it's needed."

Her answer is directed at Gail, but I *know* those words are for me. I embody every trait she mentioned. *I* am her ideal instructor.

Gail's mouth forms a flat line. "Leopold is a traditional school, and our training concentrates on classical, baroque—"

Ivory turns to the keyboard and busts out the hardest section of Balakirev's Islamey.

If she doesn't intend to go to school here, I don't know what she's trying to prove. Nevertheless, the shivering intensity of her performance bangs through the room with gusto. There are no rhythm, note, dynamic errors. Every sound she produces is flawless.

All three judges lean forward in their chairs, eyes wide, mouths parted. Yeah, they're impressed. They fucking should be. I bet they've never seen someone attempt Islamey in an audition, let alone pull it off with immaculate skill.

Ivory cuts the piece short and raises a brow at them. I feel my pride all the way to my toes.

Gail rests her fingers over her mouth then smooths back her hair. "Okay, Miss Westbrook. You have our attention."

Wearing a private smile, Ivory rises, straightens the black dress, and steps toward them. "I've spent my entire life saying, 'I want to get into Leopold.' Most musicians do, you know? But I've been selling myself short. There are some brilliant piano instructors outside these walls. I can happily spend the next however many years perfecting my skill without moving to New York."

My heart thumps so loudly I wonder if they can hear it across the room. I climb to my feet and step beside Ivory, hands clasped behind my back in silent support.

Gail stands, her expression etched in determination. "I need to converse with my colleagues..." When both men nod to her, she hardens her voice. "We would be honored for you to join us."

Ivory nods. "Thank you, but I've made my decision."

Extending an arm, Gail hands her a business card. "It's an open offer. If you don't find the instructor you're looking for, this year, next year, or anytime in the future, we'll have a seat for you."

Goodbyes are exchanged, and Ivory and I walk silently through the halls, my head pounding with questions.

When we reach an empty courtyard outside, I can no longer hold my tongue. "Tell me why you did that. What the hell changed your mind?"

She wraps her arms around her waist and shudders against the chill in the air. "I don't want to live here. It's too cold."

I hear the smile in her voice and shrug off my jacket,

draping it over her shoulders.

She burrows into the wool, keeping her steps in pace with mine. "When I sat behind that piano, I imagined what it would be like learning from an instructor, a mentor, who isn't you. Then I played the song that fit *me* instead of the requirements. A song that expresses passion and voice, something I've never felt through the textbook pieces. The judges didn't approve, and that's when I knew." She stops and blinks up at me. "If I enrolled here, I would be forced to conform under the instruction of someone who doesn't *know* me while practicing music that doesn't touch me."

Tendrils of warmth spread through my chest, but I wonder if she's considered all the ramifications. "You won't receive a degree under my tutelage. If you're still aiming for that seat in the symphony, you won't have the pedigree and prestige to put you there."

She shrugs. "A symphony, a theater, a stadium...the *where* isn't important. I want the lights, the audience, and the music. I guess I have a lot to figure out, and if it turns out that the degree is necessary, I'll get it." She holds up the business card and smiles.

"That's why you played Islamey."

"Backup plans are good to have. You never know. My current instructor might set his eyes on another student." She smirks. "High school teachers have a way of falling fast and ignorantly in love."

My hand flexes, burning to slam against her ass. "You amaze me."

She grins. "I try."

As we meander into the next building, I give her a proper

tour. Her interest in the campus focuses on where I spent my
time rather than how the facilities would help her if she ever
changed her mind. She seems well and truly at peace with her
decision.

Since it's the weekend, the halls are dark and vacant. Still,
we maintain a professional distance, walking side by side as I
point out my favorite stomping grounds and share memories
about the people I hung out with.

"I don't get it." She follows me into a dead-end hallway.
"I've known you for eight months, and I've only ever heard
you play old-guy rock on the piano."

"Old-guy rock?"

"Guns N' Roses, Megadeth, AC/DC... I mean, that's your
jam, so how did you handle the classical training here if
you're not into it?"

"I was just about to show you."

At the end of the empty hall, I wiggle the handle on the last
door. It opens, and I herd her inside, shutting and locking it
behind me.

My hand hits the light switch in reflexive memory, and the
overhead fluorescent buzzes to life.

The spartan, soundproofed practice room is big enough to
hold the upright piano and two people. She glances around
and gives me a confused look.

I lean against the upright. "I spent every day in here,
practicing the songs I enjoyed without the rigid instruction of
my mentors. I sat right there with my headphones on and my
playlist on repeat. This is where I fell in love with metal on
the piano."

She runs a hand along the covered keyboard, inching

toward me. "Every day? On this piano?"

"Yes."

Slipping off the jacket, she drapes it over the bench. "Alone?"

"Of course."

She stops just out of arm's reach. "Did you ever bring a girl in here?"

"Just one." My cock twitches. "Her panties are in danger of being ripped off."

"I'm not wearing panties."

Fuck, I'm hard. How did I miss her bare pussy when she was straddling me in the limo?

I glance at the door and remember I locked it.

A wicked grin twists her lips. "Did you jack off in here?"

I cough through a laugh.

She steps in front of me and grips my tie. "You did."

I totally did.

She glances down at the piano, nibbling on her smile. "I bet you squirted on the keys. I wonder if there's still—"

"You want to see my come?" I grip her wrist and hold her palm against my erection, desperate for relief. "You can watch it drip out of your cunt."

My other hand goes to her hair, tangling in the thick strands as I pull her mouth to mine.

The kiss slips past gentle and plunges straight into hard, aggressive strokes. Her fingers squeeze me through the slacks, spurring my hips into motion, rocking against her hand as my tongue lashes and licks in her mouth. I bite down hard on her bottom lip and holy fucking hell, her nails dig into my balls.

I spin her toward the carpeted wall, chest to chest, and pin her arms above her head. She gazes up at me, her lips pouty, sensual, and swollen with lust. It's that sexy-as-hell look she always gives me after I've kissed her into a daze. The kind of kiss that makes her entire body heavy and limp with desire.

Grinding my cock against her pussy, I trail my tongue along her neck. "Remember the first time we were in this position?"

She arches her neck for my mouth. "In the hall on the first day of school. Not quite the same position."

"I wanted to restrain you just like this and bite your smart mouth." I sink my teeth into her bottom lip, mercilessly, and release her.

Her breaths quicken. "You scared the shit out of me that day."

"And now?"

"You scare me in a different way." She kisses the spot over my heart, making my pulse race. "In the best way."

"Flatten your palms against the wall."

As she follows my order, I lean my weight against her, confining her while I tackle my belt, fumbling to loosen it. Christ, I need her. I'm shaking with the urgency to bury myself inside her and thrust hard, fast, and unapologetically. I don't even care where we are.

I shove my slacks and briefs to my thighs and fist my dick, stroking with one hand as I yank up her dress with the other.

My fingers find her bare, soft, and soaked. Thank God, because I'm already lining up and... Ahhh! Fuck, that first thrust inside her always steals my air. She's so tight, so wet and warm. I let go, not holding back as I slam into her, again and again, lost in the snug clasp of her body.

Her hands stay on the wall, her thighs trembling against mine.

I lift her, hook her legs around my waist, and drive my hips, deeply, viciously. "I fucking love your pussy."

With a moan, she bows her back, ankles crossed against my ass, those dark brown eyes dilated and locked on me.

My body tightens with my desperation to come. She feels too damn good, too fucking perfect wrapped around my cock. I want to explode.

I grip the back of her head and press her mouth against mine. Not kissing. I'm too wild and frantic for that. I lock our lips, holding us tightly together, savoring her breaths, as I groan and thrust and fuck her to climax.

Her chest heaves through a series of rising moans, her hands sliding up and down the wall. The instant she clenches around me and her body shudders in release, I come so fucking hard my head spins. "Fuuuuck!"

I drop my brow to hers and hold her against the wall, lazily kissing and panting through the lingering vibrations of pleasure.

She wraps her arms around my neck, lips parted and teasing mine. "You're all I want."

I stroke my tongue against hers. "You're all I need."

"Mmm. I love that."

I pull from the warmth of her body, knowing I'll be back in it by the end of the day. "We only have twenty-four hours. Time to see the city."

By way of the limo, I give her a whirlwind tour from Central Park to the Statue of Liberty. We walk the crowded streets of Times Square. We dine at a fancy restaurant I had to book two months in advance. Not my thing, but it's something I wanted her to experience.

Late that night, we lie nude in bed in the Presidential Suite at the Four Seasons Hotel. I've been inside her for so long my dick's numb. But in about twenty minutes, I'll be ready to go again.

She watches me with heavy-lidded eyes, her arms extended above her head, wrists bound together with my belt. She doesn't bother moving them or asking me to untie her. I'm not sure she has the energy to speak.

I slide down her curves and kiss her hip, nipping at the bone with enough pressure to make her tremble.

"How did you get into..." She twists her wrists in the shackle of the belt. "This?"

Crawling back up her body, I undo the strap and massage her arms. "When I was fifteen, I found some books stashed away in my dad's office."

Her eyes widen, waking with alertness. "Like dirty sex books?"

I curl my fingers around one of her tits, trussing it up to roll my tongue around the nipple. "BDSM books. Kink. Master/slave stuff. I was instantly"—*hard as a fucking rock*—"intrigued. The next few years, I researched it. Obsessed about it. But I wasn't bold enough to try anything until I went to college."

The vein in her throat pulses. "With a girl here in New York?"

"No one important." I don't even remember her name.

She relaxes against the soft sheets, her fingers mindlessly combing through my hair as I lick, kiss, and caress her tits.

She's so damn beautiful I can't keep my hands off her.

Her fingers still in my hair. "What risks did you take today? If I would've accepted a spot at Leopold, what would've happened with your job and the dean?"

"The risks are null. I want you to focus on graduating." I give her a steely look. "Trust me."

"Okay."

Bringing her here didn't put her education at risk. I knew the judges would accept her. If Beverly Rivard is double-dealing behind my back, it won't prevent Ivory from graduating from Le Moyne or achieving the future she wants.

There's only three weeks left of school, and Beverly believes I've already pushed Prescott's enrollment past the application process. I haven't, and I'm not going to. He'll get into a conservatory. It just won't be Leopold. By the time Beverly learns this, Ivory will be graduated and I'll have my resignation turned in.

I've done a lot of soul-searching over the past few months. Ivory wants to learn, and I want to teach. We'll get those things from each other. Then?

She has a very specific image of what her end goal looks like... The lights, the audience, the music. My aspirations aren't much different.

I know exactly how I'll make our dreams align.

# EMERIC

The Monday following our New York trip, I find myself sitting in Beverly Rivard's office, exchanging glares with her across the desk. I have no idea why I'm here, only that I was summoned after second period. Is this about Leopold? Andrea Augustin? Prescott? Every possibility is a vindictive intruder trying to penetrate my defenses and steal away my future with Ivory.

The eight months that I've known Ivory have been a goddamn war, the entire world against her and me. But Shane is located—working as a grunt for a construction crew in Tennessee. Lorenzo is still *MIA*—my PI is embarrassed to report the trail went cold.

I've been waiting for the final shoe to drop.

Beverly draws out the silence, watching me with sharp eyes, probably an attempt to make me squirm.

I'm fighting a high-adrenaline battle on the inside, but I hold my posture loose and force a bored look on my face.

She straightens the long sleeves of her suit jacket and pats at the gray-blonde bun at her nape. When she finishes her preening, she looks down her nose at me and sniffs. "I have some unfortunate news."

Whatever it is, she seems downright smug about it. That

doesn't bode well for me.

I settle back in the chair with exaggerated casualness.

She unlocks the tablet on the desk and meets my eyes. "One of your students was expelled this morning."

I have dozens of students, but deep down I know, *I fucking know* who she means, and it's an excruciating punch in the gut.

The second punch comes when she rotates the tablet and slides it across the desk.

A soundless video plays on the screen. It's grainy and dark around the edges, but the Le Moyne theater stage shines beneath the overhead lights. Front and center is Ivory, rising from the piano in a yellow and white daisy printed dress.

I watch in horror as she steps off the stage, walks to the edge of the screen, and kneels between a disembodied pair of legs. Darkness shrouds everything in front of her. The face, clothes, shoes, nothing identifies the person sitting in the shadows of the front row.

But I remember the seductive look in her eyes before the video shows it. I remember her words before her lips move silently on the screen.

*I will crawl to you. Bow to you. Whatever you want, I want. Just...give me this.*

My insides harden into fiery embers, hissing steam through my veins. If Beverly's gaze wasn't burning into me, if the consequences of this video weren't boiling me into combustible rage, I would watch the remainder of it with a stiff cock and a hungry smile. Instead, I force myself to watch it as the man Beverly thought she hired. A jaded, insensitive teacher who only cares about his own agenda.

I pace my breathing and mask my expression, elbow on the arm rest, chin resting on a loosely fisted hand. I would turn off the video, but I need to know if the camera angle captured me when I exited.

The footage shows an indistinguishable hand in Ivory's hair and her head bobbing up and down in a lap. It ends with her following an obscure silhouette into the dark.

Nothing on the video incriminates me. Hard to find relief in that when Ivory's been kicked out of school three weeks before her fucking graduation.

Beverly studies my face, her mouth pinched in a line. She's looking for a reaction from me. It takes every ounce of control I have to not give her one as a rapid-fire of questions riddle my thoughts with bleeding holes.

I'm not Ivory's only teacher, but I bet I'm the only one Beverly called in for a video viewing. What does she know? The footage is five months old. How long has she been sitting on it? Why is she just now using it?

Some of those answers might reveal themselves if I understood how and why the theater was equipped with a live camera.

I cock my head. "Signed parental consent is required by law to photograph or film a student, especially when it invades her privacy. What are you thinking? You know those laws are there specifically to protect student misconduct from public attention."

She turns her glare to the tablet in front of me. "The school didn't place the camera. It was someone's personal device."

There we go. That someone is either Andrea Augustin or Prescott. Both knew I moved Ivory's lessons to the theater, and both have a reason to fuck me over. But if they set me up, they would know it was me in the footage.

My pulse hurtles as I push a dispassionate tone through my voice. "Did you interrogate Miss Westbrook before you sent her home?"

"Yes, of course. She refused to...participate."

"Explain."

"She didn't say a word after I showed her the video." She shrugs. "It's her funeral."

Christ, Ivory must be freaking the fuck out right now. Why hasn't she called me?

My temperature rises, but I maintain a cool façade. "She wouldn't tell you the identity of the boy in the video?"

Beverly huffs. "She wouldn't answer *any* of my questions."

In a student-teacher affair, the student is a victim and therefore immune to school punishment or criminal action. All Ivory had to do was say my name, and she would've been exonerated.

Instead, she let Beverly assume her sexual misconduct was with another student, knowing it would result in her own expulsion. Four years at Le Moyne, and she gave up her high school diploma. A Le Moyne diploma. One that her father sacrificed everything for her to receive.

And she walked away from it.

*To protect me.*

I'll rectify that right now.

"That's me." I tap the video screen.

Beverly blinks. "Mr. Marceaux—"

"Surely you figured that out based on the substantial size of the cock." I grin. "I can pull it out if you need proof."

She looks like she's going to throw up, but beneath the disgust, there isn't a hint of shock. "I don't know what you're up to, but I don't believe for a minute you intend to ruin your career and go to jail for that...that..." She winces at my murderous glare. *"Girl."*

The evidence of how deep I will go for Ivory is rotting at the bottom of a Louisiana swamp.

I pull the phone from my pocket and call her.

Beverly stretches an arm across the desk. "What are you doing?"

"Emeric." The sound of Ivory's tear-soaked voice makes my chest cave in.

I press the phone tighter to my ear. "Where are you?"

"Sitting in the parking lot." Her tone rises an octave. "Oh God, Emeric. I wanted to call you, but I was afraid you would be with the dean and—"

"I'm with her now." I smile at the sight of Beverly viciously grinding her jaw. "Come back inside."

"But I'm—"

"You're not expelled. Go directly to her office." I end the call.

Beverly jerks forward, hands fisted on the desk and eyes hard and tapered. "I'm going to turn you in to the authorities."

Except she hasn't made the call yet.

Because she still needs my referral for Prescott. And because misconduct between a student and teacher would be bad publicity for Le Moyne.

"Let's get to the point, Beverly." I set the phone on my knee and drum my fingers against it. "It's clear you pulled this video out of your arsenal to get rid of Ivory. Tell me why you chose today, of all days, to do it."

She straightens and draws in a deep breath. "I received a disturbing call last night." An angry flush rises up her neck. "You took her to Leopold. For an audition."

My assumptions were right about her double-dealing connections. "Who called you?"

"Someone who has access to the admittance records. The Leopold faculty is all in a buzz about the young virtuoso from Le Moyne. Yet not one person there has mentioned Prescott's name."

I'm going to go out on a limb here. "Prescott set up that camera and gave it to you months ago. You didn't want to use it because you didn't want the scandal. Now you're panicking, because you realized I have no intention of pushing your worthless son past the auditions."

One, he's not good enough for Leopold. Two, I've drawn attention to myself after Ivory's audition. The Leopold faculty would question why I didn't bring Prescott for an audition as well. Someone would dig, and it would lead to my mom's involvement.

Beverly called me in so she could deliver Ivory's *unfortunate news* herself and gloat over having the upper hand. She expected me to let Ivory take the fall alone and push Prescott through to keep my job.

Now, in a weak grasp at straws, she's threatening to call the authorities. Except the video doesn't implicate me.

She's got nothing.

I pull the tablet closer and launch a browser. "Ivory will graduate from Le Moyne, and you will treat her with the utmost respect."

"No!" Beverly glares at me so hard I think her eyeballs might burst. "I want her out of my school."

Logging onto a cloud storage platform, I access the account I set up in the event Beverly decides to be a bitch.

Kicking Ivory out of school? Definitely a bitch.

I cue up the first video and turn the tablet, rather enjoying the symbolic turning of tables.

Beverly snatches it from my hand. As she stares at the screen, her fingers clench around the plastic casing.

A fist knocks softly on the door.

I leave Beverly to watch her husband pile drive Deb's ass and open the door. I'm met with huge brown eyes, red-rimmed and swollen.

Ivory silently steps in. I shut the door, tangle our fingers together, and guide her to one of the chairs in front of Beverly's desk.

We sit side by side, hand in hand. She moves her gaze from our fingers to Beverly then to my face, her eyebrows lifting in question.

I would love to kiss her, but that might be pushing it. "Beverly was just about to tell you to return to class."

Beverly looks up from the screen, her complexion a sheet of white. She doesn't cry or rage or freeze up. I suspect she already knew her husband cheated. But given her strong need to maintain an image that captivates and impresses everyone around her, she wouldn't want anyone to know her marriage is a steaming pile of shit.

I imagine right about now she's mentally shitting herself as she thinks through the fallout if those videos were ever made public. Her career as dean? Fucked. Her husband's face on all his car commercials? Forever associated with the money shot on Deb's ass. Prescott's connections to other colleges? As worthless as his musical ability.

With a look of defeat, she powers off the tablet and sets it down. "What do you want?"

I squeeze Ivory's hand. "I already told you."

Beverly sets her jaw. "I can't allow this..." She waves a hand between us. "To go on in my school. End things with Miss Westbrook."

*Like hell.* But I'm willing to compromise. "Ivory stays. I'll submit my resignation immediately."

Ivory flinches beside me. "Emeric, don't—"

I cinch my fingers around her wrist in a tight shackle, reminding her to trust me. I have her.

My unwavering gaze narrows on Beverly. "Tell Ivory to return to class."

Beverly stares at me from across the desk, her eyes deep cauldrons of hatred. "Miss Westbrook, return to class."

# IVORY

I wake the same way I do most mornings. Drowsy, happy, horny. Except today is different.

Today, I'm a drowsy, happy, horny Le Moyne Academy *graduate.*

Yesterday's ceremony was held in the campus theater. The very same theater that almost cost me that diploma. Stogie and Emeric's parents were there. The dean demanded Emeric not show his face, though I'm certain I glimpsed his fedora in the crowd. When I asked him about it, he kissed me into a warm, gooey stupor. I'd love one of those kisses now.

I reach behind me, expecting to bump into warm skin. Instead, I encounter cold, vacant blankets.

Blowing out a breath, I sit up and glance at the clock. *7:13 AM.*

Damn him. He told me the morning workouts would stop. I hate waking up alone.

I climb out of bed, wrap a robe around my nude body, and set off to find him.

Ten minutes later, I come up empty and check the garage. The GTO is gone. Maybe he's picking up breakfast?

As I shuffle into the kitchen, something moves in my periphery. "The hell?"

I spin just as a tiny streak of black darts across the floor and disappears around the island. Is there a rat in the house?

Cautiously, I tiptoe around the corner and gasp. "Oh my... What?" I cover my smile with trembling fingers.

One look at those bright yellow eyes turns my vision into a wet blur.

A kitten. He brought a kitten home. My throat closes up.

Coal black fur covers the cat's body from the peaks of the ears to the tip of the tail. I press my lips together as a sob rises up.

In the next heartbeat, I'm fucking crying. A damn mess of soggy snivels, runny nose, and noisy hiccups for no reason that makes sense. I did the same thing when my dad gave me Schubert.

I wipe my cheeks with the backs of my hands and slowly lower into a crouch, careful not to scare... Him? Her? Knowing Emeric, he'd want another male in the house.

Excitement races through me when I spy two charms hanging from the black collar.

I offer my hand in greeting. He sniffs my fingers, marks them, and makes me his. I melt.

Scooping him up, I nuzzle him against my neck and sink into the vibrating purr. I missed this so much.

With shaking fingers, I examine the silver charms. The first is a round ID tag with a name engraved. *Kodaline.*

The Irish pop band I played at my audition.

I shake my head, grinning. God, I love that man of mine.

The second charm is a heart-shaped locket with a raised treble clef on the front. I open the latch and a tiny folded note falls into my palm.

# DARK
## NOTES

Sliding into the nearest stool, I set Kodaline on my lap and unravel the teeny piece of paper.

It's an address in the French Quarter. Scrawled beneath the street name in his sexy male penmanship is, *Don't keep me waiting.*

What has he done now?

I smile as I shower, fix my hair, and slip on a casual black rockabilly dress with gray rose print. The strapless bodice seductively hugs my cleavage. A flirty bow ties at the waist, and the skirt flares at the knees. I pair it with comfortable red pin-up pumps—as comfortable as heels can be anyway. The flats would be more practical, but I want to look good for him, for whatever he has planned.

My grin grows bigger and bigger on the drive there, making my cheeks ache in its refusal to go away. Smiling is as much a part of me as the clothes he picks out, the pain he pleasures me with, and the music he resonates in my heart.

With the address mapped on my phone, I follow the directions to a popular breakfast place in the French Quarter. The warm breeze kisses my face as I walk quickly along the flagstone passageway, surrounded by the ambiance of New Orleans' salient history and architecture.

Sunlight glints off the steeples, gables, and dormered rooftops. Dew clings to the gas lamp posts. Eager tourists gather around the vendors setting up booths beneath the blooming trees in Jackson Square. It's a beautiful southern morning. How could I have ever moved away from this?

I step into the restaurant and immediately spot him in a corner booth sipping his coffee. His blue eyes find mine, and for the second time this morning, I melt.

He watches me intently as I cross the busy dining room, his gaze roaming up and down and deep inside me.

When I reach the table, he stands and laces our fingers together. "You look ravishing."

Black hair falls over the cropped sides in disheveled strands, no doubt molested by his fingers since the moment he woke. His cobalt blue button-up matches his eyes and hangs open over a white t-shirt. The relaxed denim of his jeans sits low on his tapered hips, a fit so perfect it's as if every thread was woven to embrace his long-legged strides and cup his impressive bulge.

He looks like a man who intends to spend a lazy day strolling along the pier. Maybe that's the plan?

"You look damn fine yourself." I smile up at him. Rather than sitting across from him, I follow him in on his side, wrap my arms around his wide shoulders, and hold my lips to his. "Thank you for Kodaline."

"Fast friends, I take it?"

"Insta-love."

He steers the conversation through breakfast, keeping the chit-chat carefree and unassuming. He hasn't told me how he spent my last three weeks of school, but his entire demeanor has been focused and fueled with purpose. When I pry, it's always the same response. *Trust me.*

I'm getting that look now, the *wait-and-see* glimmer in his eyes. I don't care what he's keeping from me. I'm content to simply enjoy his company, holding his hand as his girlfriend and kissing his lips in public. No more hiding or living in fear. We're finally free.

After breakfast, we meander along the narrow streets of the

French Quarter, fingers intertwined, sharing lingering glances and smiles.

With shops below and homes above, the rows of buildings dazzle with scrolling brackets of hand-wrought iron, fluted ionic columns, and balconies famous for bead tossing.

He stops in front of one of these structures, pulls a keyring from his pocket, and tilts his head up. I follow his gaze and lose my breath.

A huge, round sign dangles on metal chains from beneath the towering overhang. Framed in black wrought iron scrollwork, the name of the business makes my mouth go dry.

*Emeric and Ivory*

*Dueling Piano Bar*

My breath returns in a whoosh, only to be taken again as Emeric swoops me off my feet. Cradling me against his chest, he unlocks the glass door and carries me over the threshold.

"Holy shit." My heart pounds. My arms shiver. My entire body floats through a dream. "How did you—? When did you—? This is ours? I can't even."

"Easy." He sets me down on wobbly legs and locks the door behind us. "Deep breaths."

My chest heaves as I take in the deep mahogany walls, Gothic mirrors, and black and ivory mosaic floor tiles. It's classy and sophisticated, trendy and cocktail lounge-ish. Right in the heart of the French Quarter, the property value alone on this place must've cost him millions. I'm stunned into stupefied silence.

Two grand pianos sit on a platform at the center, facing away from each other. The keyboards are close enough together to share the long bench between them. Those will be

*our* pianos? Where we'll play together? With the lights, the
audience, the music?

"Oh my God, Emeric. Pinch me."

He does, right on the nipple, hard enough to make me
yelp.

Leading me to the ornate wrap-around bar, he leans
against the edge. "When I bought it a few months ago, I tried
to find a loophole, but because of this"—he points at the
shelves of liquor on the wall—"your name won't be on the
business license until you're twenty-one." He lifts my hand
and presses a kiss to my fingers. "By then you'll be Mrs. Ivory
Marceaux."

My heart sings a swooning melody. "You sure about that?"

"You bet your sweet ass." He slams his palm against my
butt with an echoing *whack*. "Go explore."

There's so much to take in I'm trembling against the
significance of it. A piano bar. Just like my dad.

Shivery, joyous tears fall down my cheeks as I make a
circuit around high-top tables, soft red velvet chairs, and
black leather settees. Candlelight chandeliers illuminate the
space in a warm glow. And the pianos...

I pause beside one of the Steinways, and my finger
instantly finds a familiar scratch on the lid. My watery gaze
latches onto Emeric across the room.

Braced against the bar, he slides a stick of gum in his
mouth and crosses his ankles. "I bought it the day I met
Stogie. It's yours."

I glance back at the piano and swallow around the
happiness swelling in my throat. "You're going to make me
ugly cry."

"I'll buy you a piano every day for the rest of your life just to see your beautiful tears." He prowls toward me, hands clasped behind his back.

That look in his eyes, the devotion rimmed in desire, is my centering pitch, my musical note, the one that induces the perfect wave of vibrations inside me, balancing me.

He moves up behind me, slips an arm around my waist, and holds me against him, his cock hardening against my ass. "Stogie sold his shop."

I glance back at him, startled.

He brushes his mouth against my ear. "Pain in the ass won't retire, but we worked something out. He's helping me with the inventory and hiring, and I set him up in one of those Creole townhouses a block away."

Overcome with emotions, I try to unscramble my brain, parsing through everything he's done and the future he's spread out before me. "What about your teaching? How does this bar fulfill that?"

"I still have you. When you outgrow me—"

"I'll never outgrow you."

"—there's a full second floor with a separate entrance in back. I'll open a School of Old-guy Rock to the public and teach metal on the piano."

Wow. He's thought of everything, which leaves me with only one thing to say.

*Thank you.* I could vocalize it a million times over, but I don't have to. He sees the salty rivers coursing down my cheeks. He feels the trembling of my body against his. He hears the rushing whistle in my breaths.

Words aren't needed because we have something better.

Our own notes. It's just us and our song, the tune pulsing between us, nourishing, fusing, and making us one.

He turns me in his arms and clutches me snugly against him. I lock my hands behind his back, rest my cheek on the warm wall of his chest, and close my eyes as he sways us to the beat of our hearts. Someday soon, we'll do this, right here, as the crowd applauds and cheers and pleads for an encore.

I sigh. Reality is better than any dream I imagined.

He hooks a finger beneath my chin, lifts my face, and puts his mouth on mine. He tastes like cinnamon and desire, his firm lips a devouring comfort of familiarity.

He passes me his gum with a roll of his tongue. The next sweeping stroke reclaims it. The bite of his teeth on my lip holds us together.

His hands slide beneath the dress and grip the backs of my thighs, lifting me to the edge of the piano so he can deepen the kiss. So he can tease his fingers between my legs. So he can rip—

There go my panties, tossed in a shred of silk behind him.

I grasp at his sexy hair as his fingers sink inside me, my tissues rioting beneath the sensual affection of his touch. His other hand yanks down the bodice of my dress. Then his lips are there, wrapped around my nipple, sucking it deep into his hot mouth.

My head falls back, my spine bowing against the brace of his arm at my back as moans spill from my mouth. Jesus, he knows how to work those fingers. On the piano. In my pussy. Around my heart.

I love this man. I love him, and when he's ninety and I'm eighty, I'll still love him. I grin at the image of his wrinkly body.

His eyes lift to mine, and his mouth releases my nipple. "What's so funny?"

I trace the wet curve of his lip with a finger. "When you're too old to get it up, I'll still love you."

He curls his fingers inside me and puts his face in mine, baring his teeth in a wicked smile. "Viagra, sweetheart."

I shake my head. He has a solution for everything.

He removes his fingers from inside me and tackles the button on his jeans. "I've spent every day here for the last three weeks." He releases his zipper and yanks the skirt of my dress out of the way. "Every day imagining fucking you here, just like this."

"You could've told me." I balance on the ledge of the piano, my bare legs trembling around his hips. "I would've come."

"Oh, Ivory." He notches the broad head of his cock against my pussy. "You're going to come."

His gaze holds mine as he thrusts. A low deep groan rumbles in his chest.

Pleasure floods my body in whipping torrents, one on top of the other, gathering into an overwhelming haze of need.

He kisses me passionately as our bodies slide together, rocking against the edge of the piano. My fingers sink into his hair. Our breaths mingle in a harmony of panting groans, and my hips absorb the impact of his as he fucks us into a wild and frantic crescendo.

His eyes never leave mine as he wraps a hand around my throat. He squeezes, and I whimper against the blissful pressure.

I love the way he holds me. "Harder."

His fingers tighten, and he drives his hips faster, ruthless in his urgency.

We strain toward each other, hands clutching, eyes locked as we soar, lost in our private world of notes and dreams.

# IVORY

*Three years later.*

People from all over the world come to the French Quarter for food, culture, and *music*. Bourbon Street is an endless party, day and night. Our dueling piano bar is smack at the center of it, booming with the overflow of enthusiastic tourists. Most nights, the line out the door snakes around two blocks.

The sound of laughter, clinking glasses, and scuffing shoes charges the atmosphere with excitement. We're so crammed in tonight the combined body heat stifles the air, made hotter by the bright lights above me.

I shudder with happy nerves and take a long draw from my beer, returning it to the shelf on my piano.

Stogie sits behind the bar, as old as the ninety-year rafters, smiling a youthful smile. Laura and Frank Marceaux sip their drinks in the seating area, surrounded by their friends.

Sharing the bench beside me, Emeric faces the other way, the shift of his hips creating a pleasurable glide against mine.

Our pianos sit in opposite directions and slightly off-center to allow elbow room as we play side by side.

He leans back against the keyboard of my piano, his eyes

sweeping over my fitted ivory dress. "You look good enough to eat tonight, Mrs. Marceaux."

I take in his jeans, white t-shirt, and gray fedora, and damn near purr with appreciation. "Hope you're hungry, Mr. Marceaux."

"Endlessly." He launches at me, gripping my hair and giving me a kiss so scandalous the crowd explodes in whistles and catcalls.

When he breaks the kiss, my body swims in his lingering heat.

I focus on his bright blue eyes. "What are we dueling first?"

Grinning, he poises his fingers on his keyboard and nudges his shoulder against mine. "Guns N' Roses."

I tilt my smile upward and shiver beneath the lights. "And Kodaline."

Then the music begins...

# PLAYLIST

Scriabin's Sonata No.9
"Toxicity" by System Of A Down
Balakirev's Islamey
"Patience" by Guns N' Roses
"Nothing Else Matters" by Metallica
"Symphony of Destruction" by Megadeth
"Smells Like Teen Spirit" by Nirvana
"Comfortably Numb" by Pink Floyd
"I Will Follow You Into the Dark" by Death Cab for Cutie
"All I Want" by Kodaline

# OTHER BOOKS BY PAM GODWIN

## LOVE TRIANGLE ROMANCE
### TANGLED LIES TRILOGY
One is a Promise

Two is a Lie

Three is a War

## DARK ROMANCE / ANTI-HEROES
### DELIVER SERIES
Deliver #1

Vanquish #2

Disclaim #3

Devastate #4

Take #5

Manipulate #6

Unshackle #7

Dominate #8

Complicate #9

## DARK COWBOY ROMANCE
### TRAILS OF SIN
Knotted #1

Buckled #2

Booted #3

## DARK PARANORMAL ROMANCE
### TRILOGY OF EVE
Heart of Eve

Dead of Eve #1

Blood of Eve #2

Dawn of Eve #3

## STUDENT-TEACHER / PRIEST
Lessons In Sin

## ROCK-STAR DARK ROMANCE
Beneath the Burn

## ROMANTIC SUSPENSE
Dirty Ties

## EROTIC ROMANCE
Incentive

## DARK HISTORICAL PIRATE ROMANCE
King of Libertines
Sea of Ruin

# ABOUT PAM GODWIN

New York Times and USA Today Bestselling author, Pam Godwin, lives in the Midwest with her husband, their two children, and a foulmouthed parrot. When she ran away, she traveled fourteen countries across five continents, attended three universities, and married the vocalist of her favorite rock band.

Java, tobacco, and dark romance novels are her favorite indulgences, and might be considered more unhealthy than her aversion to sleeping, eating meat, and dolls with blinking eyes.

EMAIL: pamgodwinauthor@gmail.com

Made in the USA
Middletown, DE
15 September 2024

61011332R00291